MW01196151

PRIMAIED CHRONICLES: BOOK 1

First edition: May 2022

Copyright © 2022 A.D. Sinclair. All rights reserved.

This is a work of fiction. All characters, organizations, and events portrayed in this novel are either products of the author's imagination or are used fictitiously.

First published and printed in the United States of America by A.D. Sinclair Publishing.

LCCN: 2022907393

ISBN: 9781958319000 (paperback)

ISBN: 9781958319017 (ebook)

For more information, visit www.adsinclairpublishing.com

A.D. SINCLAIR

PRIMAIED CHRONICLES

BOOK I

PROLOGUE

The walls of the villa trembled as a resounding, bone-shaking clap of thunder rolled over the expansive estate. Aurelia Lucio shot up in bed with a gasp, her chest heaving. Outside the bedroom window, no rain fell. No stars shone, and only the faintest arc of moonlight was visible, though it was masked by a wall of clouds that otherwise went unnoticed in the black sky. Aurelia's husband, Marcus, sat up beside her and groped around the bedclothes for her hand. Aurelia automatically pressed her palm to her swollen abdomen and edged closer to him, seeking comfort in his presence.

"Did you hear that?" she whispered.

"Even a deaf man couldn't miss such a thing," Marcus muttered. "It's probably just thunder, Aurelia. Go back to sleep. Don't agitate the baby." He, too, patted her stomach, but Aurelia was not reassured.

"It isn't storming," she pointed out, voicing her earlier thoughts.

Taking in her pale face and trembling hands, Marcus finally gave a long, tired sigh and rolled out of bed. Both donned thin robes and sandals, and Aurelia hurriedly pinned her thick blonde hair up as she followed her husband out of the room. Several bleary-eyed slaves milled about the halls, scuttling from adjacent rooms to huddle together at the main doors. An air of tense curiosity hung about the villa, reaffirming Aurelia's suspicions that this was no ordinary storm. The overseer, Clavus, nervously approached Marcus and Aurelia.

"Did you hear it, too?" he asked.

"What about the light?" piped up another slave.

"What is this? What light?" Marcus demanded.

1

Glancing over his shoulder at the doors, Clavus wrung his hands and explained, "Several of the slaves were awoken by a flash of light beyond the southern field. It occurred at the same time as the noise. Those who saw it claim it was brighter than any of Jupiter's bolts."

"Look outside! It cannot be thunder or lightning," Marcus snapped. "Jupiter has no reason to wreak havoc upon us tonight. Now, you say it came from the southern field?"

"Yes, master. I was going to take a group of slaves to investigate."

"I shall join you, Clavus. Fetch some spears; it could be an intruder, or perhaps a wild animal." With that, Marcus swiftly strode toward the doors of the villa and threw them open. The soles of his sandals slapped loudly against the cobblestone veranda as he walked outside. He was quickly followed by Clavus and a trio of spear-wielding slaves. Aurelia watched them go, praying to the gods that they would be safe from whatever vandal or creature had wandered onto their estate. She felt a small kick from her unborn child and took a deep breath, pressing her hand to her belly again.

Did Marcus remember to bring his father's pilum?

She knew they had spears on hand, but the old pilum that Marcus had inherited from his father, Maximus, was an ancient and blessed weapon. Aurelia briskly returned to their bedroom and stopped in the doorway. The pilum was mounted on the wall above their bed, its long, slender blade shining in the moonlight. During their first few years of marriage, Aurelia had lain awake for hours each night staring up at the spear, worrying that the thing would swing down and slice into her head. Now its presence was familiar and almost comforting.

"Mama! Mama!"

She loosed a yelp of surprise as a quivering shape slammed into her leg, almost knocking her over. Aurelia looked down to see her young son, Maximus, clinging to her skirts. Although he was named for Marcus's father, a renowned soldier, he was a small, sickly little boy who was frightened by the entire world. Maximus sniffled and whimpered, "Mama, what was that? Is it a monster?"

"No, Maximus," she said gently, bending down and scooping up her youngest child. Careful to avoid pressing the boy to her belly, she balanced him on her hip and added, "Monsters only exist in stories."

Her two daughters, Vena and Marcia, darted to her side as well, and the latter teasingly poked Maximus's chubby arm.

"Sylba knows a man who saw a sea monster once!" the girl exclaimed. Aurelia pursed her lips and rolled her eyes.

"That's silly," Vena interrupted with a sneer. "How do you know Sylba's telling the truth?"

"She told me so! Slaves can't lie to their masters," Marcia declared. Aurelia cursed under her breath and made a mental note to speak to Clavus about discipline; the slaves were there to work and maintain the villa, not fill each other's and her children's heads with far-fetched stories.

"Is the monster going to eat us, mother?" Maximus asked fearfully.

"Yes!" Marcia crowed delightedly at the same time Vena scoffed and snapped, "No." The two girls glared at each other, and Aurelia carefully set Maximus down on the floor. She let out a tired sigh when he continued clutching her leg.

"Vena's right, children," she said, and her eldest daughter beamed at the praise. "There is no monster, and none of us will be eaten. But I am going to check on your father and see if he's found anything. I'll bring him the pilum while I'm at it."

She pried her son off her leg and entered the bedroom, where she hopped up onto the bed and pulled the javelin down from the hooks that suspended it. A film of dust puffed up, disturbed from its resting place across the weapon. The pilum was long, unwieldy, and awkward in her inexperienced grip, and she had to carefully maneuver around her children to avoid hurting them.

"Just send a slave with it," Vena suggested.

"Like Sylba! She probably knows how to—"

"Hush, Marcia. I won't hear another word of Sylba," Aurelia interrupted sternly. She bit her lip and glanced around the villa. Perhaps it would be safer to take Vena's advice and have a slave deliver the pilum instead. But when she observed the sea of dirty, frightened faces, she felt a pang of disgust for the workers. Marcus would never stand to see his father's pilum touched by one of them.

They would steal it, or at the very least filthy the handle. I am the only one besides Marcus himself who should lay a hand on it.

Yes, she would go. It was the only viable option. She gathered up the folds of her robe and hurried toward the open doors of the villa with the pilum in hand

3

and her children trailing behind her. Just as she stepped out onto the veranda, however, a terrible scream tore through the night, chilling her to her very core and making the tiny hairs on her arms stand straight up. A slave woman bolted around the corner of the villa, almost smacking directly into her. The woman was sobbing and screaming, and through her hysterical state, Aurelia recognized her as Sylba, the avid storyteller.

"Sylba, what is going on? What have the men found?" she demanded, grabbing the woman's arms and trying to hold her steady. Sylba just blubbered and stammered and shook, and her knees gave out, pulling them both to the floor. Aurelia cringed as the pilum clattered on the cobblestones, but she still held Sylba tightly and stroked her hair in an effort to calm her hysterics. It took nearly a full minute of this before the slave was able to force comprehensible words from her lips.

"P-please don't be angry, mistress, I-I was frightened! It would have killed me!"

She curled over on her knees in a fetal position and clutched Aurelia's skirts. Aurelia grimaced as the woman sobbed against her legs. Her robe was clean white linen, and this woman was ruining it! But she fought back her disgust and took Sylba's hands, lifting her up so she could meet her eyes.

"I can't understand what you're trying to tell me, Sylba. Calm yourself and talk to me," she encouraged gently. She had often observed Marcus adopting a calm, regal persona whenever he was instructing the slaves, and she now worked to assume the same demeanor.

"There's something in the field. The southern field," Sylba whispered through her tears. "I don't know what it is, but it's not human."

Aurelia pursed her lips and glanced over her shoulder at her three children. They were huddled at the edge of the doorway, watching the interaction with wide, wary eyes. She found it hard to believe Sylba's words, but if it was an animal of some sort, she needed to see it for herself. Perhaps bringing the pilum to Marcus was the right course of action after all. But she couldn't allow her children to be involved if the beast was hostile. Coming to a hasty decision, Aurelia pulled Sylba to her feet and began giving her calm, clear instructions.

"Sylba, I want you to take my children and hide. The kitchens, the slave quarters, the stables, anywhere that has an easily accessible escape route. I want you to stay with them, and no matter what happens, don't come out until you know for certain that the villa is safe. Do you understand?"

4

"Y-yes, mistress," Sylba gulped, wiping the tears from her eyes.

"Good. Now go," Aurelia commanded.

Sylba quickly gathered up the children and dashed into the villa. Aurelia watched them leave, and a bolt of fear sliced through her heart. Was this the last time she would see them? Their faces flashed across the forefront of her mind one by one: Vena, who, at such a young age, was as beautiful as any grown woman; Marcia, with her bright eyes and soaring spirit; and little Maximus, who might someday live up to his namesake despite his innocent fragility. She thought of the fourth child growing inside her and wondered if it would ever see life. She whispered a prayer to the gods and, after taking a deep breath to calm her nerves, abandoned the safety of the villa and ran to the southern field.

"I don't know what it is, but it's not human."

Sylba's words echoed in her ears, and Aurelia wondered what they meant as she picked up her pace and rounded the corner of the country house. She'd heard of wolves and even bears wandering onto other estates, but Sylba would have simply told her if it was either of those things. What was out there? Did Marcus face danger from this creature? When she finally came around to face the southern field, the clouds broke overhead, bathing the land in the silvery glow of the moon. Aurelia froze in her tracks and her jaw dropped.

Standing in the tall grasses, surrounded by Marcus, Clavus, and the other men, was a monster.

The beast towered over all of them, easily two-and-a-half men tall and roped with full, hard muscle that stretched across its entire body. Its arms, unnaturally long and jointed by two elbows each, hung at its sides, and the powerful legs on which it stood looked akin to the hind limbs of a wolf. In the moonlight, she could see that its leathery skin was a deep shade of brown, like oiled wood, and vicious scars marred the creature's body from head to toe. Glowing golden eyes pierced the night like bonfires, swiveling from person to person as the beast studied the men who surrounded it. Long horns sprouted up from the top of its head, and large, sharp ears twitched with intelligent awareness. The most striking thing about its appearance, however, was a lizard-like frill circling the back of its head like a crown and covering its neck. Two smaller frills lined the sides of its face, one right below each ear. The large neck frill was flared up, and a long, cat-like tail lashed about behind the creature's legs.

Aurelia stared at the beast, her mouth agape and her eyes bulging in terror. Great Juno, what *was* that thing? Which of the gods would ever create a monster like that?

A shout broke her from her horrified stupor, and she watched as a slave jabbed a spear up at the beast. Its lips pulled back from its wolfish snout to reveal gleaming white fangs, and it flicked a single hand at the man in a sharp smack. It barely touched him; even Aurelia could see that, despite her distance. But the monster's sheer strength hurled the slave through the air until he crashed into the wall of the villa and fell to the ground, dead.

The other men advanced on the creature, jabbing their spears. It backed away from them, holding its hands out and letting loose a string of growls, snarls, and guttural clicking noises. Clavus darted forward and managed to stab a spear into the creature's left leg. The beast roared and fell to one knee, then struck a hand across Clavus's face. The overseer went flying—just like the previous slave—and even from afar, Aurelia could hear the *crunch* of breaking bone.

Before she realized what she was doing, her feet were moving again, carrying her across the field as if she wore the winged sandals of Mercury. She held her belly stable with one hand, but did not slow. The creature's back was toward her; it was distracted by the men and its wounded leg, oblivious to her approach. She ran closer and closer, all but flying over the grass. Marcus's eyes widened and his lips started to form her name, but she didn't hear him. The beast turned its head at the last moment, and those burning golden eyes locked onto her as she thrust the pilum high over her head and into its neck.

The sound the creature made when it died was like no other, tremendous and sickening. It was a horrible, howling wail of agony that quickly tapered as it choked on a fountain of purple blood. The creature stumbled and fell back, knocking Aurelia into a shallow ditch in the grass. She immediately thought of her baby and was able to turn onto her side as she hit the ground, arms cradling her midsection. She screamed when she felt her ribs strain and crack beneath the creature's weight; even with only part of its body stretched over her, she was pinned down by its enormity. She was only barely aware of the fact that, had she fallen flat onto the ground instead of into the curve of the ditch, her entire body would have been crushed and her baby's life ended.

Still, she could feel the creature above her thrashing, shuddering, and tearing open its own throat for air as it desperately clung to its last threads of life. The pilum had snapped and splintered upon hitting the ground, and tiny shards of wood dug painfully into Aurelia's skin. One of her arms remained trapped beneath the creature's broad back, but with a desperate surge of energy, she freed the other and flailed it weakly above her head, crying for help.

"Marcus! Clavus! Help me!" she screamed. She choked on her words when the creature's steaming blood dripped from the wound on its neck and into her mouth. She reflexively swallowed and tried not to vomit as the vile fluid trickled down her throat. She was unable to escape the stream for another moment longer before she finally twisted her arm around and shielded her face from the flow. She glimpsed Marcus hurling his own spear into the creature's chest. He planted a foot on its midriff for leverage and began twisting and shoving with all his might to get the blade through the tough skin. Although the monster was already dead, he struck it with more rage and ferocity than Aurelia had ever seen in her husband. He managed to wring out a few more limp twitches before the creature went still.

"Aurelia!" he cried, kneeling beside the beast's fallen body and clutching her hand. His face was contorted with fear and confusion, and in her delirium, Aurelia felt a wave of guilt wash over her when her gaze landed on the snapped pilum.

"I broke it," she croaked, pawing weakly at the javelin.

"Pay it no mind, my love. It is only a spear," Marcus said gently. He kissed her fingers and stroked her hair, which had fallen free during the struggle. The two remaining slaves worked to hoist up the monster's body, but they were unable to move it more than half a pace. They called other workers over, and even then it took nearly an hour before they were able to move the beast and free Aurelia from the ditch. Her heart both rose with joy and sank with humiliation when her children came running across the field toward her.

"Mama! Mama!" they cried. Aurelia gripped Marcus's arm and tried to hide her haggard appearance behind him. She didn't want her children to see her like this, weak and soaked with that monster's blood. Nonetheless, they darted past their father and wrapped their tiny arms around her, crying into her robe.

"Mother, are you hurt?" Vena demanded.

"What is this?" Marcia whined, prodding at the violet blood that soaked Aurelia's clothing.

"Did father kill it?" Maximus asked nervously, staring at the huge creature in shock. Aurelia exchanged a grim look with her husband, and a few silent words passed between the two of them. Marcus would not take credit for a heroic deed that another had carried out.

"Your mother ended the beast," he declared at last. "She killed it with your grandfather's pilum. But the creature landed on her when it fell, and she is now in need of rest, children. We need to make sure the baby inside her is safe."

Behind them, the slaves were filtering out of the villa and gathering around the fallen monster, once again huddling together and whispering amongst themselves. The whispers soon turned to murmurs, then grew to triumphant yells. Two of the men fetched a pair of axes and began hacking savagely at the creature's neck. It took them several minutes to force their way through the thick skin, muscle, and bone. After working strenuously for some time, they finally separated the grotesque head from the body, then dragged it away to reveal steaming lavender flesh and the jagged, chopped end of a wide spine. The slaves shoved two of the remaining spears and a long rod into the base of the ruined head and mounted it ceremoniously above the ground. They could find a better place for the trophy later.

"We killed the beast!" one of the slaves hollered happily.

"The monster is dead!" chanted another. Aurelia found she couldn't look away from the creature's lifeless face; as she stared, she noticed small details about its head and body that she hadn't seen before. Its eyes were wholly unnatural, with each golden iris pierced by a sharp feline pupil and set within an inky black sclera. A patch of small spikes endowed its forehead around the base of its horns. Six long digits protruded from each hand.

What is this thing?

"The filthy creature should never have wandered onto Lucio lands!" a slave cackled. Aurelia covered her children's eyes and turned away with a disgusted grimace as the man lifted his tunic and urinated on the exposed flesh of the monster's neck. Marcus also frowned at the indecent act, but he didn't leave his wife's side to stop the man.

"We'll get you to Aribus's villa," he murmured to Aurelia, gathering her frail body up in his arms. "You, the children, and I will spend the rest of the night there. We shall have to take a couple of slaves with us, of course, but the rest

8

can remain here to clean up and tend to the creature. I want its body on full display for the world to see when I return."

"It really shouldn't have wandered onto Lucio lands," Aurelia said weakly, repeating the slave's words.

Marcus chuckled and responded, "No, it should not have. It may have been a great and terrible beast, but it was obviously not a very clever one."

"Father, can I have one of its horns?" Marcia begged.

"Me, too!" piped up Maximus.

"Why not?" Marcus exclaimed. He snapped his fingers at one of the men who was working to hoist up the creature's arms and ordered, "I want both horns sawed off that thing's head when we return. And pry some teeth out while you're at it! My children need souvenirs!"

The slaves all laughed merrily and crowded around the fallen beast. After poking and prodding hesitantly as if making sure it was truly dead, they joined in the effort of taking it apart while Marcus called a few over and commanded them to ready the carriage. Not long after, the Lucios were on the road to a neighboring country house owned by Aribus Neptium, a good friend of Marcus. Aribus was a portly, jovial man who welcomed them with open arms and immediately assigned a pair of servants to fuss over Aurelia and her baby.

"You are welcome to stay for as long as you need, my friend," he said to Marcus. "Until then, I would love nothing more than to hear your story."

"Send for some drinks, Aribus. I have quite a tale."

Marcus sat down on a plush sofa in the dining room with Maximus balanced on his knee and recited the recent events that had shaken their family.

While Marcus regaled his friend with the story of the great and terrible beast, Aurelia lay on a cot in a guest room with clean bandages wrapped around her chest and her daughters on either side of her. With a bucket of water and a set of damp rags, Vena and Marcia gently washed the creature's blood from their mother's hair and skin. Aribus had offered slave women to do the job, but the girls had insisted that they alone would care for Aurelia.

"I thought you were very brave, mother," Vena murmured.

"Yes, I thought so, too!" Marcia chimed in. "I snuck away from Sylba to watch your battle, and I've never heard of anyone fighting such a horrible beast as bravely as you did!"

"That's kind of you, my daughters," Aurelia groaned, wincing and pressing a hand to her ribs when pain shot through her torso. She didn't have the energy to reprimand Marcia for leaving Sylba.

"Don't strain yourself, mother."

"Yes, you're injured enough as it is! You have to be careful."

"I'm trying, girls."

When she could safely be moved again, the slaves carried her to a soft bed and tucked her beneath the covers. Her daughters were shown to another guest room, and after dropping Maximus off with them, Marcus joined Aurelia in their borrowed chambers.

*****

That night, as Marcus stroked her hair and held a hand lightly over her belly to feel their child's kicks, Aurelia recalled the flash of light and the noise that had awoken them.

"Where do you think it came from?" she asked.

Marcus shrugged and replied, "I don't know. Perhaps the gods sent it as a test."

"But who were they testing?"

"If they were testing you, my love, I think we can safely say that you passed," Marcus assured her with a wry smile. Aurelia smiled back, but the whole event was still an utter mystery to her. Her husband seemed to sense her unease, and he added, "We'll go back to the villa tomorrow morning and sort this mess out. This discovery could be tremendously beneficial for the Lucio family. You might even be written into a legend."

"Oh, I doubt that. Only great heroes get legends," chuckled Aurelia bashfully.

"You may be a woman, but are you not a hero?" Marcus countered. "You are more than worthy of a legend, my love. Making you my wife might be the smartest decision I've ever made."

Aurelia laughed and snuggled closer to him, and sleep came easily after that.

Her sleep was not restful, however; visions of blood and war danced through her dreams and screams echoed in her mind until the sun rose the next day. Despite her pain and Aribus's assurances that they could stay longer, Aurelia was anxious to return to the villa. A sense of overwhelming dread followed her throughout the entire morning, and it didn't dissipate even when the slaves helped her and her family into the carriage and prepared their bags for the short journey home.

"I wish you well, my friend!" Aribus called as the horses trotted away with the carriage in tow. "I should like to see this creature with my own two eyes when you get everything sorted out!"

"I'll be sure to save you a tooth!" Marcus responded with a laugh.

Despite the men's shared mirth, Aurelia's trepidation only deepened as the carriage trundled along the road, and she found herself gripping her husband's hand so hard that her knuckles went white. She closed her eyes and leaned back against the cushioned seats, trying to calm herself.

The monster is dead. My family is safe. My baby lives.

"Stop the carriage!" Marcus shouted suddenly, snapping Aurelia out of her litany of safety. Her husband threw the door open and leaped out, and when their children looked out the window, they began to scream. Although fear tickled the hairs on the back of her neck, Aurelia scrambled to the open door—as swiftly as her injuries and pregnancy would allow—to peek outside. Her eyes widened and one hand flew to her mouth in shock.

Crimson swathes of blood coated the tall grasses, turning the golden-green blades to a shiny copper in the sunlight. The villa had been razed to a pile of scattered rubble as if struck by a vicious tornado. Littering the remains of the estate were dozens of corpses. Some had been torn limb from limb, others were impaled over the ground on their own spears. Aurelia even saw one unrecognizable body hanging from the branches of a tree.

The slaves who had remained at the Lucios' villa overnight had all been slaughtered like animals.

And the monster's mangled body and head were gone.

I

The Rhithien pack raced across the desert, kicking up clouds of harsh red sand in their wake and stirring the occasional ground-dwelling creature from its resting place. The two suns were scorchingly hot, turning sweat into steam and bearing down upon the eight Rhithien with relentless force. There was no wind, not a single breeze to shift the blistering air or push them towards their destination. It had been three days since the pack left behind the relief of water and forested shade that bordered the Red Desert. Longer still since they'd run down any prey worth more than a mouthful, but they persevered nonetheless. Rhithien were built for enduring stretches such as these, and their goal was far more important than parched tongues, empty stomachs, and sore muscles.

As the pack slid down into a valley formed by two sandy dunes, their alpha came to a halt and held up a hand, signaling the others to do the same. He squinted irritably up at the two suns and shielded his icy cerulean eyes from their blinding glare. His scarred blue skin had been burned to a light indigo hue during their long trek, but the discomfort was bearable. It would fade in time, he knew.

"Five minutes," he called to his pack, and there was a collective sigh of relief from all of them. He climbed to the top of the next dune and scanned the horizon. Sand, dunes, more dunes. . . There! His ears pricked up and his tail swished happily when he spotted the tiny but distinct silhouette of the Oasis wall in the distance. They were closer than he'd dared to hope.

"Salidus."

His ears flicked towards the sound of his name, but he didn't turn around as his third-in-command strode up to his side.

"Aremaeid," he returned amicably, offering his subordinate a curt nod. Aremaeid returned it and followed Salidus' gaze to the horizon. Salidus pointed to the distant Oasis and let a small, relieved smile cross his face as he said, "We're almost there. I imagine we'll arrive by nightfall at the latest; without too many more breaks, that is."

"How do you define 'too many more breaks'?" Aremaeid inquired.

"None, if we can help it. Inform the others."

"They won't be happy about that."

"I'm not happy about it, either, but you don't hear me whining about it, do you?"

Aremaeid snorted and turned away to rejoin the others. Then he paused and gave his alpha a long, weary look. Salidus glanced at him sideways and asked, "Is there a reason you aren't promptly informing the others?"

"Do you really think this is the right course of action?" Aremaeid asked, lowering his voice so the rest of the pack wouldn't hear. "If everything goes according to plan, we will be directly responsible for the slaughter of millions. *Billions.*"

"You're really voicing your doubts now? When we're less than a day from the Oasis?" Salidus demanded sharply, meeting his third's hard golden eyes.

"I haven't had the opportunity to speak to you in private. I know it's late to be bringing this up, but it needs to be said. You are my alpha, and you know I would follow you into death, but I want to be sure. I want *you* to be sure. Is this really worth the cost of so many lives?" Aremaeid was usually stoic and reserved, but now his tail was curled around his legs, his ears were pinned back against his head, and his face was set in an expression of uncertainty. Salidus placed a hand on his shoulder and looked him straight in the eyes, keeping his tone smooth and confident as he responded.

"It is worth everything, my friend. Have faith." He jerked his head towards their packmates in a silent command, and although Aremaeid still looked unconvinced, he obediently returned to the group. Salidus understood his doubts—he'd experienced them himself—but he had already made peace with the gruesome results that their task would beget. Without wasting another thought on the matter, he clasped his hands behind his back and gazed out over the sea of rust-colored sand that lay between them and their destination.

*****

Aremaeid had been correct in assuming that the pack wouldn't be pleased with their orders. Upon hearing that they would have to run for the rest of the day without stopping, groans and mutters of protest rose among the group until

13

a Rhithien named Orniell spoke up. He was tall and imposing, his presence amplified by two sheathed daggers strapped to a leather belt around his waist. A patch of faded scars covered his left eye socket and stretched down the side of his face far enough to mar his upper lip. His remaining yellow eye regarded the pack with disdain.

"Settle down, all of you. It's a long way, but we've seen longer. I'm sure we will be allotted some time to rest when we arrive." Orniell was the oldest member and unofficial peacekeeper of the pack. Certain Rhithien in their group were quick to anger, and he was often the one who subdued fights. The chore was relatively easy for him due to his rank as second; he answered to no one but Salidus.

"If by 'rest' you mean five more minutes, then you're probably right," growled Vegra, the largest of the eight.

"Oh, hush. It's better than nothing," scoffed Ridaion, a lean, green-eyed Rhithien. He had ashy grey skin dappled by small, white freckles on his face, shoulders, and back. With his petite stature, delicate features, and unique patterning, he was considered by many to be highly desirable. No one in the pack was allowed to touch him, however; that privilege was reserved for Salidus, to whom Ridaion had been both consort and confidant for almost twenty years.

"Better than nothing, you say?" Vegra grumbled, baring his teeth. "We will all be little more than nothing if we continue at this rate."

"What's wrong? Can't handle a hike?" teased Ridaion. Vegra lunged towards him, snarling furiously and lashing his tail.

"I didn't ask for your input, whore," he hissed. Instead of backing down, Ridaion rolled his eyes and crossed his arms.

"Nobody does, but you're the only one who's an ass about it. Now stop complaining. Orniell's practically a fossil, yet he's the one telling everyone to shut up and stick it out. How about you do us all a favor and listen to him?"

"How about both of you listen to him?" suggested Ziiphan, who was sprawled out at the base of a nearby dune with one arm draped over his eyes. "Some of us plan to use those five minutes." Another Rhithien trotted over to where Ziiphan lay in the sand, this one sporting inky black skin and crimson eyes that always seemed to hold a hint of amusement.

"You are all very entertaining," the red-eyed Rhithien commented. "Am I the only one who isn't close to keeling over and dying from exhaustion because of a short jaunt through the desert?"

"Fuck off, Ornathium. You won't have to worry about death from exhaustion if you keep talking. Being cursed with these idiots as packmates is bad enough, but I won't tolerate you trying to boast your supposed superiority," Vegra snarled. Ornathium didn't respond, but his gleaming red eyes remained locked on the older male. He didn't shift his gaze even when Salidus slid down the side of the dune to join them.

The alpha scrutinized Vegra and growled, "No one is killing anyone. I don't like our circumstances any more than you do, but now is not the time for bickering. There are many more important things at stake here. Now quiet down and prepare yourselves; we are not stopping again until we reach the Oasis."

No one argued. As far as the pack was concerned, their alpha's word was law, even if they didn't like it or agree with it. They rested in silence for a few minutes longer before resuming their journey across the desert.

*****

They reached their destination as the two suns were dipping below the horizon, just as Salidus had predicted. This Oasis, like all Oases across Primaied, was a massive expanse of trees containing buildings, a lake, and areas of cleared ground for livestock. It spanned hundreds of dynnsopions across the desert and was surrounded by a colossal wall of red stone. Oasis walls took many dilunar cycles to build and were impenetrable by physical force. Thanks to constant guard rotations, the only viable point of entry was a vast wooden gate built neatly into the arrangement.

As the pack approached, the gate slowly rolled upward into a recess in the wall above it, accompanied by a chorus of creaking wood and groaning metal. Salidus led his weary pack inside, where they were met by a pair of female Rhithien. The older of the two was stiff and stern-faced, whereas the younger was grinning and quivering with excitement.

"We expected your arrival earlier," the older female snapped.

"You have my sincerest apologies for our tardiness, Fiiorha," replied Salidus. He bowed his head respectfully and explained, "We were held up in the brinkwoods by a group of Omelae, and the Red Desert is unyielding in its harshness to those who would pass through it. Now, if it pleases you, my pack is

15

tired and hungry, and we would be grateful for time to recuperate. Any food and water you are willing to provide would be appreciated."

"I assumed this would be the case," Fiiorha sniffed haughtily. She swished her tail, irritably rattling the large spikes that protruded from the end, and turned away from them. As she left her place by the gate, she called over her shoulder, "We have a set of pack chambers cleared out in the Typig Building. Follow me. You too, Tanja."

The younger female, who had been shamelessly ogling the eight males, immediately leapt to Fiiorha's side with an excited squeal. As the two females led the pack through the Oasis, Aremaeid glanced over his shoulder to watch the gate roll shut behind them.

No turning back.

They followed a dirt path that wound through the dense foliage and ended by the sandy shore of a broad lake. As the group headed towards one of the arched wooden bridges that crossed the water, Aremaeid looked over and spotted close to a dozen cubs wrestling and splashing in the shallows. Three females—likely their mothers—watched over them from the bank. All Rhithien cubs believed themselves to be the center of the universe, untouchable and superior to all. These ones were no different; they paid no heed as the pack passed by.

Aremaeid turned his attention back to the front as Fiiorha stopped and addressed them.

"Salidus, you will follow me to the Knowledge Center. You may bring your second if you wish. Tanja will escort the rest of you to the Typig Building." Tanja eagerly hopped forward, but Fiiorha grabbed her ear and yanked her back, hissing, "Hands to yourself this time, girl. You know what their job is."

"But *Fiiorha—*"

"No 'buts'. Show them to their chambers, have food and water sent up, and leave them to rest. They are not here to bother with silly cubs like you."

"I'm not a cub!" Tanja whined. Fiiorha shoved her towards the pack with a scowl.

"Then don't act like one. Off with you, now."

Ignoring her student's pouting, Fiiorha led Salidus and Orniell away from the pack. Tanja sighed and gazed longingly at the remaining males.

"Come with me," she said flatly. The bridges that went over the lake met in the center at a four-way crossroads, and while Fiiorha kept going straight, Tanja

16

turned left and headed for a towering cylindrical building that stretched almost as high as the Oasis wall. They entered the structure through a wide doorway that led out onto the main floor. Several clusters of females, cubs, and a few smaller males looked up as they came in. Tanja guided them to the very center of the room, where a spiral staircase disappeared into the ceiling. As they left the main floor behind, Aremaeid's ears twitched in response to the sound of excited murmuring from the Oasis residents.

The pack made their ascent in silence. Every fifteen steps, the tight corridor opened into a wide, circular floor. Open doors lined the far walls on all sides, and Aremaeid could see moonlight filtering into the various rooms through outer windows.

"I've never seen a Typig this large before," he commented offhandedly. Tanja blushed and smiled shyly up at him.

"Yes, our Oasis is bigger than most. This Typig took over a hundred and fifty years to build, and it's been around since Rhala's time. The wall took nearly twice that. Don't worry, though; your pack is on the fourth floor."

"Thank Callii," Ziiphan muttered.

It wasn't long before they reached their designated level. Tanja guided them across the room to one of the larger doorways, chattering happily as she went along.

"The big ones are the pack chambers. Each floor can hold up to fifteen packs at once. The smaller ones—twenty on each level—are private rooms for the alphas, healers, and scholars. The second floor is reserved for the elders."

"We know the layout of Typig Buildings, girl," Vegra growled. Tanja gaped at him in astonishment, like she hadn't thought any male would dare speak to her in such a tone. Then she narrowed her eyes, bared her teeth, and dashed her tail spikes menacingly against the stone floor.

"Who's the guide here, packer?" she snarled. She didn't wait for Vegra to respond. "That's right, me! So unless you want to sleep on the hundredth floor, keep your mouth shut and do as you're told! I don't have time for males who think they own the world." Tanja puffed up and rattled her tail spikes, looking pleased with herself. Though she was fierce, Aremaeid detected no real anger from her. It sounded like a rehearsed pitch, likely practiced under Fiiorha's instruction.

"I apologize for my packmate's arrogance," Aremaeid interjected. Vegra glared at him, but Aremaeid ignored the sour look and maintained, "The fourth floor would be wonderful. Please, continue."

This made Tanja swell with pride, and she merrily spun around and led them to their quarters. She stopped by the doorway and stood off to one side so they could enter.

Repeating Fiiorha's earlier command, she recited, "I'll send up food and water. Your alpha will be stationed across the hall from you when he returns."

"Thank you," Aremaeid said, nodding respectfully. He waited for his pack to enter the room first. Tanja's energy unnerved him, but he knew it was his job as third to act as a representative while Salidus and Orniell were occupied.

"Will you be needing. . . anything else?" Tanja asked hesitantly. She swished her tail and rocked forward expectantly, and Aremaeid blinked in surprise when his nose caught a whiff of musk emanating from her pores.

"No, thank you," he said quickly, dashing into the room. She frowned up at him, looking slightly hurt, but nodded and trudged dejectedly away. Aremaeid shut the door and exhaled. Even if Salidus and Fiiorha had permitted them to engage in dalliance, Tanja looked like she was still a juvenile. He knew it wouldn't be a problem for many other Rhithien, but he preferred partners who were closer to his age. He probably had at least two hundred years on her.

"You aren't really supposed to reject them, you know. Especially when they're that eager. Five minutes together, a handful of words exchanged, and she was musking for you," Ziiphan drawled. He had already claimed one of the woven grass rugs piled up in the corner. The main room was small and cramped, but it branched off into three separate sleeping chambers. Aremaeid was grateful to have a small semblance of privacy, even if sharing was still a necessity. Some Typig Buildings had only a single room for one pack.

"That's not what we're here for," he responded curtly as he grabbed two of the woven mats. Ziiphan rolled his eyes and carried his rug into one of the small chambers. Aremaeid stepped past Ornathium, who was scampering to join Ziiphan, and headed for the room where the lowest-ranking member of their pack had gone. Thoughtful violet eyes looked up at him as he entered, and he grunted "Torraeid" in greeting. He handed his packmate a rug and sat down.

Although he was Aremaeid's age, Torraeid was easily the smallest member of the pack. He had spotless white skin that was nearly translucent in sunlight, and

18

his eyes were a deep shade of purple. Few Rhithien had those unique blood-hued eyes, but Aremaeid wasn't bothered by them like many others were. He was accustomed to his brother's odd appearance.

"What are your thoughts on this?" he inquired. He kept his voice down, but none of their packmates outside seemed interested in their conversation.

"Hmm. It looks well-made from a distance, but based on the fraying and uneven rows, it has to be the work of a juvenile. Someone Tanja's age, probably," Torraeid replied matter-of-factly, holding up the woven rug and pointing out various imperfections in the stitching.

Aremaeid snorted and elaborated, "I'm referring to the plan."

"Ah. That." Torraeid frowned and hummed pensively, still inspecting the rug. "I'm not sure my opinion on the plan accounts for much, Aremaeid."

"I want to know."

Torraeid pressed a claw lightly against the rug and sighed when it pierced the weave easily. He rolled it out on the floor and seated himself cross-legged upon it.

"I think it's a mistake," he confessed at last. "It's not our planet. It's not our home. We could go about our lives never knowing that it exists, and nothing would come of it. All Primaied knows that it exists, of course, but still. . . If crossing paths with them is inevitable, I don't think genocide is the answer. It would be much more beneficial in the long run if we took a non-violent route."

Aremaeid chuckled and rubbed his temples. Seeing his reaction, Torraeid's ears flattened and he demanded, "What? What's amusing?"

"I'm just glad I'm not the only one."

Torraeid's ears perked back up, and Aremaeid continued, "My loyalty is to Primaied, but that doesn't mean I agree with what we're doing."

"What are you two chattering about?" interjected a voice from the doorway. They both looked over to see Ridaion sauntering in with his mat.

"Are you really staying in here?" Aremaeid grumbled.

"The other chambers are taken."

"Everyone else is sharing," Torraeid pointed out, and Ridaion scoffed.

"I am *not* sharing a room with Vegra. Orniell can be in there when he gets back."

Aremaeid rolled his eyes and suggested, "Go to Ziiphan and Ornathium, then."

"Ornathium's a fucking creep. The last time I slept near him, he sat up and stared at me all night. You two are stuck with me."

"I outrank you, Ridaion," Aremaeid said sharply. "I could order you to go to a different room." This elicited a snort of amusement from the younger male.

"I've never known you to be so petty. You won't have to deal with me for long; I'll join Salidus in his private chamber when he returns." Despite his packmates' protestations, Ridaion unrolled his rug and stretched out on it with a contented purr. Then he scrutinized the two of them and asked, "What *were* you talking about when I came in?"

"Nothing of importance," Aremaeid responded stiffly.

"Fine. Have it your way." Apparently unbothered, Ridaion curled up on the rug and closed his eyes without another word. Aremaeid and Torraeid exchanged a glance before they both lay down as well. Aremaeid stared up at the ceiling, listening to the snoring and steady breathing that drifted through the chambers, and thought about what Torraeid had said. Despite his exhaustion, it was a long while before he finally found sleep.

*****

Aremaeid was roused by the sound of the door creaking open. He leapt to his feet, body tense and claws at the ready. He spared a glance to his right and saw that Torraeid had reacted the same way. They both relaxed when they peeked out into the main room and saw that it was only Salidus entering with Ridaion in tow. The latter had left the pack chamber when Salidus and Orniell came back from their meeting with Fiiorha, and he'd been quick to join his alpha in the private room after eating some of the food provided.

"Up, all of you! It's time," Salidus commanded. The Rhithien emerged from their sleeping chambers and abandoned the pack quarters. They headed down the spiral staircase, out of the Typig Building, and across the lake to where the broad, domed Knowledge Center awaited.

"Pick up the pace!" bellowed Fiiorha, who was waiting for them up ahead. "You've been fed and rested, you have no excuse to lag!"

"Apologies, Fiiorha," Salidus called back. The eight males sped up to a trot.

Fiiorha growled and spun around, stalking quickly towards the doors of the knowledge center. Outside, a scrawny male awaited them, scribbling something on a sheet of parchment and muttering indistinctly to himself. Fiiorha smacked his parchment up into his face and lashed her tail spikes at him as she passed, and he hopped to her side with a startled yelp.

"Apologies, Fiiorha. I prepared the portal stones as you asked," he stammered. He almost tripped over his own feet in his efforts to keep up with the female's long strides.

"You males are nothing more than clumsy fools. I've seen over seven hundred dry seasons, yet I've never figured out why we allow any of you to be scholars. Or healers, for that matter," she growled.

"Of course, Fiiorha," the small male whimpered.

Aremaeid looked around the large building as Fiiorha led them inside. It had been a while since he'd seen the interior of a Knowledge Center. The dome overhead was made of sandy glass warped by time, weather, and the desert's relentless heat. The central atrium was filled with tables, mingling scholars, and shelves crammed to the limit with books, scrolls, and journals. The shelves were arrayed throughout the room and covered every besosopion of the walls. Aremaeid saw several scholars on high ladders with stacks of books wobbling precariously in their arms. When Fiiorha strode through the atrium, her presence was met with varied reactions: one Rhithien in her path yipped and darted to the side, accidentally ramming into a shelf; a cluster of juveniles at a table went silent and dipped their heads to avoid her gaze; a scholar who was scaling a ladder nearly dropped her books and fell to the floor. Fiiorha scowled at the lot of them as though they were little more than pestilent insects.

"Saebien!" she roared, stomping over to one of the tables. Three juveniles were pouring over a pile of books, and supervising them was an older female who looked up as Fiiorha approached.

"What do you need, Fiiorha?" she asked calmly. The juveniles fell from their chairs to hide behind her, peeking around her legs.

"Where is Nexus? She agreed to meet me here at this time."

"Where do you think?" Saebien replied. A tiny grin danced across her lips. "She's downstairs with her creatures. Go easy on her, Fiiorha. You know how she is when Rhithien raise their voices at her. Especially you."

Fiiorha snorted and grumbled, "I'll speak to her how I please. Return to your studies."

Saebien rolled her eyes and helped the three juveniles back onto their chairs as Fiiorha led the pack away. They headed through a side door and down a long,

21

twisting stairwell. As they descended deeper underground, Aremaeid felt the air cooling on his skin. They at last came to a long, dimly-lit hallway lined by windowed doors. Aremaeid could hear scratching and animalistic vocalizations behind them. They followed the hall to a small room crowded with a too-large desk, cupboards, more books, and containers of various foodstuffs. The smell was overpowering, and Aremaeid just barely resisted the urge to cover his snout.

"Hush, little fluff. You had your breakfast today," a short, hunched Rhithien said. She spoke to a squawking bird that fluttered agitatedly around the room. Then her bulbous eyes fell on Fiiorha and the pack, and she let out a frightened whimper.

"You did not tell me there would be so *many*," she cried.

"There's only eight of them, Nexus," snapped Fiiorha. Nexus flinched and whimpered at her tone. Fiiorha ignored her, grimacing at the state of the room and adding, "When was the last time you cleaned up in here?"

"I know where everything is. Cleaning does not need to be done."

"Whatever. They're here to see your 'special ones'."

"They will not hurt them, will they?" Nexus asked nervously. She shrank away and curled her hands up against her chest when Salidus stepped forward and spoke to her.

"We are not going to harm your creatures. We only want to see and learn from them," he explained gently. Nexus studied him suspiciously for a moment, then slunk towards another door on the opposite wall. The pack followed her, accidentally whacking cupboards and clumsily knocking things over with their tails. Nexus glared at them and winced with every clatter, but she said nothing until they reached the door.

"Please keep your noise down. My special ones are easily frightened."

"Just fetch one of the damn things," Fiiorha ordered, rudely shoving Nexus into the next room. The smaller female screeched at the unwelcome physical contact and slammed the door shut. The pack was silent for a long, awkward minute before Ridaion spoke up.

"Is she coming back?" he asked cautiously.

"Yes. Just be patient," Fiiorha snapped. Sure enough, after another few moments, Nexus slipped back into the room. For the first time since he'd laid eyes on her, Aremaeid thought she looked relaxed and almost happy. She crooned at a bundle of cloth cradled in her arms, then carefully set it down on the desk in the center of the room. She pushed the fabric aside to reveal the creature within.

Aremaeid and the rest of the pack had spent the last twenty years fervently learning about humans—their cultures, their myriad of languages, their technology, their weaknesses—but it was another thing entirely to see one alive and up close. Aremaeid found himself edging closer to the table to get a better look, and he wasn't the only one. The human was a tiny thing, little more than half the size of a Rhithien. It was hard to believe that they were the dominant species on their planet. This thing had spindly limbs, a mop of coarse hair on its head, and no claws or fangs to speak of. Vegra leaned forward and grabbed the human's arms, yanking it roughly towards himself so he could get a better look. The thing started shrieking and babbling in one of its Earthen languages, and Nexus slashed her claws at Vegra with a snarl. The sudden attack made him release the human, and it scuttled back into Nexus's arms.

"Do not touch my special ones!" Nexus roared at him.

"That thing is about as sturdy as a leaf. I could've snapped that arm without even trying," Vegra scoffed.

"DO NOT TOUCH MY SPECIAL ONES!" Nexus wailed again, her voice growing in pitch. The trembling human whispered something unintelligible, and Nexus's fury immediately died. She pulled the human against her chest, stroked its hair, and purred softly.

After a moment she said in a softer tone, "They are much stronger than they look. Not alone, of course, although one could hold its own against something small. A human's mind is its greatest weapon. Very clever things. And quite friendly once you get to know them. This one was very hostile when she was first brought in—almost clawed my assistant's eyes out—but it took only a year for her to warm up to me. Very cuddly, she is. We've studied hundreds of humans at this Oasis, and many tame ones helped us flesh out some of the scholars' language translations."

"They know this, Nexus," Fiiorha sighed. "All eight of them have learned English and. . . what did you say the other one was?"

"Mandarin," Salidus replied.

"Yes, that one. Not all of them are familiar with the writing systems, but they know the spoken languages." Fiiorha seemed to suddenly realize that she hadn't insulted them in a while, so she sniffed and added, "Most of these males are illiterate fools."

Nexus's face lit up and, switching from Rhithos to English, she excitedly asked, "Are you all fluent? Or do you only have a handful of words and phrases?"

"We are fluent," Salidus replied proudly in English. The human's eyes bulged, and its jaw dropped open in shock. Aremaeid used the opportunity to glance into its mouth in search of hidden fangs, or any form of natural defense; he quickly gave up upon realizing that there was nothing but flat, useless teeth.

"What the fuck!" the human yelled, cowering against Nexus. "How many of you know English? What do you want with me?"

"Hush, little thing. They are only looking. Curious, they are," Nexus explained.

"I'm not a fucking freakshow attraction!" the human snapped. Aremaeid was surprised by its bravery. How could something so fragile afford to be so bold? Unperturbed by its outburst, Nexus clicked her tongue in disapproval and shook her head like it was a disobedient cub.

"Put that thing away," Fiiorha commanded in Rhithos. Both Nexus and the human flinched at her sharpness, but she didn't ease her tone. "It's vulgar, and they've seen enough."

Nexus nodded sullenly and wrapped the human back up in the blanket. She carried it out of the room and returned with an oddly happy expression.

"You are leaving now?" she inquired hopefully. There wasn't an ounce of subtlety in the question.

"Yes, yes. We're leaving. Go back to your little beasts," Fiiorha growled. She didn't wait for a response as she ushered the pack out of the room, back through the hallway, and up the stairs.

As they crossed the central atrium and headed for another door, Fiiorha began lecturing them.

"Nexus has the mind of an air-headed child, but she knows more about humans than anyone on Primaied. Over the last two millennia, we've sent thousands of reconnaissance groups to gather data from everywhere they can: maps, books, humans themselves, anything they could get their hands on. Larger Oases like this one all over Primaied have even captured and bred humans for study. And although pack Rhithien aren't the sharpest tools in the crate, I trust all of you are aware of the portals."

24

"Of course. The portals are the only way to access Earth," Salidus responded. Fiiorha gave him a begrudging look of approval before continuing.

"Yes. And you, like everyone else on Primaied, have heard the tales of Rhala. Rhala the Conqueror, the Warrior, the King. Long-dead scholars discovered the gateway during his brief but prosperous rule over Armenthaal, and Rhala decided to go through and see this new world for himself. As great as he was, he had the narrow mind of all other males, and he foolishly decided to go through alone. Thanks to some faulty counsel from his advisors, he was killed by a group of humans he encountered. The Lucio family. That event began the setup of the extensive surveillance network we have today, which was initially put in place to track the movements of the Lucio lineage. Humans are stupid little creatures; they are easy to follow, and most insist on having two or more names."

Aremaeid tuned her out. The pack had heard it all before and she knew it, but scholars her age liked to hear themselves talk. They soon entered a large side room with nothing inside save for a small stool, upon which was a bowl full of pebbles and a pair of leather pouches.

Fiiorha grabbed one of the bags and handed it to Salidus. It was strung on a flexible cord and no bigger than his palm. Objects rattled around inside.

"Are these..." Salidus asked in awe, his voice trailing off as he peeked inside the pouch.

"What do you think, *labyll?*" Fiiorha snapped. "The preserved remains of Rhala himself. Knuckle bones, specifically. I'll tear your head off myself if you lose even one of them."

Salidus tied the ends of the cord around his neck and pulled the mouth of the bag shut. Fiiorha nodded in approval and handed the second pouch to Orniell. She narrowed her eyes at him and hissed, "You will carry the portal stones in here. If you lose these, your entire pack will be stuck on Earth. Our scholars can't risk an extensive search. Failure is not an option. Do you remember the instructions I gave you last night? They were very clear, so I will not be repeating them."

"I remember," Orniell replied stiffly. He selected a small handful of the pebbles from the bowl. Aremaeid squinted at an array of peculiar symbols and runes carved into their smooth faces.

"Now, I know there are holes in some of the cultural and lingual studies you took on these creatures. If you see anything you don't understand, simply observe and adapt, then recall it for us when you finish the mission. Here, give me the stones. I know where you're going, and you have a better chance of securing your target if you end up in the right spot. Hopefully you can avoid. . . certain *issues*."

"Issues?" Aremaeid asked with a frown. Fiiorha growled irritably and gave him an exasperated glare.

"Even after two thousand years, the science of the portals isn't perfect. The teams of scholars we have working on them are still figuring out some of the more delicate intricacies. The chance of anything going wrong is minuscule, however, so I wouldn't worry about that. And Orniell, remember, once you move the stones from where they lay on the ground, you will have about ten seconds to go through before it closes. Since you're carrying them, I suggest you go last."

Fiiorha held the stones close to her mouth and whispered, "Nuncan. The Lucio house." Then she tossed them onto the ground, where they landed with several hard *thuds.* They did not bounce as normal pebbles might, but simply fell like hunks of metal. The runes on the stones glowed white for a few brief moments before a resounding *bang* tore through the room, startling the eight males and making Fiiorha's eye twitch with irritation. A huge circle of swirling light formed above the portal stones, so bright that Aremaeid's eyes watered when he tried to look directly at it.

"This is it," Salidus declared, turning to address his pack. His face shone with anticipation. "This is what we've been training for. What we've been selected for. Our mission is vital, but simple: find the target, get back to Primaied, and finally. . ." He paused and gripped the bag that hung around his neck. The knuckle bones within clicked softly against each other. He took a deep breath and finished, "We carry out the ritual."

"Lovely speech," Fiiorha commented dryly, her voice dripping with sarcasm. "Nice and short. You really enjoy listening to your own voice, don't you? Shut up and get a move on, now. If we wait another two thousand years, the humans will have destroyed Earth or evolved too quickly for Primaied to pose a threat. Orniell, are you certain you can be trusted to use those properly?"

"Yes, Fiiorha, I know the process," Orniell said tiredly as he tied the portal stone pouch around his neck.

Salidus was the first to step forward and disappear into the churning gateway. Aremaeid moved up next. He didn't hesitate to enter the portal. He refused to think about the repercussions of their mission that would befall Earth, that would befall an entire species. He could not allow himself to feel anything for those creatures.

My loyalty is to Primaied.

The gateway engulfed him. That blinding light seared into his brain, emptying his mind. It was burning agony and cool relief at the same time, and he barely registered the sensation of stepping out onto soft, damp grass.

II

It was a quiet evening in the small town of Nuncan, Montana. The streetlamps illuminated the darkened windows of houses and the neon signs of closed stores and restaurants. The occasional lonely car trundled through an intersection or sped along the interstate, slowing only to watch for deer crossing the road. The majority of Nuncan's population, however, were tucked snugly away in their homes for the night.

Maisie Arberon was one of said majority, although she was still hours from sleep. She sat at her kitchen counter with a mug of coffee beside her elbow and a stack of papers in front of her. Whenever her eyelids began to droop or she would start to think about how soft and warm her bed was, she took a sip of the life-saving beverage and rapidly clicked her favorite green pen until her energy returned. Staying up late into the night to grade her students' work was a long-established routine for her, even though the daytime procrastination that led to this point was devastating for her sleep schedule.

"Oy vey," she groaned as she flipped to a sheet covered in what looked like the scribblings of a dyslexic chimp. Maisie took pride in the knowledge that she never disliked any of her students, nor did they seem to dislike her—as far as she was aware—but a few of them had convinced her that they had no idea what the word "penmanship" meant. Leaning back in her seat, Maisie ran her fingers through her long, red hair and stretched her arms out over her head with a groan. She glanced at her old dachshund, Roller, who lay across the sofa in the adjacent living room with his head on the armrest. His vacant, heavy-lidded eyes seemed to be asking her to turn off the lights and let him sleep.

Maisie snorted at the thought and muttered, "I wish." The dog's ears perked up, but she ignored him. She grabbed her coffee mug and lifted it to her lips, then frowned when she saw that there was no more than a drop left in the

28

bottom. Standing up with a loud, tired sigh, she moved to her brewer to retrieve the final dregs of stale coffee from the pot. It was then that a tremendous, resounding *bang* went off outside, accompanied by a flash of blinding light that shone from the back of her house. Maisie yelped and ducked behind the counter, accidentally dropping the coffee pot in her panic. Glass and coffee exploded all over the laminate floor.

"Shit!" she yelled, whimpering and flapping her hands at the mess, and she hastily grabbed a dishtowel hanging from the oven handle. The oven door fell open as she did so, making another loud crash. She leaped back with a shriek, hitting her head on the cupboard door below the sink and cutting her hands on the broken glass.

"Shit, shit, *shit!*"

Tears of anxious frustration filled her eyes, and she wiped them away with a small, gasping sob. Roller hopped off the couch and waddled into the kitchen with a sympathetic whine.

Waving him away, Maisie cried, "No, dumbass, you're going to cut your feet! Stay!" Roller obediently stayed while Maisie gathered up the glass shards, dropped them into the kitchen trash, and wiped up the spilled coffee with her towel.

Deep breaths. Be calm. In, out. In, out. Remember Dr. Frasier's advice. Deep breaths. Be calm.

She crawled across the kitchen floor and scooped Roller into her arms. The old dog wagged his tail and licked her chin, and she buried her face in his coarse, scruffy fur.

Deep breaths. Be calm.

When she finally settled down enough to focus on the situation at hand, she cautiously stood, still cradling her dog against her chest, and peeked out the kitchen window. Was that sound a gunshot? No, she knew what gunshots sounded like. Perhaps it was someone's tire popping? She soon gathered the courage to place Roller back on the ground, tug on a light jacket, and walk to her front door. She stepped outside onto the porch and saw her neighbors doing the same thing all the way up the block. A small crowd was gathering in the middle of the street, the people all clad in robes, pajamas, and slippers. Maisie shut her door as she left to prevent Roller from escaping and then ran out to join them.

"...was getting up for some tea to help me sleep..."

"...fell out of bed..."

"...damn near pissed myself..."

Maisie's ears were assaulted by at least ten different voices telling similar stories as she jogged over. Catherine Lucio, a short blond woman who lived across the street, dashed up to her. The woman's face paled with worry.

"Maisie, what was that? Where did it come from? Was it a gun?"

"I don't know what it was, but it wasn't gunfire," Maisie responded tiredly. "Whatever it was, it scared the hell out of me."

"There hasn't been any gang activity here in decades," said an older man who lived a few houses down. Maisie had often seen him tending to the flower beds at his windows. "I don't think the base up north has anything that could make that sort of noise, either. Not so close to our neighborhood, anyway."

"It sounded a little like thunder. Maybe it's just an unexpected storm moving in," suggested a slender woman who had a grumpy-looking cat clutched to her chest.

"It's not storming. There was no indication of bad weather on any of the channels or radio stations," pointed out a man who could often be seen through his living room windows with his eyes glued to the TV. His comment was met by uneasy murmurs of agreement, but people still squinted up at the night sky in search of ominous clouds.

"What about that light?" Catherine piped up. The neighbors frowned at her.

"I didn't see a light."

"Me, neither."

"There *was* a light," Maisie agreed, and Catherine gave her a grateful smile. "How did no one else see it? It could have blinded someone."

This new information was met with nervous whispering. The group steadily grew larger and more restless as people continued filtering out of their homes, and they didn't quiet down until old Reverend Pate stepped up and addressed everyone.

"I don't know exactly what that was," he said with a calm, careful tone, "but lock your doors and shutter your windows tonight. The sheriff is a good friend of mine. I'll call him over for a quick look around, and I'm sure this will be cleared up by morning." Though the crowd remained unsettled, his reassurance calmed them somewhat, and everyone began to gradually disperse. It was late, they were tired, and no one wanted to stay up investigating this mystery when they

30

could simply leave it to the authorities. Maisie headed back up the street with Catherine, and as they were about to part for their respective houses, the woman turned and regarded her wearily.

"Are you still good to come over tomorrow?" she asked. "Layla's been doing so much better in school since you began the tutoring sessions."

"Oh, absolutely," Maisie replied without skipping a beat. "I'm always happy to help you guys out, Catherine. I want my students to succeed."

Catherine gave her a quick hug, bade her goodnight, and returned home, where her two children were waiting with her half-asleep husband. The elder of their offspring, Layla, waved from the doorway, and Maisie returned the gesture with a smile before climbing the steps back to her own house. She walked inside, hung up her jacket, and didn't notice anything out of place until she saw that Roller wasn't in the kitchen or the adjacent living room.

Probably got scared and went to the bedroom, Maisie assured herself, but she felt a strange nag in the pit of her stomach. She cautiously walked down the hallway, checking the bathroom and then her room. No Roller. She finally went to the sliding glass door in the back of the house—which was where the light had come from, she remembered—and found her dog staring out into the yard. His small body was tense, his hackles were raised, and his lips were pulled back from his gums in a vicious growl.

"Roller?" Maisie asked nervously. He didn't look up at her. She'd never seen him like this. She bit her lip nervously, squinting past the glass and into the unlit yard. Though terrified of what she might find, she carefully unlocked the door and slid it open, overcome by a strange urge to keep her movements quiet. She groped blindly at the side of the house for the switch that would turn on the porch light. There were no streetlamps back here, preventing her from seeing anything beyond her hand, and her earlier panic renewed as she failed to find the light switch. Groaning through her teeth, she reached out farther, sliding her hand along to where she knew it should be—there!

She grabbed the switch and pushed it up, flooding her lawn with pale fluorescent light. There, standing in the middle of her backyard, was a monster.

Roller started barking furiously. Maisie stumbled back with a gasp, slipping on the doormat and falling hard on her rear. The monster was huge; a quick estimation put it at close to twice her height. It began to approach her at an alarming pace, stalking forward on muscular hind legs and staring straight at her

31

with simmering golden eyes. Maisie scrambled back and tried to push herself up, but she was slow and clumsy in her panic. Her leaden limbs weighed her down; every movement was like trying to wade through water. It was a waking nightmare. Roller's barking turned into terrified whines as he tucked his tail between his legs and ducked behind her. His terror was enough to snap Maisie out of her hysterical state, and she managed to push herself to her knees and lunge for the door.

She was fast, but the creature was faster.

The thing leaped forward and shoved the door open just as she was closing it. The edge of the door slammed back against the wall with a *thud* that made the glass quake. Maisie let out a small cry of fright and crawled back down the hallway on her hands and knees. Roller darted by her faster than she'd ever seen him move, disappearing into her bedroom and leaving her alone with the monster. The loud thumping of its footsteps had her scrambling to her feet. She started forward, almost slipping on the floorboards, and made a break for the front door. Calling someone would take too long. She needed to get outside, find a neighbor, *anything*—

Something grabbed her hair and yanked her backward, then pulled her down. Maisie tried to scream, but she was cut off when a six-fingered hand the size of a dinner plate clapped over her mouth and nose. The monster crouched over her, holding her thrashing body tight with an iron grip. Desperate for air, Maisie clawed at its hand and kicked at the floor. She elbowed and scratched at it, but all in vain. The creature's strength was unyielding. Her lungs burned and her head pounded, and she realized with sudden clarity that she was dying. As she quietly suffocated in the dark recesses of her house, she wondered how long it would take for someone to discover her body.

*****

Aremaeid had to give the human credit for trying to put up a fight, even if its efforts amounted to nothing. His skin was too tough for its blunt nails to penetrate, and he barely felt it when those useless little teeth scraped his palm and dug into his middle finger. It was little more than an itching nibble. But the creature's energy was quickly fading due to the lack of air, and he used the opportunity to tighten his grip.

32

"I'm sorry, little one," he murmured in Rhithos. Because she needed to die, there was no point in using a human language, but the kill wouldn't sit right on his mind unless he said it. "You don't deserve this."

The bitter scent of fear hung around the human like a dark, festering cloud, and it thickened when he spoke. The creature was utterly terrified of him, and it was probably true that the little thing didn't deserve to die, but he had no choice. The secrecy of his pack's mission was vital above all costs, and this human had seen him.

The creature started to go limp, and Aremaeid thought it was close to death when it suddenly kicked again. He sighed. This was taking longer than he had anticipated. He tightened his grip on the human's head and prepared to snap its neck. He reflected that he should have done this as soon as he'd gotten his hands on the little thing. It was much quicker than suffocation.

Suddenly, a different set of teeth snapped into his tail. These teeth were sharp, unlike the human's. Aremaeid whipped around and snarled at the fuzzy little beast he had glimpsed just a few moments earlier. It scrambled away from him with a yelp and barked fiercely from a safe distance. He took a moment to study it, trying to puzzle out why this small, seemingly cowardly beast would attack him with such fire. But his attention shifted once more when he realized that he'd dropped the human in his distraction. It was crawling away from him, gasping and coughing, and he lunged forward to tackle it onto the ground again. He had it trapped on its back this time, and he didn't hesitate to lock his jaws around its throat. A messier death than he'd intended, but quick and necessary. His teeth were just about to break through the skin when the human spoke.

"Stop! Please, stop!" it begged. The desperation in its voice made Aremaeid pause, but he didn't pull away or release his grip on its neck.

The human apparently saw this as a victory, albeit a small one, and maintained, "You don't have to do this. Please, just. . . I'll do whatever you want. I don't know what you are or if you can understand me, but whatever you want, you can have it. Take my money, take my house or something, I don't care. Just don't. . . please don't k-kill me." The human's breath hitched and its throat bobbed against his teeth. It let out a quiet sob, and Aremaeid's ears twitched at the sound. It didn't know what he was. It didn't know why he was there. It had taken little to no effort to make the human submit to him, even though he hadn't even been aiming for such a reaction.

Kill it. Kill it now, before it calls for help. If you let it go, you could ruin everything.

But if it really was as terrified as it sounded—and based on the ever-increasing stink of fear that surrounded it, it was—then maybe he didn't have to kill it. He at last pulled away from the human's exposed neck and covered its mouth again, but he was careful to leave the nose exposed this time. He glanced over his shoulder at the door through which he'd entered. He had come out of the portal alone. He scanned the immediate area for his packmates but found not one of them. He briefly entertained the idea that they were still close by until he remembered something Fiiorha had told them before they'd left.

"Even after two thousand years, the science of the portals isn't perfect. The teams of scholars we have working on them are still figuring out some of the more delicate intricacies."

Aremaeid snarled a curse and, ignoring the human's muffled yelp of fright, looked wildly around the house as if it would provide some sort of solution to the problem at hand. He dug through his memories of the portal studies the pack had taken part in and recalled that one of the more common complications was "scattering". If this was what had happened, then it was likely that none of them were near the target or each other. The chances of this were "minuscule," Fiiorha had said. What were the odds that it would happen right when it was least convenient for them? He took a deep breath in an effort to soothe his rising frustration and looked down at the human. He would need to search for the target *and* his pack now, and he had no idea how long that would take. Perhaps this endeavor would be easier if he had a consistent place to lay low. He leaned down until his snout was just a few annosopions from the human's face and waited for it to meet his gaze.

"I am going to release you now," he said in English. The human froze and its eyes widened, but he continued before it could try responding. "If you scream, run, or attempt to call for help, I will kill you and the tiny beast that defends you. Do you understand?"

The human was shocked into stillness for so long that he started to wonder if he was speaking the right language. Maybe he had an accent that the human couldn't understand? Just as he started considering Mandarin, the human relaxed and nodded compliantly. He pulled his hand off the human's mouth and sat back on his haunches, allowing it to slowly rise into a seated position on the hard floor. Its scruffy companion dashed to its side and leapt into its arms, where it threw a final defensive bark at Aremaeid. The human squeezed the tiny beast and rocked shakily back and forth. It was then that Aremaeid paid attention to its breathing; it was rapid and panicked, and he felt a pang of guilt for scaring the little thing so badly. Still, if fear tactics were necessary, he would use them.

"You speak English," the human whispered at last.

"Yes."

"What do you want from me?" it whimpered. "Why are you at my house?"

Aremaeid's eyes narrowed, and it occurred to him that he may have ended up in the right place, even if his packmates hadn't.

"What is your name?" he demanded, and the human recoiled at his sudden harshness.

"M-Maisie. It's Maisie."

"And your family name?" he pressed impatiently, edging closer.

"Arberon. Maisie Arberon."

His shoulders slumped, and he rubbed his temples. He hadn't found the target after all. He looked back down at the human and studied its appearance. Staying in this house until he could locate his pack still seemed like the most viable option for the time being, so perhaps familiarizing himself was the best course of action. For now, at least. The human had long hair that was a unique shade of orange-red, and its eyes were a soft brown. Aremaeid also noticed the distinctive fleshy lumps on its upper torso that characterized human females. This individual was a female, then. He'd always found sex identification to be difficult when it came to these creatures; although female Rhithien didn't have those peculiar glands, their tail spikes and shorter horns made them easy to distinguish. Humans, on the other hand, all looked the same at a glance.

"I did not intend to come to your house," he admitted. "I apologize for any disruption I have caused."

"Disruption?" the human repeated with a hollow laugh. "You tried to kill me."

"Yes. I am sorry for that as well."

"Just. . . Just sorry? Nothing else to say?"

"What would you like to hear?" inquired Aremaeid, cocking his head to the side. The human—Maisie, he reminded himself—opened her mouth, then closed it. She swallowed hard and tried again.

35

"There was a weird sound a few minutes ago. A really loud one. And a light. Was that you?" she asked at last. When Aremaeid nodded in confirmation, she shakily whispered, "Are you an alien?"

He almost informed her that no, *she* was the alien, but stopped himself when he remembered that he was the one invading her planet.

"To you, I suppose," he conceded.

"Oh," she breathed, hugging her furry beast tightly. "Oh, jeez, I need a minute. You're like. . . from another planet?"

"Yes." Aremaeid once again looked over his shoulder towards the glass door and asked off-handedly, "Have you seen any others?"

"Others?"

"Like me. More of my kind," he clarified. The human gasped and scooted away from him.

"There's *more* of you?" she squeaked.

Aremaeid mentally smacked himself and tried to think of a quick response that wouldn't scare her off.

"We are not here to harm you or anyone else," he lied, holding his hands out passively.

"You just tried to kill me!" the human cried. Her breathing quickened again.

Aremaeid hastily countered, "Only because my pack's mission was meant to be secret. In all honesty, we are not yet ready to reveal ourselves to your kind. The only reason I ended up here is that a problem arose in our transportation and we were separated."

"Oh. So, this is supposed to be like. . . what? Some sort of scouting mission?"

"Something like that," Aremaeid agreed with a nod. The human still looked nervous, but she was slowly starting to relax.

Thank Callii, she believes me.

The human scrutinized him in silence for several seconds before shifting onto her knees and straightening her posture. She was still afraid of him, but the smell of her terror had begun to dissipate.

"Why did you let me live?" she asked, narrowing her eyes with suspicion. "What do you want from me?"

She yanked on a strand of hair, and Aremaeid took a deep breath. Would she allow him to stay? And if she did, would she keep his presence a secret?

"I need somewhere to hide while I search for my pack," he answered. That part wasn't a lie; he really did need to find them. But Maisie wasn't convinced. She edged away and pressed herself against the wall, quivering like a cornered rhego.

"Why here? Why me?" she demanded. "Couldn't you go find somewhere else?" Aremaeid straightened up from his hunched position and slunk closer, making her shrink down into a terrified ball.

"You have seen me," he growled. "No other human knows I am here. I do not want to kill you, Maisie Arberon, but I will if I must." Maisie stared up at him, trembling with fear. Her furry companion whined and wriggled nervously in her arms. After a few moments, the human gulped and responded.

"How long?" she whispered, her voice barely audible. Aremaeid hesitated before providing a rough estimation. Surely his packmates couldn't be *too* far away.

"A week."

"A *week?*"

"At the very most. It may not take that long."

"And you're leaving as soon as you find them?"

"As soon as I find them," he confirmed.

Maisie looked down at her hairy companion as if consulting its opinion, and after a beat of cautious hesitation, she nodded. Aremaeid exhaled slowly, relieved that there was no need to kill her. He knew she would have to die eventually if their mission was to succeed, just like all the other humans on her planet, but that didn't mean he had to enjoy it. He backed away and allowed her to stand up before following her down the hall to a stairway. She released her little companion, which ran away as fast as its stubby legs could carry it, and guided Aremaeid down the stairs. She led him into a small, cluttered room and flicked a switch on the wall that activated a spotty yellow bulb.

"You can stay down here. I don't usually get visitors, but when I do, I never bring them into the basement." She threw constant peripheral glances at him like she thought he would lunge at her again." I'm usually gone during the day, but you can come upstairs if you need anything. I'll, um. . . I'll try to answer whatever questions you have."

"I will not come out in the day. It would be too easy for more of your kind to spot me."

"Oh. Right. Okay."

The space was full of boxes, dusty books, and old furniture that Aremaeid doubted would hold his weight. He had to stoop to fit under the low ceiling, and even then, he couldn't help whacking his horns on wooden beams that stretched overhead. Maisie flinched with every bump.

"Thank you," Aremaeid said sincerely, bowing his head.

Maisie returned it with a curt nod and started to leave, but stopped just before heading back upstairs.

"What's your name?" she inquired.

Aremaeid blinked in surprise. It was such a simple, standard question, yet he hadn't really expected her to ask it of him.

"I am called Aremaeid," he replied. Maisie nodded in acknowledgment. She remained in place for a few awkward seconds, opening and closing her mouth as if she wanted to ask more, then scuttled back up the stairs, leaving him in the basement. Recalling the switch on the wall, Aremaeid strode over to it and inspected the small plate. It was common knowledge that human technology advanced quickly and made up for their lack of magic, but seeing its efficacy in person was fascinating. He pushed on the tiny rod with a single finger and jumped back when it flicked sharply downwards. The room darkened instantly. His vision automatically switched to compensate for the change, allowing him to see his surroundings in varying shades of grey.

Oases were the only places he knew of that had luxurious articles of furniture like the ones around him. Was this typical for human dwellings? He experimentally poked the cushion of a wide chair, and his claw pierced the soft covering easily. He was tempted to sit down on it but decided that this course of action would not be in his best interest. Just as he was turning away, something on the cushion caught his eye: a tiny hair, almost imperceptible in the darkness. He plucked it from the chair and sniffed it hesitantly, then drew back when he recognized the faint odor of Maisie's beast. Did it use furniture as she did? Did she consider it an equal? Perhaps she was raising it for food, as Oases did with livestock. But if that was the case, wouldn't more creatures be running around?

Aremaeid pushed those questions aside for later pondering and searched for a noisemaker. He wouldn't be able to sleep until he could ensure that Maisie wouldn't attempt to sneak away. He eventually uncovered a round, palm-sized bell that tinkled with every movement. He slunk up the stairs—being careful to make minimal noise on the creaky floor—and sniffed around until he located Maisie. She had shut herself inside a room in the hall, and if the smell was any indication, her beast was in there as well. He gingerly placed the bell against the door, ensured its stability, and returned to the basement.

Satisfied with the rudimentary but functional alarm system he had set up, he ducked into a cramped cavity beneath the stairs. It was far from comfortable, but it would do. He, like most Rhithien, was a light sleeper and would be woken immediately if Maisie tried to flee. He doubted she would, but one could never be too careful.

Aremaeid knew his top priority was locating his pack and their human target, but he didn't know how much time he had until dawn, and he didn't trust Maisie to keep quiet about her predicament if he left her knowingly alone in the house. But as long as she believed he was in the basement, she would hopefully be deterred from seeking aid. Feeling as secure as he could under the tenuous circumstances, Aremaeid closed his eyes and waited for sleep to take him.

III

Layla Lucio sat on her bed, clutching a bulky flashlight and whispering excitedly under a blanket with her younger brother, Tyson. He had started to cry when they were all awoken by that boom, but Layla was proud to admit that she hadn't shed a single tear. She hadn't even been all that scared. She had, in fact, been nothing but excited; once the irritation of being roused in the dead of night wore off, she'd realized that their neighborhood had been granted a great opportunity. The way she saw it, there was only one logical explanation for what had happened.

"Do you have any idea what that was?" Tyson asked, wringing his hands and staring up at her with his fearful brown eyes.

"I know exactly what it was," Layla scoffed. "You seriously haven't figured it out?"

"The government?"

"No, stupid! An *alien!*" She knew her little brother was unfortunately dense at times, but had he really not considered the obvious truth?

Tyson's eyes looked like they were going to pop out of his skull as he asked in awe, "For real? How do you know?"

"It's the only way to explain what happened. That weird noise? The light? Come on! What else could it have been?" Layla explained. "We should look for it. Just imagine, Tyson: we could be the first people to ever see an alien!"

"You don't think it could be anything else?"

"Well, I guess it *could* be something else, but that's not as exciting. Aliens are cool. I bet there's one in Nuncan right now."

"That might not be a good thing."

"Come *on!*" Layla insisted, giving him a playful shove. "Where's your imagination? Let's just pretend for a second that we know it's an alien; wouldn't that be exciting? We could make friends with it!"

"It might be here to take over Earth, though," her brother pointed out. She waved her hand dismissively.

"It probably came in peace, or it would have attacked right away and blown Nuncan sky-high. Besides, you're missing the point. How cool would it be to see an actual alien? If we could get a picture, we could show everyone and become famous and rich!"

Layla sighed wistfully. She was not unique in her twelve-year-old aspiration of being famous. She longed to have paparazzi scrambling after her, adoring fans begging for her autograph, and all her peers fawning over her in endless admiration. She knew aliens were supposed to only exist in movies, but how cool would it be if there really *was* one in Nuncan? Would it want to take over Earth, as Tyson suggested, or would it be more interested in peace? She didn't know, but she could easily picture herself as an ambassador to creatures with bald green heads and big black eyes, or perhaps as a hardened and clever survivor of the apocalypse, scarred by her tragic experiences. With these two images in her head, Layla decided she would be fine with both options.

"Yeah, I guess," Tyson relented. He still sounded unsure but seemed to be warming to the idea.

"You *guess?*" Layla exclaimed in disbelief. "This could be the biggest moment of our lives! We could go to parties, have friends besides each other for once, and buy all the puppies we want! Mom and Dad wouldn't have to work, so they could spend all their time at home! Wouldn't that be great?"

"Yeah," Tyson conceded, but he held up a finger before Layla could continue. "But that's only if it really *is* an alien that's coming in peace."

"Don't be so *cynical*," Layla scolded, taking pride in her use of the word she'd learned the other day. She wasn't entirely sure she was using it right, but Tyson didn't have to know that.

"Cynical?" her brother repeated, his brow furrowing. He began to play with a knotted-up length of yarn in his lap. This was nothing new; whenever he was confused or agitated, he tied knots into whatever string he had on hand.

"It's like the opposite of excited," Layla explained. "I'm super excited about what could happen when we find the alien, but you don't seem excited at all. We could be famous, and you're all like, 'Yeah, but it might not be a nice alien.'"

"But it might not be," he insisted. She rolled her eyes and sighed exasperatedly. She enjoyed her brother's company—he was her only real friend, after all—but she often thought that he had no creative vision. The only thing he ever got excited about was tying knots.

"It probably is, though. Like I told you, it would've attacked us as soon as it got here if it was evil. And if it turns out that it was waiting for a specific time to invade Earth, we'll just beat it up! It can't be too tough."

"How would we even find it, though? It could be anywhere."

The two siblings were silenced by a thump above their heads, and Layla thought she heard a faint growling noise. Her bedroom was on the second floor of the house, right below the attic, making that the only place where such a noise could come from. She grinned at Tyson, who once again looked terrified and had begun frantically knotting and unknotting his yarn.

"Looks like we don't have to," she said.

They slipped out of Layla's room and quietly padded down the hall until they reached the narrow staircase that led up to the attic. Tyson balked at the foot of the steps, and Layla frowned.

"What's your problem?" she hissed. "The sound came from above us, dumbass." Normally Tyson would have started giggling hysterically at her use of a forbidden word, and the two of them would exchange foul phrases behind their parents' backs, but now his face was devoid of amusement. Even in the dark Layla could see that he was pale and trembling.

"I know it came from above us, but do we really have to go up there? I don't like the attic," he whined. Layla rolled her eyes, but she understood his complaints. She didn't particularly like the attic, either. A few years prior, their parents had made plans to renovate it and turn it into an office or guest bedroom. They'd even gone so far as to transfer most of the cardboard boxes of keepsakes and antiques from past generations down to the basement. The project was abandoned, however, when Dad went back to college and later started his current job as an accountant. So the attic remained dusty, unused, and likely full of spiders.

"I don't like it any more than you do, but you want to be famous, right? Or at least rich? Think of all the sad puppies we could save from shelters and stores," Layla encouraged, her voice a gentle whisper. Tyson bit his lip and glanced back in the direction of Layla's room, but followed his sister up the stairs despite his obvious trepidation, fiddling with his string all the while.

Layla reached the door and opened it slowly, wincing as it gave a creak that sounded painfully loud in the quiet house. It was a good thing their parents were hard sleepers. She walked inside, squinting through the dark at the silhouettes of old chairs and a dusty wooden card table. Behind her, Tyson shuddered and moved closer to her side. Layla understood his fear. The attic was spooky enough during the day, but nighttime rendered it absolutely terrifying, full of deep shadows cast by pale moonlight that was filtered through a single high, dusty window. The unused furniture formed dark, lurking shapes that seemed to move when she looked at them out of the corner of her eye. She had to do a double-take at a tall, broad armchair that sat in the corner of the room. She could have sworn she saw something move behind it, but she shook her head and decided it must have been her imagination.

"Go get the flashlight. I left it in my room," she ordered. She knew Tyson couldn't handle much more of this. He nodded and raced down the stairs, skipping the last two and landing with a loud *thump* that made Layla cringe. As she waited for Tyson to return, she found her gaze drawn once more to the big armchair in the corner. It looked a little like what she imagined a throne would look like, with a wide seat and low armrests. The back of it arched high into the air with intricate curls and spirals carved into the wooden frame. The thought of a real throne in her attic eased Layla's fear, so she tiptoed over to it and sat down, experimentally posing at the edge of the chair and straightening her spine. She could easily picture herself as a queen, majestic and beautiful, looking over the heads of her devoted subjects.

She was unaware of the tall, dark shadow that rose behind the armchair to tower over her, black as a moonless night.

"It suits you," purred a soft, deep voice.

Layla leaped out of the chair with a yelp, falling to the floor and whipping around to look behind her. Paralyzed by a set of glowing red eyes, she could just make out a tall, hunched silhouette with a pair of long horns.

The figure seemed startled by her reaction, and it, too, jumped back. It held its hands out before it and said quickly, "I mean you no harm! I did not intend to scare you. I am sorry." It really did sound sorry, and Layla found herself relaxing. The thing no longer seemed to loom over her as it had before, and those scarlet eyes no longer seemed quite so menacing.

"What are you?" she asked, her voice coming out in a whisper.

"I am not of Earth," the creature informed her. Layla's fear was quickly replaced with her earlier excitement. Was this real?

"You're an *alien?*" she asked enthusiastically. The alien seemed to sense her sudden ease, and it crouched down to her level to get a better look at her as she demanded, "What's your name?"

"Ornathium is the name I was given," the creature replied.

"Do you want to know my name?" she prompted when the alien didn't return the question. She bounced on her feet, looking him up and down. She was fairly certain it was a "him."

"Sure," he replied absently. He didn't seem particularly invested in knowing her name as he looked around the small room and poked at the old furniture, but Layla knew he'd probably never seen a human house before, so she overlooked his apparent disinterest.

"My name's Layla," she declared proudly. "Layla Lucio."

Suddenly she had the creature's undivided attention; it was almost frightening how quickly those unblinking crimson eyes locked onto her.

"Lucio, you say?"

Ornathium's voice was filled with renewed gravity. Still crouched down, he shuffled a few steps closer to her and cocked his head to the side like a curious dog. Layla wasn't threatened by his approach, despite his shift in mood, so she nodded and smiled.

"Yep. Why are you in my attic?"

"Because—" Ornathium shut his mouth, then looked around once more. There was a calculating expression on his face for a moment before he smiled back at her, revealing a mouthful of sharp teeth, and replied, "Because I was participating in a transportation experiment. I did not mean to come here. Have you seen others? I arrived with a pack."

"There's more of your kind?" Layla gasped delightedly.

"Yes. Seven others. They are not here?"

"No. Did the experiment fail or something?"

"It appears so," he answered with a heavy sigh. His ears drooped and Layla saw a long tail curl tightly around his legs. Thumping sounded on the attic stairs then, and panic chilled her. Was it Mom or Dad? She exhaled when Tyson burst through the door, grunting and hefting the large flashlight.

"Sorry I took so long," he whisper-shouted. "I had to go to the bathroom, and—" His voice came to a halt when he turned the bright beam on Layla and the alien she had discovered. Layla dashed over to him and clapped a hand over his mouth before he could scream. She shushed him harshly and yanked the flashlight from his grasp, then shone it on Ornathium so she could get a good look at his appearance. Although he was crouching and hunched, he was bigger than any human she'd ever seen. His pitch-black skin reflected a slight gray hue when she shone the light directly on his muscled form. A large frill covered the back of his neck, and two ribbed horns jutted up from his forehead and curved slightly backward. The cat-like tail she'd noticed earlier twitched and flicked behind his legs. Layla pressed a hand to her mouth to suppress a giggle at the sight of how long his arms were. Then she noticed the awkward way they were bent and frowned.

"What's with your arms?" she demanded.

"What about them?"

"Are they broken?"

Ornathium blinked in surprise and studied his arms thoughtfully. It took Layla a moment to realize that they were not broken. Rather, he had two elbows on each one.

"They do not feel broken," Ornathium mused. Layla trotted closer and circled him, intently studying his legs. His first knee joint was bent like a person's, but he had a second one lower on his leg that was inverted. She thought at first they were normal digitigrade legs, but he also had raised ankles similar to that of a dog. Two knee joints on each leg, just like his elbows. And while his hands were human-ish—despite having twelve digits instead of ten—his feet looked more like paws. He was like some sort of cross between a human and an assortment of unrelated animals.

"Woah," Tyson breathed from the doorway. He opened his mouth, then closed it again.

"I know, right?" Layla squealed, bouncing back to her brother. "I thought that noise was an alien, but I didn't *really* think it was an alien, you know? Just imagine what this could mean for us!"

"We should tell Mom and Dad," Tyson said seriously. His face didn't display a single ounce of mirth.

"I guess we could do that. Yeah, we should, actually! Then they could tell their friends, and then the newspapers, and when everyone knows we discovered an alien, we could be famous, and—"

"No!" Ornathium interrupted suddenly. Both children jumped at his sharpness, and he said in a softer tone, "No, please do not do that."

"Why not?" Layla whined.

"What do you think your parents would do if they found me here? They might drive me away. They might tell everyone and claim all the credit. It was you who found me, Layla, was it not?"

Layla nodded, seeing the sense in his words. Mom was always trying to make convoluted deals at work, and Dad was unstoppably ambitious in his efforts to search for a better job. An image popped into Layla's head of her parents standing by Ornathium, smiling winningly as they shoved their daughter—the real hero—out of the spotlight. Cameras snapped wildly, microphones were thrust forward, and Layla got none of it. She was the one who found Ornathium, wasn't she?

"On another note, I told you earlier that I came here with a pack. No one is meant to know about our mission. The fact that you two already know is bad enough, but. . . If an entire human town were to find out, I could get in serious trouble," Ornathium elaborated.

"That's okay, you can just stay here with us!" Layla offered happily, but he shook his head.

"You do not understand. I could be killed or exiled simply for talking to you."

"Why are you still here, then?" demanded Tyson, who was looking increasingly suspicious of the alien.

"I am unable to leave without my pack," Ornathium explained. "It seems we were scattered during the transition. I need to find them before I can return to my world."

Tyson narrowed his eyes and inquired, "How long will that take?"

"Don't be a jerk," Layla scolded her brother. "If he needs to stay here, he can. He's nice."

"He's scary," muttered Tyson. His fingers flew across his knotted string at a breakneck speed.

"Would it be alright if I stayed here for a few days?" Ornathium asked hesitantly. His ears suddenly drooped, and he turned away with a sigh. "I understand if you do not want me to. I can find somewhere else to stay while I search for my pack. You need only ask it of me."

Tyson opened his mouth to respond, but Layla hopped to Ornathium's side and answered before her brother could make a peep.

"Of course you can stay! We won't tell our parents or anyone else, we promise. Right?"

Layla gave her brother a hopeful look. He didn't say anything at first. He just stood in the doorway, playing with his string and staring at the floor. When he glanced up, Layla gave him her best puppy dog eyes. Tyson looked reluctant, but he finally nodded in assent, dropping his gaze to the attic's dusty floorboards once again.

"Fine," he conceded. "But only until you find them."

"Of course. I will search for them every night," Ornathium said with a grateful smile. But Tyson didn't offer a smile of his own, instead turning around and heading back down the stairs.

"I'm going to bed. You should, too, Layla," he mumbled.

"I will, I will!" Layla assured him. "Good night!" She watched as Tyson disappeared, finally offering her a chance to talk to Ornathium in private. She wanted to know everything; everything about him, the planet he was from, the technology they had, and more.

"I assume you have questions?" he prompted, sensing her enthusiasm.

"Yes!" Layla exclaimed. "What's your planet called? Where is it? Do you have fancy technology? Are there people on your planet? Do you have dogs? How did you get here? What's your species called?"

"Slow down, child! I can only answer one at a time," Ornathium interjected hastily.

"Fine. What's your species called?"

"We are called Rhithien."

Rhithien. What a weird word, Layla thought to herself. But she didn't slow down; there was so much more she wanted to know.

"What's your planet? How did you get here?"

"My planet is Primaied. My pack and I came here through a portal that connects our world to Earth."

Layla stared at him. When he said portal, did he mean a magic one? She immediately envisioned dark gateways, people sliding through wormholes, and round tunnels tearing through the fabric of the universe. Was it truly possible that these aliens, these *Rhithien*, had magic or some weird, advanced technology that could do such a thing?

"Do you mean a magical portal? Or a techy portal?" she asked, voicing her thoughts aloud.

"Magic, of course."

"Oh my God. Oh, wow." Layla took a moment to gather her thoughts. This was huge. Not only did aliens exist, but magic did as well. She took a deep breath and inquired, "Is there other magic on. . . How do you say it? Prim—?"

"Primaied. And yes, there is," Ornathium replied.

"Do you have magic? You have to show me!" Layla begged, eagerly jumping up and down and almost forgetting to keep her voice low.

"I do not have any. The only Rhithien who have magic are alphas and healers. I cannot show you the portals, either. Special stones are required to open them, and I do not have those stones."

"Aww!"

Disappointment settled heavily in her chest. She was grateful to meet a legitimate alien, but it would have been cooler if he had magic.

"I am sorry I have upset you, little queen," Ornathium said somberly. Layla gave him a puzzled expression.

" 'Little queen'? What's that supposed to mean?"

"Oh, nothing, just a stray thought. I tend to speak my mind. But when you first came in here, you looked rather dignified in that chair. Quite elegant, for one so small. Like. . ." Ornathium paused, as if letting his words sink in, and a shy smile spread across Layla's face as he finished, "Like a queen, perhaps?"

"Yeah," she confirmed with a slow nod. "Like a queen. It's just a nice chair, is all. I don't think I could actually be one."

"Whyever not?" Ornathium asked, sounding genuinely perplexed.

"I dunno," she replied with a shrug. "I don't have any royal blood or a fancy last name or anything. I'm just a Lucio."

The Rhithien was silent for a moment before he softly commented, "I think it is a perfectly fine name."

Layla blushed and rocked back on her heels, clasping her hands behind her back. Who would have guessed that humanity's first encounter with an alien would go so well?

"How long do you think it'll take to find your pack?"

"I cannot say. It could be a few days; it could be a few weeks."

"Well, the longer the better," Layla decided with a grin. Ornathium smiled back at her and held out one of his large hands. A small part of Layla quailed at the sight of sharp, curved claws on the tip of each finger, but she ignored her unease and took his hand.

"Friends?" the Rhithien offered.

"Friends," she agreed.

After a few more minutes in the attic, she returned to her room and splayed across her bed contentedly. The longer Tyson kept his promise and stayed quiet, the longer Ornathium could live in their attic. There was still so much more he could tell them, and Layla wanted to hear it all.

There was an alien in her house. An alien who had magic and said she looked like a queen and wanted to be her friend.

And he was her own personal secret.

IV

Torraeid had never liked heights. He'd been shorter than everyone around him his entire life, and he'd grown comfortable with that shortness. Standing on top of raised platforms or looking out the window of a Typig Building terrified him. His feet were no longer on the ground, and even if he was only a few besosopions up, it looked so far away. Aremaeid and the others didn't seem to have a problem with heights, however, so he had neglected to share his fears since joining the pack. Still, even something as simple as climbing a tree made his stomach churn and his head spin.

Because of this, he felt that panicking was a perfectly reasonable reaction when he came out of the portal in free-fall.

One moment he was trapped in the swirling light, and the next moment there was nothing but cold wind whipping around him. The safe, solid ground he had expected was nowhere to be found as he spun and careened through the air. Sheer terror overtook him and he screamed, but the wind swallowed the sound as he plummeted towards Earth's surface with all the grace of a heavy rock. Luckily, he didn't have too far to fall; a dense forest canopy rushed at him, and then his body crashed into it, tearing through the leafy growth. Leaves crackled and whooshed at his passing, bristling twigs clawed at his skin, and a large branch snapped beneath his weight, sending him to the ground with an undignified *whump.* He lay face-down for several minutes while he caught his breath and allowed his fear to dissipate. Despite his painful landing, he was relieved to have dirt and dry leaves beneath him.

"Fuck. Me."

Torraeid pushed himself up, groaning, and sat back on his haunches. He looked around in bewilderment, taking in the thick foliage around him. Tall trees covered with spiny green needles surrounded him, and a bird twittered somewhere in the distance. Was he supposed to be here? He couldn't smell or hear any human activity. How were they supposed to find and capture the target if they were nowhere near it? He lifted his nose into the light breeze and sniffed, searching for something he could rely on.

Trees. . . other plants. . . birds. . . no humans. . . no—

Torraeid tensed when he realized that he couldn't smell his packmates. He strained his ears to listen for them and scoured his surroundings, but they were nowhere to be seen.

"Aremaeid!" he called, hoping his brother would respond. "Ridaion! Orniell?"

No luck. He then remembered Fiiorha's warning and rolled his eyes with a growly sigh.

Of course we've been scattered. Right when it could ruin trilunar cycles of research, training, and planning, we get scattered.

Keeping low to the ground, Torraeid made his way through the woods, sniffing along in the dirt and into the wind for any sign of the other Rhithien. His ghostly white complexion made blending in a difficult feat, but he made an effort to stay within shadows and slink behind bushes. He couldn't afford to get caught. He couldn't afford any sort of delay if he wanted to see Primaied again. He had no doubt that his pack would leave him on Earth if faced with the choice of waiting for him or completing the mission.

Suddenly, his ears pricked up and he froze. He could hear a voice; a Rhithien voice.

"Salidus! Orniell!"

He started laughing in relief and scampered quickly towards the source. At least he had one of his packmates. But his joy was immediately squashed when he slipped through some trees, rose to his feet, and spotted Vegra standing alone in a clearing.

Great Callii, not him.

Alas, he had no choice but to be civil. Not only did Vegra outrank him, but the older male was obviously in the same scattering situation if he was calling out to the others.

"Vegra," Torraeid greeted stiffly, lowering his head respectfully.

"Oh, it's *you,* runt," Vegra growled. His brutish face twisted into a disgusted grimace. He was far from a refined intellect, but he had a quick temper and was a ruthless, battering force in combat. His aggression had earned him a set of jagged claw marks across his throat that turned his voice into a loud, angry rasp.

"I am glad to find someone else here," Torraeid said in a hesitant bid for polite conversation.

"Go fuck yourself," grunted Vegra in response. He sneered and added, "It's not like anyone else will."

Torraeid rolled his eyes and muttered, "Nice to see you, too." He hunched his shoulders in anticipation of a blow as Vegra came stomping over. Rather than hitting him, however, the older male grabbed his frill and yanked him backwards. A blaze of sharp pain stabbed through Torraeid's body, and he shrieked as Vegra slammed him down against the ground and tore into his frill with his claws.

"Don't take a fucking tone with me, freak. Remember how well your last act of insubordination went?"

"Let go!" Torraeid wailed, scrabbling at Vegra's hand. "I'm sorry! I'm sorry, just let go!"

Vegra released him with a snarl and stepped away. Torraeid, clutching his mangled frill, crawled away from him with a low whine of pain. Why did frills have to hurt so much?

"Fucking pathetic," Vegra hissed. Torraeid just nodded, only half-listening as he reached behind his head and gingerly poked at his frill, trying to gauge the damage. It was still throbbing painfully, as it always did whenever it was injured, but it didn't seem especially bad. Vegra had barely pierced the thin veil of skin with the tips of his claws.

Stalking away to stand in a patch of moonlight, Vegra squinted up at the sky and rasped, "Have you found any of the others? I came out of the portal alone."

"Just you," Torraeid replied bitterly. "I'm pretty sure we've been scattered. The portal erred like Fiiorha said it might."

"You think I can't figure that shit out for myself?" snarled Vegra. Torraeid suspected that no, he hadn't figured that shit out for himself, which was probably why he was so pissed at an off-hand comment. But Vegra was always pissed about something, and voicing those thoughts would get him killed.

"I never said that."

"You fucking thought it, though."

The older male stomped over and yanked Torraeid up to his feet by one of his horns.

"I swear I didn't!" he lied. "I was thinking about the scattering. Now, I know you don't like me any more than I like you, but we're stuck together until we find the others."

Vegra dropped him and suggested, "I could just musk over all the trees and wait for them to come here."

"That's disgusting, Vegra."

"Shut up, you purple-eyed twat!" the older Rhithien snapped. He smacked Torraeid's damaged frill, eliciting a pained yelp from the smaller male. "If you're so bloody clever, what would you suggest?"

Torraeid knew Vegra just wanted to discuss options without appearing to be considering someone else's opinion, but he didn't question it. That would be suicide. It was a relief, anyway; Vegra never asked for his input ordinarily.

"The others might not be anywhere near this spot, and they're probably out looking, as well. They could be moving farther away from us for all we know. I think it would be best if we stuck together and searched this area. We don't know how big these woods are, and two Rhithien can cover more ground than one."

"I think it would be best if you shut up and let the Rhithien with the better rank make the plans, runt," Vegra growled. Torraeid clenched his jaw and nodded sullenly. Vegra looked around, and after a moment declared, "Here's what we're going to do: we don't know how big these woods are, and I suspect the others are already searching for us, maybe even moving farther away. We need to look for them. And as much as I hate your filthy fucking guts, two Rhithien can cover more ground than one."

"Excellent plan."

"I know. Now shut your mouth and go that way. I'll go this way. We shall return to this spot at dawn and reconvene. Move your ass!"

Torraeid didn't wait for any further instruction. Relieved to be rid of Vegra, he dashed off into the woods in search of more tolerable company.

*****

Ridaion wasn't sure what he was expecting to see when he came out of the portal, but it wasn't what he got. He arrived on Earth in the middle of a large room built of boards that looked like they'd been cut from dead trees. There was a furry rug on the floor beneath his feet made from the pelt of some large beast, and he cringed at the overpowering smell of rot emanating from it. Mounted on the walls all around him were strange animal skulls, poorly-stuffed carcasses that still carried moldy flesh, and several of the long, awkward-looking weapons he had learned about in his human studies.

"The fuck?" he whispered, slowly turning in a circle to take in the entirety of the room. He found the décor oddly disturbing—especially when he realized how many of the creatures had antlers or horns. But overshadowing it all was the centerpiece of the room, a bed big enough to fit at least three Rhithien. Parts of the frame were carved from wood while other parts looked more like bone, and the headboard was bedazzled with polished skulls and rows of sharp teeth. Ridaion stared at those skulls for a moment before turning around and searching the room for an exit.

"Fuck this," he muttered as he stalked towards a door opposite the bed. It was unlocked, thankfully, and when he ducked past the low frame he was met with a long, dimly-lit hallway. Every anxious warning bell in his head was ringing violently, and he hesitantly called out, "Salidus?" His alpha had to be around here somewhere. Ridaion took a cautious step forward, wincing as the moldy floorboards creaked under his weight, and he nearly jumped out of his skin when he heard a door open somewhere else in the house.

Fuck fuck fuck fuck…

He heard footsteps accompanied by a tired yawn, and his panic increased when the shadow of what appeared to be a human started ascending the stairs at the end of the hallway. Ridaion was faced with two options: hide in the skull room with the dead creatures, or throw the human down the stairs and run out of the house before it knew what was happening. Before he was even aware of making a decision, he was back inside the skull room, shutting the door as softly as he could. He looked wildly around the carcass-filled space in search of a good hiding spot.

First, he checked the underside of the bed, but it didn't take a genius to figure out that he wouldn't fit. There was a tall shelving unit full of drawers in one corner of the room, but the human might notice if it was moved to make space behind it. There was a closet with two large doors, but he would have to double himself over to fit inside, and there was no guarantee that the human wouldn't need something from it. Not knowing what else to do, Ridaion just stood awkwardly behind the door, hoping he could quietly slip out after the human came in.

The door suddenly slammed open, smacking straight into him, and without thinking he yelled, "Ow, what the fuck!" There was a scream of fright, and the human who obviously lived in the house dashed past him, heading for the large bed. Ridaion tried to skirt around the door, but he slipped on the rug and fell to the floor with a clumsy *thump.*

"You're not taking my soul! With God as my witness, it ain't my time!" the human screeched, and Ridaion's eyes widened when it pulled one of those long weapons—a *gun,* he recalled—from beneath the bedclothes.

"Hang on, you do not want this, I can—" he began in English, but he flattened himself to the floor with a yelp just in time to avoid a loud shot from the weapon. A scattering of tiny bullets embedded themselves in the wall above his head, and he was out the door before the human could reload. He ran through the hall, down the stairs, and ended up in a large foyer lined with doors and windows. His ears and frill flattened tightly against his scalp as he whirled around and tried to hastily guess which one would lead him outside.

"I swear on the Bible and God himself, if you don't get out of my house, I'll send you back to Satan!"

Ridaion whimpered and ran to the door directly ahead of him, but it opened into a tight closet full of coats and trunks. He slammed the door shut and sought his next option. His search was interrupted by a second deafening blast from the gun, this one splintering the floor where he'd stood just a few seconds ago.

Hobbling down the stairs and reloading the weapon, the human cried, "You'll never take me, devil! Not while I've got the Bible at my side!"

"I do not know what the fuck that is!" Ridaion yelled back.

"It's the word of God! And in his name, I'm sending you back to Hell where you belong!"

Ridaion dodged the third shot and desperately opened a door on the other side of the foyer. Furious barking erupted within, and he shrieked at the sight of a snarling beast bouncing around the room and flicking slobber everywhere. The jowly creature saw him and bolted for the door, foaming and howling, and Ridaion yanked the door shut just in time. The animal threw itself against the barrier and scratched at it from the other side, still woofing angrily, but its strength was no match for his.

Suddenly there was a fourth gunshot, and the round, black pellets sprayed across Ridaion's skin. He cried out and stumbled away from the door. Most of the beads had planted themselves in his chest and shoulder, but several had hit his neck and even his jaw. The bullets wouldn't kill him or leave noticeable scars—the tiny things had barely penetrated his skin—but they hurt like a dozen harben stings.

As the human reloaded its gun once more, Ridaion gave up looking for the correct door and went to a window. When it didn't open right away, even with heavy force, he simply crashed it open with his elbow. Glass shards and broken bits of frame sliced through his skin, but he barely felt it. He ran away from that house faster than he'd ever run before, and it was only when he stopped for breath nearly a full molosopion away that he reflected on what happened.

"I could have just killed that thing," he panted, scowling at the trees. Humans were remarkably easy to kill, even with their weapons. This particular specimen had looked old and weak, too; it probably wouldn't have put up much of a fight if he'd gotten close to it. Even by himself, he could have—

Well, shit. I'm by myself.

Ridaion put his hands on his hips and took in his surroundings, letting out a bitter laugh. This would complicate things. If he had to look for his pack *and* the Lucio heir, this mission would be about ten times harder.

"Three moons, Salidus. You just *had* to volunteer us for this," he growled, kicking a rock and wishing it was that human's face. Twenty years at his alpha's side—pleasing him, sleeping beside him, confiding in him—and this was one of the few times he'd ever been fed up with the older male. Sure, they had a brief spat now and then, but he rarely opposed Salidus's decisions in their entirety. Ridaion didn't like the mission they were tasked with, and even if they hadn't been the ones selected out of hundreds of other volunteer packs, he wouldn't have been completely on board with eradicating a species. But this. . . After two dilunar cycles of studying, training, and coping with the guilt of instigating genocide, the fuck-up with the portal was a real pain in the ass.

He threw his hands up and exclaimed, "You'd think using some basic two-step magic would be easy as extending your claws, but *no!* Why would it be that simple? Stealing a human should be the easiest task in the world, and we've already managed to fuck it up! I've heard you have a merciful streak, Callii, but I'm not seeing it right now." He sighed and began to carefully pick the small bullets out of his skin. The sting of it was unpleasant but bearable.

His ears twitched at the sound of that beast baying and the human shouting in the distance, and he groaned.

Not again.

Ridaion briefly debated hiding and waiting for the human to approach so he could kill it. That drooly creature, too. The human had seen him, after all. But did he really *need* to kill it? It seemed to live alone, aside from its animal companion, and its words indicated that it thought him to be some sort of malevolent being trying to take its soul. That line of thinking wasn't far off from the truth, he knew, but if the human didn't know he was invading its planet, then it couldn't spill his secret. Ridaion realized he was stretching his logic a bit, but he wanted to avoid killing humans for as long as he could. He would follow Salidus to the ends of Primaied and Earth, but that didn't mean he had to love every part of their mission.

Then again, this particular human was aggravating his already irritable mood. Maybe just a small beating—

No. I'm not a savage.

His moral compass was admittedly flawed in some areas, but it was at least consistent. This human was just afraid of him. It didn't deserve to die for defending its home, even if that home was littered with animal remains and facing a rather unflattering state of dilapidation.

"Fine, you can live," Ridaion said with a sigh. He listened for another minute to pinpoint where the human and its creature were approaching from, then promptly ran in the opposite direction. He would worry about human interference when it became an unsolvable problem, but for the time being, he would stick to his self-imposed rule of not killing them unless mercy was too inconvenient. Even if the little creatures in question got on his nerves.

*****

Salidus felt nothing but pride and elation when he stepped through the portal. After trilunar cycles of development, the plan was ready, and his pack had been selected to carry out the most important mission of their generation. The honor that came with the position was unmatched. He'd even been entrusted with the remains of Rhala himself, a Rhithien who had been all but a god in life.

Right as Salidus stepped into the gateway, he thought, *This is it. This is why I'm here. This is what every part of my life has led to, even my darkest times. It's all guided me to this very moment.*

Would his name be remembered, like Rhala's? Or would he and his pack eventually fade from all historical records? It was a question that had been nagging him ever since it was decided that he would be the one to lead the mission to Earth. He would be fine with either option, he supposed. This was far more important than his ego.

I just need to keep everyone together until it's over.

He knew that several of his subordinates didn't wholly agree with the moral integrity of their task, and he understood their doubts, but they remained loyal to him despite their unsurety. He was especially proud of Ridaion, with whom he'd debated the matter several times. The younger male made some good points, and although he made it clear that he didn't like the plan, he promised he would remain by Salidus's side until the end.

"Are you sure you want to go through with this?" Ridaion had asked him one night. It was a week before they were to arrive at the Oasis, and the two of them had lain side by side, staring up at the sky and arguing playfully about which constellations were which.

"Yes. We've discussed this, Ridaion, this is something we must do for the good of Primaied. I am willing to die for this mission if that's what it takes," Salidus had answered firmly. Ridaion sat up and glared down at him.

"Don't say that," he'd growled, his sharp green eyes narrowing. "It'll really piss me off if you die. Fucking moons, I'd resurrect you just so I could kill you myself."

"We wouldn't want that," Salidus chuckled, pushing himself up and nuzzling Ridaion's neck.

"No, we wouldn't," Ridaion had agreed angrily. Then his tone softened and he confessed, "I don't want to go. I don't want *you* to go."

Salidus sighed and conceded, "If you wish to stay at the Oasis when we arrive, you can. I'll understand. I'd like to see Earth for the first time with my entire pack behind me, but if you really don't want to go—"

"No, I'll go. I still don't like this, but I want to be with you."

"You won't leave me?" Salidus had asked, taking Ridaion's hand and gazing into his eyes.

"Never."

That conversation had softened the remaining threads of tension between them and arrested Salidus's final qualms about the mission. He'd never been more certain about anything in his life than when he stepped through the portal and braced himself for what was to come. He could handle anything as long as he had his pack with him.

That confidence disappeared when he emerged in the middle of a river.

Water immediately filled his nose and blinded him, and a strong current dragged his body downstream, raking him over silty rocks. Salidus almost gulped down a mouthful of water in his shock, but he managed to gather his composure and kicked up from the stony bottom. The river was chilling and powerful, and he had to stroke hard to move upward. He surfaced long enough to spit out a fountain of water and suck in a breath before the merciless force of the current pushed him back under like it was deliberately trying to drown him.

Years of childhood swimming lessons instinctually kicked in, and he methodically moved with the river's natural flow. He allowed the water to cool and calm his mind as he switched his stroke and aimed diagonally for the muddy bank. He concentrated his magic and held it at the ready as he swam, but he was reluctant to use it; he didn't want to exhaust his supply in case he needed it for other threats.

Almost there. . .

Salidus had just reached the shallows and was grasping at sturdy tree roots for a handhold when he felt the leather cord around his neck loosen. Before he could react, the small, weighty bag that contained the knuckle bones was gone. He didn't hesitate for a single moment. He didn't even risk stealing another breath of air. Surfacing would mean losing sight of the bag, a travesty that would compromise everything Primaied had worked for. He could hold his breath for a few more minutes. He dove back into the current and locked his gaze on the leather pouch. The opening had come loose, and six round bones were tumbling out, their light weight easily carried by the raging river. Salidus reached deep inside his mind and soul, gathered his magic into a powerful, crackling force, and stretched out threads of it to enclose the bones. They halted in place as if time itself had stopped around them. He held the bones and the bag with his magic long enough to swim to their location.

Grasping the strung bag and closing his fist securely around the six knuckle bones, Salidus once again propelled himself towards the riverbank. When he reached it, he employed his magic again to lift himself out of the water and onto the wet grass. His chest heaving and his eyes wide, he cradled the bones and fearfully scrutinized them for damage. They were wet but intact. He breathed a sigh of relief, returned them to the bag with every ounce of precision and care he could muster, and tied the cord back around his neck. He made sure the knot was secure by tugging on it experimentally, and when he was satisfied, he fell back onto the grass and shut his eyes.

"Haven't done that in a while," he murmured. He couldn't remember the last time he'd swum so hard. He had taught Ridaion how to swim in a lake a few years back—the younger male wasn't very good at it and had clung to him like a starving laictyn the entire time—but Salidus hadn't needed to paddle through a current in over a hundred years. He didn't want to flatter himself, but he thought he'd done pretty well after such a long break.

The bones, he remembered suddenly, and he clutched the small bag against his chest like a lifeline. The damage he could have caused by losing them was immeasurable. Why had he ended up in a river, anyway? Salidus sat up and stared at the water, dumbfounded, then studied the trees around him.

"Shit," he groaned, flopping back onto the grass. "Of course. Why not?" Of course they'd been scattered. The odds had been in their favor, especially with three portal stones—one stone would have been risky for such a large group, but the more they had, the stronger the gateway was. And they'd had *three.*

Salidus sighed and assured himself, "I'm fine. This is fine. I just need to get the pack back together, find the Lucio heir, and we can get back to the Oasis. Very simple."

But he had no idea how long that would take. He'd known that scattering was a risk—the whole pack knew, the scholars knew, everyone fucking knew—but while they'd been warned about it, the odds were so low that they hadn't really expected or prepared for it. He had no way of contacting his pack members, nor could they contact each other. He didn't even know where he was.

Where's Ridaion? Is he safe?

A bolt of fear ripped through Salidus's heart at the intrusive thought, but he subdued it fast. He couldn't allow himself to panic; not now. Despite his petite stature, Ridaion could hold his own surprisingly well in a fight. That was one of the initial reasons Salidus had accepted him into the pack. Wherever he was now, he could take care of himself.

A loud, shrill bird call jerked Salidus back into focus, and he rose with a groan. He needed to find the others, and fast. The longer they were stuck on Earth, the more likely it was that they would be discovered and thwarted by the humans.

He squeezed the knuckle bones one final time for luck before heading into the trees to begin his search.

V

Franklin Rayblue's cellphone rang loudly, jerking him awake. The noise pierced the silence of his home office, and that cheery ringtone seemed more passive-aggressively insistent than ever before. He snorted and groped around the desk with his eyes still closed, cursing as he knocked the phone onto the floor. The damn thing continued to yell impatiently at him, and Franklin grumbled under his breath as he reached awkwardly under the desk to grab it.

"I know, I know," he muttered, yelping when he whacked his head on the underside of the desk upon coming back up. He rubbed his head and stared dumbly at the screen. A colorful, rather blurry profile picture was calling him. Franklin shoved his glasses carelessly onto his face and glanced briefly at the caller's name before quickly answering. He never ignored Parker's calls.

"Hey, Franklin. How're you doing, man?" came his younger brother's voice, tinny and garbled through the speaker.

"Good, good. I'm really good. What's it? What is it? Why are you calling?"

Franklin sighed. Even he could hear the chronic sleep deprivation in his voice.

"Jesus, you sound terrible. Did I just wake you up? You're at home, right?"

Shit, what day is it? Saturday?

"I'm, uh. . ." Franklin glanced at his surroundings. He sat at his desk in his home office, surrounded by too many screens and too many tabs that had been open for weeks. "I'm in my office. At home, yes. What do you want?"

"When was the last time you got any sleep, Franklin?" Parker's voice was strained and tired, but he didn't sound surprised. He and their older sister, Avery, knew Franklin hadn't been getting as much sleep as he would have liked. The benefit of freelance was that he could arrange his contracts and work at his own pace as long as he got everything done by a designated deadline. He enjoyed the methodical yet artistic technicalities of software building, and he'd recently begun dabbling in webpage design. The problem was that an emerging company had found out, and this company was unreasonably picky.

"You still there, bud?" Parker asked on the other end of the line. Franklin blinked in surprise as his brother repeated, "How long has it been since you slept?"

"I just woke up from sleeping. I'm good, really," Franklin replied with a yawn.

"Christ, you sound terrible. Go take a nap or something, this can wait."

"No, no, no," Franklin stammered, trying—and failing miserably—to sound more awake. "I'm up, I can talk. What's going on?"

"It's just. . . well. . . aw, man, I really don't know how to say this. Um, how are things going with Nancy?"

Franklin groaned at the mention of his girlfriend. It was not going well. With this current commission hanging over his head like a guillotine blade, Nancy hadn't been getting the attention that she usually demanded from him. She called him at least once an hour and sent him about fifty texts a day—most of which went unanswered—asking if he was finished yet. And each time he would tell her, with all the lucidity and civility he could muster, that no, he was not done. Her impatience was starting to get on his nerves, but he always made an effort to keep his cool around her. One of them had to be rational.

"We're good," he lied. "Why do you ask?"

"Well, I was talking with a buddy of mine last night, and he started bragging about how he. . . may have. . . slept. . . with a woman. . . who was named Nancy. He showed me a picture, and this Nancy just so happened to look a lot like your Nancy."

Franklin sat in silence, taking a moment to process what his brother was saying to him. Then he moaned and let his head thump down onto the desk.

"Jesus, Parker."

"Look, I'm sorry, man, I didn't realize how busy you were. I thought the commission would be cleared up by now. This probably wasn't the best time to tell you."

"There's never a good time to tell someone that," Franklin muttered. "Did this buddy of yours know that Nancy isn't single?"

"I don't think so. He's one of the new park rangers who got transferred to our team in the Dennisons. I met him on one of those big capture-and-release tagging escapades the college kids from Missoula do every semester. The

Fisheries and Wildlife majors, remember? Anyway, this dude's an out-of-towner. Hasn't gotten to know anyone yet. Doesn't even know I have a brother."

"Alright," Franklin said with a heavy sigh, closing his eyes and running his fingers through his messy brown curls. "Thanks for letting me know, man." He hung up without another word, rested his head atop his arms, and closed his eyes. All he wanted was a few hours of sleep. Just a few hours to ignore his responsibilities. Was that really too much to ask?

He strongly considered doing that very thing, but he knew he had to deal with this latest fiasco before he could move on with his life. The damn webpage could wait thirty minutes.

During the occasional breaks he'd taken throughout this project to check up with Nancy via phone call or text message, she was far from pleasant to talk to. Before the company had decided to contact him and begin the lengthy process of chipping away his soul, he'd been what Nancy teasingly referred to as a "full-time boyfriend." That meant his job was to enjoy getting dragged along on shopping trips (wherein he was expected to carry the bags and pay for any purchase over fifty dollars) and take her out to dinner every other night. As her full-time boyfriend, he was also the chauffeur, butler, and pack mule for her friends.

Franklin had never minded being a full-time boyfriend for the various partners he'd had throughout his life, but the problem with Nancy was that it was never enough. In the past three years, she had managed to completely consume his life, cutting into the allotted time he reserved for his hobbies, his siblings, and even his self-enforced work schedule. Whenever he would reach a tipping point and politely ask her to let him get a few hours of work done, she would pout and cry and question if he really cared about his job more than her. If that didn't work, she would scream and throw her plethora of perfume bottles at him until he was on his knees, apologizing and comforting her. As much as it stung to know that she was cheating on him, it wasn't a surprise.

"It's because I took some time for myself, isn't it?" Franklin snapped as he grabbed his keys, pulled on his coat, and headed out to his car. "And those days weren't even for me. They were for a commission that this fucking corporation is too damn prissy to accept. Set after set of color schemes, layouts, the whole nine yards! Hours upon hours of work. *Weeks* of work. I've been living on coffee and fast food for a month! What more do you want?"

He ducked into his beat-up old car, turned the engine until it roared to life with a smoky cough, and headed down the street, the path to Nancy's house ingrained in his mind.

Ignoring the fact that neither she nor anyone else was in the car, he ranted, "You couldn't call and say you wanted a break? Hell, you could've just texted! What's the point of a 'full-time boyfriend' if you're just going to sleep with some guy you pick up at a bar? Good Christ, woman."

When he finally pulled up at her house, he was forced to park on the curb because of a sky-blue Volkswagen taking up the driveway. Franklin knew very well that Nancy wouldn't be caught dead driving that thing. He glowered at the offending vehicle as he walked up to the front door and knocked.

"Just a minute!" called a voice from inside. Franklin heard someone shuffling around before the door was finally opened by a half-naked man who appeared to be in his early forties. He had a round, average-looking face and a receding hairline. Franklin would never classify himself as uniquely attractive, nor was he a star athlete, but he at least had the assurance that his appearance was Nancy-approved. Not to mention that he was close to her age; he was two years older, but they were both in their early thirties. He'd watched her ogle other men loads of times. He knew what her type was. She rarely so much as glanced at men who were obviously older than her.

Parker said he's a decent enough guy. I know he's sleeping with my girl, but he may not know she isn't single. Go easy on him.

Despite the constraints that he secured around his temper, Franklin's irritation spiked when the guy narrowed his eyes and demanded, "Who are you?"

"I'm Nancy's boyfriend. Who are you?"

The guy blinked in surprise, then frowned.

"That's funny. She told me she broke up with her most recent man just yesterday. If you're one of those dudes who doesn't take no for an answer, you can piss off, buddy."

"That didn't happen, and I really need to talk to her," Franklin insisted, ignoring the threatening jab. "I'm fine waiting out here, but can you get her, please? She's got some explaining to do. You can listen in if you feel more comfortable that way. It makes no difference to me."

He opened his coat and turned his pockets out to show that he was unarmed, then retreated down the porch steps. The guy squinted suspiciously at him, but nodded and closed the door again. Franklin heard muffled voices, then the guy reemerged with Nancy in tow. She was wearing her fluffy white bathrobe, and her long brown hair was sopping wet as if she'd just gotten out of the shower. She looked disgruntled and close to a tantrum until she realized who was standing on her front porch. Her face paled and she put a hand over her mouth.

Franklin crossed his arms and prompted, "According to your latest catch, you're single. That's news to me." Nancy stepped outside, wincing as her bare feet touched the rough cement.

"Baby, I can explain," she began, but he held up a hand. Her jaw dropped and her eyebrows went so high they looked like they were trying to fly off her face. He never cut her off so brusquely. However, before she could launch into one of her usual rants, he spoke.

"I don't care what you thought or what you told him. I don't care why you did it. We're done. Lose my number and get his, if you haven't already," he said. He jerked his head at the guy behind Nancy, who was now staring down at her with his face contorted in a mixture of shock, hurt, and anger. As Franklin headed back to his car, he glanced over his shoulder and called, "Good luck, man. You'll need it."

"What the hell, Nancy?" the guy demanded.

"Go back inside, Darryl. I just need a minute," she snapped, and Franklin rolled his eyes when he heard her stomping across the pavement after him.

Here we go.

"Franklin, stop!" she yelled. He didn't stop. He continued to his car, only coming to a halt when she dashed in front of him.

"There's nothing to say, Nance," he declared calmly. "I told you; we're done."

"You don't get to say when we're done, asshole! I said it weeks ago! We aren't even together anymore, really. You haven't said a word to me for a month!"

"You didn't say shit about being done, and I've been talking to you every damn day."

As expected, Nancy's lower lip began to tremble and her face turned pink like it did whenever she was about to throw a fit.

"You act like I'm to blame for this. *You* were the one who wasn't paying attention to *me*. I was isolated and lonely, Franklin. For a month!"

"You weren't isolated," he protested. "We talked on the phone literally every day, and you told me you were spending a bunch of time with your friends. And

I told you I had a really important job to do. The company just kept rejecting my sets, so I had to keep trying. I'm on contract for this, you know. For a lot of money."

"I don't care about your fucking contracts!" Nancy screeched. "You barely said a word to me, you weren't taking me out, you weren't doing *anything!* I want to be with you, but I can't if you keep treating me like this!"

"So you're saying you want to break up?" Franklin asked, raising an eyebrow. Nancy opened her mouth, then closed it again, realizing her mistake. Franklin brushed past her and got into his car, saying over his shoulder, "Excellent idea. Have fun with Darryl."

"You bastard!" Nancy howled, stamping her foot on the ground. Tears started rolling down her reddened cheeks and she threw herself dramatically onto the grass with a loud sob. Franklin knew what was coming, and he was quick to lock his doors and roll up his windows. She had two emergency strategies to make him concede in a fight: the first was to flop herself around as she was doing now and fake a breakdown to try and gain sympathy points. If that failed, she would lash out and start hitting, clawing, kicking, or even biting. Franklin had been with her long enough to recognize when she was about to erupt and switch to her wild animal technique.

Sure enough, as he started to drive away, he heard Nancy's sobs recede into silence. He was forced to slam on the brakes when she dashed in front of his car. She stared right into his eyes as he halted just a few feet from where she was standing, scowling viciously and looking like an angry cat that had just climbed out of a bathtub. Then she screamed and threw herself across the hood of the vehicle.

"Help!" she cried. "He hit me! He hit me with his car!"

"Most of the houses on this block have cameras, Nancy. Your house has cameras. Darryl's standing on your front porch. That crap ain't gonna fly in court," Franklin yelled through the closed window.

Nancy got up and looked back at her house, where Darryl watched the altercation wide-eyed and open-mouthed. She seemed to realize that her victim act wasn't going to work this time, so she smacked the passenger window in rage.

"You're a piece of shit, Franklin!" she spat. "You're a bastard! You don't deserve me! I hope the next girl unlucky enough to stumble over you manages to sort out her brain cells real quick! That's right, asshole; I'm breaking up with you! You'll never find another girl like me!"

Franklin rolled down his window a fraction of an inch, barely enough for her to menacingly shove her fingers through, and called, "That's the idea, Nance."

"You were like a goddamn sex doll in bed!" Nancy screeched, evidently determined to have the last word. "I've had more fun with a vibrator!"

"That poor vibrator," Franklin said sympathetically. "Did you yell at that thing whenever it reminded you that it had a life of its own, too?"

"Fuck you!"

"Yeah, yeah. Have a nice day." He waited until she finally turned around and stormed away before putting the car back in gear. But he couldn't resist rolling his window down further and sticking his hand out to wave goodbye with his middle finger.

Franklin grinned at the sight of Nancy's utterly enraged face growing smaller and smaller in his side-view mirror. God, how had it taken so long for him to dump her? The knowledge that he was single again didn't hit him as hard as he'd thought it would. Had he really loved Nancy? Maybe he had, in the beginning. He remembered the first time they'd exchanged words, the first time he'd asked her out, and the shy smile she'd given him when she accepted his offer. But after three long years, the good times were too few and far between. Although he couldn't pinpoint it, he knew there must have been a point where he'd fallen *out* of love with her rather than *in*. The longer Franklin thought about it, the more convinced he became that she was the most hellish thing he'd ever experienced. · He had meant it when he'd wished Darryl luck. Hopefully the poor guy would be smart enough to recognize shark-infested waters and get away before blood was spilled.

Franklin's phone rang just as he was pulling into his driveway, and he jumped in surprise. He quickly parked and fumbled with the device, taking a moment to push his glasses further up his nose and inspect the screen.

Don't be Nancy, don't be Nancy, don't be Nancy. . .

"Avery," he greeted with a rush of relief.

"Hey. Parker told me about you and Nancy. That sucks, bro," she said sympathetically. Franklin chuckled, ruffling his hair and grinning.

"About fucking time, if you ask me. That woman was psychotic."

"You just needed a reason that she couldn't guilt you out of, huh?"

68

"Pretty much," Franklin admitted. He was already feeling lighter, as if he'd dropped an immense and unfulfilling weight that he'd been carrying around for too long. Three years, to be exact.

"What're you going to do with your heaps of money and free time now that it won't all be spent at Kohl's or that expensive restaurant you hate? What was that place called? 1000 Stars, or something?" Avery asked.

"1000 Stars," Franklin confirmed, cringing as he recalled how many times Nancy had made him take her to dinner there. He'd never been a fan of the food, anyway. He much preferred Naked Bear Bar and Grill, but she hated that place. "I really don't know. I guess I'll have to pick up some new hobbies. Find a new girl, maybe."

"We should get together, man! This is cause for celebration, in my humble opinion."

"Maybe another time, Avery." Franklin's smile weakened as he reminded her, "I've still got that contract to deal with."

"Ugh, they're still not happy? You emailed me some of your designs the other day, and I thought they looked great! I'd use them if I started a business."

"You're my sister, you have to say that."

"I may be your sister, but I don't have to say anything. If I thought they were ugly, I would tell you. Without hesitation. You know I would."

"Yeah, I guess you would," Franklin admitted with a laugh. "They haven't even told me what's wrong with them. They basically just said, 'Hey, this isn't what we want. Do it again.'"

"Jesus. Why exactly are you still putting up with this?"

"Money."

"Ah. The age-old motivation."

He and Avery talked for a while longer, and despite the sour subject of his declining financial state and the lengths he was going to in an effort to fix it, his mood was vastly improved. When he finally hung up and headed back inside his house, he felt lighter than he had in years. If—or hopefully when—he found someone new, they were sure to be better than Nancy.

VI

Maisie didn't get a single wink of sleep.

All she could think about was the alien in her basement.

Every logical part of her brain screamed at her to call 9-1-1, tell a neighbor, or even shoo Aremaeid out of her house with a broom. Not that she thought the latter would work, of course; he'd already proven that he could overpower her easily. Despite this, she'd started to dial the emergency number three separate times—but every time, she hung up her phone and chucked it onto the bed like it was a hot iron. She wasn't sure how good Aremaeid's hearing was, and she was petrified by the thought that he could kill her and disappear long before the police showed up. Their fragile truce was not reassuring.

So she stayed awake, alternating between snuggling Roller, pacing restlessly, and crawling on all fours with her ear pressed to the carpet to see if she could hear any sort of activity from the basement. Sometime around 2 a.m., she'd heard a muffled *thump,* and she'd been so alarmed that she had stayed crouched where she was, taut as a bowstring and staring at the door with wide eyes. She was convinced he would burst in any minute and finish what he'd started. But when Aremaeid didn't show up after half an hour of waiting or make any more suspicious sounds, she managed to relax.

When Maisie finally realized that she might as well catch up on grading, seeing as she had nothing better to do if she wasn't going to sleep, she searched for her stack of papers for nearly five minutes before remembering that she'd left them out on the kitchen counter. She quietly cursed herself and gave the door a longing glance before hopping back on the bed with her dog and curling into a ball. They could both sense each other's distress, and Roller was just as eager to snuggle as she was.

She'd set her 6:00 a.m. alarm by habit, even though it was a Saturday, and she and the dog almost shared a heart attack when it finally went off. Another thumping noise and a muffled snarl from the basement made her want to cower under her bed. But, against her better judgment, she turned off her alarm, took a deep breath, and readied herself to brave the quiet house. She slowly pushed the door open, but gasped and slammed it shut when it thumped against something and a loud, tinkling peal filled the hall. After a moment of hesitation, she opened the door again and stared down at a bell that had been expertly placed outside her bedroom.

Bastard! He booby-trapped my door!

Mustering her courage, she kicked the bell into her room and stepped out into the hallway, finding relief when she didn't see Aremaeid's hulking shape lurking about in the dark. The floor was cold on her bare feet, and she was hyperactively aware of every creak and groan the house made. She continued until she reached the living room and the adjacent kitchen, skittering past the basement steps like a frightened crab.

Roller hopped on the couch and splayed himself across it as he usually did, giving Maisie two half-hearted tail thumps when she joined him in the living room. Then his tail went rigid and he sat up with a low snarl.

"What was that noise?" came a deep, growly voice from behind Maisie. She shrieked and whipped around, almost falling over in her surprise. Aremaeid was standing only a few feet away, having somehow approached without making a sound.

"Don't *do* that!" she hissed, flapping her hands agitatedly.

"Sorry," Aremaeid muttered, but Maisie thought he sounded rather disingenuous. "You did not answer my question. What was that noise?"

"It was just my alarm," Maisie explained hastily. He probably hadn't meant to scare her—even if he didn't seem too apologetic about it—but given the circumstances, it was an easy thing to do. "It tells me to wake up at a particular time. Speaking of which, how do you move around without making a single fucking noise? You're enormous, and you were creaking all over the floor last night! What the actual hell?" In her sleeplessness and shock, she forgot to tread lightly with her tone, but Aremaeid didn't seem to care.

"Habit," he replied with a shrug. "We are taught as cubs how to keep our footsteps light." He nonchalantly stepped past her and looked around the living room. When he approached the couch, Roller offered him a single growly *woof,* but the dog didn't seem brave or energetic enough to do much more than that. Maisie glared at her pet and mouthed *"lazy"* before grabbing his food bowl and taking it to the kitchen counter.

She had been preparing Roller's breakfast for years now, so the process didn't require much concentration. Therefore she was able to focus her attention solely on Aremaeid, who was exploring the living room. He studied the various photographs placed around the room with the attentiveness of an art critic, poked curiously at a dusty glass figurine of a bluebird that rested on the mantle, and nudged the couch with a single toe like he was worried it would grow teeth and attack him. Maisie vigilantly watched every one of his movements, and she froze when he peered down at Roller. He cocked his head to the side and knelt to the dog's level.

Oh, God, is he going to hurt my dog?

"Please be careful with him!" Maisie blurted out, and Aremaeid's golden eyes flicked up to her face. She wrung her hands, debating whether it would be a good idea to intervene, and added, "He's a good boy. He just. . . doesn't like strangers."

"Why do you keep this thing in your house?" Aremaeid asked. Maisie exhaled in relief. He wasn't going to hurt Roller.

Deep breaths. In, out.

"He's. . . a pet. Don't you have pets on your planet?" she inquired.

" 'Pet' is a term used for an individual who is possessed by someone of a higher rank, most often for copulatory purposes. It is typically used regarding a male who has been claimed by a female for breeding season. Some places also breed livestock for food, but those creatures are not considered persons as we are, nor are they 'pets.' I assume you do not house the term under the same definition. Now tell me, why do you have this tiny thing? It does not seem to serve a significant purpose."

Maisie tucked some hair behind her ear and explained, "His purpose is to keep me calm. He's not a very good guard dog, but I take care of him and he takes care of me in his own way. My therapist recommended something affectionate, soft, and willing to be cuddled, so I got Roller."

"I see. So your pet is essentially a substitute for human connection?" Aremaeid mused.

"No. Yes. Kind of. It's not like that, it's—ugh, it's hard to explain," grumbled Maisie. "Don't describe it like that, it's depressing. Not all people get pets for that reason. There are guard dogs, service dogs, guide dogs, and other things like that. I got him because he keeps me from panicking and I like having him here, and that's all there is to it." She'd never imagined that it would be so awkwardly difficult to explain the purpose of having pets.

Aremaeid hummed thoughtfully but didn't respond. He slowly reached one hand out, hovering it over Roller, and both Maisie and the dog flinched when his claws retracted into his fingertips with an audible *shink.* Roller lifted his head to stare at Aremaeid for a few moments before apparently deciding there was nothing he could do if the alien wanted to pet him, and he flopped down onto the couch. Aremaeid carefully lowered his hand, placed it firmly on Roller's small, round body, and whispered in a fascinated tone, "Dog."

Maisie sighed in relief as she watched the interaction and reassured herself that her dog would be safe. When she was finished preparing his breakfast, she tapped her finger on the side of the bowl and called him over. He hopped off the couch and waddled into the kitchen, and as Maisie stood protectively over him, she pretended not to notice Aremaeid looming beside the couch like a gargoyle. She didn't relax until he returned to the basement.

*****

Maisie always looked forward to Saturday afternoons. Catherine Lucio, who lived across the street, had asked her at the beginning of the school year to come over and tutor her daughter, Layla, once a week. Maisie was grateful for the extra money she earned from it, but payment wasn't her priority when it came to her students. It was more than a job today, anyway; it was a relief. She'd never wanted to get out of her house more than she did now. Maisie and Layla already knew each other from regular classes, so they were familiar with their respective ways of teaching and learning. They'd gotten to know one another quite well through their two-hour tutoring sessions, and although Layla wasn't always the most attentive student, she and her family were good company.

Maisie went to her basement stairs and called down, "I'm going out." She was just zipping up her coat when Aremaeid appeared at the bottom of the steps. The lights were off, and a jolt of fear gripped Maisie's heart at the sight of his gleaming eyes peering up at her from the shadows. His behavior and appearance were unsettling, to say the least—he spoke in an unexpectedly human way and was clearly a creature of advanced intelligence, but at the same time, he was so animalistic and *alien* that Maisie would nearly forget he was fluent in English. She gulped, hugged her arms, and took a cautious step away from the stairs.

"Where?" Aremaeid demanded. She wasn't surprised that he was agitated about it. It had been part of their agreement that she wouldn't tell anyone about him, after all, and they both knew he couldn't stop her from revealing him if she left the house.

"Just out. I have to meet up with a friend of mine."

"For what purpose?"

Aremaeid ascended one step, and that was enough for Maisie to dart backward and stammer, "I'm not going to tell anyone! When I make a promise, I keep it. Even though you did threaten me."

His eyes glowed dangerously and scrutinized her for a few seconds, but he ultimately slipped back into the terrifying void that her basement had become.

"Very well. I shall remain here," he declared, his low voice floating up from the shadows.

"No, it's alright. You can go wherever you want. Whenever you want," Maisie said, pulling a pair of thin gloves from her pocket and tugging them on. Maybe if she encouraged him not to tether himself to her house, he would leave. But on the off chance he decided to ignore her encouragement, she added, "I'm just letting you know where I'm going to be for the next couple of hours."

There was no response, but she assumed he got the message. She silently prayed that he wouldn't demand to know the location as she headed for the front door. She paused with her hand on the knob, just to be sure it was safe, but when Aremaeid didn't stop her, she let out a shaky breath and stepped outside.

The Lucio house was the largest on the block, consisting of two main floors, an attic, and a basement. It was common knowledge among their neighbors that they were rich; Catherine was a successful realtor while her husband, Dennis, was an accountant and aspiring novelist. With their well-trimmed lawn and charming personalities, they were seen as a perfect nuclear family. The only problems they had, ironically enough, were their children: Tyson, who was a socially-inept ball of anxiety; and his older sister, Layla, who avoided children her age like the plague and was failing all her classes. Hence the tutoring.

Maisie strolled up the driveway, passing an assortment of decorative flower pots along the way, and ascended the steps to the front door. Despite being told multiple times that she was welcome to walk in—since the door was usually unlocked when someone was home—she rang the bell as she always did. The door was flung open a few seconds later, and she was met with Layla's pixie-like face beaming up at her.

"Miss Arberon, we've told you a million times that you don't have to ring. Dad doesn't work Saturdays, I have nothing better to do than this, and we always keep the house open for you. You can stop using the bell!"

The girl stepped aside as she delivered the playful scolding, allowing Maisie to enter and toe off her sneakers. She removed her coat as well and hung it up on a peg beside the door.

"And I've told *you* a million times, Miss Lucio, that when we're outside of school, it's okay to call me Maisie. We're friends at this point, aren't we?" she retorted. Layla grinned and pranced away. As the girl led her through the living room, Maisie spotted Dennis sitting on the couch with his laptop open and a mug of coffee in his hand. He looked up as she walked by and lifted a hand amiably.

"Hey, Maisie!" he called in greeting, taking a sip of his beverage. "Good to see you again. Catherine still bullying you into doing these tutoring sessions?"

"You know it," she returned with a grin.

"She's blackmailing you, isn't she?"

"Mm-hm. The woman's relentless," Maisie agreed with a theatrical sigh. She threw a hand dramatically over her forehead and added, "She'll ruin me if I don't pull her child out of the deadly pit of Fs and Ds!"

"You have my sympathies, Ms. Arberon," Dennis assured her somberly, placing a hand over his heart. Maisie laughed and sat down on the couch beside him while Layla continued to the kitchen. A stack of books on a nearby stool caught her attention, and her breath hitched at the sight of glowing eyes peering out of the dark on one of the covers. *Night Terrors,* the book's title proclaimed. She turned away before a burst of anxiety could take over. Tempting as it was to beg Dennis to call the police, the Lucios were safer if they remained uninvolved in this mess.

Deep breaths. Be calm. It's just a creepy book cover. . . that happens to have a monster that looks like my current houseguest.

"It's good to see you, Dennis," she said at last, forcing a smile. "I've been meaning to ask about your novel, by the way. Catherine called a few days ago and said you were almost finished. How's that going?"

"Yes, well, my wife does like to stretch the truth a bit," he said with a fond smile, turning his attention wistfully back to his screen.

"Is it not done? She said—"

"It's just the second draft," he clarified, scratching his beard. "I shared it with my editor, and I still have a bunch of changes to make before it'll be ready for the public. I like working at the bank well enough, but I don't exactly have oodles of free time, so it's slow going. But it's going, at least."

"I get that," Maisie murmured sympathetically. She understood the struggles of balancing work and hobbies. Suddenly Layla poked her head back into the living room and glared irritably at the two adults.

"Dad, she doesn't want to hear about your book."

"Well, that's a shame," drawled Dennis with a mischievous grin, "because I was just about to start reading the first chapter for her. I was going to make it nice and loud, too, so that all the neighbors get a chance to hear it." He cleared his throat and bellowed, " 'IT ALL BEGAN ON A PLEASANT SUMMER EVENING! JOSIE RULIO WAS SITTING AT HER DESK. . .'"

"Oh my God, Dad, stop!" Layla pleaded through repressed bouts of laughter. Maisie couldn't help letting out a few giggles herself as Layla dashed over and started swatting her father's shoulder. He laughed and leaned away from her, sinking into the couch and throwing his hands up in surrender.

"Alright, alright! Are you sure you don't want to hear the rest of chapter one?" Dennis asked, cocking an eyebrow and giving her an amused grin.

"No, God no! I need to do my math!" Layla shrieked.

"Whatever you say," her father relented with a smile, ruffling her short blond hair. As Maisie stood up to follow Layla out of the room, he turned to her and added, "I'm right out here if you need anything. Drinks, snacks, whatever. I'm not on shift today. You good?"

I have a giant, potentially murderous alien bunking in my house. I need you to call the police because I'm too scared to do it myself.

"I'm good. Thanks, Dennis."

With that, she and Layla walked through the house to the kitchen, where the girl's math book was open to the assigned pages. The counter was scattered with papers, pencils, a calculator, and several smudged erasers. Maisie only barely managed to suppress a cringe at the mess, but she pulled out a chair and took a seat beside Layla. As she looked over the problems, she recognized them from an assignment she'd given out three days earlier. She raised an eyebrow at her student.

"This is from Wednesday, kiddo. You don't have to wait until Saturday to ask for help, you know."

"Yeah, but I don't like having to stay after school with the other kids. They're all morons," Layla whined. Maisie neglected to point out that Layla needed more help than most of the students who took the time to stay after hours.

"Needing some extra help doesn't make someone stupid."

"You're a teacher. You have to say that," countered Layla. Before Maisie could protest, the girl tapped the math book with her pencil and stated, "I think it's the graphing part that I'm having trouble with. I don't get slope. What is slope?"

"Didn't I explain it in class the other day? Rise over run?" Maisie asked with a frown. Layla rolled her eyes and gave her a patronizing look.

"Yeah, but it's not my fault that it's so hard to listen to someone talk for twenty minutes."

"There's a point to me talking for those twenty minutes," Maisie maintained. "There's a lot to learn in this current unit. I used those twenty minutes to explain—with numerous visual examples, I might add—what slope is, how it can be represented on a basic line graph, and how to find it. I can give you the lecture again if you like."

"Please, no!" Layla begged, waving her hands. "Just walk me through some of the problems. I learn by doing, okay? I know you showed some examples in class, but. . . well, I wasn't really paying attention, honestly. I need to see it again."

Maisie rolled her eyes and leaned over the open book. She walked Layla through the first problem, beginning with plugging the given values into the formula, solving for x, and translating it onto a graph. Maisie found it to be a pleasant distraction from persisting worries about Aremaeid as they repeated the process for the second problem. They went on until Layla shushed Maisie halfway through her tutorial and completed the final three problems herself. She tossed the pencil down onto the paper and leaned back in her chair with a sigh.

"When am I even going to have to know this stuff? Will it help me pay my taxes?" Layla demanded, turning to her teacher. Maisie opened her mouth and closed it again as she tried to think of a reasonable answer.

"Well," she started, "slope probably won't do much for your taxes, but there are other things you can use it for. If you go to a butcher, for example, and you have two hundred dollars in your pocket, you'll need to know how much meat you can buy."

"Who walks around with two hundred dollars in their pocket?" Layla interrupted. Maisie gave her an exasperated look.

"Drug dealer!" called Dennis from the living room. They ignored his input.

"Let me finish. Let's say you're buying venison, and a pound of it costs—for argument's sake—eighteen dollars. Eighteen is the slope and your budget of two hundred is the y-value. So, if you put your equation together, you get 200 = 18x. To figure out how many pounds of venison you can buy, you just divide eighteen from both sides to get x by itself. So that's two hundred over eighteen, which gets you. . ." Maisie paused to run the numbers in her head. "A little over eleven pounds."

Layla stared at her for a moment, then grabbed her calculator and punched in the numbers.

"It's 11.11 repeating," she declared.

Maisie smiled proudly. She hadn't been very skilled in mental math until college, but she was fairly good at it now that she was settled into her career. Being able to provide an estimate at the least was all but a requirement in her profession. But Layla wasn't finished.

"You didn't answer my question. Who walks around with two hundred dollars in their pocket? That's stupid. You'll get robbed or something."

"Maybe you need eleven pounds of venison," Maisie said with a shrug. "You never know."

"Who the heck needs eleven pounds of venison?"

Maisie's thoughts automatically turned to Aremaeid and that mouthful of deadly teeth.

Without thinking, she blurted, "Maybe you have some kind of large carnivore living in your house. Like. . . a wolf. Or a tiger."

"Right," Layla said in a small voice, averting her gaze and inspecting her fingernails. Maisie silently cursed herself; the girl was undoubtedly going to ask what sort of large carnivore she had in her house, and if Maisie told her, Layla would think she was insane. Just then, there was a *thump* from overhead that made them both jump.

"What was that?" Maisie asked sharply. "Did something fall over?"

She stood up, and Layla immediately hopped off her chair. Maisie thought she looked unusually nervous, almost frantic.

"That's probably just Tyson. He, uh, likes being up in the attic. Sometimes."

"Isn't there a second floor between us and the attic, though?"

"Yes! That's definitely where he is, not the attic! I don't know why I said that," Layla amended. She offered an innocent smile, and Maisie lifted an eyebrow. It was obviously a lie, but she chose to drop it, since she didn't know—or particularly want to know—why Layla would feel the need to lie about something thumping around in the attic. So she sat back down in her chair, giving the ceiling a final skeptical glance before turning to the math book. Layla, who looked immensely relieved that she hadn't asked further questions, returned to her seat as well.

"So, what's next, kiddo?" Maisie asked in hopes of easing the mood. Layla was silent for a moment before giving her teacher a strange, desperate look.

"Do you believe in aliens?" she blurted, and Maisie blinked in surprise.

Oh, no. Deep breaths. Be calm.

Yes, she believed in aliens. For a brief moment, she could feel Aremaeid's hand over her face as he suffocated her, and she swallowed hard. How could she answer this question in a way that made her sound informed and clueless at the same time?

"I think it's selfish to believe that, in the entire expanse of the universe, our planet is the only inhabitable one. Yes, I believe that there is alien life out there somewhere. But I don't know how likely it is that aliens are ever going to visit Earth."

Very likely.

Maisie ignored the intrusive thought and asked, "Where did that come from? What's on your mind, kiddo?"

Layla shook her head and muttered, "It's nothing," before switching her attention back to her homework. Could she possibly know that there were aliens running around Nuncan? No, there was no way she could know. She would have told her parents, who would have told the authorities, and soon the whole town would be in the loop. It was just an impromptu question posed by an imaginative girl. Maisie exhaled with relief at the thought that her secret was safe, and she, too, focused on the schoolwork at hand.

There was no possible way that Layla could know. And as long as Maisie was busy maintaining her own secrecy, she had no time to worry about whatever her student was keeping up in that attic.

VII

Tick, tick, tick, tick.

Franklin had his bloodshot eyes locked on his laptop. The lights were off in his home office. The only illumination came from the three screens set up on his desk. His laptop, the centerpiece of the setup, had forty-two different tabs piled on top of each other—all of which he was too tired to look at and too afraid to close—and the tab that was currently open displayed his email inbox.

An email from his current clients had come in today. He was still gathering the courage to click into it, hoping beyond hope but not really believing that they had finally accepted his latest design set. He'd been staring at his inbox for about five minutes, his mouse hovering over the notification and the clock on his wall ticking away serenely.

Tick, tick, tick, tick.

Don't get your hopes up, don't get your hopes up, don't get your hopes up, Franklin warned himself as he finally clicked on the email. A small, traitorous part of him didn't listen, and despite his cynical discouragement, his hopes were piled so high he couldn't see the top of the stack. He took a deep breath, pushed his glasses up his nose, and squinted at the tiny script. There were several long paragraphs packed with polite, flattering garbage that he'd heard several times before. He was so sick of this job that he merely skimmed the words. His eyes floated wearily over the email, then stopped on one sentence that he had to reread three times before its message finally sank in:

"We are pleased to inform you that our board of directors has accepted your most recent submission."

They had accepted it.

Tick, tick, tick, the clock agreed.

After weeks of slaving over his monitors, hyper-aware of that clock ticking away the precious seconds of his life, they had accepted one of his design sets. Franklin stared at that one sentence for a moment longer, his jaw hanging open, before leaping out of his chair with a wordless victory screech, not even bothering to read the rest of the email. He pointed a finger at the clock, his eyes full of wild excitement, and laughed into its glassy face.

"It's not my fucking time!" he yelled, hardly aware of what he was saying and not caring that he was bragging to an inanimate object. "You can shut up, because it's not my *fucking time!*"

He cackled and danced around the room some more, and when he finally calmed down, he flicked the lights on and returned to his desk to finish reading the message. The rest of it was just more empty company jargon, thanking him sincerely for his time and saying that it was a pleasure doing business with him, yadda, yadda, ya. Franklin gleefully screenshotted and archived that email before archiving all the others he had received over the course of this project. He knew he'd have to send a polite response, but that could wait. He began chortling triumphantly as he then closed every tab across his three screens, each click of that red *x* a weight lifted from his soul.

He'd broken up with Nancy and gotten over her in the span of a few hours that morning, and now he was finally finished with the project that had been eating away at his sanity for a month. There was a reason Saturday was his favorite day of the week. Franklin switched off his monitors and left his office, feeling lighter than ever.

This is what freedom feels like.

He wanted to call Avery, but not with his cell phone. He needed a break from screens. He instead employed the landline, dialing his sister's number and waiting impatiently for her to pick up. When she finally did, Franklin felt tears of relief spring from his eyes as he informed her of the latest developments.

"I finished, Avery," he whispered.

"That big soul-sucking commission?" she asked, and Franklin could hear the surprise in her voice. He understood that surprise; after all he'd been through for this corporation, he hadn't expected them to finally end his suffering.

"Yes, the soul-sucking commission!" he crowed triumphantly, and Avery let out a delighted squeal on the other end of the line.

"My baby brother, working with the big dogs!"

Any other time Franklin might have been offended or embarrassed, but because of everything the day had brought him, he could only grin stupidly and agree.

"I've burned more weight today than I have in two years," he breathed, and Avery laughed.

"I'm happy for you, man."

Suddenly an idea struck him, and he exclaimed, "Tell Parker we're having dinner at my place tonight. Don't expect anything fancy, though; I don't have the brain capacity to look at a recipe or guess which ingredients will go well together right now. But do come over, because this is a cause for celebration!"

"Alright," Avery said eagerly. "As soon as I can get out of the precinct, I'll let Parker know that he should wear a suit and expect the finest gold cutlery."

Franklin laughed as she hung up, and he set the phone back in its cradle. He silently wished Darryl some more luck. He knew the poor guy was unlikely to be having as good a day as he was, so he sent him a mental prayer and headed to the kitchen to prepare dinner. He yanked open his fridge door with enthusiastic force, sending some magnets clattering to the floor, and peered inside.

Maybe an egg salad would be good enough? Not too simple, but not too fancy. Franklin scoured every inch of the refrigerator, but there were no eggs. He frowned at the sight but refused to let his good mood be quelled. He knew his siblings would support him and eat whatever he cooked. Hell, they would probably be fine with something even as simple as toast. It sounded like a great idea to him. Unfortunately, he discovered another problem upon seeing that he was out of bread, even after opening every cupboard in the kitchen and pillaging the pantry.

Franklin inhaled deeply and took a moment to gather his composure, letting his arising stint of agitation ebb. He wouldn't let a few empty shelves ruin this get-together. It had been a while since he'd gone grocery shopping, but that could be fixed in the morning. He hadn't spent a lot of time with his siblings lately, so he was excited for this despite the sleep deprivation. He made a mental note to go to Grader's Home Grocery the next day before scrounging around in the cupboards, wherein he managed to find an unopened box of pasta and a can of store-brand spaghetti sauce. Franklin set a pot of water on the stove to boil and pulled some dishes out to start setting the table. Spaghetti was a bit more involved than he would have liked, but it would do. He was going to enjoy this dinner if it was the last thing he did.

*****

Franklin realized halfway through preparing the food that he hadn't told Avery when to come over. Luckily, he was just transferring the pasta to a large bowl when he heard his sister's notoriously loud jeep pull up in the driveway. He grinned giddily and ran to open the door before either of his siblings were even on the front porch.

"Franklin!" Parker called ecstatically, waving his hand. He'd always been the most optimistic and excitable between the three of them, but even Avery carried an air of happiness today. It was an unusual—but not unpleasant—change from her typical sullen cynicism.

"Thanks for coming, you guys," Franklin said, embracing them both.

"Avery told me about the commission. That's awesome, bro! That thing must've shortened your life by, like, twenty years," Parker said.

"I don't know," Avery muttered skeptically, flicking her fingers through Franklin's hair. "I'm not seeing any of the white streaks I expected. But I'd say it sucked up at least a decade."

"At least," Franklin agreed as he let them inside. Although they wiped their feet on the doormat and checked their soles for excess grime, neither of them bothered removing their shoes; it wasn't a rule that Franklin enforced. The way he saw it, the floor was just going to get dirty eventually whether they had bare feet inside or not. He led them to the kitchen, and Avery whistled at the sight of the spaghetti bowl and the pot of sauce on the stove.

"You've been busy," she commented. "You're supposed to be relaxing." Franklin shrugged and handed her a plate.

"This wasn't too bad. There's a big difference between making pasta and wasting hours of your life behind a computer screen for a project that you've lost all interest in."

"That bad?" Parker asked with a sympathetic cringe.

"Worse. But I suppose it paid off in the end since it got Nancy to leave."

"I thought *you* left *her*," stated Avery dubiously, cocking an eyebrow as she dished herself some pasta. Franklin handed Parker a plate and grabbed one for himself, moving to the end of their short line. Even if he didn't care for the no-

84

shoes rule, he dutifully practiced the tradition of allowing guests to select their food first, family or otherwise.

"I did, but I don't think she saw it that way. Did I tell you that she jumped on my car and tried to make it look like I hit her?"

Avery and Parker both burst out laughing, and Franklin maintained, "It's true! Darryl was standing right there on the porch, too. He saw the whole thing. Hell, I wouldn't be surprised if the whole neighborhood came out and saw it. She was throwing a serious fit. As much as I hated that contract, a company that can't decide which degree of fuchsia they want is easily the lesser of the two evils."

"Fuchsia? Really? Has that been the problem this whole time?" inquired Parker, raising an eyebrow.

"Among other things. Fonts, colors, placements, accessibility, things like that. They wanted me to redesign their logo, too, but I had the sense to say no to that one."

"Jesus," Avery muttered, frowning as she ladled some sauce onto her pasta.

They all took their seats around Franklin's kitchen table with their plates of food, and for a few minutes, there was silence while they ate. Parker was the first to speak up.

"Avery also told me that, according to you, it was 'about fucking time' when you broke up with Nancy. You seem to be in a pretty good mood right now, so it checks out, but how're you handling this whole thing? Breakups can be nasty."

"I can't remember the last time I didn't feel like I was dropped in the ocean with my feet stuck in a cement block," Franklin replied truthfully. "That woman was an absolute nightmare. Feel kind of bad for Darryl, though, if I'm being honest."

"Same here," Parker said with a sigh. "Based on everything you told me about Nance, he's in for a bumpy ride. It's a shame, really. He seemed like a pretty good guy."

"Hopefully he's smart enough to crawl out of the sink before he gets pulled down the drain," Avery added.

"You know what? I thought that same exact thing," Franklin said. Then he shuddered and grumbled, "I just hope Nancy doesn't come to my house at 3:00 in the morning trying to get me back. I don't want to see her standing outside my window."

"Would she do that?" Parker asked, his eyes going wide.

"Knowing her? It's not improbable."

"If she ever comes near your house again," Avery commented, twirling some spaghetti around her fork, "you call me up, and I will punt that bitch into Canada." Franklin and Parker began snorting and giggling at her words like a pair of teens at a sleepover. Suddenly Avery's eyes brightened and she added, "Oh, Franklin, something interesting happened at work today. Parker already knows, but I need to tell you about it."

"Really? Was it more interesting than speeding tickets and shoplifters?" Franklin asked, lifting an eyebrow.

"Yeah. A very angry Karen called in about some nasty roadkill on the interstate out near Goldcreek. Dead fox. Part of one, anyway. I called Parker, and as it turns out, the rangers that patrol the Dennison Woods have noticed a massive influx of dead things, all mauled and mostly eaten. It started last night."

"That's right," Parker chimed in. "We're pretty sure it's bear-related, because those are the only things around here that could inflict the kind of damage we saw, so you should be extra careful next time you go out hiking. I'm not too worried about Avery, but you're skinnier than a fire pole, Franklin. A good-sized grizzly could whack you in half with one swipe."

"Haha. I'll tell you what: I'll make sure to find a tall girl. She can protect me from the bears."

"Heh, yeah. Well, anyway, it's good to hear that you're finally getting your life back together, dude," Parker concluded with a small, sad smile. The upbeat tone that was usually in everything he said suddenly deflated, and Franklin leaned forward with a frown.

"Hey, what's up, man?" he inquired, and Parker shook his head.

"It's nothing," he muttered.

Avery jabbed her fork at him, and he threw her an exasperated and slightly hurt look.

"That reminds me of something I wanted to ask you about," she said through a mouthful of food. "How are you and Trent doing? Usually, you can't stop talking about the man, but you haven't said a word about him in days."

Like Darryl, Parker had met Trent at work through his ranging group, and the two of them had been dating for close to three months. It wasn't nearly as long as Franklin and Nancy's involvement, but they'd seemed quite infatuated with each other. Franklin had hung out with the pair several times, and Trent was a nice enough guy.

"That's. . . That's the nothing," Parker admitted.

"What happened?" demanded Franklin.

"He's been kind of distant for the last couple of weeks, but I figured that if something was wrong, he would just talk to me about it. Well, he did talk to me about it. Thursday afternoon. He just said all the usual things: that I was a great guy, but we just don't have enough in common, and it would be in our best interest to take a break and 'focus on ourselves.'"

"Oh, dude," Franklin groaned, sitting back in his chair. Parker poked at the pasta with his fork, and Avery patted him comfortingly on the shoulder.

"I'm sorry, man," she said. "I thought it was going so well."

"So did I!" Parker shouted, his sudden change in volume making his siblings jump. "I don't even know what I did wrong, but I must have done *something*, right? He didn't tell me what it was, of course, but I'm pretty sure it was me."

"You didn't do anything wrong," Franklin assured him.

Parker snorted and muttered, "He sure made it *sound* like I did."

"Then Trent is the idiot, not you," Avery insisted, and the look Parker gave her was akin to the face of a kicked puppy.

"He probably just needs to figure himself out," Franklin said gently. "From what I saw of him, he really did seem to care about you, so I doubt he was trying to hurt or blame you with that. There might be something going on in his life that he doesn't want you involved in. Who knows? Maybe when he gets all of that sorted out, he'll try to reconnect."

"And then *you* can reject *him*. Keep reeling him in, then casting him back out. Make him squirm," Avery added with a maniacal grin, and Parker couldn't seem to hold back a smile of his own.

They continued talking long after they had all finished first and second helpings of pasta. By the time the plates were clean, Parker was in a better mood. It was dark enough for Franklin to turn on the porch light when his siblings returned to Avery's Jeep.

"Good night, guys! I'll call tomorrow!" Franklin called, waving to them, and they returned the sentiments. Still smiling, he watched them drive away before heading back inside to clean up. Despite Parker's hang-ups about Trent, this Saturday had been the best day Franklin had had in weeks. Nancy was out of his life, as was the contracted assignment he'd had to do, and he would never have to worry about either of them again. He went to sleep content that night, completely convinced—at least for the time being—that nothing could possibly go wrong for him again.

VIII

Maisie was exhausted by the time she finally got into bed. After her tutoring session with Layla, she resolved to spend the rest of the day cleaning her house in a subtle effort to look too busy to interact with Aremaeid. But if he got the hint that she didn't want to talk to him, he didn't care, because he used the time to follow her around and ask endless questions about various household objects. The bathroom and kitchen were full of especially interesting things that he simply *needed* to learn about, and Maisie begrudgingly indulged him.

While she wiped down her kitchen counter, he pointed at the coffee pot and demanded to know its origin and purpose.

While she swept the hallway and living room floor, he inquired about how the lamps and light switches functioned. This led to a half-assed, unintelligible explanation of electricity that she rambled on through until he got bored and lost interest on that topic.

While she sponged and sprayed her shower to immaculacy, he asked where the sink water came from and how the temperature changed.

The questions went on forever. Maisie wasn't opposed to lengthy queries, especially when they came from her students, because it was her job to teach people about the world. She admittedly relaxed as Aremaeid asked about more and more things, but the problem was that he hovered. At one point she was on her hands and knees, scrubbing between the tiles on her bathroom floor with an unused toothbrush. When she sat up, she nearly jumped out of her skin upon seeing that Aremaeid was arched over her and obsessively toggling the faucet handle of the sink.

He was especially riveted by the toilet once Maisie uncomfortably explained what it was for. Where did the water come from? Where did everything go? Why was it so small? For the last question, Maisie politely reminded him that the toilet only looked small because it was built for a human being, and Aremaeid was twice the size of its intended users.

The vacuum was also quite captivating, but not in the same way. At first, he crouched over it curiously while Maisie set it up and plugged it in. But as soon as she turned it on to vacuum her living room rug, the noise startled him so badly that he leaped backward to get away from it and ended up impaling the wall with his horns. The sudden outburst petrified Maisie and Roller, and after a solid two minutes of collective panic between the three of them, Aremaeid freed himself from the wall and the cleaning resumed. He stopped hovering so close to her but remained lurking in the hallway, watching with flattened ears and silent, suspicious attentiveness as Maisie ran the vacuum over the floor.

The questions came much less frequently after that incident.

The more she spoke to him, the more she started to see flaws in his understanding of humans. He had an extensive vocabulary and used words that she didn't even know the meaning of, as if he'd swallowed a dictionary, but he often stumbled when she employed certain idioms or used a word's alternative meaning. "Cool" and "neat" were especially stumping debacles. Although the questions about technology slowed after the altercation with the vacuum, he wasn't shy about demanding clarification on her English usage. As she helped him through it, her discomfort around him slowly ebbed until she began to think of him as a giant talking housecat and had to consciously remind herself that he could change his tune at any given moment.

That night, Maisie thought she would be unable to fall asleep just as she had the previous evening despite her growing ease, but she winked out like a light as soon as her head hit the pillow. She woke up sometime around midnight to what sounded like the sliding glass door in the back of the house opening, but when she stumbled out of her room with a pillow clutched defensively in her hands and Roller on her heels, the door was closed and there were no signs of any intruders. She went back to bed and didn't give it another thought until the next morning.

Waking up about fifteen minutes before or after 6:00 was habitual even without the alarm, as she had been doing it for years. Her morning routine was always the same; get up, make the dog's breakfast, take him out to do his business, and then prepare her own meal. But when Maisie opened her fridge, she found that she was completely out of dog food.

"Shit," she muttered, shutting the fridge with a sigh and leaning against it. Roller watched her expectantly from the couch, unaware that she had no food for him. No dog food, at least. She reheated a container of leftover chicken and dumped it into his bowl alongside crumbled pieces of a muffin. She called the dog over, and Roller, upon seeing the surprise delicacies, wagged his tail and gave her a pleased lick on the knee.

Maisie sighed and grumbled, "Yeah, yeah. Don't get used to it, you little turd."

She grabbed a thin hoodie off the back of a kitchen chair and zipped it up to her chin. Grader's Home Grocery, the store closest to her house, didn't open until 8:00, but Maisie didn't consider that a problem. She often filled the empty morning hours by hiking the trails in the Dennison Woods. The woods were close enough to her house that she didn't need to drive—the walk there was fifteen minutes at the most—and she always had plenty of time to cover a few miles before turning around.

I should let Aremaeid know.

Maisie chewed her lip nervously and glanced at the basement steps. He would probably think she was going to spill his secret if she left the house without telling him. The idea of him being like a big housecat had disappeared overnight, leaving her back at square one. Despite her fears, however, she went to the stairs and called down, "Aremaeid?"

She descended, flicking the light on and glancing around. It wasn't a very large space, and his size made him hard to miss, but he was nowhere to be seen. Maisie stepped down onto the cold floor and looked around anxiously, even checking the dusty alcove behind the stairs. She found some cobwebs and spiders, but no sign of Aremaeid.

How does someone that big just disappear?

She vaguely recalled her scare in the middle of the night, so perhaps he had left? Where to and why, she had no idea, but a final check in every room of the house proved that he was gone. Her anxiety was immediately replaced with relief. Was he truly gone? She happily called Roller to her side as she headed for the back door.

"Alright, bud, time for you to go out and have yourself a little squat. With no scary aliens around this time." She frowned when she saw that the door was already unlocked, but quickly shrugged it off. Aremaeid had probably gone out that way to avoid the attention he might have otherwise gotten on the street.

She opened the door and moved aside to let Roller waddle happily out of the house.

When the dog was finished and safely back inside, Maisie turned her back to the yard and stuffed her feet into her sneakers. She tugged up her hood and grabbed a pair of gloves as well. Autumn was beautiful in Montana, but it came with a subtle chill that could easily numb exposed fingers and ears. It was still dark out, so she grabbed a small handheld flashlight and stored it safely in the pocket of her hoodie.

She closed the door behind her, turned around, and clapped a hand over her mouth to keep from screaming. Aremaeid stood only a few feet from her, having approached with his normal technique of disturbing silence. Maisie pressed a hand to her chest and exhaled shakily, leaning back against the door.

Deep breaths. Be calm.

"I told you not to do that. You scared me," she hissed. Aremaeid shifted his weight awkwardly and regarded her with mild suspicion.

"What are you doing?"

"I'm just going for a walk. I like hiking up in the woods now and then. What were *you* doing? When did you leave the house? I thought you were gone. Like, legitimately gone."

"I was hunting," Aremaeid explained with a shrug.

"You could have left a note or something!"

"Sorry." He didn't sound very sorry. Aremaeid pointedly shifted his eyes to the door, then back to her. Maisie sighed and moved out of his path so he could enter the house.

"Don't kill my dog while I'm gone."

"Fine."

As Maisie walked through her yard and traveled up the back road that led to the Dennison Woods, she faltered mid-step and studied her surroundings. The night he arrived, Aremaeid had told her that there were others like him in Nuncan. Were they in the woods right now? If they truly weren't on Earth to start a fight, then running into one shouldn't raise any problems for her, but Aremaeid *had* tried to kill her. She was reluctant to turn around and stay at her house while waiting for Grader's to open, but she was at least somewhat familiar with the alien who was renting her basement. She didn't know any of the others, and there was no way of anticipating whether they would show the same hesitation he did.

He's not going to do anything as long as I keep him a secret.

Maisie rocked on her feet and looked around, nibbling her lip and debating for a moment before going back to the porch. There was nothing wrong with being cautious. Finding his packmates was Aremaeid's entire goal, and as soon as he accomplished that goal, he would leave. She could walk through the woods as much as she liked after that happened, but she decided that, for the time being, it would be best to hunker down and wait out the storm.

* * * * *

Grader's Home Grocery was a quiet, friendly place. Maisie didn't even have to lock her car when she got out and strode across the small parking lot. Most of the employees were either friends and family of John Grader or acne-ridden teens searching for a part-time job. Everyone was chatty and amiable, and although Maisie was the type of person who entered a store, got what she needed, and left as quickly as she could, here she often took her time so she could enjoy the positive vibes.

Maisie yanked her hood down as she walked through the automatic doors and shivered in the crisp, uniform air that all grocery stores had. She went straight to the pet section and scanned the aisle for Roller's preferred brands. The furry little walnut was frustratingly picky when it came to dog food, and Maisie had learned long ago that he only found certain kinds acceptable.

"Food, food, food," she muttered, running her fingertips along the various cans. She always had to go for wet food rather than a more convenient and easily preparable kibble, since Roller had only three teeth left due to past medical issues. Maisie groaned when she finally spotted his favorite kind on the top shelf. She could have sworn it had been near the bottom a month ago, but this wasn't unusual. It seemed that John Grader was never satisfied with the arrangement of his products, as he frequently moved things around.

Maisie cursed, grumbling, "Damn tall people. . . Fucking goliaths. . ." as she stretched up on the tips of her toes to paw at the cans. The smiling dogs adorning the labels seemed to be mocking her shortness, and she glared spitefully up at them. Everyone knew that grocery stores were rigged to serve people over six feet.

"Uh, ma'am? Do you want some help with that?"

Maisie jumped and looked over to her right. The man who had approached her was tall, skinny, and sporting a pair of wide-framed glasses that looked like they were going to fall off the tip of his long nose at any moment. He looked hesitant and tense, like a rabbit that had spotted a cat; it was as if he thought she was going to pounce on him and claw his face off.

"Oh. Um, sure. Thanks," Maisie said, stepping back and allowing him to approach the shelf. She didn't like asking for help from strangers, but he was taller than she was and could grab things she couldn't, so any assistance on his part would be appreciated.

"Which ones?" he asked, studying the various cans.

"That one there. Just one can."

"Sure you don't want any more?"

"Nah, this will hold him off until I can do some real shopping. The chunky stuff, if you don't mind."

"Mmm. Delicious."

"Yep," Maisie agreed with a smirk. "It smells real great, too."

The guy chuckled and handed her the cans, asking, "What kind of dog you got?"

"Dachshund. Picky one, too. He only eats this brand."

"He got a name?"

"Roller."

"Really? Roller?"

"I didn't pick it out; he's a rescue."

The guy crossed his arms, leaned on the shelves of dog food in what might have been an attempt to look suave, and grinned at her.

"You know something funny?" he mused, showing off several rapid eyebrow wiggles that almost made Maisie drop her can as she snorted back laughter. "I know what kind of dog you have, the food he likes, and what his name is, but I've got no idea who you are. Tell me your name, and I'll happily pick every top shelf in this store clean for you."

"I don't need some *man* to grab stuff off the top shelf," Maisie said sarcastically, drawling the words. The guy chuckled, but he continued to look at her expectantly. She bit her lip and answered, "It's Maisie."

"Huh. I didn't think horse girls grew out of middle school."

"Shut up! You don't get to make fun of my name unless I get to make fun of yours," she protested with a laugh.

The man nodded somberly and conceded, "Fair enough. Franklin."

"And you really thought you could make fun of my name? As if 'Franklin' belongs anywhere but on some 18th-century nerd with a permanent resting bitch face?"

The two stared at each other for a moment before bursting into laughter.

"You know what? That's fair. But, like your dog's name, I didn't choose it," Franklin chuckled. His face took on a boyish grin, and Maisie couldn't help returning it with a smile of her own.

They walked through the store together, chatting all the while. Once Franklin acquired a carton of eggs and a loaf of bread, they headed for the checkout lanes. Maisie got through the register with her dog food first, and she knew she could have left during the time it took him to purchase his own items, but she waited by the exit instead. When Franklin approached her, she chewed her lip and hesitantly spoke up.

"Just out of curiosity, are you doing anything tonight?" she asked. The threat of Aremaeid's presence still lingered in her mind, but that didn't mean she had to cease all human contact. She just needed to keep Franklin from entering her house until her guest left. Assuming he agreed, of course.

"I'm afraid I am. I need to take care of some business transactions. But I'm free tomorrow at 6:00 if that works for you?"

"There's this place I haven't been to in a while, I don't know if you've heard of it. It's called the Dancing Bear Café. You interested?" she edged hopefully. Franklin grinned again, and she noticed that he had slightly crooked teeth. It was a flaw she found strangely endearing.

"It's been a while for me, too," he admitted. "I'll meet you there, horse girl."

"Sure thing, Benjamin."

As they left the store and parted ways, Maisie felt unusually giddy. It was a different sort of anxiety, one that she hadn't felt in a long time. It had been years since she'd gone on a date. She had been so focused on her job and her hobbies that she hadn't taken the time to explore her social possibilities in Nuncan. Sure, she had friends, like the Lucios, but she didn't consider finding a partner to be a huge priority. It still wasn't, but it could be fun to try. She needed a healthy distraction, anyway, with the circumstances being what they were.

Just got to keep him out of my house until Aremaeid leaves.

With the date set up, Maisie returned to her house with a spring in her step and the fresh dog food held lovingly in her arms.

IX

"What did you say your species was called?"

Layla sat cross-legged on the cold attic floor, paying no attention to the folders of homework she'd brought up with her. Her original plan had been to finish it in Ornathium's company, but she'd been immediately sidetracked by tales of his home world and the creatures that lived in it.

"Rhithien," he replied. He was sprawled out in a patch of sunlight beneath the attic's dusty window, his red eyes half-shut and his voice carrying a dreamy, lethargic tone, but he seemed happy to answer whatever questions Layla had. She thoughtfully tapped her chin with her pencil as she considered her next inquiry.

"Do you have humans on Primaied?" she asked at last.

"Not that I know of. Why?"

"Oh, no reason." Layla couldn't help feeling a tad disappointed. Rhithien were cool, but it would have been even cooler to see actual people from a whole other world. "I was just wondering if there were other things besides Rhithien that could talk and think and stuff."

"I did not say there were no others like us."

"Wait, are there?"

"Of course. There are four closely related dominant species on Primaied: Rhithien—which is what I am—Serrhithien, Viprhess, and Omelae. All are intelligent, although we Rhithien and the Serrhithien are typically considered superior to the other two in our respective cultures and magics."

"What are the Serrhithien like?" Layla prompted, scooching toward Ornathium. This was an unexpected turn. Were these "dominant species" simply different races of the same thing, or were they entirely different creatures?

"They are like us, but they have gills and tend to be bigger. Most of them live on the coasts, but some Serrhithien traders travel across continents. I have only met a few myself, and in all honesty, I know not much about them. I cannot recall ever successfully conversing with one; they and the other two dominants speak in different tongues than we do. However, the Serrhithien have a language in hands, and I picked up a couple of signs from some traders I came across."

"What are the signs? What do they mean? You have to show me!" Layla demanded. Ornathium sat up with an amused smile and nodded. He lifted his hands and began twisting, shaping, and waving them in sharp, fluid motions. Layla made him repeat the short phrase until she could precisely mimic it, and when she managed to form the silent words on her own, she gave him a dubious look and asked, "What does it mean?"

"I do not know," Ornathium admitted with a shrug. "They just made those signs frequently. As I said, I never conversed with one. I simply observed."

"Huh."

She found her hands falling into the same motions again and again, and she decided that she enjoyed the smoothness of the wordless language. But Ornathium had mentioned two other species, and if the Serrhithien were this interesting, the others were bound to be, as well.

She looked back up at Ornathium and queried, "What about the Viprhess?"

To her surprise, Ornathium scoffed derisively and rolled his eyes.

"Nothing more than air-headed little birds, they are. Viprhess are the smallest dominants, although, to their credit, they are the most difficult to catch."

"Catch? Do people hunt them?"

"Some do. Their wing bones and horns are sold on many Serrhithien markets, I am told. Yes, very difficult to catch, they are. Even more so than Omelae. They have soft little wings that carry them up, up, up, forever and ever up. . ." Ornathium's voice trailed off and he rolled onto his back with a nostalgic hum. Layla giggled at his odd behavior, but he didn't seem to hear her. His eyes were glazed and content as if he was reliving his most delightful memories. All of a sudden the glaze disappeared and he sat up again, his eyes narrowing as he hissed, "But it is most definitely possible to bring a Viprhan down. Oh, yes. Pretty birds cannot fly if someone breaks their fragile little wings."

Layla gulped and edged away from him. The mood shift had come out of nowhere, and for the first time since they'd officially declared themselves friends, she felt a twinge of unease.

Run, whispered a little voice in her head. Layla silenced the voice and took a deep breath. She would not be afraid of Ornathium. He was her friend.

"Um. . ." she interjected hesitantly, and relief coursed through her when Ornathium's expression cleared. His ears perked up with a small, expectant smile, and she continued, "You said they were called Viprhess, but you just called them Viprhan."

"Viprhess for many, Viprhan for one. Not like 'Rhithien'," he explained, waving a hand dismissively. "It is the same for Omelae. Omelae for many, Omelaen for one."

"I guess that makes sense. What are the Omelae like?"

"I can only tell you what I have heard from others, as I have never met one. I know that they are skilled blacksmiths, but are otherwise a very primitive species. They live by violent instinct and care little for the goings-on of other creatures."

"But if Serrhithien have gills and Viprhess have wings, what's special about Omelae?"

"They are the largest of the dominants. I have heard that the largest Omelae can grow to twice the size of a Rhithien."

Layla had to take a minute to process that fact. She stared across the room with unbroken concentration as she tried to imagine two Ornathiums stacked on top of one another. But one thing still didn't seem to fit: what was unique about the Rhithien? Serrhithien had gills, Viprhess had wings, and Omelae were big, but Ornathium had used his own species as a mere comparison to display the others' differences. What did the Rhithien have that no other species did?

"You said Rhithien were superior," she prompted, and Ornathium nodded. After a beat of hesitation—was it rude to ask such a question?—she mused, "but what makes you guys different? Why are you better than the others?"

"Well, unfortunately, it is the one thing that I cannot show you. We have the strongest magic, and can beat any foe in a contest of ability."

"Then why don't *you* have magic?"

"I told you the other day, little queen, only alphas and healers have magic. Anyone can become a healer with practice and proper training. All dominants have healers. But each dominant has a specific magic that can only be harnessed by an alpha of that species. All normal Rhithien, myself included, are forbidden from learning such power."

"Oh gosh, this is a lot," Layla said, rubbing her temples as she processed all the details.

"I was told that you humans have no magic, but I want to hear it from you. Are you aware of any magic here on Earth?"

The question caught Layla off guard. There were magicians, but all they had were practical tricks meant to impress an enthusiastic audience. She'd heard of fortune-tellers and mediums, but her mother had informed her that every one of them was a greedy fraud who didn't know how to make "real money." Layla wasn't sure how true that was, but she saw no reason not to take her mother's word for it.

"No," she confessed with a sigh. Reality on Earth was depressingly dull and magic-less.

Ornathium hummed thoughtfully and inquired, "May I ask you something, little queen?"

"I guess," she replied with a shy smile. Even though it was far from the first time he had used that nickname, her face flushed and a small, happy shiver ran through her body.

"Do you know the significance of the name 'Lucio'?"

Layla was completely taken aback by the question. Why would Ornathium, a space alien, know anything about some random human's last name? Surely he was mistaken.

"No," she responded after a moment. "Why?"

"Did you know it is the only human name in Rhithien history?"

That was news. Layla didn't know alien history could include anything about humans. She eagerly slid forward from where she was seated on the floor and demanded to hear more. As mind-blowing as it was just to have Ornathium in her house, the discovery of the Lucio name superseding Earth's boundaries was a hundred times more significant.

"What happened? What did we do? You need to tell me!"

"Another time, perhaps," Ornathium purred with a sly smirk. "I am tired, little queen. I was awake all night searching for my pack."

"No you weren't, I didn't hear you leave! C'mon, you can't just leave me hanging like this!"

"If you were able to hear me leave, I would not be very good at hiding up here," he pointed out. He curled up and rested his head on his arms, closing his eyes. Layla nagged and poked at him for another five minutes, pushing for the story, but received no response. When she finally realized that he wasn't going to talk, she stomped out of the attic with an irritated growl. If he was unwilling to tell her about her family lineage, she would have to get the information from another source. But where?

As Layla left the attic and headed down the hallway, she had a troubling realization; she had no idea what her family history was like. She knew all about Nana's and Poppa's lives, of course, but nothing before that. It wasn't something she had ever wondered about, as she had always considered old people and stories about old people to be rather dull.

It might not even be my *family. There're probably hundreds of Lucios on Earth.*

That could be true, but Ornathium had appeared in *her* house, hadn't he? And he'd decided to share stories of his planet with her instead of finding someone else, hadn't he? It had to mean something, but if she wanted to find out on her own, she needed to do some digging.

"Mom?" Layla called, ambling down the length of the hall. She knew she'd gotten the surname from her mother. Her father often joked that he'd married a Lucio so that he could avoid being called "Dennis Pissink", which was his previous name.

"In here, Layla."

Her mother's voice drifted calmly from the sewing room, which was situated at the back of the house. Layla grabbed the doorframe and swung inside, inhaling the comforting aroma of cinnamon-scented candles. The sewing room was her mother's favorite place, and when she wasn't doing chores, filling out papers, or stressing about work, she could almost always be found stitching away at old clothes and embroidering squares of fabric. Layla liked the room, too; piles of cloth stood haphazardly on every surface, from chairs with flattened cushions to dressers overflowing with materials and tools. The desk on which the sewing machine rested was covered with thread spools, ribbons, and scraps from previous projects. The fabrics and yarns were of all shades and textures. Despite the room's chaotic nature, Layla found it cozy and comfortable.

She went in and sat down on a faded blue loveseat where her mother was hand-stitching the hem of a checkered skirt. Setting the garment on her lap and putting an arm around her daughter, she asked, "What do you need, sweetie?"

"I know this is a little random, but I was wondering about our family. The Lucios. How far back do we go?" inquired Layla, getting straight to the point. Her mother frowned, and Layla felt a twinge of embarrassment. Maybe it was weird to ask about something like this.

"Is this for a school project?"

"Yeah," she lied. "I have to record a family tree for one of my classes, and I'm supposed to go as far back as I can."

"Well, as a matter of fact," her mother said, setting aside her sewing and rising from the small sofa, "your great-grandmother happened to keep an old document on that very thing. Not too many people have a record quite like hers. I'm not sure how many times it's been copied, but the version I have is from the mid-1700s. Our lineage can be traced all the way back to Ancient Rome. I keep it in a trunk in the basement. We can dig it out if you'd like."

Layla couldn't believe her luck. A family tree? Going back to Roman times? She only barely managed to contain her excitement as she followed her mother out of the sewing room and down to the basement. It was like the attic, but stuffier and full of even more dusty knickknacks. The space overflowed with cardboard boxes, battered board games, unused furniture, and mysterious heirlooms that looked like they hadn't been touched in years. Her mother shoved things aside until she uncovered an old chest with rusted hinges and a torn leather covering on the lid. Layla sneezed as a waft of dust floated up and blew into her face.

Her mother opened the chest and unearthed an ancient-looking book that was thicker than Layla's arm. It was bound in ripped, weather-worn leather, much like the trunk it was stored in, and Layla could see the moldy pages curling and yellowing at the edges. It looked old enough to crumble into papery ash at the touch of a light breeze, and she winced as her mother opened it with a series of loud, crinkly pops. She set it gently on the floor, and Layla eagerly knelt beside her.

"According to this date here, it hasn't been updated since 1957," her mother explained. "Your Great-Grandma Rosalee was the last one to do it. I've been meaning to make some current entries for us, but I haven't spared this old thing a single thought in a long time. Work's been pretty busy lately."

Layla was impressed by the sheer amount of content. She gingerly flipped through the middle section of the tome, squinting hard at the tiny, rumpled handwriting.

"You said this goes back to Ancient Rome?" she asked, and her mother gave a nod of confirmation. "Why didn't you ever tell me we had this?"

"You never seemed interested. And in all honesty, my mother and I weren't too invested in it, either. We kept it because it was important to Rosalee, but I actually haven't looked at it since before I married your dad. It's been in the family for generations. Like I said, this copy is from the eighteenth century."

Layla nodded, hardly listening. She attentively scanned each entry, searching for someone who stood out. Each name included family details—who they married, how many kids they had, and more—as well as a short paragraph describing something important that the person accomplished or experienced. Her excitement was replaced with disappointment when the entries stopped about two-thirds in. As if sensing her pursuit, her mother flipped to the very beginning of the book and tapped the name that headed all the rest.

"Who's that? I can barely read this," Layla grumbled.

"You're not the only one," her mother laughed. "This is Aurelia Lucio, the woman who started the tree. The original record that she started is long gone, but this version is pretty accurately translated from what I was told. Only our direct line is traced—just the people who kept the family name—but we probably have distant relatives all over the world. Aurelia had four kids: Vena, Marcia, Maximus, and Petra. They all grew up to get married and have kids as well, and so did their kids after them, and so on. You can see here that Petra is our ancestor."

"Wow," murmured Layla. She tried reading through Aurelia Lucio's short biography, but the wording was completely incomprehensible. She pointed out the strange dialect and asked, "Is this even English?"

"Of course it's English. It's just old. Well, it was originally written in Latin, probably, but this copy was translated into English. People just spoke differently back in the 1700s. It describes how a bear wandered onto the family's estate in the country, and Aurelia killed it to defend her family. But it also says the bear's body was lost, so she probably just wounded it and ran it off. She had her fourth child, Petra, soon after that. History has a funny way of getting embellished by the people who live to tell about it."

Was it really a bear? Layla could feel the wheels turning in her head. The book said it was a bear, but there was no body. No body, no proof. She thought about Ornathium's hesitation. What didn't he want to tell her? If he was at her house for a reason, could it possibly connect to this? What if the attacking creature wasn't a bear, but something else? Something from Primaied?

Is that why Ornathium didn't want to talk about it? Did my ancestor kill a Rhithien?

She clapped the book shut with a *slam* that made her mother flinch.

"I'll copy it," she blurted, eliciting a look of surprise from her mom. Layla quickly gathered her composure and maintained, "I have plenty of time to start it today. I can spread it out over this week when I'm not doing homework."

"I don't know kiddo. It's a big job, and, well. . . this is a pretty important family heirloom."

"I won't damage it or mess it up, I promise!"

"Maybe you won't, honey, but this is the sort of thing that takes weeks, even months. Do you have any idea how many names there are here? And I haven't even gotten started on how much paper you'd need."

"I can just type it up on my computer," Layla insisted, her hands now itching to grab the book. "I know how to make documents. I'm not a very fast typer, but this book isn't totally full, and these pages are thick, so it might not take *that* long."

"Alright," her mother conceded with a sigh. "If you think it won't be too hard, you're welcome to tackle this thing. Great-Grandma Rosalee's probably smiling down at you right now. But feel free to come get me if you need help or lose interest. I'll find a way to make myself available."

She gave Layla a final skeptical look before heading upstairs to return to her sewing. Layla remained in the basement, studying the family tree. She knew it would take several days, perhaps even an entire week, and while she hadn't come downstairs with the intention of volunteering for the rewrite, she was now determined to see it through. Fishing an old pen out of a nearby dresser drawer, she neatly printed her grandparents' names after Great-Grandma Rosalee's entry, then her parents. She finished by scrawling in her own name:

Layla Violet Lucio

Smiling at how the words looked on the old paper, she gently closed the book and lugged it up to the attic to show Ornathium.

X

An angry chittering sound roused Ridaion from a terribly pleasant dream. He blearily looked around at the small, shaded place where he lay. After traveling for most of the previous night and day, he'd welcomed a concealed spot beneath a tall, broad tree. He'd fallen asleep almost as soon as he was on the ground, and he would've been happy to stay there for the rest of the day. But someone apparently had a problem with that. He growled and squinted up through the canopy of needle-like leaves that sprouted from the rough bark. High up in the topmost branches, he spied a tiny creature with red-brown fur and a bushy tail. It saw him staring and chattered again, though it didn't move closer to his level.

"Would you still be yelling at me if I came up there?" Ridaion called grouchily, to which the little beast replied with an insistent churr. He knew it wasn't worth his time, but damn it, that thing was pissing him off. He rose and began to scale the tree. The branches creaked under his weight, but he didn't stop until the tiny thing went silent, scampered across a limb, and leaped to an adjacent tree, where it proceeded to scold him again. Ridaion braced his feet against the trunk, tightened his body, and then sprang up through the branches towards the little beast. Any other day he might have let it go, but he was hungry and in a foul mood, and although this thing wouldn't make more than a mouthful, it was better than nothing.

He slammed against the tree that held the little creature, making it dash away again. But it had nowhere to run as the tall trunk bowed beneath Ridaion's force. It scampered to the end of a branch, but he lunged forward, reaching as far as his arm would allow, and closed his hand around the meager prey. It let out a terrified screech that pierced his ears like a blade, but he ignored it. He flexed his grip, extending his claws further until red blood sprayed out between his fingers. He was so startled that he almost fell out of the tree.

105

"What the fuck!" he yelled, throwing the tiny thing's limp, crushed body to the ground. He gagged at the startling crimson fluid and waved his hand wildly to flick the vile stuff off. It took him a moment to recall that it was normal for Earth blood to be that peculiar shade of red.

Ridaion's face flushed with embarrassment, and he looked around the area as he hopped down from the tree, hoping that no one had noticed his inane panic. Once he was sure that he was indeed alone, he retrieved his food from the ground, brushed off the dirt and tree needles, and promptly consumed it. The taste was strange, utterly unlike anything he'd eaten before, but it wasn't awful. It was just meat. The thing was gone in a single bite, as he'd predicted, but despite his persisting hunger, he felt strangely satisfied by the knowledge that he'd shut the tiny beast up. Had it deserved such an end? Probably not. But did it feel good to kill that bothersome little shit? Absolutely.

Regardless of the brief triumph, he was far from content, and he heaved a tired sigh as he looked longingly back at the spot where he'd been napping. He could try going back to sleep, but the natural thrill of chasing even the smallest prey now had him wide awake.

If I'm going to stay up, I might as well keep looking for the others.

Ridaion turned away from the tree and trudged on through the woods, occasionally lifting his nose and sniffing at the wind. He wasn't really expecting to find his pack at that point, so he focused on seeking out some decent prey.

"Not that I wouldn't mind finding another Rhithien. Anyone, really," he muttered aloud. "Some company would be nice. Not Vegra, though. He's an ass. And probably not Ziiphan, either. I don't think my sanity would last long if I had to put up with his arrogant correshit by myself. And not Ornathium. No, definitely not him. The creepy bastard would have his hands around my throat as soon as I turned my back. Okay, so maybe 'anyone' is a bit of a broad statement. But anyone other than those three would be great. Except for Orniell. And maybe Aremaeid and Torraeid. They're nice, but they're also boring."

Ridaion stopped and sighed as he realized that his fastidious complaints about his packmates narrowed his choices down to one good option: his alpha. He knew that Salidus was the only one whose company he could truly enjoy through the current inconvenient circumstances.

Is he safe? Is he anywhere near me? What if we're all just moving further away from each other?

He might have been able to ignore these troubling thoughts if he could talk to someone other than himself. But he was alone. He'd never liked having to listen to his own mind wander and speculate. Being with Salidus would come as a welcome distraction. Perhaps things would even be better than before they'd left Primaied; after all, they hadn't had a single moment of privacy since their pack was selected for the mission.

Ridaion was too busy thinking about Salidus to notice a familiar scent carried on the wind until it assaulted his senses like a wave of noxious water. He snorted and stumbled back, one hand flying up to his snout as he gagged on the overpowering stench. It was a warm, sultry smell that spread easily and would probably stick around for days. Someone was musking all over the woods, and it was so strong that it took Ridaion a moment to figure out who it was. He tentatively sniffed the breeze, grimacing at the heavy odor. A small release of musk could be enticing, but this much of it was horridly unappealing. It was a strategy commonly used for claiming large stretches of land as private territory. It was easier, faster, and classier than pissing on everything in the immediate area.

"Ziiphan!" Ridaion roared, holding his nose as he stomped through the trees. Of course Ziiphan would do something like this. Sure, he might be alerting every nearby human with a functioning nose that he was on Earth, but that was perfectly acceptable as long as he felt comfortable.

Ridaion sped up to a jog, grumbling, "Fucking idiot," under his breath. The egotistical bastard was probably proud of himself for covering so much ground in just a few days.

"Hello?" called an innocent voice up ahead. It was coming from a dense grove of trees. Ridaion narrowed his eyes and shoved through the foliage. He came out in a spacious clearing that was neatly protected by the surrounding forest and cut in half by a thin, burbling stream. Sprawled out in the sun beside the water was none other than Ziiphan.

"You seem to be enjoying yourself," Ridaion hissed, stalking towards him. Ziiphan flashed a lazy smile and laid his head back down on the ground. His dusky orange skin was a soft golden color in the sunlight, and the large, dark spots that patterned his body looked brown rather than their natural black.

"I am, actually. I was starting to doubt that the musking would work, but it brought you right to me. I am so very clever, aren't I?"

107

"Oh, yes. You're going to bring our pack and every human on Earth right to this spot. Forgive my bluntness, but are you insane? Or are you just the stupidest piece of shit on Primaied?"

"Don't fuss, Ridaion," he tittered. "Humans have terrible noses, remember? They couldn't smell a puddle of piss if they were drowning in it."

Ridaion growled and sat down about half a sopion away from him, scowling judgmentally at the trees around him. It was an admittedly nice place, with access to water and ample hunting grounds. As frustrating as Ziiphan was, he knew how to pick locations. Ridaion glanced at the stream and swallowed. He was thirsty, and hungry, too, but not enough to give his packmate the slightest hint that his choices had benefits.

As if sensing his dilemma, Ziiphan sat up again, spread his legs, and said with a smirk, "If you suck my cocks, I'll hunt something down for you. You won't even have to lift a finger."

"You can suck your own cocks just fine."

"Would you say the same thing if I had pretty blue skin?" Ziiphan teased. An image of Salidus flashed through Ridaion's mind, and his lips twisted into a disgusted snarl.

"Even if I was with Salidus and no one else, I wouldn't be in the mood. Not with all this musk floating around. How did you release so much in such a short span of time, anyway?"

"It's rather impressive of me, isn't it? You don't like?"

"There's a point where it becomes a turn-off."

"Mm. That's a shame. Your loss, I suppose."

"I would hardly call it a loss," Ridaion scoffed. Ziiphan rolled his eyes and flopped onto his back with a mocking sigh of dejection.

"You're a real bitch when you don't have a pair to sit on, you know that?" he drawled.

"Oh, I know," Ridaion agreed sarcastically. "A good fuck really mellows me out. You ought to try it sometime."

"Sounds fun. I'd love to mellow you out."

Ridaion stood up and stomped one foot on Ziiphan's stomach. Ziiphan yelled and curled up on his side, but he was grinning like an idiot and letting out bouts of wheezing laughter.

"Isn't that why you let Ornathium follow you around?" Ridaion grumbled. Ziiphan gave him a perturbed look.

"You really think I'd stoop to that level of desperation? I'm not sure he even knows what sex is. Don't you remember what he was like when he first joined the pack? He sticks to me now because I was the only one who was willing to talk to him back then, but he doesn't seem to want much more than ear scratches and the occasional cuddle."

"Then I guess you'll just have to continue spending your nights alone."

"It's not nighttime," Ziiphan pointed out with a patronizing smile. "And I'm not exactly alone, am I?"

"You are now. I'm going hunting," growled Ridaion. He promptly stood up and walked away.

"Aw, seriously? You've only been here a couple of minutes!"

"A couple of minutes is about as much of you as I can handle, Ziiphan. And that time frame wouldn't be any different if I decided that I was interested in getting you off."

"Okay, that was uncalled for."

Ridaion rolled his eyes and left the clearing, ignoring his packmate's incessant chatter. He couldn't deal with Ziiphan on an empty stomach. He tried searching the air for any scent that indicated prey but gave up when all he found was a certain Rhithien's musk. He ended up having to travel six dynnsopions in order to track anything, and even then it took another hour to find the trail of a large enough creature.

Tired and irritated, Ridaion followed the trail to a meadow of long grasses that fluttered and whispered in the wind. The trees thinned out—and, mercifully, so did the leaves on the ground—and he was forced to approach on all fours to survey the scene. Standing at the edge of the meadow, just before the tree line of the forest, was an antlered beast that looked similar to a corrhega. It was half the size of one but would be enough to make a decent meal as long as Ziiphan didn't try to usurp his hunt.

Deciding once and for all that this creature would be his next kill, Ridaion lowered himself to the ground until his chest scraped against the dirt. He pulled up his haunches and rolled his shoulders, then testily flexed his claws. He took a few more slow steps to bring him closer to the creature, then went as still as a statue, waiting for the opportune moment.

One.

The creature raised its narrow head and looked around, every muscle in its graceful body tensed.

Two.

It didn't detect him and apparently figured that the coast was clear to continue grazing.

And. . .

Ridaion was about to pounce when he heard a roar behind him. Ziiphan leapt out from a grove of trees and charged towards the creature. It immediately bolted, and Ridaion, seeing no other option, bounded after it as fast as he could. This race was not just against the antlered beast, but also against Ziiphan. He needed to beat them both. He sprinted through the tall grass on all fours and quickly came upon his prey's rear. He was going to catch it, and by some miracle, his packmate was nowhere in his peripheral field of view. He was close, so close, he could just about grab it. . .

That was when something hard slammed onto his back, throwing his stride off and sending him face-first into the ground. Ridaion spat out a mouthful of grass and glanced up just in time to see that Ziiphan had used him as a launching pad and had flown far enough through the air to land directly on the creature. His body weight was enough to crush its slender frame, but he snapped its neck for good measure. When the animal was dead enough to appease him, he smiled the smuggest smile Ridaion had ever had the displeasure of seeing.

"Oh, hello," Ziiphan called amiably. "I just caught this thing. Would you like to share? I noticed that you looked hungry earlier."

"You fucking *birg*," Ridaion hissed, pushing himself to his feet and stomping over. He jabbed a finger at the fallen beast and snarled, "That was mine! I tracked it down, I was about to jump on it, but *no!* No, you just *had* to cut in and take it, didn't you?"

"Oh, darling, if I had known that you were aiming for this very creature, I would have let you take it! But as I said, I am willing to share. Feel free to pull off a leg."

"A *leg?* That entire thing should have been mine!"

"But it's not, is it?" Ziiphan crooned, deliberately and tauntingly tearing away one of the limbs.

"You disgusting, arrogant, fang-lipped piece of shit!" Ridaion screeched. That was enough. Despite his youth, he outranked Ziiphan, and as per the universal pack rules, he had the right to put him in his place. He leapt at the older male and knocked him flat on his back, kicking away the fallen prey as he did so. He locked one hand around Ziiphan's throat and balled the other into a fist, which he slammed into his jaw with all the force he could muster.

Ziiphan growled and grabbed Ridaion's wrists, then lodged one foot against his belly and kicked him over his head. Ridaion smacked into the ground, but he didn't have time to collect his thoughts. Moving meant staying alive. He rolled to his feet in time to meet his packmate head-on, and he dodged two subsequent punches before bringing his knee up into Ziiphan's abdomen. Ziiphan doubled over from the blow, but he jerked his head upwards, scraping the sharp point of one horn across the side of Ridaion's face. Ridaion barely registered the blow even as vibrant purple blood sprayed across his vision, and he instinctively swiped his claws towards his packmate's throat. Ziiphan stepped back just enough to keep his neck safe, but he still received a set of long gashes across his chest.

The two jumped away from each other and circled the recent kill, snapping and snarling. Both had their frills flared up, and their tails lashed angrily behind their legs.

"It's just a bit of meat, Ridaion," hissed Ziiphan.

Ridaion narrowed his eyes and growled, "Then back off. It would have been mine if you hadn't jumped in and fucked things up! Don't you remember who's in charge when Salidus, Orniell, and Aremaeid are all gone?"

"You've only got a significant rank because you're riding our alpha's cocks every night!" Ziiphan snapped. Ridaion recoiled with a hiss as he continued, "If Salidus decided he wanted to find some other hole to fill, you wouldn't last a day!"

"I lasted ten years in this pack without him, didn't I?"

"Not without attracting some attention. Don't you remember Mariykaed? He was rather fond of you, was he not?"

Ridaion's ears flattened against his scalp, and he had to concentrate to keep his teeth bared and his frill spiked up. He hadn't thought about Mariykaed in a long time, and he didn't want to think about him. That Rhithien had made his first few years in Salidus's pack a waking nightmare.

"Don't you remember what happened to Mariykaed?" he finally retorted. "He didn't last a day once Salidus found out what he was doing."

To his annoyance, Ziiphan scoffed and sneered at him.

"That's because Salidus stepped in and saved your ass, just as he always fucking does! You didn't lift a damn finger to protect yourself."

"What was I supposed to do?" Ridaion demanded, throwing his hands up. "I was new to the pack, he was older and stronger than I was, and he usually had Vegra with him. What does this have to do with you stealing my kill, anyway?"

Ziiphan opened his mouth to respond, then closed it again.

"Fine," he conceded at last. "You can have two legs."

"I want all four."

"Two."

"Four!"

"Fine, three."

"Done," Ridaion snapped, and before Ziiphan could move, he dove upon their prey, pulling away three of the limbs and leaving the rest to his packmate. Ziiphan glared at him but didn't protest as he knelt down and ripped into the beast's soft underbelly. They ate in tense, uncharacteristic silence. Ridaion didn't want to be the one who gave in and spoke first, but neither did Ziiphan. However, once the meat was gone and they had nothing to do but gnaw on the bones, Ridaion gave up on the competition.

"As reckless as your musking strategy is," he relented, "it's effective. Now, whether we like it or not, we're stuck together. The odds are good that more of our packmates will find us in the next few days, but we can't afford to split up. So if you quit being such an insufferable ass, I'll try to avoid being a vindictive bitch. Deal?"

Ziiphan glowered at him long and hard, and after a few seconds, he nodded.

"I quite enjoy being insufferable, so no promises, but you've got yourself a deal. At least until we find the others." Then he smirked and added, "I knew you'd come around. Normal packers are just as good as alphas, you know."

"Shut up. Come on, we can clean up back at the stream."

Their bickering didn't cease when they returned to Ziiphan's campsite, but they managed to avoid killing each other. Once they cleaned the wounds from their squabble, they settled down to wait for the others.

XI

Maisie left Pine Summit Middle School with a tired sigh, not flinching once as the heavy double doors slammed shut behind her. Her purse hung haphazardly from her shoulder and a briefcase of schoolwork swung at her side, smacking against her leg with every step. Despite the late autumn weather, she hadn't bothered buttoning up her coat in her rush to leave the building. As much as she enjoyed her career, it was the most exhausting job she'd ever had. She typically tried to get out at around 4:00, but today she'd ended up staying until 5:00.

It had all started when a boy named Trevor walked up to her desk at the end of class and nervously asked to stay after school. He'd always been a bit behind, particularly in math, and it came as no surprise to Maisie that graphing was especially challenging for him. He was close to tears over the homework by the time the bell rang, and Maisie had heartily agreed to his request.

"It's my job to help you learn this stuff, Trevor," she'd told him gently.

"Okay," he'd sniffled in response. As it turned out, many other students were having trouble as well, and the moment they saw that someone else needed help, they'd gathered the courage to request further assistance after school. In a matter of minutes, almost half the class had confessed a lack of understanding of the material and began calling their parents to tell them about the schedule change.

With more homework assignments and extra credit work being turned in all at once, Maisie desperately tried to get some of it graded when the number of kids finally began to dwindle sometime after 4:30 p.m. Even after the last one left her in the classroom alone, she remained hunched over her desk with her pen flying across turned-in assignments. She'd completely lost track of time, and when she finally realized how late it was, the only people left in the school were the janitors and a small handful of other staff members.

Maisie tugged the folds of her coat together against the chill of the evening air as she strode toward her car. When she reached it, she set her briefcase on the ground, opened her purse, and fished her hand around inside.

"Keys, keys, keys," she muttered to herself. Just as her fingers closed around the jingling keyring, the tiny hairs on the back of her neck prickled and her arms shivered with goosebumps. Maisie's stomach turned, and without even knowing why, she lifted her head and glanced around at the remaining cars. Her eyes stopped on a black vehicle parked across the lot. It was sleek and expensive-looking, with heavily tinted windows and shiny paint. No one at Pine Summit drove anything like that. She squinted at the license plate, but in contrast to the car's apparent newness, the numbers were worn and scratched up to the point of unreadability. The headlights were off, but she thought she could hear the faint rumble of an engine.

Maisie turned her back on the mysterious car and unlocked her own battered CRV. She yanked the door open so hard and fast that a part of her worried she would pull it off the frame, and she jumped in so quickly that she almost left her briefcase outside on the ground. Once she and her things were safely inside the vehicle, she locked the doors and started the engine. Terrifying thoughts sped through her mind, each one worse than the last. Was that person here for her, or someone else? Would they follow her? Her car seemed to be running just fine, but had the tires been slashed? She couldn't recall seeing any damage while standing outside, but she rarely paid the tires any mind unless there was an obvious problem with the car's movement. Maisie allowed herself to relax somewhat and let out a sigh of relief when she rolled out of her parking space unhindered.

Glancing in the rearview mirror as she turned onto the main road, she saw that the black car hadn't moved from the lot.

Deep breaths. Be calm. Nothing wrong. Maybe a new staff member. Deep breaths. Be calm.

Only when she was driving safely toward her house did her mind begin to conjecture about the car. The way she saw it, nothing screamed "government" louder than a polished black car with tinted windows and unreadable plates. Did they know about Aremaeid? He'd told her the other day that his species was called *Rhithien*. Did the government know about these Rhithien? He had made quite the spectacle the night he'd come through the portal, so it was possible.

The idea of being followed by the CIA or another secretive bureau was somehow more terrifying than having a carnivorous alien renting her basement.

The painful rigidity that tensed up Maisie's whole body didn't ebb until she pulled up into her driveway, got inside her house, and locked the front door. On a whim she darted around, bolting every window and making sure to secure the back door. She shuttered the blinds and closed the drapes, and when every entry point was shut tightly, she collapsed onto the living room couch and leaned back with a slow exhale. Her house was safe. No one could get in.

Drawn by her distress, Roller waddled over from the kitchen and put his front paws up on the couch cushion.

"Hey, dog," Maisie said with a weary smile, leaning down and helping him up. Because of his age and arthritis, Roller often had difficulty getting on and off the furniture by himself. He could jump up on chairs and the sofa, but Maisie didn't like leaving him to struggle on his own. As she scratched the small dog behind the ears and assured him that he was a good boy, she felt her gaze drawn to the basement stairs. She was slowly becoming accustomed to Aremaeid's presence, but she still wouldn't trust him not to kill and eat her if he was starving.

Maisie swallowed and hesitantly called, "I'm back." She wasn't really expecting an answer. There were times when she wasn't even sure he was home with her. *What if he's outside right now?*

As if on cue, she heard a polite tapping from the back of the house. She gasped and leaped to her feet, almost knocking her poor dog off the couch. She ran to the sliding glass door and shrank away when she saw Aremaeid waiting patiently outside. She'd been in such a panicked state when she'd gotten home that she hadn't considered the prospect of him not being inside, and she had locked the door without hesitation. Maisie hurriedly unlocked the door, slid it open, and stepped out of the way so he could duck beneath the frame.

"Sorry," she said guiltily. "I didn't realize you were out there."

"Do not worry yourself. Thank you for letting me in."

"Sure thing," she murmured, giving him a curt nod and heading back down the hall toward the kitchen. Roller needed dinner. She thought about making something for herself but remembered the date she had with Franklin and decided otherwise. She briefly considered offering something to Aremaeid but brushed off the notion. He said he hunted regularly. Besides, he had zero qualms about threatening her into housing him for a week, so he would no doubt let her know if he needed food.

To her surprise, however, Aremaeid followed her instead of going back downstairs. While Maisie went to the kitchen with Roller's bowl, the Rhithien wandered into the living room and placed one large hand on top of the dog's head. Despite his unnatural height, his arms were long enough that he didn't have to lean down. Roller didn't seem to mind the attention, and as long as Aremaeid was getting enough food on his own, Maisie was fairly confident he wouldn't eat her dog. The Rhithien glanced over at her and opened his mouth to speak, but closed it again.

Maisie sighed and assured him, "I didn't tell anyone. Work just ran late today. I'm going out again tonight, just so you know. I'm meeting up with someone I met yesterday."

"I was not concerned about that," he responded. "I was just curious about. . . You are normally earlier."

"You want to know about my day," Maisie said flatly. It was more a statement than a question, but Aremaeid nodded anyway.

"If you do not wish to speak, I understand."

"No, no, it's fine. I just wasn't expecting you to care."

"Just curious," Aremaeid muttered. He sat down on the couch beside Roller, and Maisie suppressed an anxious grimace as the furniture groaned loudly beneath his weight.

"I'm a teacher," she began, and those burning golden eyes locked onto her. "I've always loved working with kids. Well, they're not *kids* kids, because they're not super young, but—"

"Juveniles?" Aremaeid offered.

"Yeah. I teach math. Anyway, one of my students is a bit behind his classmates. He wasn't understanding a certain concept, so he arranged to stay late with me and figure it out. A bunch of other kids wanted to do the same thing. I just got caught up and lost track of time."

"I see." A long, awkward pause weighed on them. Then Maisie spoke again.

"Any luck with your pack?"

"No."

Another pause. Maisie rolled her eyes and set her dog's food bowl on the floor.

"One person can't carry a conversation, you know. You're the one—Roller, come get your dinner—who wanted to talk."

"I have nothing to say," Aremaeid admitted with a shrug. He watched as Roller hopped off the couch and ambled into the kitchen, lazily wagging his tail at the sight of a full food dish.

"Are you kidding?" Maisie scoffed. He frowned at her, and she elaborated, "I'm not sure if you know this, but we humans haven't discovered any kind of alien life. At least none that's been shared with the public. So the fact that you're staying in my house—and that you're on Earth in the first place—is a pretty big deal. I don't know anything about you or your planet, so the way I see it, there's a lot you could say."

"There is only so much I am allowed to disclose, but what would you like to know?" Aremaeid inquired after a beat of silence. Maisie had to think for a few seconds; there were so many things she could ask about.

"Well, um. . . Tell me about your pack. Or packs in general," she prompted at last. Aremaeid seemed to perk up, and he straightened his posture.

"My pack consists of eight members, including myself. Each pack has an alpha, a second, and a third, which is my position. The others have loosely ordered ranks, but they change much more frequently than the top three. Our alpha is Salidus, and his second is Orniell."

"What's Salidus like?" Maisie asked. Aremaeid had to think on that one for a few moments, like he'd never been asked to describe his pack members.

"Salidus is. . . respectable. Of the alphas I have met, he is the most approachable. The most reasonable. He also has the strongest set of morals. He does not stoop to levels that alphas before him have."

"And the second? Orniell?"

"Orniell. . ." Aremaeid sighed, and like with Salidus, it took him a while to figure out what he wanted to say. "He keeps the pack orderly. He offers Salidus his counsel when it is needed. But it is all very impersonal for him, and despite his age and the length of time in which he has been with our pack, none of us know much about him."

"How old is he?" Maisie asked as she poured herself a glass of water and took a long draught from it.

"I do not know the exact number, but I believe he is somewhere in his mid-seven hundreds."

Maisie choked on her drink and stared at the Rhithien in astonishment.

"Seven *hundreds?*" she echoed.

"Yes, that is what I said," Aremaeid confirmed. He said it like it was the most obvious thing in the world. Then his ears went back and he awkwardly amended, "I apologize. I forget how different our life spans are. You humans age very quickly."

"Okay, I guess we can just gloss over that," Maisie muttered, shakily taking another sip of water. "Are there any other 'respectable' Rhithien in your pack? Or ones that would be higher-ranking if there were more than eight of you?"

"Ridaion, maybe," Aremaeid answered. He shifted his weight with discomfort and added, "Although I doubt he would have risen in rank on his own. He is our youngest member, and although he makes up for his smaller size in combat ability, he does not command the same respect that Salidus, Orniell, and I do."

"That doesn't make sense. If he can't move up on his own, how would he be anywhere near the top?"

"He has been Salidus's personal consort for around twenty years now."

Maisie choked on her water again, but Aremaeid didn't seem to notice. His lip curled with slight distaste upon mentioning Ridaion's exact position. He obviously didn't approve, and if his previous words were any indication, neither did the rest of the pack.

"So. . . Would he be considered a 'pet' by your standards?"

"Yes, but Salidus does not call him such."

Did not expect to hear this sort of thing from an alien, Maisie thought as she took another sip of her water. Perhaps it was time to shift the subject.

"Is a pack like a family? Or is it more like living in a frat house?" she asked.

"I do not know what a 'frat house' is, but we are not family. We fight together, hunt together, and sleep beside one another, but we do so only to survive and compete with other packs. I enjoy the company of some of them, but if a certain few died, I would not grieve the loss."

Aremaeid snarled the last few words and narrowed his eyes.

A guilty part of Maisie liked hearing people rant about folks they didn't like, but it would probably be in her best interest to avoid such a thing with Aremaeid. It was light conversation, nothing more, but she was flying blind. On the kitchen floor, Roller finished his dinner and leaned his front paws on her leg, so Maisie set her water glass down on the counter and scooped her dog into her arms. She looked up when she felt Aremaeid's eyes focus on her again.

"How long have you had that thing?" he asked.

"I've had him for about ten years now, but he's fifteen or sixteen. That's pretty old for a dog, if you need context."

"How does a creature like that survive on its own?"

"Um. . . He doesn't. Dogs are all descended from wolves, or some similar canine ancestor. It's like I told you the other day: there are different breeds for different purposes. Rottweilers and Dobermans were bred as guard dogs and attack dogs, greyhounds are racers, and dachshunds like Roller are just pets. I think they were originally hunting dogs, but I don't know anyone who uses them for that now. Roller's technically a bunch of different dogs, but he's mostly dachshund."

Aremaeid blinked uncomprehendingly at her. Realizing that he probably had no idea what most of those words meant, she snuggled her dog closer and muttered, "Never mind."

"Why do you live alone?" the Rhithien demanded suddenly. "I was informed that humans are social creatures. You live in a community. Why are you alone in this house?"

"I dunno. Most of my family stayed back in Boston, but I wanted a smaller town, so I came to Nuncan. And I guess I just never found someone who I wanted to share my life with."

"'Share your life with' as in. . . a mate? Do humans mate for life?"

"A mate. Ah, I don't really. . . like that word. In that context. Talking about people. It makes me uncomfortable. But yes, that's what I meant. Some people find partners they love, and those people get married, but not everyone does it. Some folks aren't interested, and some just never find the right person."

"Married?"

"Yes, marriage." Maisie frowned and explained, "People say their vows at a wedding ceremony, fill out some paperwork, and move in together unless their jobs require otherwise. Most couples who get married will have kids, but again, it depends on the people. Everyone has different priorities. Don't you have something like that on Primaied?"

Aremaeid didn't answer right away, and the distant, somber look in his eyes indicated that he had stopped listening. Maisie waved her hand to get his

119

attention, and he blinked a couple of times before responding in a disarmingly soft tone.

"We do not have a ceremony for such a thing due to its rarity. It is almost unheard of, especially among Rhithien, but there are some who find partners with whom they may experience a lifemate bond."

"Do you have a lifemate?" she asked.

All the warmth in Aremaeid's expression that had slowly built up throughout their conversation immediately melted away. His face went blank, and Maisie had a sick feeling that she had said something very wrong.

"No," he replied flatly. Then he stood and left the living room without another word.

"Wait, I'm sorry!" Maisie called.

He stopped at the top of the basement stairs but didn't turn around. She scratched Roller's ears and stammered, "I know that sort of stuff can be hard to talk about, but I'm willing to lis—"

"My personal life is no concern of yours. It was a long time ago," Aremaeid interrupted sternly. With that, he disappeared into the basement, leaving Maisie alone upstairs.

XII

Layla sat on her bed, hunched over the Lucio family tree in unbroken concentration. The ancient tome sat open beside her laptop, which displayed a document she had been adding to ever since she'd gotten home from school. It was the only thing she had been able to think about; she zoned out during all her teachers' lectures, doodled over her homework, and smacked into six people while ambling distractedly through the halls. As soon as the bell rang, she bolted out the door as fast as she could, backpack slung over one shoulder. Her house was only a few streets down from Pine Summit, so she arrived home in a matter of minutes.

Her excitement was quickly subdued, however, upon discovering that rewriting the family history was a difficult and tedious chore. Her pecking technique on the keyboard only caused further delays, and it certainly didn't help that the people who had made and added to this copy seemed to all be participating in a silent competition of who had the least legible handwriting. She had spent nearly an hour up in the attic on Sunday talking to Ornathium about the book, but she hadn't actually started the copying process then. Now that she had finally begun, it seemed like an impossibly daunting task. Still, she pushed through. She typed without a break for the first two hours up in the attic until her fingers cramped and her eyes burned. Then she moved to her room.

Layla stretched and groaned, grateful for the softness of her bed rather than the hardness of the attic floor. Checking the clock, she realized that she had spent an additional thirty minutes in her room typing up names and their corresponding life summaries. She blinked rapidly to refocus her aching eyes.

"Layla?"

She jumped and whipped her head around. Tyson stood in her doorway, looking more fidgety and nervous than usual. He hadn't spoken to her since

121

Friday night, but she'd been acutely aware of him sulking around the house and watching her unhappily from a distance, always fiddling with his string.

"What do you want, booger?" she demanded, hoping he would throw an insult back at her. It was a sort of code between them, one that Layla had picked up from her classmates and shared with her brother. It wasn't mean if they both thought it was funny.

Tyson didn't retort, however, nor did he retreat. Instead, he stepped into her room and closed the door.

"We need to talk," he said flatly.

"About what?" inquired Layla with mocking innocence. She knew very well what.

"The weather. What do you fucking think?" Tyson snapped with uncharacteristic seriousness. Layla blinked in surprise. He usually swore for fun, during playful banter or when gossiping about someone. But now he was using the words like a grown-up, and Layla wasn't sure she liked it.

"What about him?" she whispered furiously.

"He's been up in the attic for almost three days now. How long do you think you can keep Mom and Dad from finding out?"

"However long we need to. He's not going to be here forever. You didn't tell them, did you?"

"Of course I didn't, but it's not easy to keep a secret that big in our own house. And you haven't been helping with that as much as you think you have." Tyson yanked hard on his string, pulling a slipknot loose. Today he had a length of blue acrylic yarn that he'd found in their mother's sewing room. Layla scowled at the yarn, then at him. There was no way she would let him get away with talking to her like that. She angrily shut the Lucio book, then her laptop.

"You're forgetting something," she pointed out. "I'm the one who wanted to keep him a secret in the first place, remember? If he wanted to hurt any of us, he would have done it by now. I know he looks kind of evil, but he's been nothing but nice. You're right that one of us is being a problem, but it's not me."

"Sure, 'cause I'm the one who's been hanging out in the attic for hours at a time. You say you're keeping him secret, but you're not exactly subtle about it," Tyson said with a sneer. Layla recoiled from the bitterness in his tone. He never spoke like this.

"So what?" she snapped back at him. "Why do you care if I want to be up there with him? He's nice. I like him. Are you jealous or something? Look, just because you don't have any friends doesn't mean I have to be that way, too." She regretted the words as soon as they left her mouth. Tyson's face twisted into an expression of surprised hurt, and the aggression he had displayed only a few moments ago melted away. Layla sighed and muttered, "Sorry."

"It's fine."

That sounded like it would be the end of it, but Tyson didn't leave. He remained awkwardly where he was, his eyes darting around the room like a frightened rabbit. Layla leaned back on her hands and regarded him with a sigh.

"Where is all this coming from? I get that you're scared of Ornathium, but he hasn't done anything to prove that he's bad, so what's your deal?"

"I'm not jealous," Tyson responded quietly.

"Tyson, I didn't mean it when I said that, I was just—"

"I'm worried about you. I'm worried about Mom and Dad. What if he's lying? What if he and his pack had another reason for coming here?"

"I told you, if he wanted to hurt us, he would have—"

"Layla, shut up and use your head for one second!" Tyson cried. "He hasn't found his pack yet! He's only staying here because he's all alone and doesn't have anywhere else to go."

"Exactly! He's all alone, and we need to help him. And who knows? If he really *is* here for something else, being nice might convince him to change his mind." Layla smiled reassuringly at her brother, but he just pursed his lips and pulled a knot out of his string.

"I've got a bad feeling about his," he mumbled. "I really don't think it's a good idea to let him stay here while Mom and Dad don't know about him."

"It *is* a good idea, and we're going to make sure they keep not knowing. Would you rather help him do what he needs to do so he can go back home? Or do you want to make assumptions and chase him out with pitchforks and torches? Doing that could risk an intergalactic war, but whatever."

Tyson looked slightly miffed as he muttered, "You don't have to be like that. I'm serious. I've barely gotten any sleep the last few days because I can hear him moving around up there. I'm pretty sure I even heard that old window in the attic open one time, and I don't think he was even in the house for most of that night!

I don't know what's going on, and whether you like it or not, neither do you. Has he told you anything else about why he came here, or where he's from?"

"Of course he has! What do you think I do all day in the attic? He told me all kinds of things about his planet. They have magic, Tyson! Real magic! That's how they got to Earth—not with technology, but with *magic!* That's pretty cool, right?"

"I guess," her brother conceded. "But—"

"And do you wanna know what he said about our family?" Layla prompted excitedly. She hefted the old book into her lap and patted the spot beside her on the bed.

"What does he know about our family?" demanded Tyson. Fresh fear bloomed in his eyes.

"Just the name Lucio. He told me it was special, but he didn't say why. So I did some digging, and I think I've figured it out. Come look, it's really cool!"

"No, Layla! Don't you see how bad this is?" he yelled. They both flinched at the volume of his voice and sat frozen in place for a moment, but when they didn't hear their parents coming to intervene, he continued. "He just so happens to end up in our house because of a supposedly failed experiment, and the name Lucio also happens to be a known thing on his planet? Wake up, Layla! Do you really think that's just a. . . a. . . ."

"A 'coincidence'?"

"Yeah, that. Do you really think it's just a coincidence?"

Of course she'd thought about it, she just didn't think it was cause for alarm. She was too excited about her family's history and the idea that her ancestor, Aurelia Lucio, might have secretly been a monster killer. Although Tyson had a point, she couldn't give him any leeway.

"I don't know," she bluffed at last. "If it was anything other than a coincidence, I think Ornathium would have told us. But like I said, he hasn't acted angry or mean at all."

"I understand mean, but why would he be angry?" Tyson asked suddenly, frowning at her choice of words. Layla perked up and happily opened the book to the first page. She just needed to switch his focus to something besides the Ornathium debate.

"You know how I said I did some digging? Well, I asked Mom about how far back the Lucios go, and she found this for me. It starts with this lady named

Aurelia Lucio. She lived in *Ancient Rome,* Tyson!" She jabbed her finger at the top of the page. Tyson bit his lip, then hesitantly hopped up onto the bed next to her. Layla showed him the entry and maintained, "It says here that in 35 A.D. she killed a bear that tried to eat a bunch of people on her estate, but its body was never found. So I started to think; what if she didn't really kill a bear? What if she killed—"

"—an alien," Tyson finished with wide eyes. Layla grinned and nodded.

"We're related to a monster killer!" she squealed gleefully.

"You didn't tell Ornathium that, did you?" Tyson asked, glancing nervously up at her. "If a bunch of aliens know who we are after almost two thousand years, then she might have killed someone important. I guess this explains why you thought he would be angry."

Layla was silent. After a few seconds of scanning the other entries on the page, Tyson frowned up at her and inquired, "You *have* kept this book secret from him, right?"

"Well. . . not exactly," she confessed.

" 'Not exactly.' What does that mean?"

"Well, it's not like I told him *everything,* but like. . . You haven't been talking to me, and I couldn't tell Mom the real reason I was excited about this, so. . ."

"Oh my God, Layla," Tyson groaned, letting his head fall into his hands.

"He wasn't upset about it, even when I told him that I thought it was one of his kind that died! He thought it was interesting!"

"Oh, God, they really *are* here for us," Tyson whimpered. He was trembling like a leaf in a tornado, and before Layla could react, he jumped off the bed and ran for the door. Layla darted after him and yanked him back just as his hand closed around the knob.

"Calm down!" she yelled.

"Calm down? *Calm down?* We need to tell Mom and Dad! What if they want revenge? Maybe their experiment did go wrong like he said, but what if they want to kill us? What if—"

"Tyson, stop," Layla ordered, holding his shoulders tightly and waiting for his hyperventilating to subside. When his anxiety had dissipated enough for her to speak, she said, "He's not going to do anything to us. I think I'm really getting through to him. He listens to me. And even if his pack tries to do something bad, I promise I won't let them touch you. Not you, not Mom, and not Dad. I'll figure

125

out what's going on, and we can work from there, but sorting this mess out is up to us. I can't have you breaking down on me, okay?"

"Okay," Tyson blubbered, nodding tearfully. He wiped his eyes on his sleeve and pulled his strip of yarn so taut Layla worried it would snap.

"Okay," she echoed. She released him and stepped back. "I get why you're scared, and I can't tell you I know everything about him. But we will figure this out, and I won't let any of them hurt you, alright? Pinky promise?"

She offered him her pinky finger. Tyson stared at her long and hard, and though his trepidation was clear, he held his hand out and wrapped his pinky around hers.

"Pinky promise," he agreed.

"Good. I'll talk to him again tomorrow and find out whatever I can. If there's something important, I'll tell you as soon as I leave the attic. Deal?"

"Deal."

"What's this deal?" came another voice from the hall, and they both looked up as the door swung open and their father poked his head inside the room.

"Noth—" Tyson started to say, but Layla interrupted him. She knew she was much better at improvising than he was.

"If he gives me half his dessert, I'll give him the white shoelaces from those sneakers I outgrew. They're still in really good shape," she lied.

"Sacrificing dessert for a pair of shoelaces? Hardly seems like a fair trade," their father teased.

"He's fine with it, he said he was!"

"If you insist. But while we're on the subject of dessert, it's dinner time. Wash your hands and come downstairs." He left the room, and Layla waited until she heard him head down to the main floor before she spoke again, this time making sure to keep her voice at a whisper.

"Everything's going to be fine," she assured Tyson.

"How do you know?" he asked pleadingly, and for a moment, the terror in his watery blue eyes almost swayed Layla from her loyalty to Ornathium. But she shook it off and held her resolve. She would find a way to figure this out while still maintaining her growing friendship with the alien. She had to.

"I pinky promised, didn't I?"

"Yeah," Tyson agreed with a deflating sigh. "Yeah, you did. Alright, let's go." With that, the two of them left the bedroom and went downstairs, leaving the Lucio book on the bed.

*****

Ornathium hummed thoughtfully and crawled away from the vent that connected the attic to the girl's room. He knew they hadn't meant for him to hear their conversation, but that made his sneaking all the more exciting. Remaining on all fours, he walked to the window and laid down beneath it, curling up and resting his head on his arms. He'd known from the night he arrived that Layla was going to be no trouble at all. She was hilariously easy to convince of his supposed innocence. The boy, on the other hand. . . That one would be another challenge.

They're cubs, snarled Kairen. *And stupid ones, too. A fucking rock could manipulate them better than you have.*

Ornathium frowned and looked around the room before remembering that Kairen only visited him in his head. He'd been mercifully silent for the last dilunar cycle, but coming to Earth had sparked his activity. Not quite to the degree it had been at when Ornathium was first recruited by Salidus's pack, but he was there all the same. And he never. Stopped. *Talking.*

You'll be lucky to keep whatever sanity you have left if you continue stalling like this. Those ugly little vermin are more annoying than you ever were.

"I need to find the others before we can carry out the mission," Ornathium irritably explained for what must have been the hundredth time. Instead of responding right away with some hateful quip, Kairen laughed that horrible, raspy cackle that haunted Ornathium's dreams. The sound bounced around his head like screeching music, and his eyes widened when he realized that it was echoing around the attic.

He sat up and furiously whispered, "You have to be quiet, or they'll hear us! Please, Kairen!"

You're fucking pathetic, aren't you? Begging me like a damn cub. You're no better than those flat-faced little brats.

"I *am* better than them," he protested, speaking more to himself than to Kairen. That hateful voice was so loud that Ornathium thought his head might split open, or his entire body would shatter like a sheet of fine glass. He had barely listened earlier that day when Layla was chattering endlessly about her

127

family's old book. The only voice he registered was Kairen's, so he had simply smiled, nodded, and pretended that he could hear her. He'd gotten very good at pretending since joining the pack.

Hmph. You're hardly better than them. At least those scrawny little rhegoes have friends.

"Ziiphan is my friend."

Don't make me laugh, Kairen scoffed. *You are less than a pet to him. You're still just as worthless as you were twenty years ago. You told the girl you were a Rhithien, but you lied. You are nothing but a mindless beast and you know it. Couldn't kill a real Rhithien if you tried.*

"I have killed dozens of Rhithien. Hundreds. And I'm part of a pack, am I not? I *am* a Rhithien."

Kairen cackled and rasped, *Keep telling yourself that, boy. You and I both know better. You're just a filthy hound wearing a mask. Anyone who looks closely can peer through the holes in your disguise. You are a soulless insect that belongs in the dirt. You are beneath Rhithien. You are beneath those ugly human whelps.*

"Shut up, shut up, shut up," Ornathium whimpered, curling into a ball and holding his ears flat against his scalp. He didn't want to listen to Kairen, but as long as that terrible voice was this active, sleep wouldn't bring any relief. No, sleep would only bring him nightmares that he could never escape from, memories that would never leave him, pain and blood but not the blood of other Rhithien, no it was his own blood his own pain his own misery all of it tormenting him eternally forever and ever and ever and ever. . .

His body spasmed with phantom agony and silent tears streamed from his eyes, but he managed to drag himself towards the large chair that Layla liked. He crawled behind it and hugged his knees against his chest.

Safe here. No one can see me. Kairen is just a voice.

I'm far more than a voice and you know it.

Ornathium closed his eyes against the burning lance of pain that tore through his skull. Kairen was wide awake now.

He's not real. He's not real. Ziiphan can't hear him, Layla can't hear him, no one can hear him. So he's not real. Not one part of him.

Maybe not for them. But for you? I will be with you until you rot.

XIII

The Dancing Bear Café was one of Nuncan's oldest establishments. It had gone through several refurbishments and name changes throughout the decades, but it remained in the same location and had been passed down through generation after generation of the same family. The current owners were Ford Montague and his wife, Tillie. Once the place passed into their hands, they renamed it from "Naked Bear Bar & Grill" to "Dancing Bear Café" and reformed every inch of the place, from the menu to the décor to the toilet seats. It was now a homey little restaurant that served tea, cookies, crepes, and various breads, and its clientele had changed just as much as its interior. Bearded, tattooed, potbellied motorcyclists and local barflies no longer downed cheap beers over the scratched pool tables. Instead, young couples with hip new clothes and shiny, parent-purchased cars congregated to sip Americanos and nibble scones.

Franklin hadn't lied when he'd told Maisie it had been a while for him. He'd not been to the place in years; not since its Naked Bear Bar & Grill days. He had lived in Nuncan his whole life, and he and his siblings had watched the restaurant shift through its management, menus, logos, and design choices throughout the decades. It was a sort of sacred place for the locals, and many of the old-timers felt it was being defiled by Ford Montague's controversial stylistic choices. But it was quite popular with the youngsters nowadays, so Franklin had hope that it couldn't be all bad.

As he pulled into the parking lot, he studied the vibrant exterior with what he knew was probably an unnecessarily critical eye. The overhang trim was striped with happy pink and yellow colors that matched the umbrellas opened over the outdoor tables. The entire building had been repainted and the windows looked like they were cleaned at least once a week, which Franklin had to admit was an improvement. Despite the chilly autumn weather, small groups of customers sat outside with tightly zipped coats, gloved hands, and floppy hats. One couple huddled under the overhang, grinning and giggling over a picture on a cell phone. Watching them together made a fresh sheen of sweat break out on Franklin's forehead, and he clutched the steering wheel so hard his knuckles went white.

Was it too early to be dating again? He'd just broken up on Saturday, after all, and then he'd gone and asked out a complete stranger the very next day.

She asked me. It's not my fault.

"But I still agreed," he reminded himself. As glad as he was to be rid of Nancy, maybe he should have waited a bit longer. In retrospect, accepting a date from a woman he'd known for five minutes probably wasn't the best idea. He knew her name, at least.

What else do I know about her?

He knew she liked dogs. He knew she was okay with some gentle teasing. He knew she probably hadn't been in Nuncan for very long, because she didn't indicate that she knew about the Dancing Bear Café's mixed history. And, yes, he knew her name. Four things about her, then. It wasn't much, but he could work with that.

Franklin took a deep breath and pulled out his phone to call his brother. It barely rang once before Parker answered.

"Franklin, I've been meaning to call. I know we just talked the other day, but I wanted to check in. How're you holding up?"

"Pretty well, actually," Franklin admitted. "Again, it was a long time coming. But I rang because I really need a jump-start on my mojo right now. I know it's pretty early for me to start looking at other women, but I met this redhead at Grader's on Sunday morning. I'm right outside the place we agreed to meet up, and I'm heading inside in a few minutes. Any advice?"

"Woah, woah, woah, back the fuck up. Where the hell have you been these last few days? Who is this woman? What's her name and why didn't you tell us about her?"

"I don't know!"

"You don't know her name?"

"No, I know her name—it's Maisie—but like. . . I don't know why I didn't tell you. I guess I just wanted to wait and see if this date was going to go anywhere. I dunno, man, she seems alright. Sane."

"Jesus, Franklin. Are you really serious about this?"

Franklin leaned back in his seat and closed his eyes. Yes, he was serious. He wasn't yet sure if this would lead to something long-term or if they just wouldn't have the right chemistry, but he was willing to try it. He opened his eyes and scanned the parking lot, then quickly looked through the café's windows to its brightly lit interior. She hadn't arrived, and it was almost 6:00.

"Yeah," he said at last, voicing his thoughts aloud. "I'm serious."

"Damn, okay. Well, here's some brotherly wisdom: be yourself. And if you spot any red flags, run. You just got done dating a red flag on legs, so you know what to look for."

"You say it like I'm crawling through a minefield."

"I don't have a ton of experience with women, but most of them really are walking minefields. Listen, just be yourself and be cool, alright? Well, no. On second thought, don't do that. The two are mutually exclusive. Just stick to being yourself, alright, bro?"

"I'm feeling the support."

"Good. Have fun." The line disconnected, and he shot a glare at Parker's contact photo before pocketing his phone, taking one more deep breath, and stepping out of the car.

I can do this, he thought, trying to look confident as he entered the café. *I've been on plenty of first dates. She's only human. And she can't be as bad as Nancy.*

A sign just inside the door told him to seat himself, so he selected a cozy booth by the window and examined the menu above the front counter. The Dancing Bear Café had clearly and thoroughly flushed out every trace of the Naked Bear Bar & Grill. Oh, well. The former establishment had had its fair share of problems that no amount of nostalgia could fix, so perhaps it was for the best.

A young, frizzy-haired waitress walked up to his table and grinned down at him with that telltale, forced-looking customer service smile.

"Hey there, welcome to the Dancing Bear Café! How are you doing tonight?"

"Pretty well. How about yourself?" Franklin returned absently.

"Horrible, thanks for asking!" the waitress replied cheerfully. "What can I get for ya?"

"Um, I'm actually waiting for someone, so do you think you could come back in, like, five minutes? Or whenever she gets here?"

"Sure thing, hon," she said. She somehow managed to smile even wider, then headed back to the counter and disappeared into the kitchen. Franklin turned toward the window again, put his chin in his hand, and studied the parking lot. A part of him wasn't expecting Maisie to show up, even though she was the one who had asked him out. Maybe she'd gotten cold feet and changed her mind? He stupidly hadn't thought to ask for her number—or her last name, for that matter—so he had no way of contacting her.

He perked up when a battered blue CRV pulled into the lot. The car parked, the door opened, and Franklin leaned against the back of the booth with a relieved smile when he spotted that bright red hair. Maisie entered the café and glanced around, biting her lip. Franklin waved his hand to get her attention, and her face lit up when she saw him, making the butterflies in his stomach go wild. She quickly came to his booth and slid into the seat across from him, tucking a loose strand of hair behind her ear.

"Hey," she greeted nervously. "I've gotta be honest; I didn't think you were going to show."

"Wasn't sure you were, either," Franklin admitted.

"I realized that we only spoke for, like, five minutes, and I want to make something clear: I don't usually do this. Just go out with people I meet in the grocery store. So I know that this whole thing was probably pretty sudden for you, but—"

"Don't worry about it. I said yes, didn't I?"

When they finally got their orders taken by the harried, ever-smiling waitress, Maisie removed her coat and set it on the seat beside her. She wore a slim indigo dress with a wide neckline and short sleeves that fell just off her shoulders. Franklin himself had worn an open suit jacket even though he knew that the Dancing Bear Café wasn't exactly a classy place. Her formality made him feel less on edge about the decision. She leaned forward, nibbling her lower lip, and Franklin shifted his feet hesitantly. What should he say? Was she the type of person to talk first, or was he expected to begin the conversation? Just as he was about to start commenting on the weather, she spoke.

"So, uh, I realized on the way over here that I don't know your full name. And you don't know mine. It's Arberon. Maisie Arberon." She held out a hand like they were meeting for the first time, and Franklin took it with a grin.

"Rayblue," he replied. "Franklin Rayblue. Now, we really don't know that much about each other, so I suppose we can start with some standard interrogation questions."

"Fair enough."

"What do you do for a living?" he asked after a few seconds. It was a basic question, but he felt that it was an important one.

"I'm a teacher over at Pine Summit Middle School. I work with the seventh graders, mostly, but I take on a select handful of sixth and eighth when their academic level matches my curriculum. I also do some tutoring on the side."

"I'm going to guess. . . English?"

"Close. Math. What about you, Benjamin? How are you surviving in this economy?"

Franklin grinned at the nickname and replied, "I'm a software designer, but recently I've been getting into web design."

"Freelance?"

"Yes. I just finished up a soul-killing contract, so in all honesty, this date couldn't have come at a better time for me. I haven't been able to relax in close to a month, so it's really nice to just sit back and take a breather, you know?"

"I get that," Maisie said, nodding intently.

Looking around the café and taking note of the new floorboards, paint job, and furniture that had all come with the brand change, Franklin couldn't help wondering how long Maisie had been in Nuncan. If he had to guess, he'd've pegged her as an out-of-towner, but he wanted to know for sure.

"Do you know the history of this place?" he asked. Maisie looked around and shook her head, so he explained the lengthy, convoluted story of the building and restaurant. When he was finished, Maisie sat back and stared at him.

"Huh," she said simply.

"Yeah. This is my first time coming here since before the change. My nostalgia's a little bitter, but I have to admit that I like the renovations."

"So. . . You were born in Nuncan?"

"Born and bred. Went to college in Missoula, but I came back here when I was done. How long have you lived here?"

"Not nearly as long as you," Maisie confessed with a light laugh. "I've only been in Nuncan for a little over four years. My family moved around a lot, so I've seen a bunch of different places, but we spent most of our time in Boston. I'm not really a fan of big cities, so when a position opened up here, I was pretty excited. As it turns out, a town with less than ten thousand people is a much quieter place to live than a city of close to 700,000."

"I'll bet."

The conversation paused as the waitress approached with their beverages. When she left them alone, Maisie took a sip of the iced tea she'd requested and continued.

"Hobbies?" she asked, swirling the ice cubes in her glass.

"Hiking. My older sister, Avery, is part of this hunting club, and sometimes they'll go on group camping trips up on the mountain trails. I tag along now and then. Also, my brother's one of the rangers who patrol the Dennisons, and he's taken me out on his RV a few times. Are you into hiking at all?"

"Oh, definitely. That was one of the reasons I scoped out Montana for jobs. What are some of the trails you'd recommend? I've been on Silver Creek and Cougar Canyon, but as a local, I'm sure you're a lot more familiar with these woods than I am."

"Have you tried the Bear Mountain Trail? It's not too challenging, but it's not something for beginners."

"I don't think I have," Maisie admitted with a frown. "But I'm noticing that Nuncan is heavy on the bear theme. Dancing Bear, Naked Bear, Bear Mountain. I'm not complaining—because I wouldn't expect any less from Montana—but how many bear-related things are there?"

"More than you'd think," Franklin chuckled, pushing his glasses further up his nose. "And probably more than Nuncan deserves. The Dennison Woods cover a lot of space up here, but there aren't too many bear sightings. Two or three a year, maybe. They're definitely around, but they never interact with people if they can help it, so as long as you stick to the marked trails, you've got nothing to worry about. Some people bring bear bells anyway, but I don't usually bother. You've seriously never been up to Bear Mountain, though? That's one of the best trails!"

Maisie snorted and swatted at him.

"I told you, I haven't lived here as long as you, and teaching's a full-time job, even in the summer. I haven't completely adopted the bearded mountain man persona."

"Do I look like a bearded mountain man?" Franklin inquired, arching an eyebrow.

"You look like you were the type of student in school who reminded the teacher to assign homework," she commented, taking a sip of her tea.

"Oh, come on, the glasses aren't *that* bad! And I actually like math, so screw that."

"You're into math?" Maisie inquired, perking up a bit more. Then she rolled her eyes and added, "I suppose if you do stuff with computers for a living, you'd have to be. What's your field of choice?"

"Algebra. I hated it when I was younger, but then I started warming up to the stuff when I realized I was good at it. You?"

"Easily trig. Sohcahtoa all the way. Triangles are the best and you can't tell me otherwise. But I can't use it with seventh graders, because most of them barely know algebra."

"Damn. Jobs are supposed to be fun."

"I'm not saying I don't enjoy it. I love working with middle schoolers! They're at the age where most of them think that all adults are 'cringey' and annoying, but they're still young enough to see me as an authority figure. Honestly, it's pretty entertaining to watch them flop between those two viewpoints. It's especially funny with the ones who think they're 'cool' or 'intimidating'."

"Nobody's cool in middle school. Especially in seventh grade."

"I know, right? I feel bad making fun of them for it, but it's just funny to me that none of them figure it out until high school."

"I'm feeling really attacked right now."

"Oh, hush. I was the same way," Maisie said with a roll of her eyes. She gave him a lopsided grin, and the whole café seemed to light up.

They talked until their food came, and when it finally arrived they continued speaking between bites. Their conversation went on for almost an hour after they finished. Franklin found that Maisie was easy to talk to. Every time they began to run out of things to say on one subject, she launched into a new one. The whole time he watched and listened to her, he began to notice small things: how she would chew her lip with an obsession that she didn't seem to be aware of, the way she impulsively tucked some hair behind her ear every few minutes, and that awkward lopsided smile. Her soft brown eyes were attentive and focused, and she never seemed to drift off when he was speaking. She was Nancy's complete antithesis and more.

When they finally left the café together, the sun had gone down, leaving only the streetlamps and neon signs to illuminate the dark road. Franklin shivered in the crisp night air and looked down at Maisie, who bit her lip and smiled up at him.

"I had a really good time tonight, Franklin. I haven't been on a date in a while," she said softly.

"I had fun, too. Are you free tomorrow, by any chance?"

"What do you have in mind?" she asked, rocking back on her heels and grinning shyly.

"You said you've never hiked Bear Mountain Trail. I'd like to take you up there tomorrow, maybe at 4:00 p.m. or whenever school gets out?" He pulled a slip of paper out of his jacket pocket and handed it to her. Scrawled across its surface was his phone number. "Just call or text whenever you get a chance."

"Damn it, I didn't bring anything to write my number down on. Can I just tell you what it is and have you put me in your contacts?"

"Sure. I've got my phone."

Maisie rattled off her number, then read through the digits on the paper he'd given her. She gave Franklin a sly smirk and asked, "How long was this in your pocket?"

"All night. Is it a date?"

Maisie hesitated for a moment, then nodded, biting her lip again and flicking a nonexistent strand of hair behind her ear. She stood up on the tips her of toes, tugged Franklin down by the collar of his jacket, and gave him a light peck on the lips.

"It's a date," she agreed. "Good night, Franklin." With that, she headed to her CRV and got in. Franklin stood there a moment longer, watching as her car pulled out of the lot, turned the corner, and faded from view. Then, with a giddy smile plastered on his face and a spring in his step, he strolled over to his own car and got in. He turned on his cell phone and scrolled through his contacts to Avery's number. She answered on the first ring, and her rapid words dug into his eardrums before he could even open his mouth.

"Oh my God, Franklin, Parker told me you were going out with some lady you met. You just broke up, dude, isn't it a bit early? Are you alright? Was she a psychopath? Do you need me to pick you up? Should I arrest her?"

"Woah, woah, Avery, chill," Franklin interrupted. His sister's panicked rant died down, and he took a deep breath before speaking. "It went really well, actually. Her name's Maisie. I really like this girl, Avery."

"Tell me about her."

Franklin told her, recounting all of the small habits that he had observed, how she wasn't opposed to light bickering, and how she latched onto every word he said. He sat in the parking lot talking about Maisie for almost twenty minutes before his sister finally interrupted him and said that she had reports to file. Even after that, as Franklin drove home, Maisie's smile was all he could think about.

XIV

Aremaeid knelt on the damp ground and brushed his fingers over the dirt, which was plastered with flat, wet leaves. It had rained just a few hours ago, so he knew the trail he'd been following was fresh. He lifted his snout to the wind and inhaled deeply. His quarry's scent was getting stronger.

He crept through the underbrush of a shallow, rocky ravine, slipping through the shadows of sizeable rocks and densely packed trees. He took care to make no sound even when he was forced to wade through runnels of shallow water. This silent approach was an ingrained habit, and it came easily despite the unfamiliar terrain and its numerous noise hazards. He climbed out of the ravine as the trees began to thin and continued along his prey's trail until he came to a wide, expansive field. He crouched in the tall grass behind a tree and surveyed the scene. In the field stood four animals with long, spindly legs and narrow faces. Potential food, to be sure, but not what he had followed.

He was downwind, so he closed his eyes and waited, motionless, as the breeze carried a myriad of fresh smells towards him. The creatures in the field, the grass itself, and even the sharp, aromatic odor of small creatures that scurried across the ground. Though unfamiliar, all were remarkably similar to scents he might find back on Primaied. But where. . . ?

Aremaeid's eyes snapped open as soon as he caught a whiff of his quarry. He lowered himself further to the ground and peeked out from the undergrowth. High up in the branches of a nearby tree was a limber, tawny animal staring intently at the prey creatures in the grass. It was close enough that it could land on one with a well-placed leap. Aremaeid had suspected the creature he was stalking was likely a predator, and now he could confirm it. If it knew he was there, it would have probably thought he had his eye on the same creatures it did. He usually tried to avoid hunting other predators due to a begrudging yet respectful understanding, but this creature's trail was the first one he'd picked up, and he wasn't the type of Rhithien to change direction mid-pounce.

He saw the creature's body tense, and he, too, readied himself to spring. Each muscle was tight. His blood was racing. He had every ounce of attention focused on his prey. The hunt was more than just a means to get food. There was sport in it, an undeniable, adrenaline-fueled excitement that he couldn't find anywhere else.

One.

The grass-eaters lifted their heads and stamped the ground nervously. Their huffing breath turned to mist in the chilly air.

Two.

The creature in the tree rolled its shoulders and flicked its tail, and Aremaeid saw curved claws flex against the bark of the branches.

Three.

The predator launched itself from the tree and, just as Aremaeid had predicted, landed right on one of the grass-eaters. The creature bugled and scrabbled to try and get away, but the predator bit into its neck, bringing it down with ease. As the other creatures dashed off, Aremaeid leapt from his own hiding spot and knocked his quarry off its kill. It spun and hissed at him, but quickly decided that fighting over this meal wasn't worth its time or its life. Even on all fours, Aremaeid was twice its size.

The beast turned and started to slink away, but Aremaeid lunged and dug his claws into its haunches, dragging it back with minimal effort. The thing yowled and spun around with surprising fluidity to swipe at his face.

Aremaeid jerked back from the flurry of claws and teeth before remembering that he was far bigger and stronger. He grabbed his prey by the shoulders and forcefully flipped it back onto its stomach, then used his body weight to press it against the ground. It whipped its head around and tried desperately to bite him, but its efforts were rendered pointless when he grabbed its muzzle and yanked its head back with a loud *snap*. The creature went still.

Aremaeid turned it over again so he could access its soft throat and belly. He bit into its neck and tasted hot, thick blood flowing over his tongue. The red blood had been a surprise when he'd first gone hunting, but he had grown used to it by now. At the end of the day, meat was meat. Who was he to complain about the color?

As he ate, he frowned over his shoulder at the fallen grass eater. He had worked for his own quarry, so he would eat it, but what about the herbivore it had killed? He hated leaving prey uneaten. It was a waste of meat and a waste of life. Rhithien didn't usually take leftovers, but perhaps he could hide it in Maisie's house until he got hungry or found his packmates? No, she wouldn't like that. Although they'd never discussed it, he knew humans weren't partial to raw meat, and she probably wouldn't be pleased if he dragged a fresh carcass through her house. Even if she allowed him to bring it inside, it wouldn't keep for long. No, taking it with him would be nothing but an inconvenience.

Suddenly his frill prickled, and he sat up with renewed alertness. Someone— or something—had its eyes on him. He rose to his full height, hoping that whatever was stalking him would see his size and decide that he wasn't worth the trouble. Most Earthen creatures were smaller and more breakable than the ones on Primaied, so his physicality alone might be enough to defend his kill.

There was no need, however; a pair of familiar red eyes adjoined to a lean, dark shape slunk out from the shadows of the forest. Aremaeid didn't relax, though, even as his packmate sat back on his haunches and gave him what was probably meant to be a friendly smile.

"Aremaeid," greeted Ornathium with an amiable nod. That wide, toothy, insincere smile didn't fade. The smaller male had learned a lot about typical Rhithien behaviors since he'd been inducted into the pack, but he still smiled too long, laughed too loudly. He showed too much of his teeth, which, in the past, had led to several misunderstandings with Rhithien who were unfamiliar with his ways. His performance was far from perfect and everyone knew it.

"It's good to see a familiar face," Aremaeid acknowledged stiffly.

"But not my face."

"I didn't say—"

"Don't lie to me, please," Ornathium said. "I know you don't like me any more than the rest of our pack does. But yes, it is good to see a familiar face." That smile still didn't waver, but his red eyes were completely devoid of emotion.

"How long have you followed me?" Aremaeid asked, trying to maintain civility.

"Not long. I caught your scent and followed it here. Many trees, there are, all telling the same story. A hunter following a hunter. I decided to jump in line, but I'm not hunting."

"Are you hungry?"

Ornathium didn't respond to the question right away, but his eyes fell upon Aremaeid's kill, and he swallowed.

"No," he lied.

"Yes, you are. Have this thing. It's fresh, but it's not mine." Aremaeid picked up the dead grass-eater and tossed it to his packmate. It landed with a *splat* at Ornathium's feet, but instead of eating, he stared hungrily down at it and let out a small, pleading whine.

Aremaeid sighed and added, "You may eat."

Ornathium immediately grabbed the grass-eater and dug into it, mercifully turning his attention away from Aremaeid. One of the oddest things about him was that he never ate unless he was alone or a higher-ranking Rhithien gave him permission with those specific words. No one was sure where he'd picked up this conditioning, and though they'd asked him numerous times, he never told them.

As the two ate in silence, Aremaeid recognized an odd smell hanging over Ornathium. It wasn't his personal musk, nor was it the natural scent of the forest and its inhabitants. It was a foreign smell. A *human* smell. He frowned and sniffed at his own arm, finding that he, too, carried that odor. Had his packmate somehow settled into a similar living situation in a human house?

He waited until he had consumed most of his kill before sitting back on his haunches and nonchalantly inquiring, "Care to explain why you smell like human?"

Ornathium froze and looked up at him.

"You have it, too," he commented.

"I have a special arrangement," Aremaeid explained stiffly.

"Special arrangement?"

Ornathium lifted an eyebrow, and Aremaeid clenched his jaw. How much should he tell him? Certainly not where Maisie lived, although his packmate could probably track him back to her house if he wanted to.

He eventually said, "I ended up at a human's dwelling when we were scattered. It discovered my presence, and I was going to kill it, but we made an agreement; if it allowed me to stay in its home, I would allow it to live."

141

"Interesting."

"How so?"

"Interesting that the human was able to say so much before you killed it. You are devoted to the mission like the rest of us, are you not? I wouldn't expect our alpha's third to show such hesitation."

Aremaeid narrowed his eyes and growled, "Yet you seem to have made the same decision if I'm not mistaken. I spared the human's life because it was convenient to do so. I shall finish the job as soon as it comes time to leave. Now, you haven't answered my question. Why do *you* smell like them?"

"Mmm. Let's just say I'm in a similar situation."

Aremaeid didn't offer a response, and Ornathium didn't elaborate. They simply stood there, staring at each other in an unspoken competition, waiting for one to reveal more information. Realizing that Ornathium wasn't going to give in, Aremaeid sighed and relented.

"This mission is taking longer than we anticipated. Have you found anyone else?"

"No one. Maybe they found each other and left."

"They wouldn't have left," Aremaeid snapped. He chose to ignore the dubious twitch that flickered across Ornathium's forced smile. The pack couldn't leave without him. There was a vital part of the ritual they needed to perform that no one in the pack knew about except for Salidus and himself, a secret that not even Orniell had been let in on.

"What makes you so sure? It's been a week since we arrived, and you are the first Rhithien I have seen."

"I hunted and fought alongside Salidus for more than a trilunar cycle before he took the rank of alpha. He knows the importance of this task, but he would never leave one of us behind."

"Not even me?"

"Not even you," Aremaeid promised. After a heavy pause, Ornathium winced like he'd been struck.

"No, they wouldn't," the smaller male whispered, seemingly to himself. His eyes glazed over and drifted past Aremaeid, who gnawed awkwardly on a bone. Aremaeid had learned from Ziiphan that whenever Ornathium went into one of these absent moods wherein he spoke to himself, it was best to let him be until he came back to reality on his own. So he remained silent until Ornathium's eyes cleared and the smaller male returned his attention to his half-eaten carcass.

"I think it would be best for us to stay close," Aremaeid probed. "Most of the others have probably assembled elsewhere by now, so it would be much more convenient if they found both of us rather than one."

"That's all well and good, but I do have some business to attend to," Ornathium said. He seemed ready for an argument, but Aremaeid thought about Maisie and nodded. She knew too much for her own good, and something needed to be done about it. There would be nothing stopping her from telling other humans about his pack once he left.

"As do I. Meet me here tomorrow, when the suns have gone down."

"*Sun,* not suns," Ornathium reminded him. "This is not Primaied."

"You know what I meant. Just take care of whatever 'business' you have and come back. With some luck, we can find the others and return home."

Aremaeid rose to his feet and returned to the woods. He didn't hear any parting words from his packmate, and he couldn't help glancing over his shoulder to make sure Ornathium wasn't following him. He only relaxed when he saw the smaller male trotting merrily away through the tall, billowing grasses. He exhaled with relief and, while still shooting suspicious looks behind him, slipped into the foliage and began the trek back to Maisie's house.

XV

One of Willard Hayes's greatest joys in life was driving up the twisting mountain paths in his rusty old pickup with his bloodhound, Foxboy, panting happily in the passenger seat. He knew these back roads like his own mind; every bump in the gravel spread was familiar, and every tree he passed by was an old friend. The only other people who knew about this trail were a couple of old-timers like himself and the rangers who patrolled the woods.

Willard parked his truck in a small, grassy clearing and stepped out of the vehicle. Foxboy bounded after him as he grabbed the wooden walking stick that he kept in the bed of his pickup. The dog's favorite place to run around right at dusk was an open field that Willard liked to call "Deer Meadow." They'd been parking in this clearing for years, and both of them knew the way to Deer Meadow by heart. Willard adjusted his cap, patted the tail-wagging Foxboy on the head, and set off through the woods.

The rangers demanded that hikers stick to the marked paths to avoid bears, but Willard had been going off-trail for years, and he'd never seen so much as a shit pile from one of the damn things. Even so, he usually made sure to talk loudly to himself and his dog, just in case there did happen to be a bear that had come down the mountains for a snack. He didn't know if his strategy of talking—and even carrying around bear bells now and then—worked, but he kept at it nonetheless.

"You know something, Foxboy?" he said wistfully. His jowly bloodhound perked up and wagged his tail at the sound of his name. "I don't think you and I will ever get too old for these here woods. Or Deer Meadow. We don't need much to be happy. Just a cabin, the trees, and some privacy. Not like them youngsters with their hiking trails, always bringing packs full of them plastic water bottles and primly packaged cookies, wearing those fancy li'l puff vests. They don't know what it means to *really* walk through the woods. But you and I do, ain't that right, boy?" Foxboy did not respond—not that Willard expected him to, of course.

But a dark shadow tainted Willard's good mood today. There was something on his mind, something that had made him bring bear bells for this hiking trip. There might not have been bears or mountain lions anywhere close to him, but he knew there was something worse.

Don't think about it. It was late. Your eyes were playing tricks on you.

A week had passed since. . . since that *thing* had broken into his house. He knew he was getting old, and it was dark that day, but still. . .

He'd gone outside to use the outhouse, and when he came back, there had been something lurking about in his cabin. A demonic entity that had no doubt stopped by to take his soul early. But he knew it wasn't his time, so he had fought back.

I fought back. Even if it was just a person in a hokey suit, I was right to be afraid. Home invaders ain't nothing to take lightly.

Yes, just a person in a costume. No righteous God—hell, probably not even Satan himself—would create something so abhorrent.

If you don't know what to make of it, don't think about it.

Willard nearly jumped out of his skin when something warm and wet touched his hand. He looked down to see Foxboy licking his fingers.

"I'm alright boy," he assured the bloodhound, giving him a pat on the head. "World's just going to shit, is all. You were very brave, taking on that demon. Couldn't have done it without ya. But you're a dog, so I doubt you remember it." Apparently satisfied with his human's emotional state, Foxboy pushed his nose into the ground and snuffled along in the dirt.

His wagging tail slowed until it came to a complete stop, sticking straight out behind him, and he lifted his head sharply. Willard started when the dog bayed loudly and took off into the woods like a brown streak of lightning.

"Foxboy!" Willard bellowed, hurrying clumsily after his hound as fast as his old, creaky legs could carry him. "Damnit, Foxboy, get back here! Ya can't just go runnin' off like that!"

Perhaps the dog had caught the scent of a rabbit or a coon. Nothing could stop him once he had an animal's odor up his nose. But Willard soon slowed down, knowing that, eventually, Foxboy would make his way up to Deer Meadow. The dog knew the path as well as his master, and it wasn't like he'd never gone off on his own before. He was a hunting dog, after all.

Willard sighed and called, "Alright, boy, I'll meet you up there." He grinned at the sound of distant baying, then headed up the path.

Deer Meadow had an intrinsic beauty at dusk when the setting sun brought out the gold in the grass and the soft pinks in the wildflowers. Willard stopped as he exited the woods, put one hand on his hip, and inhaled that sweet, nostalgic scent of nature. A light breeze blew his way, and he happily welcomed it, turning his face into the wind. Then a strange, cloying smell hit him and he jerked back with a snort, squinching up his nose.

"The hell?" he muttered. He followed the overwhelming stink across the field, and the creases in his face deepened at the sight of a bloody red patch in the golden grasses. He continued toward it anyway, and just as he reached that red spot, he heard Foxboy bay again. The dog sounded much farther than before.

Willard gagged at the sight of stripped animal remains covered in a writhing black carpet of flies. Through the cloud of buzzing insects, he could just make out gleaming white bones coated in strips of pink flesh and patches of blood. There appeared to be two broken skeletons—both looked roughly deer-sized, but one skull looked more like that of a mountain lion. What could have killed the lion? Based on the state of the remaining flesh and stray organs, they couldn't have been more than a few hours old. Willard's blood chilled in his veins.

Foxboy. Where's Foxboy?

Willard patted his thigh and whistled, then shouted, "Foxboy! C'mere, ya big dumb dog! I'm waitin' for ya up in Deer Meadow!" He heard Foxboy bark and felt a surge of relief when the sound seemed closer than the dog's earlier baying. That relief froze and shattered when he heard a loud yelp of pain. "Foxboy!" he cried hoarsely, and he rubbed his wrinkled throat with a wince as his voice cracked from the strain.

The demon! It's come back!

His bloodhound suddenly came bounding out of the trees on the opposite end of the field, and Willard could have sobbed with joy. But he quickly noticed that something was wrong; the dog's gait was off like he was limping, and he left a shimmering scarlet trail in his wake as he tore through the grass. Was he injured?

Willard hobbled forward to meet Foxboy, but the dog ran straight past him, almost knocking his master over in his haste. Nothing had ever made him run that fast in his life. Fear bubbled up in Willard's gut, but rage soon replaced it. Demon or not, if someone or something had hurt his dog, there was going to be more blood tonight, and he knew damn well it wouldn't be his.

"Who the hell hurt my dog?" he yelled, hoisting up his walking stick like a spear. "Get your ass out here! I swear I'll beat the tar out of you!"

A creature emerged from the trees as if responding to his challenge, and all the blood drained from Willard's face. It was the demon—or something similar, at least. Even from afar, he could see that it was huge, easily over eight feet. It had a wolf-like face but stood on two legs with the comfortable poise of a person. Unlike the thing that had broken into his cabin, which had had green eyes and speckled gray skin, this creature was distinguished by a hide blacker than ink and eyes redder than a stoplight. It might not have been the same beast, but it was surely coming for him just as its predecessor had. Willard let out a terrified, wordless yell and stumbled backward. He started to turn around, hoping to outrun it, but his knees gave out and he collapsed to the ground.

A shadow towered over him, blotting out the fading light. Willard was forced onto his back, putting him face-to-face with the creature. He stared into those burning crimson eyes and screamed in a pitch that he hadn't been able to reach in decades.

Oh God, how did it get across the meadow so fast? Dear God, it's gonna kill me, it's gonna tear my soul right from my body, dear God, have mercy, sweet Jesus—

The creature bared its teeth and raked sharp, curved claws across Willard's face, eliciting a hoarse cry of pain from the old man.

"Save your whimpering, I have barely touched you," a deep voice purred, and it took Willard a moment to realize that the creature was *speaking* to him. "Now, I think you should know that this is nothing personal. But *he* has given me a command that I cannot deny."

"What? Who's 'he'?" Willard pleaded.

"No talking," it crooned, clapping one large hand over his mouth and leaning in close. "If I wanted you to speak, I would ask it of you. All I need you to do now is scream."

Then the demon ripped into him, tearing at his belly, separating his limbs from his body, and spraying blood across the grassy field. And Willard screamed; he screamed with unbridled, animalistic agony until the sun went down and his voice broke. The creature didn't allow Willard Hayes to die for almost an hour, and when it finally ended his life, there wasn't much of him left to kill.

*****

Torraeid sat in dejected silence, watching Vegra feast on their most recent prey. The sounds of flesh tearing and bones crunching were so tantalizingly close, yet so agonizingly far. Technically, Torraeid was the one who had tracked, chased, and caught this prey, but technicalities didn't mean much when one was at the bottom of the pack. He politely waited his turn as he always did, despite knowing that Vegra would intentionally overeat to leave as few scraps as possible. It had happened before, if not with Vegra then with Ziiphan, and occasionally Ornathium. At least when Ornathium did it, it didn't feel like a personal attack. That Rhithien always ate like it would be his last meal.

He perked up when Vegra ripped a front leg from their prey and tossed it aside so he could gain better access to the meat of the creature's chest. Torraeid cautiously slunk forward and reached for the limb, but was met with a defensive snarl and a set of claws slashing at his face. He leapt backwards with a yelp, his ears and frill flattening down and his tail curling between his legs. Vegra hissed and dragged the leg back to the rest of the kill.

Torraeid had been hungry for the past week, but Vegra consistently allowed him just enough so he wouldn't starve. There were plenty of incidents on Primaied recounting Rhithien going mad from hunger and becoming little more than mindless beasts, turning to cannibalism without a second thought, and both Vegra and Torraeid knew that a starving Rhithien was not a problem they needed. Thus, food would undoubtedly be shared, but there wouldn't be much of it. Torraeid shifted uncomfortably in his spot, trying to ignore the nauseating hollowness in his stomach. A meal usually mellowed Vegra out, so perhaps he could be reasoned with, even in a somewhat defensive state.

"I know you're not finished yet," Torraeid began slowly, eliciting an irritable scowl from his packmate, "but you never eat the legs. If I could just have—"

"Wait your turn, runt," Vegra growled, extending his claws and dragging them menacingly through the dirt.

"I *am* waiting my turn. But—"

"How about I rip one of *your* legs off and beat you with it?" snarled the older male, rising to his feet and stepping over the kill.

Torraeid scuttled backwards on all fours and shook his head wildly.

148

"Never mind. I can wait," he conceded.

"That's what I thought. Shut up."

Torraeid curled up against a tree and didn't say another word as Vegra continued eating.

A carcass suddenly plummeted from the foliage and landed with a splattery crash before Torraeid. The two Rhithien jumped to their feet, claws out and teeth bared, but relaxed when Orniell, Salidus's second, stepped into the clearing. He had a second kill slung over one shoulder, and his single yellow eye regarded them coolly. The twin daggers sheathed on either side of his waist thumped softly against his hips in their leather holsters.

"You can have that," he grunted, nodding at the creature he'd offered. Torraeid gave him a grateful nod and crouched over the carcass, dragging it away from Vegra to reduce the risk of having more food taken from him. Orniell knelt as well, groaning at the strained creak of his joints, and started on his own meal. Nearly a full minute passed before Vegra spoke up.

"How did you find us?" he demanded. "How long have you known where we were? We could have used stronger numbers on our hunts."

"I found your trail this morning, but I figured I would find something to contribute before joining you," Orniell explained with a shrug.

"Thank you," Torraeid mumbled, to which Orniell responded with a curt nod of acknowledgment.

"Hang on, we're just going to slide over this? It's been a week since our arrival—a fucking week—and you're the first Rhithien we've seen besides each other! Where the fuck is everyone?"

"If I knew where everyone else was, I wouldn't be taking the time to share a meal with you. Calm down and eat, Vegra. You aren't terribly good company when you're hungry."

"I swear, Orniell, if you didn't outrank me, I'd—" Vegra began, but Orniell was immediately at his throat, grabbing his neck and slamming him face-first into the ground. He pressed one of his large knives against Vegra's back in a silent warning. Orniell was the only one in their pack who used weapons, but no one dared call him a coward for it, and with good reason. He'd carried those knives for hundreds of years, and he knew how to use them.

Torraeid went still, hoping his statue technique would keep him out of the squabble. He wanted to eat but feared that even the slightest movement would attract unwanted attention.

"What would you do?" Orniell growled, lifting his frill. "I don't need two eyes to have you begging for a healer. So what would you do, Vegra? I'm curious."

Vegra started to bare his teeth, but thought better of it and slowly relaxed.

"Nothing," he muttered at last. Orniell eased away from him, sheathing his blade as he did so.

"Good. Remember your place."

The two older males returned to their respective meals, and Torraeid waited until they were both eating before turning back to the kill Orniell had provided. He didn't know what it was, and he didn't like the smell or taste of Earthen meat much more than he had a week ago, but it was better than nothing. The three of them were quiet until Torraeid, halfway through a meaty leg, looked up and saw Vegra scowling at him.

"I'm sure you are well aware of pack etiquette at this point in your life," Vegra nonchalantly said to Orniell.

"Of course I am. I have been part of this pack for over six hundred years."

"Then you know that normal circumstances don't see the second—or even the third—sharing his scraps with the dregs of the group."

"These aren't normal circumstances," Orniell pointed out. "This is not something I usually do, but we should eat as quickly and fully as we can. Although I'm sure I don't have to tell you that, Vegra; you are less than a trilunar cycle behind me in age. I have no doubt that you understand how the current situation complicates things. So leave Torraeid alone. There are more important matters at hand than petty dislike, and losing our only healer would be terribly inconvenient."

" 'Petty dislike'?" Vegra hissed indignantly. He flexed his claws and dug them into the soft dirt beneath his feet, but backed down again upon receiving a sharp look of warning.

"Just quit being an ass, at least until we get back to Primaied."

Suddenly, Torraeid's ears flicked towards a distant sound. He sat up, looking around and sniffing the air.

"Did you hear that?"

The two older males stood at attention. When the sound drifted into the clearing again, all three of them heard it: screaming. Someone or something was screaming, and it didn't sound like a Rhithien.

"Is that a human?" Vegra demanded.

Ignoring him, Orniell abandoned his meal and crept through the foliage to follow the noise. Torraeid started to trot after him, but Vegra shoved him aside and bared his teeth, so he lowered his head and allowed the older male to go first. Though they sped swiftly through the dense forest, it took close to an hour to finally reach the origin of the sound.

"Three moons," Orniell groaned as he took in the sight before them. The woods opened up into a large meadow, which might have been a pretty sight if it wasn't filled with bloody carnage. The tall, golden grasses were stained red. The area was scattered with limbs that had been pulled from a body at various lengths. Bits of torn cloth and flaps of mangled skin littered the ground, and at the center of it all, a Rhithien crouched over what might have once been a human. The pitiful slab of meat had a skinless, eyeless face, and its broken body spasmed with post-mortem twitches as its tormentor sliced the tip of a knife through its bare chest.

"Ornathium!" Vegra snarled, stomping over to the gruesome scene, and their packmate looked up in surprise.

"Oh, hello!" he called brightly, waving a blood-soaked hand. Vegra grimaced down at the human and gave Ornathium a disgusted glare.

"Ugh, you signed it and everything. You don't even know how to read!"

"Ziiphan showed me how to make my name. He also showed me numbers."

"Where did you get the blade?" Orniell queried, gesturing to the small knife in his hands.

"I borrowed it."

"Were you planning on eating that?" Torraeid inquired, to which Ornathium shook his head.

"No, I already ate. Aremaeid gave me food."

"You've seen Aremaeid?" asked Torraeid hopefully. His ears pricked up and he stepped forward, but Orniell grabbed his arm and pulled him back with a growl. Torraeid sighed and stood quietly in place, allowing his superior to approach instead.

"Where is he?" Orniell demanded.

"I don't know. He said he had business to take care of. I do, too, so we agreed to meet back here tomorrow night." Ornathium dragged his claws down the human's ruined face and smiled dreamily as small spurts of blood bubbled up in the fresh slices.

"What *business?*" hissed Vegra suspiciously.

"Well, he said he's been staying in some human's den, and—"

"*What?*" Orniell roared, stomping closer and grabbing Ornathium by the throat. His frill rising in anger, he shook the smaller male viciously and snarled, "He's been staying *where?*"

"I-I don't know where exactly, he didn't tell me, but he said—"

"And you didn't follow him? You didn't try to correct him? Surely you have at least an inkling of why his decision is a poor one!"

"What was I supposed to do?" Ornathium cried, pawing at Orniell's hand. "He outranks me, and I'm not as good at tracking as he is! I couldn't have followed him if I wanted to!"

Orniell snarled and released him. Ornathium stumbled away with a yelp, clutching his neck. He fell to the ground and pulled himself into a quivering ball, his frill pinned tightly back and his tail curled anxiously around his feet. He rocked rapidly back and forth, muttering under his breath, "No, there was nothing. . . It's not my fault. . . No, it's not."

"You said you have business to take care of as well," Torraeid said gently, gathering his courage and stepping between the two males. He could feel Orniell's disapproving glare boring into his back, but he focused his attention on Ornathium and placed a hand on his shoulder. The red-eyed Rhithien recoiled with a surprised hiss as if he had forgotten they were there. Torraeid met his eyes and questioned, "What 'business' do you have, Ornathium? If this mission is going to work out, you need to talk to us."

"Have you been staying with a human, too, freak?" Vegra laughed.

Ornathium opened his mouth to respond, then closed it again and averted his eyes.

"No," Orniell said sharply.

"Wait, are you really? How the fuck did *you* manage that?"

"No. Absolutely not. One Rhithien staying with a human is bad enough. You will remain with us," Orniell ordered.

Ornathium shot to his feet and desperately grabbed the older male's arm.

"Wait, you don't—"

He stopped and backed off when he was met with a vicious growl, but he stood tall and continued speaking. Excitement spread over his features as he explained, "I found the heir."

"What?"

"The Lucio heir. I found her! Our pack was scattered, but I ended up in the right place! I have the heir!"

"No fucking way," scoffed Vegra.

"Yes, fucking way! I found the heir!"

Orniell's eye traveled from Ornathium to the human he'd mutilated, and he stiffly said, "It better not be that one."

"No, of course not! This human I saw wandering around the woods. But I found the heir!"

"You mentioned that."

"Yes, I found her! She is my friend. I'm a very good liar."

"No, you're not," Vegra said with a derisive snort. "Humans are just stupid."

"Shut up, Vegra," growled Orniell, and he calmly turned to address Ornathium again. "Alright, let me get this straight: you met up with Aremaeid."

"Yes. And I found the heir."

"And you two agreed to part ways long enough to dispose of your temporary human companions."

"Yes. And I found—"

"I know, Ornathium. And then. . . you will both return to this spot?"

"Yes. Tomorrow night. With the heir."

"Very well. We shall do the same, then." Orniell beckoned his other two subordinates and left the way they had come, evidently satisfied with the plan, but not before glancing over his shoulder and adding with distaste, "Clean up your mess."

Torraeid felt his gaze drawn to the mangled remains of the human. The poor thing hadn't stood a chance. He sighed and turned away, following Orniell and Vegra back into the woods.

XVI

Maisie lay on the living room sofa with her slipper-clad feet pulled up on the cushions and a book balanced upon her knees. Roller was sprawled across her stomach with his head resting on her chest, and despite her continuous page-turning, he was fast asleep. A small fire danced in the hearth, casting the room with a soft orange glow. Maisie glanced at the clock on the mantle. 9:27. Aremaeid was usually back by around 10:00, so she still had some time to herself.

This evening had been the most fun she'd had in years. She'd gone on another date with Franklin, this time to their local theater for a rerun of *Jurassic Park*. They and the rest of the audience participated eagerly, cheering for the opening credits, da-da-da-ing along to the main score, and screeching at the characters to go faster. That movie had been one of Maisie's favorites as a kid. It was the type of movie that she could rewatch over and over and never get bored of. She hadn't put it on in years, however, so seeing it on the big screen was mind-blowingly nostalgic. The only problem she faced now concerned the book in her lap: *Moby Dick,* another classic that she hadn't touched in a long time. She still liked the story and the perspectives it offered, and she also liked whales, but now she couldn't help thinking that the book would be much more interesting with a megalodon or some other prehistoric giant.

Maisie looked down when Roller's front paws suddenly twitched and he began to make small, popping barks in his sleep. His nose wiggled, his ears flopped up and down, and his tail even thumped a couple of times. Maisie was overcome with the temptation to snuggle him hard enough to pop his tiny head, but she managed to stay completely still until the barking stopped and he opened his eyes.

"Hi," she whispered. Roller turned his face up to look at her, and she happily scratched him behind the ears. "You were dreaming," she informed him. "Was it a nice dream? Did you get to chase all those nasty bunnies? You haven't been able to do that in years, bud!"

The dog wagged his tail and stretched his neck out to lick her face. Maisie giggled and leaned away. "No face kisses, I know where your tongue's been."

They both glanced into the hallway at the sound of the sliding glass door opening. As per usual, Maisie heard Aremaeid before she saw him; she'd nagged him enough that he no longer walked around the house in complete silence, therefore minimizing the risk of giving her a heart attack. But with how loud and weighty his non-sneaky footsteps were, she was amazed by the fact that he was ever able to move without making a single noise.

"Hey," she called. When she received a wordless grunt in response, she marked her page and leaned over the back of the couch with a frown. Aremaeid had been in her house for only a week, but the tension between them had ebbed enough that they mutually engaged in somewhat friendly conversation, and he was usually more polite than that. By the time he came into view, he was already disappearing down the stairs. Maisie managed to catch a glimpse of his frill, which was flared up. Something was wrong. She peeled Roller off her chest, set him down beside her legs, and asked, "Everything alright?"

"Yes."

"Did you find one of your packmates?"

There was a long pause, then, "No."

"Liar. Isn't regrouping your entire goal?" Maisie inquired, lifting an eyebrow. Another pause. Then Aremaeid came back up the stairs and leaned on the banister.

"Why do you care?" he demanded in an unusually clipped tone. Maisie blinked in surprise before a hurt scowl crossed her face.

"It's called being nice. This is what we do, isn't it? We ask how each other's days are? Now, something's obviously getting under your skin, and I know it's not me because I've been doing nothing but sitting here. So tell me what's wrong."

"I cannot tell you. It is strictly confidential."

"So you *did* find one of your packmates," Maisie said, and he nodded. Setting *Moby Dick* aside, she continued, "I hate to sound like I'm trying to kick you out, but why didn't you stay with him? You've been searching since you arrived."

"He said he had business to take care of. We are meeting again tomorrow. Until that happens, I will need to prolong my stay here."

"Ah." Maisie scooped Roller onto her lap and patted his bony head. There was another long, awkward silence, but it was broken when Aremaeid switched the subject.

"How goes your courting?"

"My what?"

"With your male companion. I cannot recall his name."

"You mean Franklin? It's going pretty well. We had a great time tonight at the movies. Have you ever seen the movie. . ." She trailed off at the lost expression on Aremaeid's face. "Oh, right. Never mind. I don't suppose you would have."

"Okay."

"But yeah, it's going well. It's only been a few days since our first date, but I'm feeling pretty good about him. Do Rhithien do. . . 'courting'?"

"Not many of us bother. I have only courted once."

"Like. . . one time ever, or multiple times but with just one person?"

"One Rhithien." Aremaeid shrugged and added, "Most see it as unnecessary effort—a delay, even—especially during breeding season. How does the process work with humans?"

Maisie cleared her throat and explained, "Well, most people call it 'dating', not courting. And you basically just find someone you like and do fun things with them. You can go to dinner, try a lowkey sport, see a movie. There are a bunch of other options, but all in all, you just do fun bonding activities where you get to know your partner and see if you like being with them. We call them 'dates'."

"Dates," Aremaeid repeated.

"Yep."

"And these dates are used to determine which two humans are compatible for reproduction?" His expression remained curious and almost scientific, but Maisie's face flushed.

"I-I mean *kind* of, but not really," she stammered, thrown off by the direction of the conversation. "I mean it *can,* but not everyone decides to go that route. It doesn't have to be about reproduction. It's just about whether you like the person or not. Lifemates, remember?"

"Ah, yes. You creatures are monogamous."

156

"Well, most of us are. Or we try to be. There are a lot of people who aren't very good at it."

"How so?"

"Some people think they're compatible when they aren't, and they get married before they figure it out. Then they get something called a divorce so they can try again with other people. And then there are the people who aren't satisfied with one loving partner, so they run off while you're not looking and stick their lying, cheating *dick* where it doesn't belong! Most of those people are named Jared."

Maisie narrowed her eyes and glared at the wall, forgetting that she was in the middle of a conversation.

"You creatures are strange."

"Fair observation."

"What is that?" Aremaeid asked, nodding at *Moby Dick*.

"It's a book."

"Yes, I can see that, but what are its contents?"

"Oh. It's called *Moby Dick*. It's a story about this boat captain named Ahab who got his leg bitten off by a whale, and he spends his life chasing it around the ocean."

"A whale?"

"It's this giant fish thing that lives in the sea," Maisie explained. "Well, it's not technically a fish, but it lives in the ocean. There are a bunch of different kinds, and they can grow to be really big. Blue whales are the biggest, and to give you some scale, their babies can be bigger than my entire house."

Aremaeid's eyebrows went up, and he looked around as if trying to gauge the size. Maisie studied him for a moment, then asked, "How big is Primaied?"

"Bigger than Earth."

"Do you have anything like whales there?"

"We have similar creatures, but I have never seen them myself. The only knowledge I have of them comes from stories. My pack has visited settlements near the coast, but I have never been close enough to see the ocean."

Maisie blinked. She wasn't sure why that was such a surprise. She enjoyed the ocean herself, and it always made her sad when someone told her they had never been to one, but she hadn't expected to feel the same sort of sympathy for Aremaeid.

"Well, hopefully you'll get to see it someday," she posed. "We have oceans here. If you ever come back to Earth, you should check them out. There are a lot of really nice beaches."

"I have heard that your planet is sick. I have heard that your oceans are polluted wastelands," Aremaeid said with sudden sharpness. There was a note of accusation in his voice, and Maisie had to suppress a surge of defensive anger.

Keeping her tone calm, she countered, "There are some places like that, but that's not all Earth is. There are a lot of really beautiful parts, too. It's like humans; there are some nasty people out there, sure, but there are also a lot of good people. Are all Rhithien perfect?"

Aremaeid's frill stiffened at that comment, though he remained silent. Maisie waited, but when he didn't say anything more, she sighed and set her book on the arm of the couch.

"Just something to think about," she concluded.

She received another grunted response—though it was much less curt than the earlier one—before Aremaeid descended into the basement. Maisie rose from the couch, stretched, and scooped up Roller. She kissed his fuzzy head and cooed, "You're perfect. You're a perfect little old man." She carried him to her bedroom, turned out the lights, and closed the door behind her, veiling the house in quiet, peaceful darkness.

*****

I should have killed her.

If he had killed her the night he'd arrived in her backyard, he wouldn't be in such a compromising situation. He could have left with Ornathium as soon as they'd met up in that field. But no, he just *had* to let the pitiful little human live.

Unable to sleep and desperate for a distraction, Aremaeid grabbed a book from a box that lay nearby and opened it up. Judging by the thick film of dust on the cover and the way the spine creaked when he turned the pages, it hadn't been read in a while. Not that he could read it. A couple of his packmates had learned some written human languages, but although they'd pushed him to do the same, he hadn't bothered. Rhithos runes were challenging enough for him. The characters always seemed twisted and jumbled, and he could never make sense of them. It seemed so easy for everyone else.

It seems easy for everyone else to follow orders, too. This mission is for the good of Primaied.

Yes, it was. Everybody seemed to think it was the right thing to do. Surely he, who had risen to the rank of third, shouldn't have a problem with the mission. But then he thought of Maisie, and guilt roiled in his gut. Was she his friend? He certainly didn't need her as one. He had his pack. Even if he wanted her as an acquaintance, they hadn't known each other very long, and he *did* try to kill her when they first met, so perhaps they weren't quite there yet. Despite this, as much as he hated to admit it to himself, Aremaeid was starting to grow rather fond of the little human, and he truly didn't wish her any harm. But she knew too much. If the plan was going to succeed, she would have to die.

It would be easy, he knew. He would slip into her room and break her neck while she slept. Quick. Painless. Her dog undoubtedly posed a risk of alerting the other humans in the area, but Aremaeid wanted to avoid hurting that thing if he could. He would kill Maisie and leave, then wait out the next day in the woods until it was time to rendezvous with Ornathium. Then he could at last abandon the human town, reunite with the rest of his pack, and carry out the mission that had brought them to Earth. And he would never again be troubled by thoughts of a tiny, red-haired human.

If it had been a matter that affected only himself, he might have considered other options, but the stakes were inconceivably high. This would determine the future of his entire planet. The good of the many came before the individual, did it not? The pack before a single hunter? So why were his mind and soul still battling so furiously over what needed to be done? It wasn't as if he'd never lost someone for whom he bore affection. All creatures died. That was the way of life.

Aremaeid growled in frustration and closed the book upon realizing that even looking at the pictures was pointless. He couldn't concentrate. He had no choice.

I have no choice.

Before he even knew he'd made a decision, he was slinking up the stairs and ghosting through the quiet house. It was dark. Even if she happened to wake up, chances were good that she wouldn't be aware of his presence. Rhithien could see in complete darkness, but humans were as vulnerable as blind cubs. Aremaeid stopped when he reached Maisie's door, and he turned the handle with agonizing slowness. Because of his efforts to remain unheard, it took him close to two minutes just to get it open. But when he was finally faced with her chambers, he ducked down and stepped inside, being careful to avoid scraping his horns on the ceiling.

Just as he had hoped, Maisie was fast asleep. But her dog wasn't. Curled up on the bed against Maisie's side, the tiny beast stared at him and cocked its head to the side curiously. Thankfully, it didn't growl or make any noises that would awaken its caretaker.

Aremaeid crept closer until he reached the side of the bed, where he loomed over the two Earthen creatures like a dark, deadly wraith. Every muscle in his body stiffened when the dog let out a low *woof* of warning. It knew Aremaeid fairly well at this point, but it didn't understand why he was in Maisie's room.

"Y're fine, bud," Maisie groaned, turning onto her front and lazily reaching over to pat the small beast. Aremaeid waited in frozen apprehension for her to wake up, to see him, to scream and try to flee. That would make things much harder than they needed to be. But to his relief, she didn't stir, and with her reassurance, her dog plopped its head back down. Aremaeid didn't allow himself to relax, however; he still had a job to do.

Just break her neck and leave. Simplest thing in the world.

He reached out and hovered one hand over the back of her neck. He'd kept his claws sheathed while moving through her house to avoid clacking, but now he extended them so he would have a better grip. Her neck was so slender that all it needed was one sharp, heavy blow. She wouldn't even have time to open her eyes. She wouldn't feel a thing. Quick. Painless.

Now.

If he was really going to go through with this—which he was, of course—this was the time to do it. He hardened his resolve. He had no choice.

I have no choice.

Aremaeid inhaled sharply and pulled his hand away like he'd been burned.

He couldn't do it. He just couldn't kill her. Killing a human with whom he wasn't acquainted would have been challenging, but doable. However, he knew this human's name. He'd watched her live her ordinary life in peace, completely unaware of the extermination looming on the horizon. He'd even come to enjoy the company of her dog, despite its innate inability to survive on its own. After debating with himself for hours, after that violent mental war, after he had finally decided to follow through with ending her life, he had gone against everything he knew by allowing her to live.

160

Three moons, what am I doing?

Suddenly he couldn't stand another second in that house. He sped from the bedroom, closed the door as quietly as he could, and headed into the backyard for a breath of fresh air. He still needed to follow through with the plan; in that matter he had no other options. But perhaps Maisie didn't have to die. Not by his hand, at least. Billions of humans inhabited Earth. What were the odds that he would encounter her when the fighting began?

His one reassurance was that once he left her house for good, he would never have to see or think of her again.

XVII

The call came in at 4:30 in the morning.

Detective Carlton Davis was up early, sitting in his car and playing a game of paper football with himself across the dashboard. He'd laid a pencil flat as a makeshift goal and had just scored a point when his radio gave a burst of static and the operator said, "We've got a 10-54 in the Dennison Woods."

Carlton's brows raised and then furrowed as the operator continued, rattling off directions and statuses. He swiped both the pencil and the little paper triangle off his dash, then buckled up and started his vehicle. The engine roared to life, and he pulled onto the street, accelerating in the direction of the Dennison Woods.

The route the victim had taken was gravelly and dusty, barely a road, and Carlton would have been doubtful that it was the right place had the man's truck and tire tracks not been found there. He stopped in a wide clearing bustling with activity, where several cruisers and news vans were gathered around a rusted pickup. An old bloodhound cowered under the truck, growling at anyone who tried to coax it out. Carlton's partner, Eric Moore, stood beside the vehicle, and he crackled into his radio, "We've got a 10-91. Can I get animal control up here?" He turned and saw Carlton just as he finished the request and strode over to him.

"You came up without me?" Carlton said stiffly. "You know procedure."

"I was picking us up some coffee. Nothing ever happens in this town, so I didn't think you would miss five minutes of me. I was already on the road when the call came in."

"Fine. What's the story?"

"Body in a field just north of here. Can't get to it with vehicles. Could be an animal attack, but Rayblue thinks it might be homicide-related. She was the first on the scene."

"How do you confuse an animal attack with a homicide?"

"It's. . . Well, come see for yourself, Davis. I haven't taken a look yet, but they're saying it's bad."

They hiked up the trail, leaving the other officers behind to deal with the cloud of reporters and the dog. The path, marked with bright cones, led to an attractive meadow. Carlton could see a group of other officers, including Avery Rayblue, crowded around a red patch in the grass that was impossible to miss. As they headed for the scene, Avery left the body to meet Carlton and Eric halfway. Her lips were pursed and her face was pale—not a good sign. A death that could shake up someone like Avery Rayblue was bound to be a messy affair.

"Who found the vic?" Carlton inquired.

"Park Ranger. Nathaniel James. My brother works with him. Said he was doing a routine check of the area when he found the guy. At least, we're pretty sure it's a guy. It's hard to tell."

"That bad, huh?"

"Worse. Keep a tight hold on your stomach."

Carlton steeled himself and strode confidently toward the bloody patch, weaving between the other officers. He glanced at a flock of journalists—all trying to sneak pictures of the macabre scene—who were restrained at a distance and yammering for commentary. He shook his head at their loud persistence and stuffed his hands into his pockets. It took great effort not to gag at the smell as he came to stand over the body.

If he hadn't been in this line of work for eighteen years, he might have gotten a second look at the toast and eggs he'd eaten for breakfast.

He could only guess that the victim was male because of the clothes the body wore. Or what was left of the clothes, anyway. The man's face was in bloody shreds, and the torn-up flesh was littered with shards of splintered bone and chunks of what looked like brain. The gooey seep of one ruined eyeball had trickled out of the broken socket and down the side of the face, forming a bloody, ruinous mess that was now dry and stiff as baked clay. One of the man's arms was missing, and Carlton spotted a colorful marker about fifteen feet away indicating its location. The other arm had been more or less ripped out as well but was still anchored to the body by a few loose strands of tissue. His legs, both pulled off and strewn to the sides, were destroyed with the same brutality that had assaulted his face. Despite all this, his torso was where the money was.

The man's jacket and shirt were cut open, and the skin had been completely—and very deliberately—flayed from his chest and abdomen. His muscles had been sliced open at his belly, allowing shredded organs to spill out all over the ground around him in messy splatters, and peculiar symbols were carved into the exposed muscles of his chest. Carlton couldn't identify what they meant—whether they were characters of a language or some kind of sick gang sign—but they were repeated in the same arrangement all over the body. He made a mental note to run a search on them when he got back to the precinct.

"Is that the left arm?" Carlton asked, jerking his head toward the other marked spot in the grass.

"Yep," Avery replied. Carlton suppressed his nausea and knelt beside the corpse.

"Sweet Jesus," Eric muttered.

Avery gave them both a tight, humorless smile and said, "You should see his back." She handed Carlton and Eric each a set of latex gloves and they worked together to carefully flip the man over. His clothing had been opened in the back as well, and his ruined skin, albeit still in place, displayed more symbols and more claw marks.

"These symbols definitely have meaning, but these claw marks look like they came from an animal," he said, tapping the vicious slashes.

"So do the wounds on the arm. There's a bite. The ranger said a bear's the only thing big enough around here that could do something like this. I've been hunting in these woods since I was a kid, and I've seen a bear only once. They scarcely go anywhere near people. I can't think of anything else that has claws or teeth like this, though."

"Can I talk to the ranger?"

Avery nodded and called the man over. He was tall and slender, with a nervous look about him, and he was careful to keep his eyes off the body as he made his way to them.

"Nathaniel James, sir," he said, holding out a hand. He saw that Carlton's gloves were sticky with dried blood and yanked his arm back.

"Detective Davis. This is my partner, Detective Moore. You said this was a bear?"

"Only other thing in Montana that's big enough is a moose, but they don't have claws. And I don't think any person could do this shit, even if they was crazy as hell."

"Did you touch or move the body when you found it?"

Nathaniel looked at him like he was insane and said, "You think I wanna touch that? I damn near threw up all over it!" He made the mistake of glancing at the body and let out a low gagging sound.

"Good to know," Carlton muttered. He stood and stepped away from the body to make the inquiry easier on Nathaniel. "About what time did you find the victim?"

"Around 4:00 this morning, I think. Maybe closer to 4:30. I wasn't exactly focused on my watch, sir."

"Understandable. But this area's pretty remote; why were you out so early?"

"Just part of the job, sir. We try to do our rounds early to avoid hikers. Boss said to check this place out, so I rode up here in the four-wheeler. It was a routine check-up, sir, I swear it on my mother! I never thought in a million years I would find something like this! So I called 9-1-1 and sat with the four-wheeler until you guys showed up."

They asked him a few more questions. Did he see anyone else when he discovered the scene? Did he know if the "bear" was still in the area? Was he aware of any previous attacks similar to this one? In the end, there wasn't much Nathaniel could tell them. Carlton gave him his card and returned to the body with Avery and Eric.

"Doesn't seem like he knows much more than he's told us," his partner commented. Carlton nodded.

"What are your thoughts on this, Rayblue?" he asked Avery, ignoring Eric's slightly hurt look. Avery frowned down at the victim and tapped the symbols drawn on his back.

"I know it's really not my job to examine the clues, but this looks a lot like writing to me. I'll agree that the biggest wounds look like the work of an animal, but what kind of bear knows how to write?"

"What kind of bear skins someone?" Carlton added.

"These were pretty clearly made by claws, though," Avery pointed out, gesturing to the slices in the man's back. Carlton frowned. They did look to be normal claw marks and seemed about the right depth, but he'd never heard of any bear flaying someone and writing on them.

"You mentioned a bite on the vic's left arm," he recalled, and he glanced up at Avery. "Can I see that?"

"Yep. Right over here," she replied, leading him to the small taped-off area where the arm lay in the grass. Carlton crouched down and squinted at a huge ring of teeth that was visible even through the scrapped sleeve. He didn't know much about bears, but that bite seemed about the right size to him.

"You said you do a lot of hunting, Rayblue?"

"Yes sir. But like I said, I've never seen anything like this."

"This is roughly bear-sized, though, right?"

"More or less," Avery admitted with a shrug. "The shape's a bit off. But that doesn't explain the rest of the wounds."

"Someone could have made a weapon or some sort of tool to imitate a bear. Claw hands, maybe a toothy headpiece?" mused Carlton, lightly touching the bite. He'd never seen anything like this, either. He'd been in New York, Boston, and had even spent a few months in Detroit, but the damage here. . . This was something else entirely.

"Possibly. M.E. can check for traces of foreign materials. But Davis, this type of speculation is *your* turf, not mine. I'm not a detective, remember?"

"You ought to be. You've got a strong stomach and a good set of eyes."

Avery snorted and turned away, leaving him to thoughtfully inspect the discarded limb.

She really should be a detective.

He'd worked with many different partners throughout his career, and had even tried dating a couple of them, but none of the positions were permanent. He'd been in Nuncan for only four years, but he enjoyed the small-town atmosphere, and the lack of crime was a relief compared to previous places. Of all the cops he'd met on Nuncan's small force, Avery was probably his favorite to work with. She was practical and down-to-Earth, and Carlton admired the stoic attitude she carried into cases. Not that he would ever admit it to her or anyone else, of course. Especially not Eric. He had her pegged as the type of person who avoided dating coworkers, anyway.

Why am I thinking about this now? Focus, man.

"Hey, Davis!" called Eric from where he crouched over the body. Carlton and Avery glanced at each other before hurrying to his side.

"What's up?" Carlton asked, and Eric brushed a gloved hand over one of the claw sets.

"This weird-ass 'bear' has six fingers, including a thumb."

"How can you tell about the thumb?"

He pointed to a clear set, where one of the outermost slices appeared shorter and separated from the others. He positioned his hand over it for a reference, and sure enough, that particular mark seemed to have been made with a thumb.

"All five of the other claws are the same distance apart, but this one's different."

"It's almost like a human hand. An opposable thumb."

"Bears don't have opposable thumbs," Avery said flatly, and Eric gave her an exasperated look.

"I know they don't, but—"

"And even if they did, they wouldn't include them when they scratch something up. You ever seen a normal bear leave five claw marks?"

"Well, this sure ain't normal, and it sure ain't a bear," Carlton concluded grimly. "Rayblue, do you know how common six-digit mutations are?"

"In bears or people?"

"This is pretty obviously not a bear, so people."

"You're asking the wrong person."

"M.E. will probably catch something we didn't," Eric interjected, "so until then we can't do a whole lot more than ruminate on it. But what are your thoughts, Davis?"

"Has Nuncan ever had any serial killers?" Carlton inquired thoughtfully.

"Not that I know of. We get an occasional stabbing or shooting, but nothing worse than that."

"Well, you might have to change that statistic. Because this ain't a bear."

"Whatever it was, it took its time," Avery murmured. Carlton nodded and glanced over his shoulder at the reporters and photographers who were being escorted from the scene. It was early enough in the day that, with Nuncan's remarkably efficient newspaper production, the murder would likely appear in the midmorning paper. Carlton switched his attention back to the problem at hand and gently turned the dead man over to further inspect his flayed chest.

The blood had long since coagulated and dried on the surrounding grass, so it had likely happened during the night or late the previous evening. But, as Eric pointed out, they would have to wait for the M.E.'s report. Carlton brushed his gloved fingers over the characters chiseled into the victim's flesh.

What do those mean?

He would read the M.E.'s report very thoroughly tonight. Then he would do some digging and figure out what those damn symbols meant, whether they were part of a language, the scribblings of a lunatic, or something else entirely. After that, he and Eric would figure out who—or what—they were dealing with.

XVIII

Layla hummed a happy, nonsensical tune as she closed her laptop and returned the Lucio family record to her bookshelf. She had woken up earlier than she usually did on Saturdays, and she'd managed to get through five whole pages just that morning. She could have done a few more, but she didn't want to push herself so early in the day and ruin her good mood. After giving the large book a final affectionate pat, she left her room and headed downstairs. She smelled bacon before she heard it sizzling on the pan, and the heavenly aroma practically carried her into the dining room.

The lights were off, but they weren't necessary with the rays of sun shining brightly through the kitchen windows. Her father was hard at work by the stove, rapidly alternating his attention between hot pans of various sizes and shoveling food onto nearby dishes. Her mother, sitting at the table with the midmorning newspaper in front of her and a steaming mug of coffee at her side, glanced up as Layla entered the room. She gave her daughter a distracted smile before reverting her gaze back to the news.

"Mornin', kiddo," her dad called. He carefully turned the bacon strips with oversized tongs, and each one crackled loudly as it was flipped.

"Hey," Layla returned cheerfully. She was pleased with her progress on the book. She was nearing the end of it and suspected that, with diligent work, she could have the whole thing done by Monday.

"Someone's in a good mood this morning," commented her mother.

"I guess. I just woke up feeling happy today."

"You got up awfully early. We heard you thumping around up there."

Layla's face flushed with embarrassment. She could have sworn she'd been as quiet as a mouse, but it seemed that such a thing was impossible when her room was on the second floor.

"I was trying to be quiet," she said, voicing her thoughts aloud.

"I know, sweetie," her mother replied offhandedly. Then she frowned at the newspaper and asked her husband, "Dennis, have you read the news?"

"Not yet, hon. By the way, have you seen the butcher knife? I could have sworn I put it back when I was emptying the dishwasher last night."

"You should see this," she said, ignoring his question and walking to the stove with the paper. Layla watched with mild concern as her dad's relaxed expression morphed into that same frown.

"What's wrong? What's it say?" she demanded.

"Nothing important, kiddo," her dad responded, giving her a tight-lipped smile. Then, as if hoping to distract her, he added, "First round of bacon's ready."

"Oh, sweet!"

Layla hopped out of her chair and skipped to the stove. She bounced on the balls of her feet as her dad transferred the sizzling strips to her plate, and once she had enough, she returned to her spot at the table and dug in. A skeptical voice in the back of her head wondered what had upset her parents so much—after all, not a lot happened in Nuncan—but she chose to ignore that voice in favor of food. Her focus wavered, however, when Tyson walked into the kitchen with a grave expression on his face.

"The government's watching our house," he said darkly.

"The government doesn't need to watch our house, honey. They already have more information on us than they know what to do with."

"No, I'm pretty sure they're watching us, Mom."

"Whatever you say, kiddo."

Although her mother calmly opened the newspaper and returned to her coffee, Layla's good spirits had been sucked away by a tornado of fright and anxiety. For a few seconds, she thought her heart stopped. Was this Tyson's paranoia kicking in, or was it possible that the government really *was* watching them? She met her brother's gaze, and based on the grim terror in his eyes, she suspected it was the latter.

Ignorant of his children's worries, her father offered, "We've got some bacon here, Tyson. And eggs are on the way."

"In a minute!" Layla interjected. She was already out of her seat and racing toward her brother, a million questions running through her brain at once.

Do they know there's a bunch of aliens in Nuncan? How did they find out? Do they have x-ray goggles? Can they see inside the house? Inside the attic? Do they know about Ornathium?

"You can see them best from here," Tyson panted as they dashed up the stairs together and pivoted into his bedroom. He led her to the window, which had its drapes drawn, and ducked down against the wall. He beckoned his sister to his side and pushed back the corner flap of the curtain. Layla elbowed him out of the way so she could peer through the glass.

"What the fuck were you so freaked out about? What am I looking for? There's no one out there," she hissed. She would be lying if she said she wasn't disappointed by the sight of a normal neighborhood street. Despite her fears, she'd always wanted to see a helicopter up close, or maybe a SWAT team.

"You see the little red car across the street?"

Layla nodded. It belonged to an old man named Burt who seemed to dislike everything in the world except his flowers, which he dutifully tended to day after day.

"I see it," she responded, imagining that she was a spy or an assassin seeking out directions for her next target. Tyson was her guy-in-the-chair. "It's always there, though. He never leaves his house."

"There's a black car parked on the curb right by his driveway."

Sure enough, a large, boxy black van was stationed outside Burt's house, right across from the Lucios' lawn. Only the government would have a van like that. Exhilarated and frightened by this discovery, Layla pressed her nose against the window until her breath fogged up the glass and obscured her vision.

"Oh my *God,* Tyson, are you seeing this shit?" she squealed, almost forgetting to be quiet.

"Of course I am, dumbass! I'm the one who showed you! Now shut up and keep a lookout. Are they doing anything?"

A quick glance told Layla that no, they weren't doing anything.

"No."

"What about the windows? Can you see inside?"

"Nuh-uh. They're too dark. Is it legal to have windows that dark?"

"The government can have as much tinting as they want, they're the fucking government!" Tyson hissed. He anxiously peeked over her shoulder and asked, "Can you see the plates?"

"Plates?"

"The license plates, Layla. Can you see the numbers?"

All efforts to crane her neck and shove her face against both sides of the window were in vain. The van's parallel parking was flawless, rendering the license plates completely hidden from view.

"What do you expect them to say, anyway?" she demanded. " 'Hey there, we're the government'?"

"That's too many letters."

"You know what I mean!"

A taut, nervous silence fell over them like a too-heavy blanket as they took turns looking out the window, waiting for something to happen, for the van to move or a person to get out. It remained on the curb, motionless and peaceful.

They watched.

The van didn't move.

They watched some more.

The van remained immobile despite their dread-filled curiosity. At last, Layla pulled away from her brother's window and leaned against the wall with a resigned sigh.

"I don't think it's going to do anything," she said.

"Shh!" Tyson hissed, smacking a finger against his lips and shushing so hard that spittle flew from his mouth. He remained glued in place, but Layla had had enough. The government's apparent meddling offered none of the excitement she'd expected, but she still needed to inform Ornathium.

The government. Is it the FBI? The CIA? The president?

She wasn't sure which of the three it was—and she couldn't think of any other letter bureaus off the top of her head—but they all sounded equally bad. With all this floating around in her mind, she climbed the attic stairs and poked her head inside the door. Ornathium's lengthy, muscled form was stretched out on the floor beneath the dusty window as he napped peacefully.

"Hey, Ornathium, can I talk to you for a sec—"

Her sentence cut out and her eyes widened when she registered that he was right in front of the uncovered window. With a gasp, she raced across the room and clambered on top of the Rhithien's back to reach for the curtains. Ornathium let out a yelp of surprise and shot to his feet, pitching Layla onto the hard floor. She recovered from the fall quickly and returned to her task. The window was too high, so she had to climb onto a chair to yank the curtains shut before some cop or spy could shatter the glass and swing into the room the way they did in movies.

The drapes are closed. He's safe. We're safe.

Layla pressed a hand to her racing heart and leaned back against the wall. Ornathium crouched a few feet away, his eyes wide and his body stiff with tension.

"It's alright," Layla assured him. "They can't see us now."

"Who can't see us?"

"The government," she replied ominously.

"I do not know who that is," whispered Ornathium.

"They run the country," Layla explained. "They know a lot about us, and probably you, too. I think they're watching the house."

"Why?"

"Because you're an alien. They kidnap aliens, lock them up, and do experiments on them."

Ornathium's ears flattened back against his scalp. He glanced fearfully at the covered window and uttered a small, throaty whine. His frill pressed down against his neck and his tail curled around his legs.

"What do we do?" he asked nervously.

"I don't know, but I'll figure it out. I won't let them get you," Layla assured him.

"Swear it?"

"Yes, I swear it! I won't let them experiment on you."

They sat in silence for a long time, both listening for any activity outside. Ornathium flinched at every noise, from the chirp of a bird to the rumbling of a passing car. The tension in the room had grown to insurmountable levels by the time one of them spoke again.

"Where are they?" Ornathium asked softly.

Layla swallowed and answered, "Right outside the house."

"How long?"

"I don't know. Tyson just pointed them out to me."

The Rhithien leaned back against the wall, scraping his horns against the wood, and murmured, "Well, this complicates things."

*****

Maisie parked in the lot in front of Grader's Home Grocery and stepped outside. She didn't usually bother driving because it was such a short distance, but she was in a rush today. She had a meeting to attend at noon, and she needed to eat something before that, or she wouldn't be able to form a coherent thought. Roller needed to eat, too, but he was once again out of food. Maisie was so hurried that she didn't notice a sleek black vehicle rolling into the lot and parking silently in the back. The driver, unseen behind a near opaquely black windshield, did not get out, but the passenger side door opened and a booted foot stepped onto the pavement.

Maisie waved a quick hello to John Grader, who was helping a line of customers at one of the registers, and headed for the produce section. She selected a bag of oranges, a bag of carrots, and a head of lettuce. She shopped a little further, throwing things into the cart at a rapid and random pace until she deemed her spoils satisfactory. As she was turning the cart in the direction of the dog food aisle, in her peripheral vision she glimpsed a man in a modestly patterned Hawaiian shirt staring at her from a few yards away. She looked up with a jolt of alarm, but quickly relaxed when she saw that he was busily inspecting the avocados. She trundled her cart past him and walked briskly to the other side of the small store.

Should I get something for Aremaeid?

No, he can get his own food.

She focused on the dog food but was spooked again when she turned to enter the aisle and spotted the same Hawaiian shirt man no more than five meters behind her, now engrossed in a rack of toothpaste. He wore sunglasses and khakis, and the longer Maisie looked at him, the more suspicious he seemed.

Is he following me?

As if reading her mind and hoping to assure her of his innocence, the man glanced up, saw her staring, and gave her a friendly wave. Maisie offered a curt nod and a tight smile in response, then dipped into the pet food aisle and all but ran across the floor toward Roller's preferred cans.

Oh God, is he following me?

Dozens of questions flashed urgently through her mind, and each scenario was worse than the last. Was he just an average shopper who liked Hawaiian shirts? Was he a creeper who had become spontaneously interested in her? Or was he an undercover agent of the CIA or some other innocuous bureau? What would happen to her and Roller if the government found out about the Rhithien pack in Nuncan, assuming they didn't already know?

They would have done something by now if they knew for sure. Maybe they just suspect?

There was no guarantee that it was someone from the government, but the circumstances were too convenient for it to be a coincidence. Aremaeid's arrival via portal hadn't exactly been subtle, after all; it had woken the entire neighborhood, and probably the surrounding streets as well. She'd kept her curtains drawn and her blinds down since then in case he emerged from the basement to wander around the house during the day, but the idea that she was being followed led her to wonder how many people knew about him.

Maisie chewed anxiously on her lip as she grabbed a can of wet food. It was thankfully within reach this week, so she took advantage of the opportunity and grabbed four more cans. She began to roll the cart away but reconsidered and grabbed two more. It was probably a good idea to start stockpiling. Just in case.

In case of what?

It wasn't a question Maisie wanted answered, so she pushed her cart away from the row of smiling dogs and headed down the aisle. Maybe she *should* do some stockpiling. She had plenty of fresh fruits and vegetables now, but those only kept for so long. Some canned goods would be a smart purchase. And toilet paper! Definitely toilet paper. . .

She nearly screamed when she turned out of the aisle and came cart-to-cart with the Hawaiian shirt man. He blinked in surprise and opened his mouth to speak, probably to apologize, but Maisie scooted around him before he could do so, muttering, "Excuse me."

He's definitely following me.

What could she do? Where could she go? A recent memory flashed through her mind: that moment when she'd left the school building and was unreasonably spooked by a mysterious car in the lot. Except it hadn't been completely unreasonable, had it? The car was unfamiliar, and it had looked completely out of place among the vehicles of her fellow staff members.

Maisie began piling her items onto the conveyor belt at a frantic pace, all but throwing the dog food cans at the cashier. She could go back for stockpiling later in the week. As the employee began meticulously scanning the bar codes, Maisie craned her neck to peer out the large store windows, searching for any suspicious-looking vehicles. The parking lot was crowded, as it always was on Saturdays, and she couldn't make out any variants. Then, just as she was ready to give up, she spotted it: a trim black car with dark windows in the very back, giving itself away with the empty spaces its driver had left between it and the nearest vehicle.

Gotcha.

"That'll be $42.57."

"What?" Maisie asked, turning her attention to the cashier, who looked at her like she was an idiot. The woman leaned forward and repeated the total in a loud, slow voice, as one might do with an elderly shopper. Maisie paid, grabbed her bags, and lugged them outside. She kept an eye on the black car as she crossed the lot. She didn't relax a single muscle even as she got into her own vehicle and pulled onto the main road to head home. The short trip was a blur of anxiety and glances in the rear-view mirror, and when she at last arrived at her house, she abandoned her groceries and dashed inside.

Maisie slammed the door behind her and uneasily called, "Hey, uh, Aremaeid?"

The Rhithien emerged from the basement with a frown.

"You need not close the door so forcefully."

"I know, but something's wrong. I think someone's following me."

In an instant Aremaeid's whole body tensed, his ears pricked, and his frill stiffened. He rushed toward her and urgently demanded, "Who is it? What do we need to do?"

"It's probably the CIA or the FBI. Hell, maybe NASA, I don't know! Just check the windows. All of them. Even the little ceiling ones downstairs. But whatever you do, don't go to the back door. They're probably watching there, too."

Aremaeid nodded sharply, and the two of them systematically went around the house making sure the windows were locked and curtained. Maisie went to the sliding glass door in the back and, for the first time that week, pushed the deadbolt into place. She pulled shut the large canvas drape that acted as a curtain and returned to the living room. Aremaeid was waiting there, silently scanning the space and the adjacent kitchen as if the government had already snuck in. Maisie wasn't sure if he knew what the CIA or the FBI were, but he didn't ask.

"I believe we locked them all."

"Yeah, I think so. You figured out the basement ones? Those locks can be a little tricky."

"Yes, I secured them."

"Alright," Maisie sighed, putting her hands on her hips and looking around. She glanced back up at Aremaeid and said, "You might want to wait a little bit to go out again."

"Agreed."

XIX

Salidus sat cross-legged on the ground facing the river, his eyes closed and his hands resting on his knees. He'd stuck close to the water for the past week even though he nearly lost Rhala's remains in them when he arrived on Earth. He had traveled upriver for the first three days, but when he emerged from the woods in a wide, mountainous landscape that was barren for dozens of molosopions, he'd turned around and had since been backtracking downstream. Now he rested, meditating peacefully without worry for his aching limbs, his sunburnt skin, or the many scrapes he had accumulated in the woods. All those sensations were familiar.

With each deep breath, he gathered bundles of his magic and stretched it passively out into the area around him. He kept his eyes closed and his other senses blinded to the world, but through his power, he could see every tree, feel passing animals, and taste the subtly changing currents in the air. When he'd first earned the rank of alpha, he had scoffed at the prospect of meditation. It seemed like a waste of magic, and all beginner alphas had so little power. But with some advice from older Rhithien and a good amount of practice on his own, he'd learned that it was the best way to exercise one's power, to expand it, to explore it. He hadn't been an alpha very long—a little over sixty years by his estimate, though he'd lost the exact count—but his magic ran deep.

About half a molosopion up the river, a long, limbless creature lunged from the underbrush and snapped its jaws around a tiny fuzzy thing. It coiled tightly around its prey, and although the sight wasn't anything new to Salidus, he turned his attention elsewhere.

A nearby grove of trees began shedding their leaves all at once at the persuasion of a gust of wind, and the dry orange sheets floated gracefully to the ground. They piled atop the dirt and scattered when hit by another light breeze.

Salidus pulled his magic inward, studying himself, regarding the knuckle bones that were safely tucked in the leather bag around his neck. Every rhythmic pulse of his heart made the bag sway slightly. The movement was imperceptible to the naked eye, but it was now a familiar sensation that he only became aware of whenever he put his magic to use. His lips turned upward in a tired smile as he encased his magic warmly around each bone.

Salidus took a deep breath and opened his eyes. He stretched deeply, then leaned back on his hands and studied the river before him. He hadn't felt the presence of his packmates anywhere, and he'd managed to push his range to nearly three dynnsopions over just a few hours.

Further downstream, then. I am picking up more human activity, so I must be going in the right direction. Perhaps they're simply closer to the target than I am?

He turned to the right to ask Ridaion for a second opinion before remembering that his partner wasn't with him. Letting out a resigned sigh, he pulled his knees up to his chest and silently wished for the thousandth time that Ridaion had emerged from the portal with him. But alas, he hadn't, so Salidus was forced to remain alone until he found his packmates.

"At least I have you," Salidus said aloud, addressing the knucklebones. They didn't offer a response. He closed his eyes again and tried to imagine what it would be like to speak with Rhala himself: an ancient being from nearly two thousand years past, larger in size than any other Rhithien and the ruler of the entire continent of Armenthaal. He could have reigned over all the Rhithien on Primaied and no one would have challenged him; challenged him and lived to tell about it, anyway.

And it was a human that killed him.

It was almost funny. How ironic that, of all Earthen and Primaiedian creatures, a human—tiny, fleeting, helpless, utterly weak—had managed to kill one of the most powerful individuals in Primaied's recorded history. Salidus knew that the human who had committed the atrocity, the one called Aurelia Lucio, was long dead, of course, but whenever he thought of it, he felt a surge of anger and frustration at the sheer unfairness of Rhala's death.

"All of Earth will suffer as you did," he promised the bones. "They will be butchered like livestock as you were."

He recalled the ritual he would need to complete at the very end of their mission once they were back on Primaied. It required writing—neat writing.

179

Perfect writing. When was the last time he'd practiced his runes? He couldn't recall. He'd learned how to read and write at a very young age, but it had stopped being a necessity once he left his childhood home and came to Armenthaal to join a pack. Whenever breeding season rolled around and the packs congregated at whichever Oases were closest to their respective territories, he enjoyed sneaking into Knowledge Centers with Ridaion and looking through the books and scrolls that the scholars forgot to store. That was just reading, though. He couldn't remember the last time he'd written anything.

Salidus carefully channeled his magic and snapped a small twig off a nearby branch. It floated obediently to his hand. He cleared away leaves and sticks from a small patch of river-moistened dirt and pushed the tip of the twig into the soil. He carved the first character, a swooping curve with three short, parallel lines running through the center. He made the second character, then the third, and continued through the entire list of one hundred twenty. Due to the care he took to make the characters look neat—as neat as they could be in the dirt, at least—the task took him quite some time. It wasn't without flaws, but the lettering was tidy, and he was satisfied with the outcome.

It can't be satisfactory. It has to be perfect.

He smoothed over the patch of dirt and repeated the exercise. Perfection was awfully difficult to achieve, however, so it took him four painstakingly careful sets to achieve a proper standard. When his hand began to cramp, he considered using his magic, but quickly dismissed the thought. It was difficult to use magic for intricate, sensitive tasks such as writing, because he would have to focus on how his utensil was held, how much pressure to use, and precisely how to move it. He would have depleted his store by the end of the exercise if he'd turned to his power.

Ridaion has nice handwriting. Maybe I can show him how to do the ritual when I find him. If he asks why, I can just say I need someone to know it for any emergencies, or in case I'm apprehended by—

Something small and sharp struck him in the back, right between his shoulders, and the twig fell from his hands. Salidus extended his magic and tore the object from his skin. He studied it for half a second—it was some sort of dart, probably carrying poison—before throwing it onto the ground and whirling to face whoever had attacked him. He warped his magic into a thin shield just in time to catch three subsequent darts. They hovered in midair before him, less than a single annosopion from his body. Salidus quietly cursed himself for his carelessness; he'd drawn his magic in quickly after meditating instead of letting it simmer around the area. If he'd done the latter, he would have sensed his attackers' approach.

His icy blue eyes narrowed when he spotted three clothed figures hiding in the distant foliage. Humans.

"Try to avoid premature interaction," Fiiorha had told him and Orniell back at the Oasis. *"I know it's hard for males to not be cock-headed fools, but remember why you're there. The only human who should see you is the Lucio heir."*

Salidus muttered another sharp curse under his breath, then sprinted away from the site, still following the river. If the humans were on foot, he could outrun them in a matter of seconds, but if they had brought one of their vehicles with them, he would have to find some other means of escape. As if they had read his thoughts, he heard the unmistakable sound of a machine roaring to life and crashing through the trees in the distance.

"Fuck!" Salidus barked. He transitioned to all fours and ran faster; he might still be able to lose them. He glanced at the river. Could he jump it? They were on his side of it, and they wouldn't be able to get their vehicles across. He'd tested the water the other day, and it ran deep. Despite his speed, he could hear the humans getting closer in their machine. How fast could they go?

Can't take any chances, Salidus thought, and an image of the knucklebones flashed through his mind. He swerved towards the edge of the riverbank until his claws were sliding through grassy mud and threatening to trip him. He built up his momentum, gathered his magic for a boost, and launched himself over the water just as the humans emerged from the trees.

He crashed onto the opposite shore on all fours, skidding through the dirt a few paces, then pulled himself up and continued running. He risked a glance over his shoulder and saw a human poking up from the top of the vehicle with one of their large, oblong weapons in its arms. Salidus quickly summoned his shield again.

The masked human aimed its weapon and shot several of those odd little darts at Salidus, but they all caught in his web of magic and dropped harmlessly to the ground. Without slowing, he swerved away from the river and into the trees, leaving the humans behind. They would have to find a way to cross the water before they'd be able to continue their pursuit. Up ahead, he glimpsed a break in the trees. A clearing or a road, perhaps? Salidus considered avoiding the possibility altogether, given the risk of being seen by other humans, but decided that distance from the immediate threat was more important. He hardened his resolve and sprinted towards it. Even if it was a mistake, he needed to get out of the woods.

Salidus broke through the trees right as a large, dark machine bulleted towards him and slammed straight into his legs. His feet left the ground and his body slammed into the vehicle's frontal pane of glass, creating a nearly opaque spiderweb of cracks. He was hurled over the top of the machine while it continued rocketing forward. He landed heavily on the ground and rolled a few feet before coming to a stop. Lifting his head with a pained groan, he peered up just in time to see the vehicle twisting around to face him with an explosion of dust from its tires. Salidus lifted his hand and threw forward a tremendous battering ram of magic. It sent the car careening off the road, where it crunched nose-first into a tree.

Salidus started to push himself up but collapsed with a yelp when pain bolted through his left leg, the limb that had taken the brunt of the vehicle's impact. He grimaced and glanced down to assess the damage. It definitely felt broken, but not enough to cripple him. He'd had worse breaks. He glanced up at both sides of the road—no one was coming—and then at the crashed vehicle. The entire front half was caved in and folded around the tree, which had apathetically sustained the damage without falling. Steam hissed out from beneath a crumpled sheet of metal that had peeled back to expose a network of dark, convoluted parts. No one stepped out of the vehicle. Perhaps the humans inside were unconscious? Or better yet, dead?

Salidus couldn't risk slowing down. He gripped his injured leg with both hands and focused his magic. He was approaching the limit of his power supply, but he didn't have a choice. His magic seeped through skin, muscle, and to the bone itself. He roved a set of invisible hands up and down the limb until he found the break; yes, it was assuredly broken and shifted slightly off its axis, but it could be mended. He just needed to use extreme care.

"Where's Torraeid when I need him?" Salidus muttered bitterly. He knew how to mend simple breaks, but he was no healer. The most he could do was line the bone back up. He was lucky to walk away with so little damage.

On three, he told himself. *One, two—*

182

He gripped the bone and pushed it back into place. Nauseating agony drilled through the entire limb, and he had to bite down hard on his hand to keep from screaming. He allowed himself a few moments to wallow in his pain before shakily standing up to test his weight on the leg. An aching, throbbing tightness in his chest indicated that he'd also taken some rib damage when his body had rolled over the roof of the vehicle. His torso would be covered in bruises later. He was far from fixed, but that was a job for a healer. His own magic, albeit powerful, could only do so much in the way of wounds.

Keep moving. Just keep moving.

Salidus staggered back into the trees from whence he'd come and headed back towards the river, a new plan now ingrained in his mind. He couldn't outrun them like this, but he had a solid chance of outswimming them. In the distance, an odd, mechanical *chunk* sounded, followed by a loud *slam*. The humans in the crashed vehicle, he realized. They weren't dead yet.

Just keep moving.

Although only one leg had been broken, the other had still taken a heavy hit from the vehicle, and his progress was so slow-going that he could hear the humans catching up to him. If he was slower than those weak little things, he was all but finished. The sounds of the river drew ever closer, however, so a chance of escape was still within reach. Sure, he would be risking another encounter with the earlier humans, but with pursuers on both sides, the water was his only viable option. He couldn't afford to get captured.

A second dart hit him with a sharp *ping,* this time in the back of his upper knee, and he ripped it out with a hiss. It occurred to him then that the gradual slowing of his senses may have been a result of not only the collision on the road but whatever was in those darts as well.

Someone was shouting. The humans had caught up, and they surrounded him in a tight ring of four. Salidus growled and readied his magic, knowing that he would be unable to kill them all manually without taking more darts, but he could feel his power straining against its limits. He didn't have much time.

Salidus concentrated his magic into four small, hard bolts of invisible force and, before any of the humans could set off their weapons, flung the projectiles into their skulls. Bone cracked open and pink flesh sprayed across the surrounding trees, and the four human soldiers dropped limply to the ground. Salidus grimaced in distaste at the sight of their gaudy Earthen blood; he still wasn't accustomed to the strangeness of that bold red. But he didn't linger long. After another moment of weary scrutinization, he turned away from the mess and continued to the river. His magic was just about spent, his legs felt like they were going to buckle at any moment, and he could now clearly feel the effects of whatever drug they'd given him, but he gripped the leather bag strung around his neck and forced himself to keep going.

Almost there. Just. . . stay. . . awake.

At long last, he broke through the trees by the river, but two human vehicles awaited him on the opposite shore. He heard a shouted command—"Take the fucker down!"—before several snapping weapons went off. Two more darts landed before he was able to form a weak shield. Even then, his power only slowed the assault long enough for him to clumsily dodge.

The darts were working. Everything seemed tilted and warped. His limbs became heavy, and an odd buzzing filled his head until he couldn't hear anything else; he couldn't hear the humans' yelling or the popping of their weapons, he couldn't hear the natural sounds of the forest, he couldn't even hear his own footfalls. He barely felt it when he stumbled forward and fell into the river.

Blissfully cool water washed over him, and he sank to the muddy bed. But he remembered that he needed to move. He couldn't recall why, just that he needed to go forward. He dug his fingers into the silty bottom and crawled across it. He had to keep moving. He had to find somewhere to hide.

Struck by a sudden idea, Salidus stopped and pushed himself face-first into the muck. He tried to summon his magic, whatever dregs of it he had left, but stopped when a sensation of warmth began building in the pit of his stomach. His head began to throb, but he wasn't sure if it was from the overuse of his power or the drugs.

Can't use magic yet. Have to. . . Have to dig.

He sank his claws into the mud and tore into the muddy bottom of the river, digging as quickly as he could in his state of sluggish delirium. Soon he was digging laterally, then away from the water and up towards the surface. He was able to push his magical limits ever so slightly to get an extra boost, but he knew he couldn't risk a burnout. He'd seen what happened when an alpha or a healer used too much without recharging. If there wasn't another magic user around, burning out was a guaranteed death sentence.

Salidus pushed the mud behind him back into place, but he was still surrounded by silty water and moist dirt, all of it pressing down and threatening to suffocate him. He continued digging upward until the soil became drier, and with the very last shreds of his magic, he created a small, densely packed air pocket around his snout. He shuddered and let out a low moan of pain as his skin warmed, then burned, then blistered. He was out of magic and out of time.

Salidus finally stopped, immobile from that horrible burning sensation as well as the densely packed earth around him. As long as that air pocket remained useable, he could breathe, but the knowledge that he had buried himself alive almost sent him into an incoherent state of panic.

Need to recharge. . . Need to. . .

Salidus's eyes clouded over white, covering all trace of his blue irises and black scleras, and his trembling, scalding body went still as he slipped into the recharge space that lay hidden beneath his consciousness. He lost all awareness of the world around him, of the situation he was in, of his burning agony. And just four besosopions above him, directly over his head, the human vehicles rumbled past, continuing their search of the river and the surrounding woods.

XX

Tyson stood at the bottom of the attic stairs, staring up at the door and breathing heavily through his nose. He hadn't come this close since Ornathium's arrival, and just the thought of climbing the flight to the alien made his gut churn with terror. His hands moved without command, pulling out the length of yarn that was in his shorts pocket. His fingers flew deftly over the string in an action of pure muscle memory.

Knot, unwind. Slipknot, pull. Bellringer, pull. Bellringer, sheepshank, pull-pull.

It was soothing and lightly distracting, and he found his nerves gradually calming down. He couldn't *not* do this. Layla certainly wasn't going to ask Ornathium the questions that needed to be asked, and telling their parents would be a disaster, so he was the only one who could do what needed to be done. Tyson lifted one foot, then planted it on the first step. He stood there, frozen, waiting for some terrible reckoning, but when nothing happened, he exhaled in relief and ascended the stairs. Just before reaching the top, however, he stopped again and looked over his shoulder, half-hoping that one of his parents would come up and ask what he was doing, unknowingly putting a stop to his investigation. But he was alone.

Tyson gripped the handle and turned it, wincing at the creak that sounded when he pushed the door open. He peeked inside and saw Ornathium poking through a cardboard box. The Rhithien's ears perked up and he lifted his head with a smile, but his face fell when he saw Tyson.

"Why are you here?" he asked.

"It's my house," Tyson replied, aiming for a haughty, unbothered tone and failing miserably. Those gleaming red eyes scrutinized him, and when Ornathium seemed to decide that Tyson wasn't a threat, he returned his attention to the box, which looked to contain some old board games.

"I suppose it is," he conceded. "You fear me, though. I can smell it on you."

He can smell it?

Tyson's face paled and he instinctively took a step back. It was no more than a nonchalant comment, but the idea of this *thing* being able to smell his fear unnerved him. He was afraid of dogs and bears for the same reason. But he steeled himself and began the list of questions he had planned.

"Layla's been spending a lot of time up here. And whenever I talk to her, it's about you or that stupid book. What's the deal?"

"Perhaps she just wanted someone with whom she could converse freely," replied Ornathium with a shrug. "Your guess is as good as mine."

That stung.

She has me to talk to. I'm her friend, Tyson couldn't help thinking, but he quickly shook off the jealousy; he didn't come up here for a pity party.

"She already has plenty of friends," he lied, knowing damn well that Layla didn't have any more friends than he did. "She just thinks it's cool that you're an alien."

"What would be cold?"

Tyson blinked, then realized what he meant and irritably explained, "It's just a saying. When something's 'cool' it's neat or interesting. But Layla doesn't really want you as a friend. I know her better than anyone, and I know that she's just living in the middle of some alien fantasy where she discovers you and gets famous and rich off it. You know that, right?"

"Then why is she so passionate about your family history?" the Rhithien countered, raising an eyebrow.

"Your guess is as good as mine," Tyson said, snobbishly repeating Ornathium's earlier words. "But while we're on the subject, I've got something else to ask you about."

"Ask and I shall answer."

"She told me about our history. She also told me about Aurelia Lucio." When Ornathium's ears flicked and his jaw clenched, Tyson knew his sister's theory was correct. "That's right. I know all a-fucking-bout our ancestor's history. Aurelia killed one of your kind. You said you weren't supposed to end up here, but I think that was a lie. Layla's obviously convinced, but did you really think we would both believe that a Lucio killed a Rhithien and then your pack came to Nuncan—specifically to our house—by *accident?*"

Ornathium remained silent, so Tyson crossed his arms and demanded, "Well? You want to explain?"

That little tidbit had been bothering him since his sister first told him about it. It couldn't possibly be coincidental. No, these Rhithien were targeting their family; he was sure of it. They wanted something. But the worst part for him was that Layla didn't have so much as an inkling of suspicion about it. She trusted Ornathium with everything.

She's got a new best friend.

The realization had hurt when he'd first figured it out, but he had gotten over that sting by now. Mostly. Once Ornathium was out of the picture, everything would go back to normal. But for the time being, since his sister wasn't going to protect their family, the duty had fallen to Tyson.

"Alright," Ornathium said quietly. "You are correct. It was no accident."

"I knew it!" Tyson cried. Then his triumphant joy was squashed as he fully processed the implications of Ornathium's confirmation. The Rhithien really *were* targeting them. What would happen to their family? To Layla?

"Why?" he demanded, and he felt a surge of self-hatred for the warbling crack that edged into his voice. Were the Rhithien planning on killing them? Or worse, taking them back to their planet for torture or experimentation or whatever aliens did with humans?

Maybe we should just let the government get him, this is bad, this is sooo bad, we're all going to die, fuck shit bitch FUCK—

In his mind, he began rattling off every cuss word he knew. His yarn dropped from his shaking fingers onto the attic floor, but he didn't bend down to pick it up. He didn't want to lower his guard for a second. Then Ornathium spoke again, and his trembling stilled.

"Aurelia Lucio freed us."

What?

Tyson opened his mouth, closed it, and finally asked, "What do you mean?"

"Yes, she killed an ancient leader of ours. But this leader. . . He was a force unlike anything Primaied had seen. Utterly unstoppable. He won countless wars, conquered countless lands, and ruled over it all with devastating brutality. He called his lands kingdoms, but they were really prisons. Rhithien were called citizens, but at that time, they were slaves in all but name. He was a cruel, hateful king, with terrible punishments and laws that commanded execution or exile if

188

anyone breathed a single critical word about him. When the portals to Earth were discovered and he went through, everyone feared what would happen to your planet. But Aurelia Lucio—indeed, your ancestor—killed him. A mere human managed to dispatch the strongest and deadliest Rhithien warrior in our history."

Tyson was silent. He hadn't allowed himself to hope for luck like this, that these aliens were truly benevolent. Could Ornathium be telling the truth?

"Why didn't you just tell us that?" he cried, throwing his arms helplessly out to the sides. "Or at least tell Layla?"

"I did not lie about the portal failing. I truly was scattered from my pack, and I wanted to reunite with them before we revealed our purpose. Revealing ourselves is something that my race has worked toward for almost two thousand years, and I feared that if I told you everything, that reveal would happen while Primaied was unprepared. We've been very careful about studying your kind, you know."

"Oh," Tyson said in a small voice.

"Yes. And I am not the alpha of my pack, so I did not want to make any significant decisions alone. It is not my place to reveal my planet's secrets to any human."

"Have you considered that if everyone knew, we could help you find your pack?" Tyson suggested. He thought it was a good idea, but Ornathium shook his head.

"That is not an option. We were told to limit our human contact to Aurelia Lucio's descendants until we received other orders."

Tyson hesitated, then asked, "Why Layla?"

"What do you mean?"

"Why did you tell her everything? Are you targeting her specifically?"

"No," Ornathium assured him quickly. "Your parents do not know about me, and you fear me. She is the only one willing to speak to me at the moment. I am not trying to steal her from you. Please understand."

"I understand," Tyson said hollowly. Ornathium put his hands out like a peace offering and stepped forward with a hesitant smile, but Tyson backed away again, almost tripping down the stairs in his haste. He shook his head wildly and said, "That doesn't mean I wanna be friends."

"Very well," the Rhithien sighed. He returned to the box of board games and pulled out a battered old Monopoly set. He gave it a small frown and sniffed it as if cardboard was the most puzzling thing in the world. Tyson still didn't trust him, but he retreated down the steps anyway, closing the door behind him. Perhaps he'd misjudged the Rhithien.

"Tyson?"

Tyson gulped at the sight of Layla standing at the foot of the stairs. Her laptop was under one arm and the Lucio book was clutched against her chest. Her brows were drawn over narrowed eyes, and her mouth was pursed in tight suspicion.

"Hey," Tyson muttered, dropping his gaze and shuffling past her. He wasn't in the mood for another tense discussion. But Layla stepped in his path and leaned down to meet his eyes.

"What were you doing up there? You haven't gone up to the attic since he arrived."

"I only wanted to ask him some things. Nothing—"

"What kind of things?" Layla demanded.

"I just asked him why he was here and what he wanted. I'm sure he can tell you everything since you two are besties now," Tyson snapped. That last part was unnecessary, he knew, and guilt immediately washed over him when Layla recoiled, her shoulders slumping and her face falling. Tyson brushed by her and left her there on the stairs, and it wasn't until he was back in his room that he remembered he'd dropped his yarn up in the attic.

*****

Ornathium studied the wide, flat box in his hands. Beneath the layer of dust, a vaguely human-looking creature skipped across a bunch of squares bordered by colorful rectangles. He squinted at the runes written across the top as if he could actually read them, but quickly lost interest and gave up. He couldn't read human writing, although Salidus and the scholars had tried to teach him. He didn't even know how to read the majority of Rhithos runes. Ziiphan had shown him how to make his name, as well as numbers up to one hundred, but he didn't know much more than that.

Don't need to know anything else, he thought with a shrug, and set the box aside. He liked knowing how to make his name. He liked putting it on his prey's skin, as he had with that human in the woods. He'd written his runes all over that male's flesh.

190

He heard soft words outside the door and strained his ears to listen:

"What were you doing up there? You haven't gone up to the attic since he arrived."

"I only wanted to ask him some things. Nothing—"

"What kind of things?"

"I just asked him why he was here and what he wanted. I'm sure he can tell you everything since you two are besties now."

'Besties'? What is that?

Ornathium thought hard about it, then decided that it must be something good because of his closeness with Layla. Some variant on "friends" perhaps? He grinned and snickered to himself. The boy really *was* jealous!

The door suddenly burst open and Layla dashed in.

"Is everything okay? What did Tyson say to you? Was he an ass?" she demanded, the questions flowing from her mouth without pause as they always did. Ornathium had gotten used to her rapid speech patterns by now. Sometimes they annoyed him, but other times he found them amusing. Perhaps she was a friend to him, but she was hardly his *bestie.*

Ziiphan is my bestie. I don't need anyone else.

"Everything is alright. We had a good conversation," he replied when she at last slowed down enough for him to get a word in.

"Like what? What did you talk about?"

"Your brother is quite the interrogator," Ornathium commented with a chuckle, and he was pleased to see Layla throw a glare at the attic door. He knew she didn't want Tyson messing with him. To avoid suspicion he added, "He only wanted to know my purpose here. When you told him about your family history the other day, he took it very seriously. He suggested that we were specifically aiming for your house when we went through the portal."

"That's stupid!" Layla protested, alight with rage. Then she quieted down and said, "That *was* a coincidence, right?"

"Oh, yes," Ornathium lied. "Both of our worlds are smaller than you think. You probably have thousands of distant relatives all over Earth."

"Oh. Yeah, sure," Layla responded. She looked strangely downtrodden by the information.

Tch, if you think you can keep this up, boy. . . growled Kairen from the back of his mind. Ornathium quickly turned away from Layla so she wouldn't see his fear.

"I know I can't," he whispered.

"What was that?" asked Layla.

"Nothing. What have you found this time?" he inquired with a pleasant smile, gesturing to the book in her arms.

Look at you, sucking up to that stupid little bitch. Kairen laughed and added, *And to think; your pack first knew you as the Bloodhound of the Red Desert. Fucking pathetic.*

Ornathium knew he was pathetic. He knew. He wanted to inform Kairen that he didn't need reminding, that he already knew he was beneath other Rhithien, but Layla happily scampered over, sat beside him on the floor, and opened the thick book.

"It's actually super interesting," the girl chattered cheerfully. "In 1824, Ramsey Lucio started the butter company Silky 'N Smooth! My parents buy that shit from Grader's all the time! Isn't that neat?"

Ornathium didn't know what "Grader's" was, nor had he ever heard of "butter" before, but Kairen was being too loud. He wouldn't be able to concentrate on the answer if he asked what those words meant, so he simply smiled and nodded.

"Very *cool,*" he said, mimicking the way Tyson had spoken the word earlier. He was slightly disappointed when Layla didn't notice his use of the peculiar term, but he didn't stop her as she continued.

"Yeah! Anyway, these things get longer and longer as they get closer to modern times. Like, it talks about how this Ramsey guy had four wives and thirty-three kids! That's insane! It also says that he bred some type of Russian hunting dog called a. . . a 'borzoi'? I don't know if I'm pronouncing that right, but I looked it up and it's kind of weird-looking."

"Mm-hm," Ornathium hummed with false interest.

You told the boy half-truths, but you've fed the girl nothing but weak lies that will be torn down if she speaks to her brother about it. How do you plan on getting yourself out of this one? Any Rhithien stupid enough to get himself twisted into shitholes like this doesn't deserve to live. Why does your pack even keep you around?

As much as Ornathium resented Kairen, the older Rhithien had a point. How would he get out of this?

Wait, I'm meeting Aremaeid tonight!

Of course! He had completely forgotten about his packmate! Tonight they would meet in the field and move on to find the rest of their pack. The fake smile he was directing at Layla's book gradually stretched and took on genuine excitement as a plan began to form in his mind. He knew what he had to do.

"Layla," he interrupted while she was in the middle of a rant about someone named Marco Lucio, "I have a request."

"Yeah?"

"We are friends, yes?"

"Duh! Hell yeah, we're friends! I've always wanted an alien as a friend," Layla answered enthusiastically. Ornathium smiled. It was perfect.

"And you trust me? You trust my judgment?"

"Sure!"

"In that case..." He paused, allowing her a moment to tremble with tension. "I think it is time I was introduced to your parents."

XXI

Layla stared at her reflection in the mirror. Her cheeks were flushed pink with excitement and her eyes glittered with joy.

"It is time I was introduced to your parents."

At last. At long, long last, she could give up the sneaking around and the secretive chats in the attic, switching instead to parties, interviews, and fame. Most likely. She wasn't totally sure how all that stuff worked, but she'd known for a long time that she wanted to be famous and rich, and now was as good an opportunity as any to make that happen.

"You will be a queen," she said firmly to her reflection, and she smiled at the thought. She'd questioned Ornathium's idea at first, thinking that it could be dangerous if people knew about him—if the *government* knew more about him—but he'd convinced her that it was time. And, after a few hours of speculation, she decided he was right. She would be the next Aurelia Lucio, but better; she would be the girl who not only discovered but also befriended alien life. And no one could take that away from her.

"Layla!" her mother called from the first floor. "Finish up in there and come down. Dinner's ready."

"Coming!" Layla shouted back. She gave herself a final once-over in the mirror before heading downstairs to join her family. She slid into her usual spot at the table, which, unfortunately, happened to be directly across from Tyson. She glanced up and met his eyes, but he immediately dropped his gaze to his plate. Layla understood; she could feel the same ball of tension in her gut. Maybe she shouldn't have pushed him so hard on the stairs, but what he said had really hurt.

"I'm sure he can tell you everything since you two are besties now."

Yes, she had a new friend, but that didn't mean she was giving up Tyson. Did he really think she wanted that? He was her brother and had been her only friend for years. If she'd been forced to choose between him and Ornathium, it might have been a problem—after all, aliens didn't just fall into one's attic every day—but that obviously wasn't the case. Ornathium was good. He wouldn't hurt anyone.

I was in such a great mood, too. Of course Tyson would ruin it.

Her father glanced at them, taking in their mutual sullen silence, then gave his wife a knowing look.

"I've got a fun story from work that I think will put some smiles on a couple of faces here," he said in a mischievous tone.

"I think a few of us could use some smiles," Catherine commented. She wore the same look as her husband; it was the look of someone who was about to reveal a fun surprise. The look of a parent who thought they'd figured out how to be cool. Layla knew it couldn't be *that* interesting, though. It was just a story from her dad's work. There was nothing interesting about a bank.

"Whatever," muttered Tyson, poking at his food with his fork and obviously sharing the same sentiment. Their father was undeterred by his mood.

"This guy came in with a seeing-eye dog today. A big ol' German Shepherd, almost completely black, with the happiest face I'd ever seen on an animal. Gorgeous dog."

"What was the guy doing at the bank?" Layla asked, trying to keep the conversation going. She didn't have a very clear understanding of what went on at her father's workplace, but she liked dog stories.

"Deposit. I helped him fill out a slip."

"Was he able to sign his name?" her mother inquired, and he nodded.

"What was the dog's name?" Tyson asked. Their father grinned.

"That's the best part. His name was Donkey, but he only responded to it when his owner shouted it with a Scottish accent. *'Donkey!'*"

Layla burst out laughing, remembered she had food in her mouth, and quickly brought a hand to her face to smother her giggles. Who named their dog *Donkey*? She hadn't seen this blind guy, but she could already guess what his favorite movie was.

"That's stupid," Tyson said critically. Their mother sighed exasperatedly.

"*You're* stupid," Layla shot back, and Tyson gave her an injured look. She immediately felt bad, but she didn't take the insult back. He shouldn't have been a prick on the attic stairs.

"Woah!" exclaimed their mother, putting both her hands up and leaning back in her chair. "Where did that come from? Both of you?"

When neither of her kids answered, she shook her head and rolled her eyes. "I swear, you two have been acting weird all week. What is going on?"

Layla and Tyson exchanged a glance, each daring the other to tell the truth. Was it the right time? Layla decided it was and opened her mouth to speak, but her father, probably anticipating an argument, interrupted with a swift change of subject.

"Apparently some guy was mauled to death by a bear last night up near Silver Creek Trail. Park Rangers found his dog hiding under his truck. It was hurt, but not too badly. The guy's dead, though. Willard Hayes was his name."

"Dennis," Layla's mother said sharply. "They don't need to hear about that."

"Are they sure it was a bear?" Tyson asked nervously. He and Layla shared a grim look. Their father shrugged as he forked a bite of food into his mouth.

"That's what the news said. Rangers figured a bear's the only thing big enough to inflict the damage they saw. They're not sure if he was dragged up there or if he went on his own, though. There're no marked trails that lead to that field, they say. But according to some of Willard's drinking buddies, he had a habit of going off-trail with his dog, although he never ran into trouble until now. Bears don't like loud noises, and Willard always made sure to talk out loud or bring little bells."

"It could have been a mountain lion," Layla suggested, but her father shook his head.

"It's like I said, according to an interview with the park ranger who found the body, only a bear could be big enough to make the wounds they found on him."

"They don't need to hear about that, Dennis," Layla's mother insisted. "Why are you telling them this?"

"I remember what it's like to be a kid," her husband replied, and he gave Layla a knowing look. "Sometimes it's fun to go hang out with your friends in the woods, or at a secret meeting spot. I just want you guys to be more careful out there from now on, alright?"

"Dad, neither of us has any friends," Layla said with a laugh.

"Maisie Arberon is your friend, isn't she?"

"Yeah, but she's a grown-up. I mean friends my age."

As dinner continued, conversation started to come easier, and the tension between Layla and Tyson thinned. Their parents finished their meals first, and Layla finished hers while they cleared their dishes. It was pork roast tonight, and because Tyson wasn't a fan of pork, he was still eating when Layla stood and hesitantly said, "Mom? Dad?"

"What is it, honey?" her mother called from the sink.

"There's something I need to show you. Up in the attic," she blurted, hurrying to get the words out before she could change her mind. A ball of anxiety settled in her belly, and she wrung her hands. Why was she so afraid all of a sudden? She couldn't seriously be thinking of backing out, could she?

Only I can make my dreams come true, she reminded herself. Then Tyson's chair screeched across the floor and he bolted to his feet, startling Layla with the noise.

"No, there's *not,*" he said sharply, giving her an alarmed look. Then he leaned over the table and hissed, "What are you *doing?*"

"I'm telling them the truth," Layla whispered back. She turned back to her parents and said, "Follow me."

Her parents looked at each other with raised eyebrows and amused half-smiles, and Layla felt a spark of annoyance in the fact that they weren't taking her seriously. Didn't they want to see Ornathium?

"No, *don't* follow her!" Tyson yelled, stomping over to Layla and pushing her roughly. She caught herself on the edge of the table. Her parents cried out with alarm, but she and her brother both ignored them. "You can't keep listening to him, Layla, he's dangerous! He's going to hurt them!"

"No, he's not! You talked to him earlier today! You know he's not going to hurt anyone! You don't even know him!"

"Maybe you don't know him as well as you think you do!" her brother insisted. "Why can't you see that?"

"Shut up!" she snarled. Her parents suddenly intervened, pulling the two squabbling siblings apart.

"That's enough," Catherine said sharply. "What are you two talking about? Who's up in the attic?"

"He's my friend," Layla said before Tyson could get a word in. "And he really wants to meet you! Please come up and see him." Her parents exchanged a dark, wary look, and Layla gave her brother a triumphant smirk. He glared at her, and the expression was full of such a volatile mixture of rage and fear that a part of Layla wanted to crawl under the table and hide.

"Catherine, call 9-1-1," her father said. "I'll check it out. You three stay down here."

"No, he said he wants to see all of us," Layla insisted.

"That's not a good idea. If there's someone in our house—"

"No, he's good! He's been here for a week and hasn't caused any trouble."

When her parents' faces paled, she realized how it sounded and added, "He's a space alien."

Her parents stared at her, then at each other, then both burst out with relieved, airy laughter. Layla scowled at their mirth. Why couldn't they see how important this was? Why didn't they believe her? Tyson also looked relieved, and Layla hated him for it. She *hated* him. It was such a deep, dark feeling that it scared her, but she remained hopeful her parents would see reason.

"Alright," Dennis said at last, smothering his final chuckles. "All of you just stay behind me, though, 'kay?"

"Sure thing, hon," Catherine replied.

"Wait, we aren't actually—" began Tyson, but their mother guided him and Layla out of the dining room and up the stairs. The four of them reached the second floor and headed for the steps leading to the attic. Layla tried to meet Tyson's eyes if only to let him know that it was going to be alright. He wouldn't look at her. She tried lightly poking his arm, but he shrank away, clinging to their mother. A worm of guilt wriggled into her heart, and she let out a small, defeated sigh as she ascended the stairs behind her father. Oh, well. Tyson was upset now, but he would forgive her eventually. As soon as he saw that nothing bad would come of this endeavor, everything would clear up.

They all held their breath as Dennis twisted the knob and delicately opened the door. He stood on the top step for a moment, blocking Layla's view of the attic, then turned and asked, "Where's your friend, Layla?"

What?

She shoved past her father and ran into the small, dusty space. She saw the old throne chair she liked, as well as the rest of the unused furniture, but

Ornathium was nowhere to be found. Why would he leave now? They agreed that he would meet her parents tonight, hadn't they?

"I. . . We. . . He was supposed to be here!" Layla cried, running a hand through her hair and desperately looking around. She turned back to see that Tyson and her parents had all entered the attic, and they were checking the space as avidly as she was. Tyson's face paled and his lower lip trembled. For a single moment, his eyes met Layla's, and they shared a mutual sense of unearthly dread. Then the door swung shut, and Layla saw that Ornathium had been crouched behind it. When it finally closed with a click, her family whirled around in time to see the Rhithien rise to his full height.

"Ornathium—" Layla began, but his lips peeled back from his teeth in a menacing grin, and without a word, he grabbed her father's shoulders and bit into his head. Blood sprayed across the room, bone crunched, and Layla could only stand there, frozen, staring at her father as Ornathium allowed him to fall lifelessly to the ground. Her mother screamed, her hands flying up to the blood splattered across her face.

"Mom—" Layla started to say, but she stopped when Ornathium grabbed her mother by the neck and flung her across the room like a doll. She crashed into a stack of boxes, which all tumbled down onto her limp form.

That finally snapped Layla out of her shock. Forgetting the fight at the dinner table, she grabbed Tyson's arm and bolted for the door, trying to skirt around Ornathium, but he stepped in front of them and shoved her back. She smacked into her brother and sent them both tumbling onto the floor.

"What are you—" she tried again, but the Rhithien's laugh cut her off.

"You were just too easy," he cooed. He dropped down to all fours and prowled toward them both. The two siblings scrambled back, crying and clinging to each other, and the Rhithien stopped just a few feet away.

"Rhala was strong. Just," he said softly, addressing Tyson. "He was not the cruel king I said he was. He was the only ruler we Rhithien ever had, but if there were others, none would have compared to him. So you can thank your ancestor for this."

"Leave us alone!" Tyson screamed.

"Perhaps I could. I only need one of you."

He grabbed Tyson's leg and yanked him forward, tearing him out of Layla's arms. Pure, selfish survival instinct kicked in, and she crawled away from them to hide behind the throne chair. There was a scream, the sound of flesh stretching and ripping, and then something warm and heavy was thrown toward her. It landed on her back and rolled across the floor, and Layla almost vomited at the sight of Tyson's head staring up at her, his face contorted in a permanent visage of blind terror. A low moan ripped from her throat, building to a loud, sobbing scream. She hovered her hands helplessly over his bloody face, tears flowing freely down her cheeks. Her head snapped up at the thudding of approaching footsteps, and she scuttled backward to put distance between herself and Ornathium.

"Get away!" she sobbed. "Get away from me!"

He stalked toward her, grabbed the large armchair, and knocked it onto its side. It landed on her and pushed the air from her lungs in one big *whoosh*. Ornathium sauntered over as she struggled beneath its weight, and when he finally stopped at her side, he lowered himself to a crouch and stared thoughtfully down at her with his usual pleasant smile.

"Y-You. . . You *lied* to me!" she cried.

"Yes."

"W-Why?"

"I needed to find my pack," he replied with a shrug. "It was pure luck that I managed to find your family, and until I reunited with the others, I could not allow you to slip from my grasp."

He rose and planted one large foot atop the chair, pressing his weight down on it until Layla was wheezing and gasping in pain. Then, just as she felt her ribs begin to strain, Ornathium removed the pressure and shoved the chair off her. She curled up on the ground, sobbing hysterically, and tried to wipe her father's blood off her face, though she only succeeded in smearing it. She could hardly breathe. Her heart felt as though it had been shredded. She couldn't think. The only images that appeared in the forefront of her mind, blocking out all else, were the faces of her family. The whole thing felt surreal, like a terrible nightmare that, if she tried hard enough, she could awake from, chilled with sweat beneath her blankets. But she did not wake up. There was no waking from this.

The Rhithien knelt down, grabbed her chin with one hand, and forcefully turned her tear-streaked face up to look at him.

"Don't touch me, don't. . . don't. . ." she sobbed, and Ornathium gave her a fond smile.

"You had better run, little queen," he crooned. "I offer you a head start. I suggest you take it." He released her, stood, and stepped away. Layla gaped up at him, bewildered. An incessant buzzing filled her ears. Her mom's scream echoed around her head, and the crunch of teeth bludgeoning through her father's skull hammered at her temples over and over again. She didn't comprehend Ornathium's words until he began to count: "One hundred, ninety-nine, ninety-eight. . ."

Layla scrambled to her feet and fled.

She sprinted from the attic. Her socks slipped suddenly in a puddle of blood. Her body fell forward, her limbs tangling as she tumbled down the steps and crashed painfully onto the floor. She cried out, but pushed herself back up and continued running.

She ran down the hallway and past her room. The Lucio book sat undisturbed beside her laptop, which was open to the copy that she had recently finished.

She ran down the stairs to the first floor. She didn't dare glance at the dirty plates on the kitchen table as she passed.

She ran past the basement steps and through the entryway hall until she slammed into the front door. Her hands shook uncontrollably and refused to grasp the handle. It took her a few tries to open it, but when she finally did, she bolted from the house. She didn't even grab a pair of shoes. She ran as fast and as far as she could from the blood, the bodies, and the monster in her attic.

*****

Ornathium watched from the small attic window as Layla fled the house. Even from this distance, he could see that she was a pathetic, trembling mess of tears, covered in blood that wasn't her own. He heard a whimper behind him and turned to see the mother weeping over her mate's body. A sadistic grin spread across his face, and he prowled over to where she sat. He knelt behind her, and when she turned to look at him, he grabbed her by the hair and shoved her forcefully to the ground.

. . . *sixty-seven, sixty-six, sixty-five*. . .

He had some time to play with this one.

The female closed her eyes and turned her head away with a wordless, animalistic plea of terror. Ornathium grabbed her jaw and turned her face upwards.

"Open your eyes, little human," he crooned. When she didn't comply, he dug his claws into her cheeks until scarlet blood dripped across her skin. Only then did she finally open her eyes.

"What do you want?" she begged, her blunt fingernails scraping uselessly at his hand. Ornathium smiled and leaned down until their faces were just a finger's length apart.

"I want you to scream," he whispered. Then, while still gripping her face with one hand, he dug his claws deep into her torso and raked them slowly downward. Each spasm of her frail body, each bloody scream that tore from her lips. . . It was ecstasy that Ornathium could never find anywhere else.

Pain like this was the one thing in the world that quieted Kairen's voice.

Ornathium ripped his claws out, tearing free chunks of muscle and sprays of blood, and as the female lay on the floor, shuddering and bleeding, he leaned down to whisper in her ear.

"Your daughter is going to be part of something beautiful," he promised, tilting her chin back and grazing his teeth tauntingly over her soft, vulnerable neck. "She will serve a very important purpose for my planet in the years to come. Unfortunately, I will be expected to keep her alive much longer than I normally would."

"Please. . ." the female managed, but blood bubbled up out of her mouth, choking away any other parting words she might have given him.

"Thank you," Ornathium said softly. He watched with a pleasant smile as she seized again and released a final, gurgling breath. The glimmer of life disappeared from her face, but he remained poised over her until the pale pink hues faded from her cheeks. Then he stood and closed his eyes, basking in the death around him. He thought of Kairen, of those red irises that were so like his own, and a single tear of relief slipped down his face. The older Rhithien was silent, at least for a brief time. He liked killing. He liked watching Ornathium kill. It was the only thing that seemed to pacify him.

"This gift is for you, father."

. . . three, two, one.

Ornathium opened his eyes, strode away from the bodies, and descended the stairs, following Layla's scent through the house. The smile on his face twisted into one of maniacal glee, and he softly purred, "Run as far as you can, little queen. Make this hunt an interesting one."

XXII

Maisie sat at her kitchen counter with a mug of coffee, a bowl of crackers, and a small pile of quizzes. She was the type of teacher who only gave out tests at the end of the week, thinking it unfair to schedule them on Monday. After all, it was a universal fact that the weekend had a magical way of making students unlearn information. Unfortunately, nearly a third of every class had been gone for the quiz due to a sporting event. She wasn't sure exactly what that event was; she'd heard conflicting reports. Some claimed it was a soccer game, others said tennis—although she wasn't sure Fairview even had tennis—and a small handful of others declared lacrosse. Her working theory was that they had coordinated a mass skipping day.

It was her normal dinner time, and she'd fed Roller accordingly, but she was too tired to cook for herself. She'd woken up that morning exhausted and had taken a short nap, but that seemed to only increase her weariness. She'd tried cleaning her kitchen to wake herself up, but the only things she had the energy for were sweeping the floor and wiping down the counter, so she finally resorted to grading with coffee and crackers as a substitute supper. It wasn't much, but putting something in her stomach helped clear her head just enough to focus on the chicken scratch her students had given her.

"Maisie."

She turned around and was almost startled out of her chair. Aremaeid loomed just a few feet away.

"I told you not to sneak like that," she muttered, turning back to the quizzes. She was almost grateful for the Rhithien's interference, though. The answers on the current test did not bode well for its corresponding student. It was the sort of score that was so bad it was almost intentional, and she always hated handing out those low grades.

"I must speak with you," Aremaeid pressed, apparently oblivious to her easily triggered anxiety.

"Is it important, or are you petitioning to get rid of the vacuum again?"

"It is important."

"Alright," Maisie said with a sigh, hopping off the chair and moving into the living room. "Let's talk in here. What's going on?"

She took her coffee with her—she knew it was late, but she was preparing for another long night—and sat down on the recliner beside the couch. Aremaeid took a seat on the sofa with a small, huffy sigh, and Roller hopped up beside him. The couch creaked beneath his bulk but, thankfully, did not break. He regarded Maisie for a moment before speaking.

"You recall that I found one of my packmates last night?"

"Yeah." Maisie nodded and took a sip of her coffee.

"I will be leaving again to meet him soon."

"Okay. You don't have to tell me when you do that, you know."

"I will not be returning."

"Oh." So the time had finally arrived. Maisie frowned and asked, "Why didn't you leave last night?"

"I have already told you."

"I forgot."

"He said he had business to take care of. I know not what it is," explained Aremaeid. "I . . . I wanted to thank you."

"For?"

"For allowing me to stay here. And for keeping my presence a secret."

Maisie stared at him. When he'd arrived, he had tried to kill her and subsequently threatened her into letting him stay in the basement. Since then he'd spent the last week lurking around the house, coming and going whenever he pleased and not paying a single dime of rent, so she hadn't honestly expected a concise thank you.

"Well, we had a bit of a rocky start," she responded slowly, "but overall, I've had worse roommates. Are you ever coming back to Earth?"

"Possibly," Aremaeid admitted, and she heard a note of discomfort in his voice that managed to slip past his mask of indifference. "Although I doubt you and I will ever cross paths again. My one request is that you keep everything I have told you about my planet to yourself."

"No problem there," Maisie said with a dry laugh. "The only people who would believe me aren't the kind of folks I want to get involved with."

"Probably for the best."

"Yeah. And hey, if you're ever in town again. . ."

"You would. . . allow me here?"

"Well, I'd much prefer if you went somewhere else, but if you really don't have anywhere else to go, just. . . knock. Or come in. The back door may or may not be open."

Aremaeid let out a short exhale through his nose that almost sounded like laughter. Maisie smiled and took another sip of her coffee, but she nearly choked on it when a scream ripped through the quiet tranquility of the evening. The two of them were immediately on their feet, and Maisie raced toward her kitchen window. The sound had come from outside. It was faint, but after a few seconds, she heard it again.

"Oh, God," she murmured, putting a hand to her mouth. She glanced at Aremaeid, whose whole body was stiff with tension. She jerked her head at the basement stairs and he was instantly gone, ghosting across the floor and disappearing in a matter of seconds. She turned her attention back to the window and peered out, looking for any unusual activity and reaching for the landline to call 9-1-1. She suddenly stopped, her hand hovering over the phone. Was it really an emergency?

Could be those kids in the blue house at the end of the block. They play in the street sometimes.

But that scream had been one of genuine, blood-chilling horror. In almost ten years of teaching, she had never heard children scream like that while playing. If there was a problem, surely someone else had already called the police? She stood frozen for close to an entire minute, chewing her lip until she tasted blood, debating the odds of whether the police would be necessary. She finally snapped out of her stupor and grabbed the phone, but was interrupted by a loud, desperate rapping on her door. She yelped, startled, and dropped the phone, letting it bounce off the cradle and onto the counter. Her doorbell rang five times in rapid succession, then the knocking resumed.

"Maisie! Miss Arberon!" yelled a familiar voice.

Maisie rushed to the door and threw it open to see Layla Lucio standing on the front porch. She didn't get a good look at her before the girl rushed into the house, almost knocking her over in her haste.

"Layla, what—"

"*Close the door!*" Layla shrieked, and Maisie shut it without question, locking it and sliding the deadbolt into place. She backed away from it as if it was a live bomb, then glanced over her shoulder to ensure that Aremaeid hadn't emerged. She was granted a small shred of relief when she saw that he was safely out of sight. Then, when she turned around to address Layla, her words caught in her throat. The girl's face was streaked with tears and what looked like streaks of blood, and her eyes held a primal, animalistic terror that Maisie had never seen in another person. She hurriedly guided Layla to the couch.

"I need you to tell me what happened, honey," she instructed calmly, assuming her teacher persona. Layla only cried hysterically and wrapped her skinny arms around Maisie's waist. Wracking sobs shook her thin frame. "Layla, I—" Maisie tried again, but she was quickly interrupted.

"Th-they're—Th-Th-They're a-all, they're a-a-all—" Layla was unable to get more than those two words out before the hyperventilating began. She clutched at her chest with both hands and gasped desperately for air. Maisie shushed her and gently patted her back.

"Honey, I need you to breathe."

"I-I can't, I c-c-can't, I—"

"I need you to try, okay? In. . . and out." She took a slow, deep breath herself to try and guide Layla through it, but it didn't seem to be working.

"I-I-I. . . H-He. . ."

"Layla, I need you to tell me what happened. I need you to talk to me. Do you need me to call the police?"

"It wasn't my fault!" Layla cried suddenly. She gripped Maisie's shirt with fierce desperation and frantically insisted, "I swear I-I didn't know what was—I thought he was—It wasn't my fault!"

"It's okay. I believe you. I know it wasn't your fault. But you have to tell me what happened, honey."

"I should have told you," she whimpered. "God, I should have told you last week. Remember that big light and the noise that woke everyone up? It was aliens, and I let one stay in my house, and I thought he was my friend, but he—he—"

"What did he do?" Maisie urged. Was it another one of Aremaeid's packmates? It had to be. As if on cue, she glanced over Layla's head and saw Aremaeid edging up the stairs, warily watching them with those sharp golden eyes. She waved him away, and he reluctantly slunk back down.

If he had anything to do with whatever's happened. . .

"My m-mom," Layla choked out through hiccupping sobs. "M-my dad. . . T-T-Tyson. . ." She let out a low, despairing whine and swiped her hands across her face. When smears of sticky blood came off on her palms, she cried harder and wiped them on her pants. Maisie gripped her shoulders and leaned down to meet her eyes, hoping that a more direct approach would get some coherent answers.

"What happened, Layla?"

"He. . . He killed them."

No. He said. . .

Maisie released Layla, who doubled over and continued to cry.

Aremaeid had lied to her. She wished more than anything that she could say she wasn't surprised. He'd told her that they weren't here to hurt anyone, that it was just a simple reconnaissance mission, that they had never planned to let a single human see them. One thought ran on a loop through Maisie's head, a common prank that she'd seen in the halls of school whilst growing up:

Did you see that the word 'gullible' is written on the ceiling?

"Aremaeid, could you come up here?" Maisie called, and Layla looked up at her, confusion contorting her features.

"Who's Aremaeid?" she asked, and Maisie nodded at the stairs as the Rhithien hesitantly emerged. Layla's eyes bulged and her mouth dropped open at the sight of him. Maisie looked him in the eye, letting all of her newfound outrage and disgust show on her face, and his ears flattened guiltily against his head.

Layla screamed and leaped off the couch. She crashed into the coffee table, collapsed to the floor, and skittered backward on all fours like a crab.

"Layla, I can explain—"

"You knew about them?" she shrieked.

Maisie flinched.

"Yes," she admitted. "But I didn't know they were going to hurt anyone. I didn't know they were going to hurt your family."

The last sentence made Layla break down again, and Maisie glared hatefully at Aremaeid, who remained awkwardly at the top of the stairs. He stretched a hand toward her and spoke.

"Maisie—"

"I don't want to hear it. I want you out of my house," she snapped, wrapping her arms around Layla and pulling her into a comforting hug.

Aremaeid's frill drooped and his arm fell to his side.

Good. I hope he feels like shit.

That was when, with a tremendous *crash,* the front door blew inward off its hinges, smashing over the kitchen counter and onto the floor. Ducking through the doorway was another Rhithien, this one with gleaming crimson eyes and pitch-black skin. His gaze was locked on Layla, and his muscled body seemed to vibrate with excited, hungry energy. If he noticed Aremaeid, he didn't show it. Roller began barking at him, and the Rhithien spared the dog little more than a glance before kicking him easily across the room. Roller let out a yip of pain as he slammed into the wall beside the fireplace and fell limply to the floor. Maisie cried out in alarm and moved to help her dog, but stayed where she was when she remembered that she needed to take care of Layla.

"You have something of mine," the Rhithien gloated as he stalked toward them.

"Don't you touch her," Maisie hissed, throwing her arms out protectively to the sides.

The Rhithien grabbed her shirt collar tight in his claws and, in one effortless motion, threw her across the room. Maisie crashed into the recliner, toppling it with her weight. The wind rushed out of her lungs as she hit the floor. She lay there, gasping, as the Rhithien prowled closer. She tried to push herself up, but he bent down, grabbed her by the neck, and lifted her to his eye level, which left her dangling three feet off the ground. Her gaze flickered to Layla, who was curled up in a trembling ball on the floor and clutching the leg of the coffee table.

"You cannot fight this," the Rhithien purred. "And neither can any other human on your planet."

Maisie's vision began to go dark around the edges. Her heartbeat thundered in her temples. Pain pulsed through her entire body. Fire filled her lungs as she clawed feebly at his hand. She couldn't breathe.

Then Aremaeid was there, his fist slamming into the other Rhithien's face, and Maisie finally inhaled with a tremendous gasp as the hand around her throat disappeared. She fell to the floor, smacked her head on one leg of the overturned recliner, and everything went dark.

*****

"What do you think you're doing?" Ornathium snarled, switching from English to Rhithos. Aremaeid glanced down at Maisie, who lay unmoving on the floor, her face pale and her breathing shallow. Had he intervened in time? Would she live?

"Leave this one," he growled. "She is of no importance. What are you doing with that thing?" He jerked his head at the child, who was still crying and clinging to the table. Ornathium gave him a confident grin and lifted his chin, looking tall and smug despite his smaller stature.

"That thing is Layla Lucio, the descendent of Aurelia Lucio. The reason we came to this planet in the first place, remember?"

"How in Callii's name did you find her?"

"I didn't have to. When we were scattered, I ended up inside her house," Ornathium explained, puffing up with pride. Aremaeid glanced back at the girl, Layla, and felt a surge of pity for her. The poor thing had no control over who her ancestors were, and she had no notion of the role she was meant to play for Primaied's future. He felt the need to lower his voice, even though she couldn't understand a word they were saying.

"Do you have any idea of the trouble you could have caused, wandering around the streets in broad daylight for any human to see?" he hissed. Ornathium's face twisted into a scowl.

"A bit of gratitude would be appreciated, Aremaeid. I just completed our entire mission on my own by securing the Lucio heir. So how about this: instead of wasting our time arguing about inconsequential things such as showing ourselves in front of a few humans, why don't we grab the girl, leave the area, and find our pack?"

"Very well," Aremaeid growled. "But you're carrying her. It's time we left this place, anyway."

"What are we waiting for?" Ornathium agreed. He brushed past Aremaeid and knelt to scoop the girl up. When Layla kicked and screamed, he yanked on her hair and, switching back to English, snarled in her face, "Shut your mouth, or I will pry your teeth from your skull."

This quieted Layla's struggle, though she still sniffed and trembled. Aremaeid gave Maisie a final glance and cringed at the sight of her limp body splayed out on the floor. Dark purple bruises had already begun to form on her slender neck where Ornathium choked her, and Aremaeid silently prayed that she would survive. He knew that one way or another, she would have to die in the future, but he wanted no part in it when that time came. Without another word, the two Rhithien fled from Maisie's house, Layla trapped in Ornathium's arms. They now had only to reunite with the rest of their packmates, and then the plan would finally come to fruition.

XXIII

Burt Rhubarb was tending to the freshly bloomed daffodils outside his wide living room window when he heard the screams. They were coming from the direction of the Lucio house. Instinctually, he shuffled away from the window as fast as his arthritis would allow and pressed himself against the wall, hoping to look inconspicuous to whomever or whatever was the cause of that screaming. He stayed there for close to a minute, heart pounding and jowls quivering as he waited for the terrifying noises outside to die down.

Crash!

He flinched, and when he finally gathered the courage to go back to the window, he saw that the front door of the house a few places down from him was gone. He didn't know a lot about the red-haired woman who lived there, but he would be damned if he was going to let someone get away with burglary or worse.

Burt ran to his basement and crouched in front of the safe in which he kept his guns and a copy of his will. He grabbed his old rifle, hobbled back upstairs, and threw on a robe before rushing outside. He hurried across the street toward the redhead's house, dread growing in his heart with every step. He realized as he reached the place that he should have called the police, but resolved to do so once he knew what the problem was.

Just as he reached the cracked doorframe, he heard glass break in the back of the house, and he almost soiled himself at the sudden sound. Despite his fear, he continued onward. He took a single hesitant step inside and peered around, clutching his rifle to his chest like his life depended on it.

"Ma'am?" he called, moving slowly past the entryway. To his immediate left was a small kitchen, and to his right looked to be a living room. "It's Burt Rhubarb, from down the street. Everything alright in here?"

He knew for a fact that it was not alright, and as he turned to inspect the living room, he gasped at the sight of the redhead lying motionless beside a toppled recliner. He rushed to her side and knelt down, grimacing as his joints popped again. The woman's face was frighteningly pale, and Burt almost threw up at the sight of a small stain of blood on the chair leg beside her head. He grabbed her wrist to check her pulse and sighed in relief when he felt steady thumping against his fingers. When he looked closer, he could see that her chest rose and fell in shallow breaths. He stood, shuffled to the kitchen, grabbed her landline phone, and dialed 9-1-1 while keeping a worried gaze trained on the redhead.

"9-1-1, what's your emergency?"

"This is Burt Rhubarb. You gots to come quick, one of my neighbors is hurt bad."

*****

Maisie opened her eyes only to immediately squint them shut again against the hazy glow of fluorescent lights. She lifted a hand to ward off the brightness and saw a thin IV needle protruding from her arm. She peered at it for a second, then turned to her right, where she could hear a faint, repetitive beeping. She stared dumbly at an EKG machine that stood beside her bed, and it slowly dawned on her that she was in a hospital.

Sorely sitting up and leaning back against the pillow, she examined her surroundings, sighing in relief when she saw Franklin. He slept in a chair beside her, leaning on the bed with his head atop his arms.

"Franklin," Maisie whispered, and she winced at the painful hoarseness of her voice. She clutched her throat gingerly to check for damage. Tender bruises lanced under her fingers, and she gasped as everything came rushing back.

She grabbed Franklin's arm and shook him, fiercely wheezing, "Franklin!" as loud as she could. Franklin snorted and jerked his head up.

"Maisie, thank God!" he cried, grabbing her face and kissing her.

Maisie allowed it for a few seconds, then pulled away and gripped his shoulders.

"She's in danger!" she rasped. She doubled over with a fit of hacking coughs before she could say more. A tight, painful dryness raked her throat as if she'd swallowed glass. Her head hammered with a soreness that felt like it reached all the way to the center of her brain.

213

"Maisie, what are you talking about? Who's in danger?" Franklin asked with a frown. Before she could answer, the door opened and a portly nurse with a pinched, unhappy expression entered the room. She perked an eyebrow to see Maisie awake and quickly shooed Franklin away so she could fuss over her patient. Maisie considered pleading her case to the nurse, but what were the odds that she would be believed? Probably very little, so she waited for the nurse to leave before waving Franklin back over and clutching his hands. His brow was furrowed and his jaw clenched as he studied her face for any hint of what could have happened.

"Maisie, who's in danger?" he asked darkly. Maisie blinked at him.

"Layla is," she answered. Wasn't it obvious? "She came to my house."

"Burt didn't see anyone else in your house, and neither did the police."

"Who the hell is Burt?"

"One of your neighbors," Franklin explained. "He heard screaming and saw that someone broke into your house, so he went over with his shotgun to check on you. He found you unconscious in your living room and called 9-1-1. Avery was one of the first officers on the scene, and she called to let me know they were bringing you to the hospital."

Maisie closed her eyes tightly and leaned back against the pillow. Why hadn't they found Layla? Had Aremaeid and that other Rhithien taken her when they'd left?

"Did they find her family?" she asked hoarsely, remembering what Layla told her.

"Yeah," Franklin said hesitantly, giving her hands a comforting squeeze. "Yeah, they found them. You know what happened?"

Maisie bit her lip and nodded, blinking back tears. She'd known the Lucios from her very first day in Nuncan. Until she settled into her job, Catherine and Dennis were her only friends. And now they were gone.

Maisie suddenly frowned and glanced around the room in search of a clock.

"What time is it?" she wheezed, pressing a hand to her throat. Franklin turned his wrist to check his watch.

"It's about a quarter to nine. In the evening, in case you weren't sure. The doctors are worried you might have a concussion, so they want to keep you here overnight. Would you be up for that?"

214

Maisie shook her head fiercely. She couldn't stay in the hospital for an entire night. She had to look for Layla. She was the only one the girl had left, and she was also the only one who knew what they were up against. Before either of them could speak, the door opened again, and two duster-clad men walked inside, flashing gold badges as they did so.

"Glad to see you're awake, Ms. Arberon," the first one said with a curt nod. He was tall and athletic, with coffee-colored skin and close-cropped black hair. "I'm Detective Davis; this is Detective Moore. I'd like to ask you a few questions if that's alright."

Maisie glanced at Franklin, who patted her hand reassuringly. He didn't know about the two Rhithien. He didn't know that she couldn't tell the truth.

You can't write 'aliens' on a police report, but I'll tell them as much as I can.

"Yeah," she conceded with a nod. Her voice, while still crackly and weak, was stronger this time, and she cleared her throat with a painful swallow, ignoring the throbbing pain in her head.

The second detective, Moore, stepped forward and calmly addressed Franklin. "If you could step out of the room with me for a moment, sir, I'd appreciate it. I'd like to ask you a few questions as well."

"Why?" Franklin demanded. "Do you think I had something to do with this?"

"Sir—" Moore began, but Maisie interrupted him.

"It's okay," she said, squeezing Franklin's arm and giving him a small smile. "I'll be alright."

He frowned dubiously at her but didn't argue. He compliantly stood and exited into the hallway with Moore, who shut the door behind them, leaving her alone with Davis. He sat in the chair that Franklin had been occupying and crossed his arms.

"*Did* he have something to do with this, Ms. Arberon?"

"Maisie's fine," she said stiffly. "And no, he didn't. He lives on the other side of town. He wasn't even at my house tonight."

"About what time did the break-in happen?" Davis asked. He struck her as someone who was straight-talking and down-to-business, and Maisie had a feeling he wouldn't take too well to being told it was an alien who had killed the Lucios and kidnapped Layla.

"I think around 6:30," she said slowly. "I wasn't looking at the clock. It might have been closer to 7, but I can't really remember."

"That's alright," Davis sighed. "Tell me what you *do* remember. Take all the time you need. I want as many details as you can give me, Maisie."

"Okay," she said with a shaky sigh, rubbing her sore neck. "I was in my kitchen, drinking coffee, when I heard screaming outside. I was going to call the police, but I didn't do it right away because I didn't know for sure if someone was in danger. The kids in my neighborhood play around in the streets all the time, and they can be pretty loud. Then I heard someone at my door, and when I realized it was Layla, I let her in."

"Layla Lucio?" Davis asked with a frown, and Maisie nodded.

"Yes. Anyway, I let her inside. She was. . . not doing well. She said. . ." Maisie stopped and swallowed, not wanting to finish the sentence but knowing that she needed to provide as much information as she could. "She said someone killed her family."

"Sorry to interrupt, but can I ask you something real quick?" Davis queried, holding up a hand. Maisie nodded. "You said there were other kids in your neighborhood. Why did Layla go to your house rather than a friend's?"

"Mine was closer, I guess," Maisie said with a shrug.

"But why did she immediately turn to you when she was in danger?"

"I've been friends with her parents for years. I also teach at her school, and I've been tutoring her for a little over six months now. Every Saturday. We've gotten pretty close, and I guess she trusts me. Plus, she doesn't seem to have a ton of friends her age. Not at school, at least."

Davis stared at her for a long time, not saying anything. It was only when Maisie started squirming uncomfortably under his penetrating gaze that he finally spoke again.

"I don't know if you realize this, Maisie, but if this is true, you are currently the last person who's seen Layla Lucio."

"What?" Maisie gasped. She'd been praying that wasn't the case.

"We didn't find her anywhere in her house or yours, and no one's seen her around the neighborhood or the rest of town. We've got a few search parties looking for her up in the Dennison Woods, but we haven't had any luck so far."

A low whimper climbed up from Maisie's throat. The only relief she had stemmed from the fact that, although Layla was missing, the Rhithien most likely hadn't killed her, or they would have left her body behind. They seemed to want her alive—though for what, Maisie had no clue. She saw no valid reason that could explain why a bunch of aliens would kill an entire family and kidnap a twelve-year-old. In fact, now that she thought about it, she had no idea why there were aliens in Nuncan in the first place. Aremaeid had claimed it was a transportation experiment, but how much of that had he lied about? What was their real purpose?

Davis sighed and said, "I'm sorry, Maisie, I really am, but I need to know if you got a good look at your assailant. Was it a man?"

"Yes."

"Do you think you can describe him for me?"

"I don't know," Maisie whispered, her voice trembling. "It all happened so fast. He knocked me out pretty quick."

"Can you try?" Davis asked, his tone pained and pleading.

What the fuck am I supposed to say?

"I can't," she responded stiffly, shaking her head. "I'm sorry, I can't."

"Did he threaten you? Maisie, I want to help, but I can't if you don't tell me what happened."

God, that's exactly what I said to Layla.

"No, he didn't. Well, he did, but—I don't know!" she cried, covering her face with her hands. Why did this have to be so hard? "You don't understand, I can't do it."

"Maisie—" Davis started.

She slammed her hand down on the bed and glared at him. Fuck it. Who cared if he believed her or not? She knew what she saw.

"It wasn't—It wasn't human. It was an alien," she snapped. It was harder than she'd anticipated to get the words out, but she felt better once they were in the air. Davis blinked in surprise, staring at her like he couldn't comprehend her response. Finally, he pursed his lips and leaned forward, and Maisie could see how strained his patience was.

"Ma'am, I know you were close with this family, and I'm sure this loss is hard to handle. But right now, you are our only lead. Between the two of us, I don't think you had anything to do with the murders or Layla's disappearance, based on the fact that we found you unconscious in your own house with all the obvious signs of a break-in. And, judging by the states of the bodies and what you've just described, it doesn't seem like Layla was responsible for the deaths of her family, either. So if that's what you're worried about, you're both clear. But I need you to tell me the truth. This is important."

"I *am* telling you the truth," Maisie insisted. "Do you want me to draw a picture or something? Because I can."

"Are you sure it wasn't just a guy in a mask?" Davis posed, and she shook her head. A muscle in his jaw flickered and he added, "He could have been using clawed gloves. Probably handmade. Stilts, maybe? A fake bear head? Anything like that ringing a bell? Concussions can mess with memory and perception."

"I know what I saw, and I know it wasn't human. It had big claws and teeth if that means anything to you. It was also nine feet tall."

That part wasn't necessarily true. Sure, she had estimated Aremaeid to be a little over nine feet, but the other Rhithien—the one that had gone after Layla—had been shorter than him by about a foot. It didn't matter much, though, so she neglected to offer that detail. Davis gave her an odd, contemplative look.

"You're saying bear-sized?"

"Yes, but it wasn't a bear."

"A man died yesterday evening. Willard Hayes. If you read the news, you would have spotted his name under the headline 'mad bear attack'. Not a ton of detail was included. Do you know if the two incidents could be related in any way?"

Maisie shook her head.

"I read about that guy's death in the news, but I don't know. That kind of thing just happens sometimes, doesn't it?"

"Yeah, I guess it does," Davis muttered, but Maisie thought she saw a glimmer of skepticism in his eyes.

"Anything else?" she asked stiffly. Taking her cool tone as his cue to leave, Davis stood and dusted off his coat. He pulled a small card from his breast pocket and handed it to Maisie. She accepted it reluctantly.

"Call if you think of anything else, Ms. Arberon," he said, giving her a courteous nod and leaving the room. Maisie stared down at the card for a moment. His full name—Carlton Davis—was written across its surface, as was a phone number. Maisie couldn't help wondering if a part of him believed her story; she knew it sounded crazy, but when he mentioned the supposed bear attack, he seemed thoughtful and almost unsure. And the description of tools that a person might have used—clawed gloves, a bear head, possible stilts—was eerily specific.

218

Franklin hurried back into the room a few minutes later, and he looked surprised to see Maisie standing up and reaching for her own clothes, though she was wobbly-legged and unsteady.

"What are you doing?" he demanded, running to her side.

"I'm checking myself out of the hospital, Franklin," Maisie replied. "Are you going to stop me?"

He gave her a long, unhappy look, then offered his arm for balance.

*****

Maisie grabbed a flashlight and shoved it into the backpack she had begun preparing. She then hurried out of the living room and to the bathroom in the hall, where she snatched a mini first-aid kit from beneath the sink. Franklin followed, standing helplessly behind her.

"Maisie, you can't do this by yourself. You don't even know if Layla's alive. Besides, you have a concussion," he said, still trying to convince her not to go after the Rhithien. She'd explained as much as she could, albeit trimming the story down, and he'd been surprisingly receptive to the information. Maisie brushed past him to her bedroom to grab an extra jacket, ignoring the persistent migraine that had continued to plague her after leaving the hospital.

"If he killed her, he would have just left her body. That's what he did with her family. But Detective Davis said she wasn't in my house when Burt found me, so chances are good that she's still alive."

"What would a bunch of aliens even want her for? Why not the rest of the Lucios?" Franklin asked, trailing after her.

"I don't know," she admitted. "But I'm not doing this to find out why they took her. I just need to find her and bring her back. I'm all she has left, and no one knows the truth about these things but me. I don't have a choice, Franklin." She zipped up the backpack, pulled her jacket on, and tied her hair back into a ponytail.

"You're really doing this," Franklin murmured, and Maisie turned to look at him. He still wore a look of disbelief, but his shoulders were now slumped in resignation. He knew he couldn't stop her.

"This is something I have to do, Franklin," she said firmly. "Layla is still alive somewhere, I know it. And I have to get her back." She turned and headed for the front door, but Franklin suddenly grabbed her arm and pulled her back

219

around to face him. She was about to protest, but he leaned in and kissed her softly.

"I find it hard to believe that there are nine-foot aliens running around Nuncan kidnapping seventh graders," he murmured, pressing his forehead against hers, "but if I really can't stop you from doing this, I'm not letting you go alone. Parker and Avery know the Dennisons better than anyone. Give me a minute to ring them up, and then we can go. I'm sure Parker will be over the moon to help, but I doubt you'll have an easy time getting Avery to believe everything you just told me."

Tears of gratitude welled in Maisie's eyes as Franklin sighed and took his cell phone out of his pocket. She wrapped her arms around him and pressed her face against his chest, holding onto him like a lifeline while he called his siblings.

"Hey, Parker," he greeted. After a short pause, he quickly said, "No, I'm good. Listen, is Avery there? Good, put me on speaker. I need to talk to both of you."

XXIV

They ran for almost two hours, Aremaeid in the lead and Ornathium bringing up the rear. Neither of them spoke, nor did the human. Even as the wind rushed by them and the woods blurred around their passage, Aremaeid could smell the child's fear radiating from her skin in a thick heat.

She must learn to control that, he thought. *Ornathium needs no encouragement.*

He knew it wasn't fair of him to be so critical of the girl—she was only human, after all—but on Primaied, one could not afford to be weak. Especially in a Rhithien pack. If a creature as fragile and helpless as a juvenile human showed any sign of submission, they were all but prey. It was something she would need to work on when they brought her to their planet.

By the time the Rhithien reached the field where they'd found each other, the lone Earthen moon was high and full, casting a pall over the woods. Aremaeid was slightly annoyed by their lack of significant progress because he knew they could have easily gone twice or even thrice the distance on all fours, but the girl might not have been as secure if Ornathium had chosen to carry her on his back.

Doesn't matter. We must keep going.

Aremaeid stopped when he heard Ornathium halt abruptly behind him. He turned around and walked briskly towards his packmate, allowing his irritation to show on his face.

"We need to keep moving," he growled. "I know you can go farther."

"We must stop here," Ornathium stated simply. Aremaeid waited for an explanation but didn't receive one. It was an irksome habit of Ornathium's. He rarely elaborated on his decisions or opinions unless someone explicitly asked for details.

"Why should we stop here?" Aremaeid inquired, trying to keep his voice steady. He was agitated enough from the incident at Maisie's house. He could still hear the wet *thunk* of her head hitting the chair leg; when he closed his eyes, he could see the finger-shaped bruising on her neck. But if Ornathium was picking up the cues, he didn't care.

"Yesterday evening when we crossed paths, I stayed out to hunt longer than you did. I found Vegra, Orniell, and Torraeid, and we agreed to meet here."

"And you didn't think to mention this sooner?" Aremaeid snarled. The human girl flinched back from his sharp tone, although she couldn't understand his words. He felt mildly guilty for scaring her, but he didn't like dealing with Ornathium. If it had been anyone else in his pack, he might have shown more patience, but the red-eyed Rhithien unnerved him on a level that he had never been able to fully understand. He always found himself on edge whenever he was forced to speak to him.

"You didn't ask," Ornathium said with a shrug.

"Because I—never mind. We will stop. But we can't stay out here in the open."

They moved through the field and into the trees, where they passed by a spot that stank of old blood. They had to break through a long strip of yellow tape that had human words written across it in black. Aremaeid doubted it was important, else it would have been harder to surpass. Once they were out of sight, Ornathium unceremoniously dropped his captive into the dirt. She yelped and tried to scurry away on her hands and knees, but Ornathium threw a sharp kick that caught her in the belly and knocked her onto her side with a cry. Gasping and wheezing, she crawled backwards until she ran into the unyielding trunk of a tree. Ornathium feigned a lunge towards her that made her shriek and cover her face, and he laughed cruelly at her reaction.

"That's enough," Aremaeid ordered, grabbing his packmate's shoulder and shoving him roughly away.

"Why do you care? She's only a human."

"You've tormented her enough. Leave her be."

Ornathium scowled and plunked down on the ground with a pouty huff. Aremaeid wasn't afraid of his wrath; he knew he could beat him in a fight if it came to that. But he didn't dare turn his back as he, too, sat down. When the pack had first found Ornathium, he'd been little more than an animal, and although the next eighteen years of socialization had tamed him to some degree, he was still wildly unpredictable. Everyone knew he wasn't above attacking his superiors for an offense as small as spoiling his fun.

It was a brisk night. Aremaeid didn't feel more than a slight chill, but the low temperature was evident in the way the girl hugged herself and shivered. He could even see her breath coming out as a soft puff of mist. He scrutinized the clothing she wore with narrowed eyes.

Why do they drape themselves in such things if they do nothing against the cold?

"Can. . . Can we light a fire or something?" she asked in a small voice. "It's really. . . I'm cold."

"No," Aremaeid responded flatly. They couldn't risk being spotted by other humans. Ornathium had caused plenty of trouble back in Nuncan, and the last thing they needed was more unwanted attention. The girl suddenly shifted away from both Rhithien, and although she seemed to be merely adjusting to a more comfortable position, Ornathium grabbed her arm and yanked her back. She screamed, loud and piercing, until he clapped one hand over her mouth and bared his teeth in her face.

"If you think about running—"

"I wasn't!" she cried. Her voice came out muffled beneath his hand. Ornathium growled and shook her roughly.

"—or attracting more humans, I will gouge both your eyes from their sockets and feed them to you. Do you understand?"

The girl nodded, and he released her. Shuddering under the force of relentless tears, she crawled closer to Aremaeid as if seeking some kind of protection. He stiffened and flared up his frill to tell her that she would get no open display of sympathy from him. She didn't seem to get the message, however, and kept coming closer until he bared his teeth with a low growl of warning. He would keep Ornathium off her back, but he wasn't interested in offering a shoulder to cry on. She finally understood and backed off, but a small dart of shame pierced through Aremaeid's heart.

"What is your name, child?" he asked in English.

"I already told you. Her name is Layla," answered Ornathium before the girl could even open her mouth.

"I did not ask you, Bloodhound," Aremaeid snapped.

"Why ask her?" his packmate demanded. He then switched back to Rhithos and added, "You've no reason to know her name. She's a tool and nothing more."

"You realize these creatures are sentient like us, yes?" Aremaeid inquired dryly. He wasn't sure why he was so argumentative tonight, but he felt the need to defend what little honor the humans had.

"Of *course* I know they're sentient," Ornathium responded, rolling his eyes. "They wouldn't be so much fun to kill if they weren't."

Aremaeid didn't bother retorting. It was easy to slip into contention with Ornathium, but it would get him nowhere. Layla stared between them as if she was trying to figure out what they were saying. Aremaeid understood her struggle. The first time he'd heard a human language, it had sounded like the babbling chatter of an animal. Complete nonsense. He'd learned since then, of course, that they used their tongues to enunciate the majority of their sounds, and what resulted was a high-pitched warble that had greatly annoyed him before he'd gotten used to it. Why it was something they needed to know, he wasn't sure, but for four years Salidus had forced the pack to speak only in human tongues, and they had all been ready to kill him by the end of it.

I suppose those lessons paid off for me.

Indeed they had. If he knew no human languages, or at least didn't know English, he would have killed Maisie without a second thought the night he arrived in her yard.

Then again, that might have been for the best.

"What was your human's name?" Ornathium asked suddenly. It was as if he'd read his thoughts. Aremaeid glared at him.

"That's none of your concern."

"Why? I told you mine's name."

"She isn't yours. And you told me her name because she's the Lucio heir."

"What could I possibly do, Aremaeid?" Ornathium flung his arms in the air and gave him a lazy grin. "We've no need to turn around. That little thing hit its head fairly hard, from the looks of it, so it's probably dead at this point. Not that it matters. The only human of importance is right here with us." He shoved Layla in a way that was probably meant to be playful, but the force of it made her fall back with a cry of alarm.

"What was that for?" she demanded.

"You looked too peaceful," Ornathium replied in English. He didn't bother switching back to Rhithos as he said to Aremaeid, "Do not take my credit for finding her."

"There is no credit to take," Aremaeid responded coolly. "Stealing cubs and killing humans is no accomplishment."

"I hid in an attic and played pretend for a whole week, so do not tell me what I accomplished," snapped Ornathium.

"You killed my family," Layla whispered, giving him a hateful glare.

He rolled his eyes.

"I know this, child. You need not remind me. Would you like it if I had killed you, too?" He grinned widely, baring his teeth, and Layla shrank away from him.

As if hoping for a distraction, she turned to Aremaeid and asked, "How long were you staying at Ms. Arberon's house?"

"Who?"

"Ms. Ar—Maisie. How long were you there?"

"A week. I arrived on Earth when Ornathium did."

"Oh." Layla pulled her knees tightly against her chest, tears brimming in her eyes, and whispered, "She didn't tell me."

"I asked her not to," Aremaeid explained. He reflected that "ask" might have been the wrong word for how he'd initially gotten Maisie to keep quiet, but the girl didn't need to know about all that. She was dealing with enough as it was. He shifted uncomfortably in place as Layla buried her face in her arms and began to cry. She was quiet about it, but he could see her shoulders quaking beneath the weight of her grief.

"You are cold, Layla. You humans succumb to exposure far too easily. Very weak, you are," Ornathium said suddenly, clicking his tongue in mock disapproval. He pulled her closer to him and wrapped one arm around her, holding her in place even as she squirmed and attempted to wriggle away from him.

"Let me—"

"Be reasonable. Would you really rather freeze than sit so close to me?"

"Yes," Layla responded with a scowl. "I hate you."

Ornathium chuckled and said, "I know, little queen."

"Don't call me—"

"I shall call you whatever I like. I am no longer trapped in your attic."

"Enough, Ornathium!" Aremaeid snapped, spiking up his frill and baring his teeth. "If I have to tell you again, I will tear off both of your ears! You obviously do not use them."

His packmate narrowed his red eyes and tightened the grip he had around Layla's shoulders.

"Why defend her? Before this, you did not even—"

"My reasons are not yours to know. You forget your place, Bloodhound," Aremaeid growled. "When I give you an order, I expect you to follow."

Ornathium opened his mouth to argue, but stopped and cocked his head to the side. He twitched his ears and lifted his nose to the wind. Aremaeid mimicked his movements, for he had heard the same sound: footsteps. They carried the light, cautious tread of hunters with a nearly undetectable softness, but they were not quite silent to a Rhithien's ears.

"It's about time," Ornathium muttered, reverting once more to Rhithos. The two of them turned in unison towards the depths of the woods, from which emerged three other Rhithien. Aremaeid was pleased to see his brother, Torraeid, alive and well, but he sighed tiredly at the sight of Vegra, looking angry at the world as he always did. It was also a relief to have Orniell's unfaltering presence. The older Rhithien's sheathed daggers thumped quietly against his thighs as he walked towards Aremaeid and Ornathium, but the soft leather muffled any noise that might have otherwise come from buckles or straps.

"This is the heir?" he asked gruffly, nudging Layla with a foot. She flinched away from him, but Ornathium grabbed her and held her up to the older male like an offering.

"Yes!" he said happily. "I found her!"

"Put me down!" Layla shrieked, smacking at his hands and kicking uselessly in the air.

"Ugh, you had to get a cub?" Vegra grimaced. "Was this thing the only option?"

"No, but I thought a child would be easier to control than an adult. And I like this one. She is my friend."

"Don't be stupid. You don't have any friends, and children are annoying."

Ornathium wilted under Vegra's criticism and dropped Layla into his lap. She immediately tried to get away from him, but he held her in place by the collar of her shirt and stroked her hair soothingly. It didn't calm the girl down, but Aremaeid suspected Ornathium was doing it more for himself than for her.

Vegra scrutinized the child and rasped, "If you annoy me, I will break both of your legs."

Layla blanched and stopped struggling against Ornathium's hold.

Smart girl. She doesn't know Vegra, but he rarely makes idle threats.

Aremaeid glanced over as Torraeid took a seat beside him. The albino's spotless white skin nearly glowed in the darkness. Though his packmates smelled like they had bathed recently, Aremaeid detected the lingering scent of Earthen blood on all of them from past meals. The odor was cloyingly strong around Ornathium, and although he appeared to have rinsed away the blood, the familiar musk of humans still clung to his skin.

"We should move on," Orniell said in Rhithos.

"If we could rest first, it would do us some good," suggested Aremaeid. "Perhaps you all can smell it and I don't need to tell you this, but Ornathium made a bit of a scene, and the other humans are likely on our trail as we speak. They're slow enough that they won't catch up to us anytime soon, but we may need to run far to lose them."

"I did not make a scene!" Ornathium protested. He yanked unhappily on Layla's hair, but the only indication of pain she offered was a wince and a small whine.

"We may not have far to go," Orniell stated. "Just a few hours ago, Vegra, Torraeid, and I caught Ziiphan's musk. We tried following it, but it carried for molosopions, so we figured we ought to collect you two before finding him."

"Ziiphan's obviously been busy," Aremaeid muttered.

"Yes. It's good that he knows how to get our attention, but the problem is that we are not the only creatures here with good noses. With as much as he was putting off, even a human could detect him by smell."

"Then we will have to move fast."

"We rest first," Vegra growled, joining the circle and sitting across from Aremaeid. "Then we'll find Ziiphan."

"I want to find Ziiphan," Ornathium contributed. Vegra pinched his frill to shut him up, and Ornathium recoiled from the touch with a hiss. After a moment's hesitation, Orniell sat down as well, strategically placing himself between Vegra and Torraeid.

There were several minutes of silence before Torraeid finally spoke up with a nudge of small talk. He spoke in English, likely in an effort to try and make Layla feel included. Torraeid had always sympathized with the meek.

"So. . . how are you all enjoying Earth?"

"I hate it. This planet reeks," Vegra snarled. He made a point to respond in the same language so that the girl would have no choice but to hear him insult her home. Aremaeid could see that she wanted to argue with the older male, but she wisely kept her mouth shut.

"It's not Primaied, but it could be worse," Aremaeid offered, trying to maintain civility.

"I like it," Ornathium said as he continued tugging at strands of Layla's hair. Vegra growled at him again and this time he submitted properly, hunching away with his frill lowered and his eyes downcast.

"I will be glad to leave this fucking rock," Vegra hissed. "It stinks of humans everywhere."

"That's my home you're talking about. This rock is my home," Layla snapped, startling them all. Aremaeid silently cursed her for her stupidity. Yes, Vegra was deliberately provoking her, but he would kill the girl for the slightest act of defiance if given half a chance. She wouldn't have a prayer of escaping him without help.

Despite the brightness of the moon, they sat in a shaded area, leaving only the faintest light cast by the glow of their eyes. Though Aremaeid could see his surroundings in varying hues of grey, Layla stared uncertainly in Vegra's direction as though she wasn't completely sure where he was. Humans were all but blind and deaf in the dark.

"I care not for your stupid home," Vegra spat, leaning into the approaching fight. "If all goes well from here and no one fucks anything up, you will never see Earth again."

"I seriously doubt that everything will go well," sneered the girl.

"Child," Orniell said with a warning tone, but she ignored him.

"And why is that?" demanded Vegra.

"Well, you guys fucked up badly enough to get separated as soon as you got here, so I think I'm pretty safe."

"Mind your tongue, girl, or I will rip it from your mouth."

There it was. Aremaeid and Orniell tensed, ready to intervene if violence erupted. Even with his obliviousness to most social cues, Ornathium seemed to sense the tension and slowly moved Layla from his lap to the ground. He scooted away, leaving her alone in the trajectory of Vegra's aggression. The bitter stink of fear wafted from the human's pores and gathered in a fog around her that was stronger than the musk of a female in heat. She, too, understood she was pushing her luck, but if she had realized the true level of danger she was in, she would have backed down immediately. She didn't.

"I don't give a shit what you do to me," she snapped. "You've already killed my family. You probably killed Maisie. I remember you saying two minutes ago that you were going to break my legs if I annoyed you, and I'm pretty sure I've been doing that. But my legs are fine, so either you're too stupid to remember making that threat or you're bluffing. I'm pretty sure my tongue is safe."

Vegra lunged across the circle with a roar and grabbed her left leg, then yanked her forward. With a sharp flick of his wrist, he broke the two bones in the lower half of the limb. Layla let out a sharp scream, which was quickly cut off as he forced her mouth open and dug his claws into her tongue. It all happened in just a few short seconds, but before he could pull her tongue out as he'd promised, Aremaeid and Orniell unlocked his grip and dragged him away.

"Rotten bitch!" Vegra snarled. He thrashed but didn't fight his superiors as hard as he could have. The girl didn't seem to hear him. She crawled away with a low, gurgling moan of pain and vomited into the grass. Ornathium made a sound of disgust and scooched away, but if she noticed, she didn't care. Blood flowed from her mouth and covered her chin like a wide red curtain, and as she cupped her lips in a desperate effort to hold all the fluid in, a long, shocked wail escaped her. But as bad as the damage to her tongue was, her leg was in much worse condition. A sharp strut of bone poked up against the stiff fabric of her pants where it had broken through flesh, and the limb twisted grotesquely outward. Aremaeid watched as a dark puddle of blood stained her clothing and oozed into the grass beneath her. Orniell barked a short curse and left Aremaeid with Vegra so he could tend to the girl.

"I'm fine," Vegra growled in Rhithos. He jerked his arm out of Aremaeid's grasp and sat sulkily back down on the ground. Aremaeid remained standing, ready to tackle him if he attacked again, but he spared an anxious glance over his shoulder to where Orniell knelt beside the human.

"I-I-I can't—I can't—" the girl choked. Her breath came out in quick, heavy bursts. Her eyes were glassy and round as she clutched her leg with trembling hands and fought to remain conscious.

"I know, child." Without turning away, Orniell snapped his fingers at Torraeid, and the albino rushed over. Orniell carefully held the human prone and asked, "How much magic do you have?"

"Plenty. This won't deplete my stores."

Torraeid first addressed the wounds on her tongue where Vegra had tried to remove it. He gently urged her mouth open, retracted his claws, and pressed his fingertips into the bloody furrows. Layla yelled wordlessly and dug her small, flat teeth into his skin, but Torraeid didn't try to pull away. Aremaeid's frill prickled as the air went heavy with magic, and Torraeid's eyes clouded over white, leaving him still and silent even as the girl's teeth cut through his flesh and spilled a small trickle of his own blood. She only released her bite when Orniell grabbed her jaw and pried her mouth open again.

One, two, three. . .

Aremaeid always counted the seconds through which his brother went under for a healing. Because Layla was so small, his estimated count was twelve. Perhaps it would take even less. Sure enough, after twelve seconds of complete silence apart from Layla's panting and crying, Torraeid's eyes cleared and he removed his hand. He moved to her leg next, where he carefully cut away the fabric of her pants with his claws and pushed the bone back into its proper place. This earned another loud, ragged scream from Layla, but he ignored it and disappeared once more into whatever subconscious realm healers went to. The pack all watched as the torn flesh knitted itself together beneath the pressure of his hand. When his eyes returned to normal and he pulled away from the wound, Layla was left with no more than a faint, pale scar where the bone had broken through her skin.

"Wh-what did you. . . How did you. . ."

The girl's voice trailed off as she fixed her leg with a dazed stare and cautiously pressed a single finger against the scar. Her other hand flew up to her mouth and she felt around on her tongue for claw marks that Aremaeid knew were little more than phantom aches; he had been through the healing process himself too many times to count. Layla slowly lifted her head and gawked at Torraeid as he returned to his spot on the ground beside Aremaeid. She opened and closed her mouth rapidly, but said nothing. Aremaeid knew humans didn't have any magic, so he understood that the display must have been a shock for her to see.

"We need to move, and fast. We've made too much noise. If there are any humans searching for her, they must be onto us by now," Orniell at last commanded in Rhithos. They all obediently stood up, and without explaining to Layla what was happening, Orniell slung her onto his back. Despite her surprise, she obediently clung to the older male's neck. Dropping to all fours, Orniell took off into the trees, and the rest of the pack swiftly followed. Although Layla's injuries were entirely healed, she huddled between his shoulders like a frightened rhego and didn't say another word for the rest of the night.

XXV

Maisie waited at her house with Franklin for what felt like hours but was probably closer to thirty minutes. A sharp spike of anxiety speared her heart with every minute that ticked by, pounding in sync with the worsening pain in her head. Franklin had asked his brother and sister to come over and pick them up, saying that he would explain everything once they arrived. Parker and Avery were confused and somewhat perturbed by the air of mystery permeating the vague request, but they agreed to drive over and help anyway. It didn't ease Maisie's nerves that Roller, from whom she was usually able to find comfort during times of anxiety, was spending the night at the local vet. She was more than grateful he was still alive, but she usually had his furry snuggles to turn to in times of distress. She resorted to pacing rapidly around the house, flapping her hands agitatedly and checking the clock every ten seconds.

"Try to relax, Maisie," Franklin said at last, obviously agitated by her restlessness. "Just watching you is giving me a panic attack."

"How do you expect me to relax?" Maisie snapped, and he flinched at her tone. "A little girl's been kidnapped, Franklin, and her whole family is dead. I'm the only one who knows what happened and therefore the only one she's got left. Every minute we spend waiting here is another minute the Rhithien have to get further away."

Franklin said nothing, just continued to watch her uneasily as she resumed her pacing. It was clear to see that he was having a hard time believing her about the Rhithien, but she was grateful for his willingness to go along.

He's helping you. Don't be a bitch. Just take a breath and apologize.

She finally paused in front of him and said with a sigh, "I'm sorry. I shouldn't be like that. I'm just worried about her, and my head is fucking killing me."

"I know. It's alright," Franklin consoled her gently. "I know you care about Layla, and we've already said we're going to help you, but you need to give us a hot minute. Parker and Avery will be here any second—I can guarantee it—but there is a speed limit, you know."

Maisie let out a short, breathy laugh and sat down on the couch beside him, wiping her sweaty palms on her thighs. She glanced at him and swallowed nervously.

I'm not sure he believes me. But if he didn't, he wouldn't be helping me, would he?

"Do you think I'm crazy?" she asked hesitantly, and Franklin snorted.

"What sort of question is that? Of course I think you're crazy. But you're also my girlfriend, and even if we've been dating for less than a week, it's my job to help you get through your craziness. Although the idea of alien-hunting is a bit far-fetched."

Maisie gave him a grateful smile and leaned her head on his shoulder. He put his arm around her with a small sigh, and they stayed like that until they heard a vehicle pull into the driveway. Maisie jumped to her feet, almost knocking Franklin off the couch as she raced to the front door. She yanked it open and rushed out so fast she nearly tumbled down the steps of the front porch.

"Slow down, Maisie!" Franklin called, and she shifted on her feet impatiently while he rose to follow her. He shut and locked the door on his way out. Maisie turned her attention to the vehicle in the driveway, a sturdy-looking Jeep Wrangler with a myriad of dents and a windshield that looked like it had never been cleaned. The license plate was scratched up and covered with grime, rendering its letters and numbers almost indecipherable.

"We're here," declared a tall woman who stepped out of the driver's seat. She had the same thick, dark hair and prominent nose as Franklin, and Maisie knew her immediately to be Avery.

"We noticed," replied Franklin with a hint of sarcasm.

"You must be Maisie!" called an enthusiastic-looking man who leaped out of the passenger seat and ran up to her. Grinning like a maniac, he pulled her into a tight hug, and Maisie let out a surprised wheeze. He released her and said happily, "We've heard so much about you!"

"That's me," she said with a hesitant smile, intimidated by his energy.

Avery, who remained by the jeep, crossed her arms and said, "You're lucky I'm off duty. My last few hours in the precinct were a mess. So are you going to explain why we had to drive out here at 10:30 at night?"

"Yeah," Frankly said, straightening his back and lifting his head. "Aliens."

Avery blinked in surprise, then repeated the word.

"Aliens."

"Yes."

"You're shitting me," she said irritably, leaning on the frame of the jeep. She obviously didn't believe it, but Parker's brows went up and he stared at Franklin with growing excitement. Practically vibrating with anticipation, he only barely managed to contain himself, like he was worried it was a hoax.

"Let the man talk, Avery," he stated. He crossed his arms just as she had and changed his face to a more aloof expression, but his eyes still gleamed with child-like enthusiasm.

"Here's the deal," Franklin explained. "Even if you don't believe the alien business—which, to be honest, I'm having a hard time with myself—that kid who went missing earlier, Layla Lucio, was kidnapped. By the aliens. Maisie knew her pretty well, so we've decided that we're going to go look for her. I was hoping you guys could get us through the Dennison Woods."

"You're fucking kidding me," Avery snapped. Her face was pinched with offended anger. "A child has gone missing, her entire family's been murdered, and you want to run around the woods looking for aliens? Christ, Franklin, you really know how to pick 'em."

"Look, Avery, I know you out of all of us don't want to believe this—"

"There's nothing to believe. If you have evidence or any record of what happened, share it with Davis or Moore. They're actually taking this case seriously."

"Those detectives don't know what they're dealing with, and right now, the four of us are the only ones who know the truth. Or most of it, at least. Avery, I wouldn't call both you and Parker out here so late if I wasn't serious about this. Neither would Maisie. You have to at least believe me on that."

"Is that why you told us to bring the rifles?" Parker asked, and Franklin nodded.

"Maisie's the only one who's seen these things."

"Solid evidence right there," Avery muttered.

Franklin ignored her and continued.

234

"I want to be prepared. And guns will probably be necessary because these aliens are apparently nine feet tall."

Parker let out a low whistle of awe and appreciation, but Avery remained stubbornly unconvinced, growing more visibly irritated by the second.

"Okay, let's say I believe this. Let's say that, for one second, I believe a bunch of nine-foot aliens came to Earth just to take one kid away from her family, and we need to go after these things with rifles because the police force—which I'm a part of, by the way—doesn't know what these aliens are and can't help us. How are you even going to find them? There's not an ounce of logic anywhere in this scenario."

"That's where you guys come in. You two know these woods better than anyone, except maybe some of the local old-timers. You also know how to track."

"That won't amount to anything if we don't have tracks to work with," Avery snapped.

"Maisie can find them," Franklin said confidently, and Maisie looked at him with wide eyes. He saw her expression, gave her a reassuring smile, and added, "She knows a lot about them. If you have any theories, babe, now's the time."

"I know that they hunt in packs. Like wolves," Maisie recalled, trying to remember everything she'd learned from Aremaeid through both observation and conversation. "They're intelligent, like us. It's kind of scary, actually. They can speak English. Fluently. They're a lot more like animals with how they move and act overall, though. They look like animals, too."

"Alright, animals. Let's start with that and see where we can go from there," Parker mused, nodding slowly as he processed her words. "You said they hunt. Do they have any specific places here where they've consistently looked for food? Since Earth is a foreign planet to them, they'll probably stick to ground they're familiar with."

Damnit, maybe I should have asked where specifically Aremaeid was going whenever he went out.

Maisie shrugged helplessly and explained, "He never told me where he went when he left, he always just said he was going hunting, and I thought—"

"Wait, stop," interrupted Avery. She held up a hand and fixed Maisie with a hard stare. "You say 'he' like you know one of them. What's the deal there?"

"How *do* you know so much about these things?" Franklin asked, and Maisie realized she hadn't told him about the part where she'd briefly been roommates with a Rhithien. The three siblings stared at her in silent suspicion, waiting for answers, and she swallowed nervously.

"One of them's been living in my basement for the past week," she confessed, and Franklin's jaw dropped. She continued before he could speak. "He's gone now, though. His name is Aremaeid, and he told me about his planet and his species. It was a different one that killed Layla's family, but Aremaeid left with him when they took her. They came to Earth through some kind of portal, but something went wrong, and their pack got separated. I don't know exactly how it all works. But anyway, Aremaeid landed in my backyard, and I agreed to let him stay in my house and keep him a secret."

'Agreed' might be the wrong word, she reflected.

"And. . . when exactly was this?" Franklin asked, disbelief coloring his features. Maisie winced at the note of betrayal in his tone.

"Friday night. Last week. I met you that Sunday."

"Why didn't you tell me?" he demanded. "Or literally anyone else? Could you have. . ." He swallowed and hesitated before finishing. "Could you have prevented this? The deaths?"

"No, of course not! You wouldn't have believed me, no one would have, and Aremaeid told me they weren't going to hurt anyone! If I'd known, I would have tried to do something to stop it! It wasn't my fault!"

"But you still lied to me."

"And I'm sorry for that, Franklin. I wanted to tell you, I really did, but I barely knew you at the time. And when I *did* get to know you, I was too caught up in everything to spill it all. But that doesn't matter now. Whether you believe me or not, Layla is gone and we need to find her. *I* need to find her."

Franklin said nothing. He looked away, his jaw clenched and his face hard. Maisie knew he was angry, but despite the leaden guilt weighing on her heart, she needed his help. She grabbed his arm, forced him to face her, and insisted, "This is bigger than us. When this is over, you can be as mad at me as you want, but we have to help Layla. We're the only chance she's got."

It was quiet for the next five seconds; ten, twenty, thirty. Then, just as Maisie was ready to give up and start the search on her own, Franklin turned back to his siblings and spoke.

"Avery, you were on the scene when that guy was killed up in the Dennisons."

"Yeah, Willard Hayes. What about him?"

"The newspapers said it was a bear attack, but I'm starting to think it might have been something else. If we started there, do you think either or both of you could pick up any tracks?"

"If there *are* tracks, sure," Parker conceded. "If the attack was from one of your aliens, they might have gone back there. Like I said, they're going to stick to territory they know."

"Wait, are we seriously doing this?" Avery demanded. Franklin and Parker ignored her and got into the Jeep, and Maisie quickly climbed in after them. Avery scoffed, slid into the driver's seat, and muttered, "I guess we are." She backed out of the driveway and started down the road, grumbling to herself all the while.

Franklin wouldn't look at Maisie. It was the closest thing they'd had to a fight in the short time they'd been together, and she hated knowing that she'd had to lie to him about something so staggeringly important.

It made her want to bury herself in the dirt and hide from the world.

*****

Can't breathe. . .

He felt crushed. Smothered. Trapped.

Can't breathe. . .

Where was he? He couldn't remember. What was he doing here, suffocating in the dark?

Can't BREATHE!

Salidus regained consciousness in complete darkness, and when he tried to open his eyes, moist dirt stung them painfully. He couldn't move with the earthen walls pressing so tightly around him. The air pocket he'd made with his magic was now stale and unusable, and he heaved and gasped to no avail. When he struggled, the dirt sifted down through the weakened magical seal and weighed heavily on his snout, filling his nose and holding his mouth shut like a muzzle.

Magic. I recharged, so I should have my magic!

Sure enough, when he dug down into that little pool within his mind that carried his power, it was full and ready for use. He couldn't afford to expend so much of it again, but he needed to get to the surface. He had no idea how deep he was, or how long he'd been under. It couldn't have been more than a day, but there was no way of knowing until he escaped. He gathered his magic and, despite not knowing for certain which way was up, pushed it outward in an invisible sphere until the ceiling of his prison crumbled away and moonlight filtered down through the newly formed hole. Salidus inhaled the fresh wave of air and leapt up to grab the edge of the pit. His limbs, stiff as those of a corpse, resisted all movement, and his broken leg screamed in protest against his efforts, but he managed to clamber out onto flat, stable ground. He stood up with a groan and blinked the dirt from his eyes.

Night had fallen. He wasn't sure if it was a mere few hours that had passed or an entire day and then some, but the one thing he did know was that he needed to move. The humans who had attacked him were nowhere to be seen, but they might have remained in the area, lying in wait for his emergence.

Ridaion. Need to find Ridaion and the others.

A brief moment of panic overcame him, and his hand flew up to his neck. He was relieved to find that the bag of knuckle bones remained safely shut and intact.

"Soon," he promised the bones. "Soon."

Exhaustion ached through his whole body even after the lengthy recharge, and his left leg throbbed terribly, but he took a deep breath, regained his composure, and set off through the woods.

This is bigger than me. I can rest when I finish my mission.

XXVI

Pale pinks and oranges crept higher, lightening the sky in the east when the pack finally came to a stop. They jumped over a fallen tree, then Orniell skidded to a halt and held up a hand, commanding them all to stop as well. Aremaeid cringed at the heavy musk permeating the air. The entire stretch of woods they'd covered for the last twelve dynnsopions reeked of Ziiphan. Musk could be pleasant and even arousing, but only under the right circumstances and only in controlled amounts. There was a point where it became unappealing, and Ziiphan had effortlessly reached that point.

"Well, at least we know where he is," Torraeid commented with forced optimism.

"No, we don't," Orniell said gruffly. "This has to be the result of several days of musking. There's no clear trail, either, so he's probably just sitting on his ass somewhere, putting out for all of Earth and waiting for us to find him."

Aremaeid raised an eyebrow. Orniell rarely cursed or spoke so bitterly. Only acts of idiocy like this drew it out of him; and, like now, it was often something Ziiphan said or did.

"I'll take her," Aremaeid said to Torraeid, holding out his arms. His brother pulled the human girl down from his back and passed her to him, and Aremaeid helped her climb up and cling to his shoulders. They'd been switching her amongst themselves because although she weighed next to nothing, they wanted to avoid tiring one Rhithien out more than the others. Carrying someone, even a small someone, drained energy over time. Orniell had notably forbidden Vegra and Ornathium from carrying her.

"Spread out," Orniell ordered. "His scent is stronger around here than anywhere else, so he must be close. Aremaeid, do not let that girl out of your sight."

"Of course," Aremaeid assented.

The group split up, and Aremaeid continued on until he was alone with Layla. He would have been content without conversation, but the girl apparently felt otherwise, because after a few minutes she began asking questions without all the caution she'd had before.

"Why are you guys really here? Ornathium told me it was to check out Earth, and you were scattered because the portals failed, but what's the real reason?"

Aremaeid remained silent as he weighed the merits of telling her the truth. She would inevitably find out once they returned to Primaied, but what if something went wrong and she escaped or was rescued by other humans? The odds of that were low, but there was still an undeniable risk to revealing the plan prematurely.

Maybe if I say nothing, she'll stop talking.

He elected to keep his mouth shut, but his resolution didn't last long. Layla gave his frill a sharp tug to get his attention, and Aremaeid yelped loudly as a hot spike of pain shot down his spine. Before he realized what he was doing, he grabbed the girl and threw her off his back. She thudded to the ground and glared up at him.

"What the hell?" she whined. "I was just—"

"Do not do that," Aremaeid growled. He scooped her back up, this time holding her in his arms so she couldn't touch his frill again.

"I just want answers. Why are you here?"

"You think I will tell you after that little stunt?" he hissed, scowling down at her.

"We don't have anything better to do, so I'm just going to keep asking shit until you tell me. Why are you here? What are we doing in the woods? Why does it smell so weird?"

Ugh, even the human can smell him, Aremaeid thought bitterly as they trekked onwards. He made a mental note to punch Ziiphan when he found him. The others were probably planning the same. The girl prattled on, meanwhile, and although her intention was clearly to annoy him into speaking—she didn't seem to realize what a stupid plan this was—he tuned her out and focused on the woods around him. His nose told him Ziiphan had to be close because his musk kept growing denser, but his mind told him that with how far the scent had traveled, it could be hours before he located his packmate.

The sooner we find each other, the sooner we can leave.

It wasn't that he strongly disliked Earth, but it simply wasn't home. Everything was strange here, from the animals and plants to the terrain and weather patterns. Even the air felt wrong; heavy and stifling, like he was drowning in it. At least it was clean out here in the woods. It had been worse in the human town. The air there smelled *diseased,* full of fumes and tasting of chemicals that burned his lungs and stuck to his tongue like noxious slime. He wasn't sure how they could stand the environment, but he'd never asked Maisie about it. Only out here, among the trees and the grass, did he feel free to breathe safely.

He knew his packmates probably shared the same sentiments, even if they didn't express their feelings on the subject aloud. A desire to return to Primaied was one of the few things they could all agree upon. As he thought more about it, he was almost grateful for Ziiphan spreading his scent around the woods, making it smell like Rhithien and therefore more like Primaied.

Almost.

One of the girl's questions suddenly pulled him from his distracted stupor.

"Were you and Maisie friends?"

He regarded the child with renewed scrutiny as he considered his answer. No, he didn't think they had quite reached the point of friendship. But he had acted instinctually when he'd prevented Ornathium from killing her, and even now a small part of his mind wondered if she survived the attack.

"Acquaintances," he replied shortly. Yes, that seemed right.

"Oh, you're ready to talk now?"

"It depends on your questions. I cannot answer everything."

The girl was quiet for a moment, then asked in a small voice, "Am I going to die?"

Aremaeid didn't respond for a long while. It took some thinking before he finally settled on a response that felt appropriate.

"We did not collect you with the intention of killing you. You will die in time, as all humans do, but this excursion will not be the cause of it."

"Why me? Why not my brother, or my mom?"

"Ask Ornathium. He selected you. All we needed was a Lucio."

"Oh," she whispered. Her eyes glistened with sudden tears, and she shuddered against him, though whether it was from the residual chill in the air or her grief,

Aremaeid wasn't sure. She looked up with her watery blue eyes and sniffled, "I want to go home."

"For whatever it may be worth, you have my sympathy, child. I know what it is to lose someone you care for," he told her gently. "But my pack and I must complete our mission."

The human didn't say anything more. She shivered and cried quietly, but Aremaeid didn't offer further condolences. He eventually returned her to his back, and she pointedly avoided touching his frill this time. With the matter settled, he turned his attention to the task at hand: finding Ziiphan. It was far from easy with all the musk the egotistical bastard had put off, but by the time the sun was at last fully visible, Aremaeid heard a pair of voices in the distance. He knew one of them had to be Ziiphan because as he drew closer, the fog of musk grew so thick and suffocating that he could see the pungent heat of it warping the air around him. He at last broke through the trees to a small clearing, where two Rhithien awaited him. One was Ridaion, Salidus's consort, and the other was—shockingly enough—Ziiphan.

"Aremaeid!" Ziiphan called in greeting, standing up and offering an amiable grin. There was an air of smugness about him that made Aremaeid want to remove his spine with extreme prejudice.

"Do not run," he growled to Layla, pulling her off his back and setting her on the ground. She wisely obeyed as he stomped over to his packmates. Ridaion remained seated on the grass beside a thin, burbling brook, but Ziiphan obliviously walked towards Aremaeid with his hands raised peacefully.

"I was wondering when you would find us. And you have a human with you, I see! The heir? I should have guessed that you, of all Rhithien, would have—"

Aremaeid's fist shot out and cracked across his face. Ziiphan stumbled away with a hiss, but Aremaeid was quick to grab him by the frill and yank him back up, snarling in his face.

"What in Callii's name do you think you're playing at?" he demanded. "You've had us searching for you for hours! *Hours!* Would you like to explain why you've made yourself at home here rather than looking for the pack or our target?"

Ziiphan pulled away with a yowl, rubbing his frill, and gave Aremaeid an indignant huff.

"I don't see what the problem is. You've found me, haven't you? And even if you hadn't, you could have just waited in one spot once you found my territory

242

and I would have made my way to you eventually. I've never known you as the petty type."

Aremaeid flared up his frill and growled at him, low and threatening, until Ziiphan dropped eye contact and stepped away. Then he rounded on Ridaion, who watched the altercation with amusement dancing in his sharp green eyes.

"And you!" Aremaeid snarled. He knew Ridaion wasn't afraid of him, but the smaller Rhithien still flinched at his tone. "How did you find him?"

"The same way you did."

"How long have you been here?"

"Most of the week," Ridaion replied. He stood, crossed his arms over his narrow chest, and shifted his weight to one hip. "I'm surprised you didn't find him sooner. He's marked up the whole forest like a cub taking its first piss on a tree."

"There's nothing wrong with making yourself comfortable," Ziiphan interjected hotly. "I didn't know how long we were going to be here. And besides, I can see now that there was no need for me to sniff out the Lucio heir. You've already found her."

He sauntered over to where Layla sat against a tree and jabbed her with one toe. She whimpered and scooted away from him.

"It was Ornathium who found her," Aremaeid explained, and Ridaion grimaced.

"Explains why she's so skittish," he muttered.

"What did Ornathium do, girl?" Ziiphan inquired, switching to English. Layla, clearly not expecting him to address her, looked up at him with frightened surprise.

"I don't want to talk about it."

Ziiphan delivered a sharp kick to her shin, making her shriek and scrabble away.

"Why not, little human? I must confess that I cared not when I asked, but now I really want to know. Did you watch him dissect helpless creatures? Did he torture you horribly? What did he do to turn you into such a frightened little rhego?"

"He. . ." Layla swallowed hard, unable to finish. She wrapped her arms around herself and tried again. "He killed my family."

Ziiphan snorted and strode away.

243

"How terribly predictable. I expected something more devious from the Bloodhound of the Red Desert."

Layla glared up at him but said nothing. Ziiphan had mastered the art of provoking others, but to the girl's credit, she managed to hold her tongue.

"ZIIPHAN!"

All three Rhithien whipped around to see Vegra stomping towards them, seething. This was nothing new—he was always angry about something—but he was no less intimidating with his towering bulk and ferocious orange eyes.

"Vegra!" Ziiphan replied cheerfully. Despite his casual tone, Aremaeid saw a touch of fear in the way his tail curled around his legs and his frill pulled a bit tighter to his neck. As soon as he reached him, Vegra swiped his claws at his face, but Ziiphan, prepared for an attack this time, dodged the attempt.

"You petulant pile of shit!" Vegra roared, grabbing him by the neck and slamming him against a nearby tree hard enough to make the trunk tremble. "I should kill you right now for that stunt you pulled! I've had to breathe in your shit for hours!"

"Is it really all that bad?" Ziiphan teased, infuriating even as his life was on the line. "Your extreme state of denial almost leads me to wonder if you're interested in my—"

"I'LL FUCKING KILL YOU!"

Aremaeid rushed forward and pried Vegra off Ziiphan. He barked sharply at Ridaion in a wordless order to help, and the two of them managed to drag the older male away. Although Aremaeid's rank was higher than his, Vegra thrashed and snarled much more than he had with Orniell, and he even tried to bite Ridaion when the smaller male trapped him in a headlock.

"You're stuck with me, Vegra, because I will live forever!" Ziiphan crowed.

"Shut up, Ziiphan! That's an order!" Aremaeid shouted.

"I'll stuff your own guts down your throat and watch you choke on them!"

"Ooh, I like it rough! You could have just asked, you know."

"You're not fucking helping, Ziiphan!" Ridaion growled. He and Aremaeid soon managed to calm Vegra down enough that they didn't need to restrain him. The older male shot Ziiphan a murderous glare as he stormed to the other side of the clearing to fume at a distance.

"I like to think I'm helping him learn patience."

"Vegra doesn't know the meaning of the word," Ridaion scolded Ziiphan. "Don't bother."

From across the clearing, Vegra whipped his head around and hissed at the smaller male. He rose and stalked forward until he stood menacingly over him. Vegra was the largest in the pack, and though Ridaion was the smallest next to Torraeid, he stood his ground without displaying a single hint of fear.

"If you weren't our alpha's personal whore, I would snap your pretty little neck just for saying my name," Vegra hissed.

Ridaion put his hands on his hips and raised an eyebrow, amused by the threat.

"I'm sure you would, but unfortunately for you, I *am* his 'personal whore', as you so eloquently put it. So, while I'm flattered that you find my neck 'pretty,' our alpha is the only one who gets to lay a hand on it." He smiled sweetly, which only seemed to feed the fires of Vegra's rage, but they all knew the older male could do nothing unless he wanted Salidus to pull his head off; it had happened once before with another Rhithien named Mariykaed. Ridaion turned and sashayed away, brushing his tail teasingly against his packmate's leg. Vegra bared his teeth, and Aremaeid could see his entire body quaking with barely restrained fury, but he didn't pursue the smaller Rhithien.

When Orniell, Ornathium, and Torraeid finally arrived at the small clearing— Orniell gave Ziiphan a long, angry lecture while Ornathium just swatted playfully at his tail—the pack prepared to move on. They had yet to find Salidus.

"Once we find him, we go back to Primaied," Orniell declared, touching the small leather pouch strung around his neck that held the portal stones.

"Why don't we wait here just a bit longer?" Ridaion suggested as he knelt down and helped Layla climb onto his back.

"And your reasoning for that?" Orniell asked. His single yellow eye narrowed with dislike. He never fought with Ridaion, but like many other older Rhithien, he was against the idea of lowering oneself to the level of a consort to climb the ranks of a pack.

Ridaion ignored his unspoken judgment and gestured to the forest around them.

"These trees reek of Ziiphan for molosopions. Chances are good that Salidus will come along on his own if we stay put. Besides, the more we move around during the day, the higher the risk of being spotted by humans."

"No one asked for your opinion on the matter, draver," Vegra snapped.

"Quiet, Vegra. He makes a good argument," Orniell conceded with a sigh. He clearly didn't like changing his orders on account of Ridaion's word, but he wasn't stubborn or petty enough to ignore the younger male because of dislike. "New plan. We stay within a seven-dynnsopion radius until sundown. Torraeid, you will wait here with the human. The rest of us will patrol the perimeter of this area. Patrol it, don't expand it, *Ziiphan*. We will reconvene at sunset or whenever we find Salidus."

They all bowed their heads in assent and started off in different directions to carry out his orders.

*****

Aremaeid had been following the rough edge of Ziiphan's "territory" for close to an hour by the time he finally slowed down for a rest and caught a familiar scent. He had known Salidus for most of his time in the pack, had been his friend long before he'd challenged their previous alpha, and his scent had become as familiar as his own. Aremaeid shifted his direction and followed the smell, hoping to happen upon him. He pushed through a tight copse of trees and almost crashed straight into his alpha. He was met with snapping teeth and slashing claws, but Salidus relaxed when he realized who it was.

"Aremaeid," he greeted with a tired sigh of relief. "It's good to see you." As he moved forward and clasped his forearm in greeting, Aremaeid noticed how gingerly he held his left leg.

"You're injured," he said worriedly. "How bad?"

"I've had worse."

"How bad, Salidus?"

"It was much worse when I got it. I fixed most of it with my magic, but it's aggravated by how much I've been moving." He sniffed the air and wrinkled his nose in distaste. "Where's Ziiphan?"

"Searching for you elsewhere. We have the target. Torraeid's waiting with her."

"Good, good. That makes things much easier." Salidus hesitated, then added, "And Ridaion?"

"Safe. You're the last one we're waiting for."

"Good. Thank you."

Aremaeid led him on the long path to the clearing. Because Ziiphan's musk was so strong, he'd had to leave a visible trail that he could follow back. He didn't like the vulnerability in the fact that anyone or anything with a good pair of eyes could trace his steps, but it was unfortunately necessary. Even while he was injured and exhausted, Salidus walked with his head high and his face stern until they arrived.

"Torraeid," he said flatly as they entered the clearing. Torraeid immediately stood from where he sat beside Layla, but before he could speak, Salidus collapsed. He avoided face-planting in the dirt only because Aremaeid lunged to his side and caught him. He half-dragged his alpha to the bank of the small stream, where he carefully set him down so his leg could be tended to. He sent a silent thank you to Callii for the fact that the rest of the pack was absent. Some, like Vegra, might have considered issuing a challenge while Salidus was in a weakened state.

"How long has it been broken?" Torraeid asked, slipping into the curt, impersonal identity he assumed whenever he was carrying out his duties as a healer.

"No more than a day, I think."

"You don't know?"

"I was attacked by a group of humans, and I was forced to use all of my magic to fend them off. I almost had a burnout. Not sure how long I was in recharge," Salidus explained tiredly. "But it's recent."

"It looks like you fixed most of the damage with your magic."

"I set it, yes. It was. . ." He trailed off, then swallowed and said, "It's not the worst break I've ever had, but it's definitely among the less tolerable ones. I needed to keep moving."

"It was stupid of you to try and fix it on your own," Torraeid snapped. He only ever spoke so boldly when he was in a state of urgency like this. Salidus raised an eyebrow at the scolding but didn't put him in his place as the albino elaborated, "If you had done it wrong, I would have to re-break it and set the bone properly."

"I couldn't walk, Torraeid."

"It was still reckless. We cannot afford to lose you on this mission."

"Noted." Salidus didn't offer any further protest to his subordinate's criticism. Torraeid might have been the lowest-ranking Rhithien among them, but with how rare it was for a healer to be recruited to a pack, his word came first where wounds were concerned. Salidus simply leaned back against a tree and shut his eyes after instructing Aremaeid, "Call the others. We cannot waste any more time."

Aremaeid nodded, raised his head to the sky, and let out a long, piercing howl. Behind him, Torraeid gripped Salidus's leg and drifted away from physical reality. His eyes went white and the healing process began. Their alpha winced as his grey-blue skin was knitted together, and Aremaeid could hear shards of bone scraping against each other beneath mending flesh. Layla didn't approach, but she stared at them from across the clearing with a look of fascination. This healing took longer than hers had, and when it was finished, Torraeid slumped over wearily. Aremaeid was always concerned for his brother when his energy waned from magic use, but he knew Torraeid would get a chance to safely recharge once they were back on Primaied.

Ridaion was the first to return to the clearing, and he immediately ran to Salidus. Their alpha opened his eyes, and his expression of pain melted into one of exhausted relief. He stood on his repaired leg and embraced Ridaion tightly. The smaller male reached up to cup his face with his hands, studying him anxiously.

"I was worried!" he cried, his voice spilling out rapidly and fearfully. "Even when I found the others, I didn't know where you were or when we would find you! Are you alright?"

"I am now," Salidus murmured. He planted a small, delicate kiss on the tip of Ridaion's snout and nipped his ear affectionately. He released him, approached Layla, and asked, "This is the heir?"

"Yes."

"She's a child," he stated curtly, giving them an apprehensive and slightly surprised look.

"Ornathium selected this one," explained Aremaeid. "He was transported to the right spot."

"Is she the only one? Surely there must be other options."

"Ornathium killed the other options," Ridaion said dryly.

"Of course he did." Salidus sighed and rubbed his temples. After a moment of hesitation, he clapped his hands together with finality and said, "No matter. What's done is done. We can work with this. I'll speak to him about self-control after the ritual, but we cannot afford any more delays for the time being."

Vegra, Ziiphan, Ornathium, and Orniell soon returned to the clearing, each of them appearing from different directions and offering respectful greetings.

"It's about damn time we went back to Primaied. This planet reeks," Ziiphan said snidely. Vegra, irked by Ziiphan's attitude even when they weren't speaking to each other, growled and swatted angrily at him. But Salidus, to the pack's surprise, nodded his head in concurrence.

"I couldn't agree more. Orniell, the stones."

*****

They'd had to abandon Avery's jeep when the road disappeared into densely wooded terrain, and they'd been racing through the trees as fast as they could for hours. Parker and Avery were having an easier time following the Rhithien tracks now that the sun was up, and their small group was slowly picking up the pace as they made further headway. Maisie was proud of their progress, but she still wished they could go faster. She hadn't done any serious running in a long time. Still, she forced herself to keep going despite her throbbing migraine, burning lungs, and aching legs. Franklin made her take frequent rest breaks, and though she was grateful for them, she also dreaded them, because more time for them to rest meant more time for the Rhithien to get ahead.

Another problem that had arisen was the fact that they were no longer chasing two Rhithien. Judging by the trail, the siblings guessed that the aliens' numbers had increased to four, possibly five. When Parker had declared this sometime around 4:00 in the morning while inspecting the trail with his flashlight, Maisie had felt a surge of gratitude for the Rayblues. They were under no obligation to help her, but they were doing so anyway. No one elected to point out the increasingly poor odds they were faced with.

"This is a hell of a lot easier with daylight," Parker panted as they jogged along a narrow footpath. "Who'd've thought it would be so hard to track a bunch of aliens in the middle of the night?"

"I'm still having a hard time believing this alien business," Avery commented from the back of the group. Although she was the most physically fit out of all of them, she had insisted on taking up the rear. "I believe that someone kidnapped Layla, obviously, but are you sure you saw it right?"

"I know what I saw," Maisie answered for what felt like the hundredth time. Franklin and Avery were still dubious about the Rhithien, but Parker, at least, was more than happy to believe that a pack of aliens was running around on Earth.

"If they don't exist, then how are we following their tracks?" he called from ahead.

"We don't know that these are Rhithien tracks," Avery pointed out. "How many Rhithien have you hunted, exactly? And how do we even know that we're following the right trail?"

"And what's that smell?" Franklin added, wrinkling his nose. Sure enough, a heavy, unidentifiable odor hung in the air. It had been gradually getting stronger for the last few miles. Maisie, however, was too exhausted to care about it. Her face was flushed with exertion and her hair was plastered to her forehead with sweat. She knew that if she took the time to stop again and focus on how sore her entire body was, she wouldn't be able to keep going.

Despite her determination, she was close to giving in and asking for another quick break when Parker turned around and excitedly shouted over his shoulder, "I think we're getting close!"

A tremendous, resonating *bang* echoed across the mountains like a cannon blast, and a bright light shone from behind a thicket of trees just over fifty yards away. Maisie recalled the night of Aremaeid's arrival and found herself picking up speed. The others slowed down and fell behind with murmurs of unease, but she paid them no mind.

"It's them!" she exclaimed, racing ahead of the group. She distantly heard Franklin call her name, but she didn't stop or slow down. All she could think about—all that mattered—was rescuing Layla. Spurred on by a burst of adrenaline, she rushed to the copse of trees, almost slamming headlong into the trunks in her hurry to get through, and once she'd gotten past them, she found herself in a spacious clearing. In the center of the area, hovering above the ground, was a large, swirling circle of white light. She was just in time to see a gray tail disappear into it, leaving her alone.

She didn't hesitate.

Maisie dashed forward, pumping her arms and legs as hard as she could, the adrenaline in her veins temporarily subduing her exhaustion. She heard Franklin and his siblings crash through the trees behind her, yelling her name, but she ignored them and dove head-first into the portal.

XXVII

Traveling through the gateway was easier than it had been the first time around. The slight weightlessness and heavy air that confounded Aremaeid on Earth transitioned to the natural atmosphere of Primaied, and he took a deep, cleansing breath.

Home.

He moved forward to his alpha's side. Although Orniell was the second of the pack, he would be the last one through because of Salidus's trust in him to close the portal properly. He heard a faint *whoosh* as Ridaion emerged behind him. They emerged in the same place they'd departed from, in the large room of the Knowledge Center where Fiiorha had initially sent them on their mission. A young scholar stood in the doorway, staring slack-jawed at the three of them. Then she dashed away, her footsteps echoing loudly through the halls, and Aremaeid heard her call to the others:

"Fiiorha! Someone get Fiiorha! They're back!"

Aremaeid glanced down at Layla, who had fallen to her knees and begun retching on the floor. He wasn't surprised that a human would have such an adverse reaction to portal travel, seeing as they had such delicate physiology. Especially a child. There was nothing left in her stomach to eject, thankfully, and after a moment she lifted her head and looked around blearily. She took in the small bowl of portal stones, the domed expanse of the room, and the sandy red stones that built the Knowledge Center.

"What. . . What is this place?" she asked. She looked up at Aremaeid and whispered, "Is this Primaied?"

Vegra, who came through after Ridaion, growled at her, "Where else would it be, girl?" He was gruff as usual, but even he seemed glad to be back home.

"Hush, Vegra. Save it for the end," Salidus scolded, albeit without much conviction. Ziiphan came next, then Ornathium and Torraeid respectively, and Orniell arrived just as Fiiorha and Nexus came rushing into the room with the young scholar scampering at their heels.

"Oh, thank Callii!" Fiiorha cried. She ran up to them, and Salidus looked touched by her concern until she snatched the bag carrying Rhala's remains from around his neck and loosened the drawstring to make sure the bones were all there. She sighed in relief and carefully closed the pouch, then glared at Salidus and slapped him across the face. The entire pack hissed and snarled defensively, and Orniell had to grab hold of Ridaion's arms to prevent him from lunging at her. Unperturbed by their reaction, the scholar bared her teeth at Salidus, dashed her tail spikes across the stone floor, and shouted, "What on the three fucking moons were you doing there? We were about to send Tembran's pack because we thought you'd been captured! What were you thinking?"

"We were scattered," Salidus explained calmly. Fiiorha snorted.

"Impossible."

"Improbable, you mean. You were the one who told us the odds were low, but not nonexistent. We were lucky not to encounter any errors on the way back."

"Do not test me, Salidus," Fiiorha growled. "You forget your place."

"I know my place," Salidus stated flatly. Before she could hit him again, he added, "We mustn't waste time. We have a Lucio and the bones. If we are going to do the ritual, it must be now."

"Oh, it is such a little thing!" crooned Nexus, who knelt beside Layla and purred softly at her. The girl cringed away, but Nexus reached out and carefully scooped her up. Layla looked more confused than frightened.

The young scholar, who Aremaeid had almost forgotten was there, leaned to the side to peer around the pack. She frowned and asked a hesitant question that made the whole room go still.

"Why did you bring two?"

"You brought *two?*" Fiiorha roared.

"Even better!" exclaimed Nexus.

"What?" said Salidus. They all turned around to see that a red-haired female had followed them through the portal. She was on her knees and panting with exertion as if she'd been running for days. Aremaeid's blood went cold at the sight of her.

No.

*****

Being transported through the portal was somewhat like falling in an elevator. It made Maisie feel like she'd left her stomach back on Earth. The light was blinding, and she was surrounded by blazing heat and numbing cold all at once. It lasted for a fraction of a second, then she stumbled onto a hard surface that was gritty with sand.

For a moment, she couldn't breathe. The atmosphere was thin and arid, and her senses were assaulted by dry, stifling heat. Beneath her feet were huge, rust-colored bricks constructing a well-paved floor. It was scattered with stray particles of sand and gravel like mud tracked into a house by dirty feet, and they ground painfully into her knees. A nearby window filled the room with scalding light, and she had to shield her face from the bright assault. She blinked her watering eyes a few times to adjust. An odd chorus of snapping and snarling filled her ears and then ceased all at once. She dropped her hand from her eyes and lifted her head to see a crowd of Rhithien staring down at her.

They were all of varying heights and skin tones and sported a surprisingly vast assortment of eye colors. Maisie recognized Aremaeid and the red-eyed Rhithien immediately. Then her gaze fell upon Layla, who gaped at her with the same expression of shock the aliens wore.

"Layla!" Maisie yelled, surging to her feet and dashing forward, but one of the Rhithien—a big gray one with painful-looking scars on his throat—grabbed her hair and threw her back onto the hard floor. It was then that all the Rhithien got over their surprise and reacted to her presence, and Maisie recoiled at the guttural snarls and roars that passed between them. As she listened, she noticed repeating patterns and fluctuations in their voices and realized that they were speaking some sort of primal alien language. The big Rhithien who had knocked her down grabbed the collar of her shirt, lifted her up, and shook her roughly. His eyes were alight with rage, and he snarled in her face.

"WHAT ARE YOU DOING HERE!" he roared. It sounded more like an expression of anger than an actual question. Maisie just stared dumbly up at him. Any words she might have offered died on her tongue. In hindsight, she realized that jumping through a strange portal might have been a rash and stupid idea.

Another Rhithien—a blue one with a noticeably larger frill than the others—snapped something at the gray one, and he dropped her with a growl. Maisie

253

deduced that the blue one was probably Salidus, the alpha of the pack. A tall Rhithien with a dozen long spikes at the end of its tail approached Salidus and said something to him. Another one, also spike-tailed, added something to the conversation. Both had the same large frills that he did. Maisie found herself completely focused on the latter of those two Rhithien. It cradled Layla delicately in its arms like an infant, crooning and purring at her.

Salidus nodded. The tall spike-tailed one rolled its eyes and growled, but didn't protest as it handed him a small bag. He opened it up and dumped a bunch of small, clinking objects into his hand, and Maisie squinted at them.

Are those. . . bones?

"Since you are here, you might as well be witness to this," Salidus said to her in the same lightly accented English that Aremaeid used. His voice was deep and rich, almost musical in tone. A tall, lean Rhithien with orange skin and bursts of dark spots approached Maisie, wound his fist into her hair, and hauled her painfully to her feet. She cried out and clawed at his fingers, but it was no use.

Salidus ignored her struggling as the taller of the two spike-tailed Rhithien handed him a piece of chalk, and he began, "One thousand, nine hundred, eighty-three years ago, a great Rhithien leader went through the portal to Earth when it was first discovered. Rhala was his name. He earned his title and his kingdom by fighting a ninety-year global war against the Rhithien tyrant Zaidryn, who sought to eradicate the other three dominant species and bring all of Primaied to its knees. For the first and only time in our recorded history, Rhala managed to unite Rhithien, Serrhithien, Viprhess, and Omelae under a single cause, a single army, a single will to survive and conquer. Serrhithien have kingdoms ruled by coljynns and coljerras, but we Rhithien have only ever had one true king: Rhala himself."

As he spoke, he knelt down to the ground, brushed aside some sand, and drew a wide circle on the red stone. It was roughly five feet in diameter, and he had to maneuver somewhat awkwardly to finish it. Next, he drew a second circle just inside it, forming the shape of a ring.

"Rhala's name has passed into legend. Stories of him are told everywhere, among all cultures, from his greatest battles to his courting of Haraena, his queen and lifemate. It is one of the earliest legends our cubs learn. But then he went through the portal. A trusted scholar convinced him to take an alphaic suppressant for fear that his magic would interfere with the portal's function. It was such a new discovery, they refused to take any risks. It is because of this that he had no access to his magic when he was challenged and killed by a human—a *human,* of all creatures—named Aurelia Lucio."

He can't be serious.

Did they really think that twelve-year-old Layla, who had been failing most of her classes less than a year ago, was related to some ancient alien killer? Maisie found it hard to believe. Even if it was true, it didn't explain why they needed Layla alive. Wouldn't they prefer to wipe out the entire bloodline for killing their king?

"Our scholars began to track that family's movements across Earth. It was difficult, but we followed them. Learned from them. This girl is one of many carriers of that bloodline. Then, one hundred seventy-four years ago, we found evidence of a ritual that could bring the dead back to life. That was when we began to wonder if Rhala himself could be brought back. So scholars began to test the ritual, trying for many trilunar cycles to uncover its secrets. In the meantime, hundreds of thousands of Rhithien packs—including my own—formed a plan. We learned all we could about human cultures and even studied a few common tongues in case of setbacks or emergency negotiations.

"But we all had hope. When the ritual was perfected, one pack would be sent to the Lucio home on Earth. We would collect one descendent and bring them back to Primaied, which we have done. Now the rest is no longer planning; it is certainty. Rhala will be resurrected and unite us once again. He will bring all four dominants together into an unstoppable army. With him as our commander and king, we will take for ourselves the planet he perished on, and we will destroy the creatures who dared to lay their hands on him."

He began scrawling strange symbols and interconnected lines within the borders of the ring, swiveling on his heels in his crouched position to build the pattern. Maisie realized it was more than linework—he was drawing neatly-crafted symbols that resembled writing. She didn't know what the symbols meant, or what Omelae, Serrhithien, and Viprhess were, but his message wasn't hard to grasp.

"We encountered a problem, however," Salidus continued. "The ritual only worked on someone who was murdered, and while Rhala fit the requirements for that, we needed both his blood and the blood of his killer. Or their descendants, at the very least. We could have collected a Lucio's blood at any time, but finding Rhala's was a challenge. Shortly after Rhala's death, some of Zaidryn's remaining followers attacked his fortress and slaughtered his pack. These insurgents were eventually stopped by loyal Rhithien, but Rhala's queen, Haraena, disappeared. Until recently, it was believed that she was killed in the attack with the rest of his court, but our scholars scoured every resource they could find and discovered that she changed her name and fled to an Oasis to live in secrecy. She had just given birth to the first and only litter she and Rhala conceived together, and she brought those cubs with her when she escaped. One of that Oasis's elders recorded her identity and the names of her children in a journal he kept. When that journal was found, the final pieces of the puzzle were put in place.

"The resurrection ritual itself was perfected over fifty years ago. It took us the remaining time to track down Rhala's current descendants and decide which pack would go to Earth, but we succeeded in the end. I regret to say that I had to keep this information from most of my own pack, but his heir is right here in this room."

The pack started muttering and turning heads, looking suspiciously around at each other. Maisie noticed that Aremaeid was the only one who remained still. His eyes were shut and every muscle in his body was tight like he was gearing himself up for a difficult task. He opened his eyes and lifted his head when Salidus said, "Aremaeid, would you come forward?"

Judging by his lack of surprise, Maisie could see that Aremaeid already knew. He stepped up beside his alpha, and Maisie's blood chilled with hard, frosty anger. This revelation somehow made all the lies he'd fed her even worse. She squirmed against her captor's grip and tried to catch Aremaeid's eye, but he seemed determined not to look at her. Salidus finished his work with two overlapping squares connecting the inner sides of the ring at eight congruent points, then beckoned forward the Rhithien holding Layla. He grabbed the girl's skinny wrist in one large hand and held her arm out over the drawing, then sliced open her palm with a single claw. Her blood dripped to the floor, and Maisie could have sworn she saw the ring pulse with a faint purple glow.

"First comes the killer's blood, then the remains of the fallen," Salidus explicated. He released Layla, who immediately yanked her hand back against her chest. Next, he knelt and carefully placed the pile of bones in the center of the drawing. Another sparking purple glow, this one slightly stronger. Finally, he turned to Aremaeid, placed a reassuring hand on his third's shoulder, and said, "Then Rhala's blood." Aremaeid faced the ring and held the point of a claw against his own hand, but he seemed to be hesitating.

Unable to hold her silence any longer, Maisie ignored the pain in her scalp and jerked defiantly against the grip of the Rhithien holding her in place.

"Aremaeid, stop!" she yelled, and all the Rhithien except him looked down at her. "They're talking about starting a war!"

"This war began when your kind butchered our king," snarled the taller of the spike-tailed Rhithien. "Be silent, little beast."

"No! Aremaeid, this is genocide! You can't do this, they're going to kill *everyone*! Entire families, an entire *planet!*"

"Shut up!" snapped the Rhithien above her. He released his hold on her hair and backhanded her across the face. The blow sent her to the ground, and for a moment she was only aware of a sharp, ugly pain in her cheek and a dull ringing in her ears. She forced herself back up to her hands and knees anyway, stumbling through the pain. She took encouragement from the fact that Aremaeid still hadn't completed the ritual. Was he listening?

"Please!" she begged him. The Rhithien above her tried to hit her again, but she dodged his swipe and crawled forward. "Who cares if you're related to Rhala? Sure, maybe his death was unfair after everything he did, but he's been gone for two thousand years!"

A foot kicked her harshly in the stomach, knocking her to the side with a cry of pain. Then the spotted Rhithien was kneeling over her, pushing her onto her back. One of his large hands clapped over her face. She let out a muffled scream of protest and scratched desperately at his rough, leathery skin, but was unable to dislodge his grip.

"With every word that comes out of your mouth, I am getting closer and closer to removing your tongue," the Rhithien growled. "You are lucky to witness this, so shut up and enjoy your final minutes of life."

"That thing does not command you, Aremaeid," Salidus hissed, and Maisie peeked through her captor's fingers to look desperately over at where they stood. Aremaeid still hadn't moved, and even though his back was to her, she could sense his conflict. Salidus could, too, and he added, "You have been one of my closest friends for many years, Aremaeid. When I tell you that you are Rhala's heir, you know I speak the truth, and you know how much it means. This is something you must do; not just for the pack, but for Primaied itself."

Maisie screamed again and kicked at the spotted Rhithien, but it was no good, and her hope was quickly failing. Aremaeid barely knew her. She'd seen how loyal he was to his pack. Maybe he was conflicted, but all her pleas and all her efforts would ultimately amount to nothing.

Then Aremaeid said one word, one single syllable powerful enough to settle a veil of silence over the room.

"No."

*****

"What do you mean, 'no'?" Fiiorha demanded, her tone colored with anger and disbelief. She had abandoned English and reverted to Rhithos. Aremaeid turned to his alpha, who stared at him with an expression of shocked betrayal.

"You can't mean that," Salidus breathed.

"This isn't right, Salidus. Yes, one human wronged us in the past, but that human has been dead for nearly twenty trilunar cycles. The fate of their world is not ours to decide."

"It *is* ours!" Fiiorha roared, shoving him roughly and baring her teeth at him. "They deserve no mercy! Do you not comprehend the importance of what we are doing here?"

"I do. But this is wrong."

"Aremaeid," Salidus said quietly, grabbing his shoulders and turning him so he could see his face. "I know this is a lot, and I understand your doubts. Please believe me when I say that. I have felt them myself. But this is bigger than us. And whether we like it or not, it's bigger than them. You've seen the scholars' reports on their planet just as the rest of us have. It's dying."

"So let it die. What difference should it make to us?"

"If we rid that planet of the disease which is killing it—humanity—we might be able to save it. We wouldn't just be avenging an ancient insult, we would be reviving an entire world! Imagine what it would mean for Primaied's future if we could give a second world to the generations yet to come! And if we had Rhala at the helm of it all. . ."

"Quit the niceties, Salidus," Fiiorha growled. "You and your pack of labyllic hounds have wasted enough time already. He doesn't want to be a willing participant? Fine. We don't need him. We only need his blood. Take it and be done with this."

Aremaeid took a step back, looked his alpha in the eye, and pleaded, "Salidus, don't do this."

Salidus's face twisted with genuine pain, then his shoulders slumped and he gave a heavy sigh. His blue eyes flicked towards Vegra, and before Aremaeid could react, the older male's fist slammed into his face. He faltered for a mere second at the sudden hit, but it was enough time for Vegra to get behind him and loop both arms beneath his biceps, pinning him firmly in place. Salidus slashed his claws across Aremaeid's chest, just below his collarbone. The cuts were shallow and stung only slightly, but it was enough to wet the alpha's claws with blood. Salidus inspected the dark purple splotches for a moment, then sent a few drops flying into the drawn ring with a single flick of his hand.

The ring began to pulse and hum at a frequency that Aremaeid could feel throughout his whole body, right down to his marrow. The markings simmered with brilliant violet light, and the knuckle bones that Salidus had placed in the middle of the drawing rattled against each other and rose off the ground. They started to spontaneously hook together, and corded muscle fibers twisted around them. The muscles linked together and were subsequently cloaked in sheets of skin, forming the shape of a hand from empty air and expanding outward into a huge arm. For a moment, Aremaeid was transfixed by the macabre display, but when Vegra's arms loosened around him, he realized what he had to do. He had only a moment while the older male was distracted, but it was enough.

He thrust his head back, and his left horn impaled Vegra's face. He felt the sharp point crack through bone, and he ripped it out with a spray of blood. Vegra howled and his grip slackened, allowing Aremaeid to jerk away. He threw an elbow back into the older male's gut for good measure. He lunged at Orniell, who, to his surprise, didn't fight back. He simply stood there while Aremaeid smacked the portal stones from his hand and snatched them out of the air. When the rest of the pack didn't try to stop him, he turned on Ziiphan and threw his full weight into body-slamming him off of Maisie. Ziiphan fell away with a grunt and sat on the ground, staring stupidly up at him.

It all happened in a matter of seconds, and before he had time to reconsider, Aremaeid scooped Maisie under one arm and broke into a run, dashing past

Fiiorha and into the hallway of the Knowledge Center. He could feel her magic crackling through the air behind him and knew he would only have a few moments to activate the portal. She roared at the pack to chase him down, her voice reverberating off the stone walls, but he didn't stop to see if they obeyed. He allowed an image to filter into the forefront of his mind: the recent memory of the woods they'd left behind, right in the clearing where he had found Ziiphan. Holding the picture in his head, he lifted the portal stones to his lips and whispered, "Earth."

He threw them onto the ground and the portal opened with a flash. He heard gasps and screams from nearby scholars but didn't address them. He didn't dare look at them. He kicked the stones away from where they rested on the ground and dove through the gateway with Maisie. Only then did he risk a glance over his shoulder. Nexus came running into the hall with Layla huddled in her arms, as did the pack. The girl's face was tight with pale defeat, and a whip of guilt raked Aremaeid's soul at the sight. Then the light engulfed him, deafened him, blinded him, and his mind went blank until he stumbled forward into frost-glazed grass.

XXVIII

Maisie let all of her loathing show on her face as Aremaeid set her carefully down on the ground and dusted some sand out of her hair. He didn't release his hold on her, however, until the portal shut behind them and disappeared. Then he took a long step back and waited for her to say something. She breathed in the silence, and it was only when the tense quiet got to him and he started to speak that she stormed forward and hit him.

"Maisie—"

"You left her behind!" she yelled, smacking his arm. "You left her!"

"I know, and I am sorry."

"No, you're fucking not!"

She balled up a fist and punched him in the abdomen as hard as she could, but it was like punching a brick wall. She yanked her hand back with a pained hiss and rubbed her knuckles. Aremaeid sighed and stood in place without protest as she picked up a rock from the nearby stream and hurled it at him. It bounced off his torso and onto the ground, and he stared wearily down at her.

"Are you finished?"

"Fuck you!" Maisie spat. Just then, she heard rustling in the trees behind her, and a collection of voices drew closer.

"She's over here!"

"But you said—"

"I know, but this is where it happened!"

Franklin came through the trees first, and he was quickly followed by Parker, Avery, and to Maisie's shock, the two detectives. The five of them stopped and stared at Aremaeid. Then Avery and Parker hefted their rifles while Davis and Moore whipped out handguns. It took Maisie a second to remember that although she'd told the Rayblues everything, none of them had actually seen a Rhithien before.

"What the hell is that thing!" Avery yelled. She didn't seem to be expecting an answer.

"Ms. Arberon, I want you to walk toward me very slowly," Davis instructed, sounding surprisingly calm despite the shaking in his hands and the paleness of his face. He sounded like he was simultaneously coaxing her out of suicide and guiding her away from a rabid animal. A fitting tone, she supposed.

"Okay, I know how this looks," she said slowly, holding up her hands, "but don't shoot him." She wouldn't have minded if Aremaeid received a healthy dose of karma for leaving Layla behind, but she still needed him. She couldn't get back to Primaied without his help.

" 'Don't shoot'? Are you fucking kidding me?" cried Avery with a breathy, anxious laugh.

"I'm not! Do not shoot, Avery!"

Maisie moved forward and attempted to grab the barrel of the gun—she realized it was a stupid move right as her fingers closed around the metal. Avery panicked at the interference and pulled the trigger. The ensuing *bang* cracked through the trees like thunder, and Maisie screamed as the bullet ripped through her hand and buried itself in Aremaeid's chest. He stumbled back with a hiss but looked more irritated than hurt. Dark purple blood oozed from the wound as he dug his fingers into the torn skin and wrenched the bullet out.

"WHAT THE SHIT IS WRONG WITH YOU!" Maisie shrieked, clutching her hand. A gaping hole yawned up from her palm, giving her a view beneath her skin that she had never wanted to see.

"Why did you grab the fucking gun?" Avery yelled.

"You shot me!"

"Jesus Christ!" Franklin exclaimed. He ran to Maisie and hovered his hands over the wound helplessly.

Maisie's throat suddenly constricted, and air became a luxury that she couldn't quite grasp. She breathed rapidly in and out, unable to get enough oxygen, and tears sprung from her eyes. Hyperventilating, she tried to recall what her therapist had told her about anxiety attacks, but his instructions stuck deep in her brain like glue. She couldn't remember. All she knew at that moment was that she couldn't breathe and there was a giant hole in her hand.

"Maisie, focus on me. I need you to breathe."

Who was talking to her? She didn't know. She couldn't think. The only thing her mind allowed her to focus on was the perforation in her palm that certainly didn't belong there.

"She shouldn't have grabbed the gun!"

"Shut up, Avery! You're not helping!"

"It's not my fault she's an idiot! She grabbed the goddamn barrel!"

Deep breaths. Be calm. In, out. In, out. Deep breaths. Be calm. In. . . and out.

Her breathing gradually slowed until she could focus enough to process her surroundings. Franklin was in front of her, and when she looked up, she saw him staring down at her, his face pale and tight.

"Alright. That's better. Are you okay?" he asked. Maisie couldn't quite form words, so she just closed her eyes and nodded while he tore a strip of fabric from the bottom of his shirt and wrapped it around her hand. Her breaths were still short and quick, but she had regained some control.

Need to breathe. Just focus on breathing.

"I hate to interrupt," Detective Moore said, "but does someone want to explain to me what that thing is?"

Maisie looked over her shoulder at Aremaeid, who stood in awkward silence a few yards away from them.

"Franklin, Parker, Avery. . . Davis, Moore. . . this is Aremaeid," she explained shakily, clutching her wounded hand.

"Did that thing kill the Lucios?" Davis demanded.

"No, that was a different one. Franklin, you remember when I said one was staying in my basement? This is him."

"Nine feet tall," Parker murmured. "You weren't joking."

"That's really what you're going to comment on?" Avery asked snidely. Franklin glared at his sister and spoke up.

"Where's the second one, then? Where's Layla?"

"They're. . ." Maisie couldn't finish.

Aremaeid seemed to sense her despair and answered the question.

"I came here with my pack. There were eight of us, including myself. They are now back on Primaied, as is the Lucio girl."

"Prim. . . Primai. . . ?"

"Primaied. My planet."

"That reminds me—You left Layla behind! Open the portal, now!" Maisie shouted. Her face hot with rage, she pushed Franklin aside and stomped toward Aremaeid.

"I cannot," the Rhithien said flatly. Maisie picked up another rock and threw it furiously at him as if a part of her anticipated a different result. They all watched as it smacked his broad chest and fell harmlessly into the grass. He gave an exasperated sigh that made her want to grab Avery's gun again so she could shoot him herself.

"Why not?" she demanded.

"There are certain stones needed to open the portal. The ones my pack and I used to come here are currently on Primaied. We cannot return unless more Rhithien come to Earth."

Maisie threw her arms out to the sides and let out a breathy laugh of disbelief. "You can't be serious."

"Why would I lie about this?"

"You lied about a shit-ton of other things."

"Yes, but I have no reason to do so now. You know that."

She did know. Why would he lie when he just betrayed his own planet? He was right, but it didn't help. It just made her angrier.

"What happened?" Parker asked. "Why did you come back? Why aren't you there?"

Maisie took a deep breath and summarized what had transpired on Primaied. She gave them the synopsis of Rhala's story and described the ritual, then finished with a recapitulation of Aremaeid's sudden change of heart.

"You left her there," she repeated.

Aremaeid's golden eyes narrowed and his jaw tightened.

"There was nothing I could have done for her."

"Bullshit. She was right there. You could have—"

"I would have had to get through Salidus, Fiiorha, and Nexus. All three of them have magic, and Fiiorha alone has the ferocity of ten Rhithien. If I had tried to fight them, none of us would have made it back here. You would have been killed or taken down to Nexus's labs to live out the rest of your days as a prisoner, and I would have been taken captive, assuming I survived."

264

Maisie shook her head wildly. Damn him! He was right again, but she didn't want to believe it. She didn't want to believe that she had come this far for nothing.

"That's *bullshit!*" she yelled, stamping her foot hard on the ground. She tried to punch him again, but he leaned down and gripped her arms, holding her firmly in place.

"I am truly sorry," he said with unexpected softness. "But there was nothing either of us could have done."

With those words, all of Maisie's anger drained away and was replaced by exhaustion. He released her, and she would have fallen to her knees in defeat if Franklin hadn't rushed forward and grabbed her. He hugged her tightly, and she pressed her face into his chest. This couldn't be real. She was the only one Layla had left, and she'd failed her.

"So that's it, then?" demanded Avery. "The kid's trapped on some alien planet, and we came all the way out here for nothing?"

"Hold up," Parker interjected, addressing Aremaeid. "If you can't open the portal without the stones, and you don't have any stones, doesn't that mean you're stuck on Earth?"

"Yes."

"Where are you going to go?"

"I will figure something out," the Rhithien said gruffly. Suddenly his ears twitched, and he lifted his nose to sniff at the air. He frowned, then looked sharply down at the humans and bared his teeth with a snarl that made them all jump.

"You called others?" he growled. Maisie gave Franklin a questioning look.

"I-I called Davis and Moore because I didn't know what to do, but I swear I didn't talk to anyone else!" he protested.

Avery spun around, studying the surrounding woods with renewed panic, and demanded, "Then who—"

"We need to get out of here," Maisie interrupted urgently. She recalled the unknown car that had been parked outside Fairview Middle School, as well as the man in the Hawaiian shirt who followed her in Grader's. She knew then that they weren't alone. She turned to Aremaeid and said, "There are some people with a lot of power who know you're here. If they see you—"

"Who did you tell?" he demanded.

"I didn't tell anyone! Unlike certain aliens here, I try to avoid lying. But these people. . . they don't need me to tell them anything. They could be here right now. You need to leave."

Aremaeid slowly backed away, studying the trees around them with wary eyes and a defensive growl.

A sharp *ping* sounded, and a small dart zipped from the foliage to strike him in the chest. He snarled and ripped it out of his skin, crushing it easily in his fist, but three more flew out and found their mark in the side of his neck. He stumbled backward and slammed into a tree, but when he still didn't go down, two more darts bulleted into his thigh. His feet slipped out from under him and he crashed to the ground.

"Shit, Aremaeid!" Maisie cried, shoving past Franklin and crouching in front of the Rhithien. His eyelids blinked rapidly over dilated pupils, then his eyes rolled back and he slumped forward, motionless. Maisie slapped his face a couple of times but received no response.

"Ma'am, I'm going to say this once: step away."

She turned to see a swarm of people materializing from between the trees, all wearing heavy-looking black uniforms, polycarbonate masks, and body armor. They pointed large guns at her, the Rayblues, and the detectives. Maisie stood and retreated from Aremaeid, putting her hands in the air. Two of the men approached the unconscious Rhithien and began to lift his arms.

Maisie gasped at a sudden prick in her neck. It felt like the sting of an oversized wasp, painful and sharp. Her vision blurred and she swayed on her feet for a moment, pawing at her neck. Everything went awash with white, and the natural sounds of the forest blended into a dull ringing. The last thing she saw was Franklin and his siblings flailing like puppets on strings and falling to the ground.

Then the world tilted abruptly to the side and everything went dark.

XXIX

Salidus stood frozen in the hallway of the Knowledge Center, staring at the place where Aremaeid disappeared. He couldn't believe it. He'd known Aremaeid since he first joined the pack, back when he sailed to Armenthaal from the Serrhithien kingdom of Bailidok and Aremaeid was just a scrawny new recruit. Then, almost a hundred years later, when he told a select few members of the pack that he was planning to challenge the previous alpha, Niabrham, Aremaeid had been the first to offer support. And before that, when Niabrham killed Aremaeid's closest companion, Salidus had been there for him with an emotional availability that few Rhithien knew how to offer.

Aremaeid had fought alongside him and saved his life in battle countless times.

Aremaeid had carried him to shelter through a blizzard when their pack was separated in an avalanche and Salidus had been badly wounded.

Aremaeid had been one of the first to accept Ridaion when he was traded to them as a peace offering from a rival pack.

Salidus had spent half his life on the continent of Armenthaal, and Aremaeid had been at his side throughout all of it, his brother in all but blood. And now he was gone, abandoning a cause that had been carefully developed and planned for generations in favor of a dying planet. Salidus wasn't surprised when the pack didn't try to stop Aremaeid. He could have stopped him with his magic, but something deep in his soul wouldn't allow it. Unfortunately for him, Fiiorha noticed his hesitation.

"What in Callii's name were you doing?" she roared at him as soon as the portal closed. She stomped forward and shoved him. "Where's your magic when it's needed?"

"I. . ." Salidus stopped before he could try to stammer out an explanation. There was no good excuse for his inaction, so he lifted his chin, folded his hands

267

behind his back, and admitted, "I did not stop him when I should have. I apologize. I expected you to accost him. As an elder, you have your own magic."

"You're a fucking *alpha*. He is your subordinate. It is your responsibility to keep your pack in line," Fiiorha hissed. "And if you can't do that, maybe you shouldn't have the title."

"Uh, Salidus?" called Ridaion.

Salidus and Fiiorha turned back to the ritual ring. The knuckle bones had formed one large arm and now began to twist and expand into the shape of a torso and neck. Salidus found himself unable to look away from the strange, grisly process. Utterly fascinated by the sight of bones forming from nothing, he gazed at the way they gleamed in the window-filtered sunlight for one moment and were shrouded in muscle the next, then finally sheathed in skin the color of dark, oiled wood. It took only two minutes for the huge body to materialize, ending with grooved horns and fully extended claws.

At last. Rhala himself, the victor of Zaidryn's War, the savior of Primaied, and the king of Armenthaal.

Rhala opened his eyes and blinked. He swayed on his feet for a moment before keeling forward and falling heavily to his knees. Salidus and Fiiorha temporarily forgot their fight and rushed to his side. He was heavy; heavier than Salidus had expected, and the sudden slack weight almost made his knees buckle, even with Fiiorha's help. Rhala was enormous, close to twice the size of a small Rhithien and nearly the height of an Omelaen. Just one of his scarred hands was the size of Salidus's head. Small tusks jutted up past his lower lip, adding to the threatening factor of his appearance, and his horns curled peculiarly at the tips. When he opened his eyes again, Salidus saw that his irises were the same vivid gold as Aremaeid's. Even disoriented and on his knees, it was easy to see why so many were willing to follow him. To Salidus, seeing Rhala with his own eyes was like looking upon a god.

"My king?" he whispered, keeping his voice low to avoid giving the older Rhithien any shock. He had just come back from the dead, after all. Rhala only groaned in response, and Fiiorha jerked her head towards Salidus in a silent signal. Together, they pushed him up to his feet, and this time he managed to stay balanced on his own. He turned to the window and brought one huge hand up to his eyes, squinting in the light of the two suns. He turned in a slow circle, blearily taking in his surroundings.

"Where—" he began, but his voice cracked from hoarseness, and he doubled over with a hacking cough. Then he straightened and tried again. "Where am I?"

"The Southern Red Desert Oasis," Fiiorha answered, clasping her hands behind her back and raising her head proudly.

"Who are you?"

"I am Fiiorha, one of the elders and the head scholar here. This is Salidus. He and his pack helped you return."

Rhala stared at her blankly, then his brow furrowed and his eyes narrowed critically.

"I have been to this Oasis before," he said, "and I don't recall your face. You say you are the head scholar? When did you replace Prahlen? He was at my fortress when I went through the gateway."

Fiiorha hesitated, then responded, "This may be hard for you to understand, my king, but—"

"Where's Haraena?" Rhala interrupted. He looked around the room hopefully, then he blanched fearfully as he touched his fingers to his temple and murmured, "I can't feel her."

"My king, what you need to understand is—"

"Why can't I feel her?" he demanded, taking an unsteady step forward and looming over them. "Where is she? Where is my mate?"

"She's gone," Salidus blurted. "I'm sorry."

Rhala's face was unreadable. He stared down at Salidus for a long, tense moment before speaking again.

"No."

"I'm sorry, my king, I truly am, but—"

"No, no, no. . . No, she can't be. She isn't. There must be a mistake."

Orniell suddenly moved forward and explained, "When you went through the portal, you ended up on a world called Earth. And when the humans attacked you, they. . . they killed you."

"Then how—"

"Our scholars discovered a ritual that brings the dead back to life. The murdered, specifically. But Rhala. . . " Fiiorha stepped towards him and placed a hesitant hand on his arm. She swallowed, and Salidus had never seen her look so unsure, so vulnerable. "That was almost two thousand years ago."

Rhala stumbled back as if he'd been dealt a physical blow and whispered, "You lie."

"I wish it were so, my king, but—"

"You lie to me!" he snarled, shoving her aside and lurching past her. Ignoring their protests, he exited into the hallway. Salidus heard dozens of gasps and startled shouts and guessed that Rhala had entered the atrium. In a brief moment of solidarity, he and Fiiorha exchanged an apprehensive look before running after him, closely followed by the pack. Up ahead, they heard him call out to his mate again: "Haraena!" Then the sound of the large doors slamming open echoed through the halls, and they sped up. They finally caught him as he was hurrying outside and looking around anxiously. The Rhithien milling about the Oasis gawked at him, but he paid no attention as he scanned every one of their faces in search of his mate. He stumbled back a few paces, overwhelmed by the bustling crowds, busy network of roads, and drifting smells from the livestock fields and smokehouse.

"Rhala, stop!" Salidus yelled. Rhala spun around, saw him, and bared his teeth. Salidus felt unfamiliar magic close around him and yank him forward, lifting him effortlessly into the air by his neck. Rhala grabbed him and snarled in his face.

"Where is she?" he roared. "Where is my pack?"

"Th. . . gone. . ." Salidus choked out as he clutched at his king's large hand. "I'm. . . sorry. . ."

Rhala dropped him, and he pressed a hand to his neck, coughing and gasping. Ridaion was immediately at his side, and he braced a hand on the younger male's shoulder until he was stable enough to stand on his own. He faced Rhala and repeated, "They're gone. We would not lie to you about this."

Rhala didn't resist as Fiiorha took his hand and led him back inside the Knowledge Center. They returned to the portal room, and she closed the doors on the murmuring crowd that tried to follow them. Once inside, Rhala turned his attention to the ritual ring that was still chalked onto the floor. He circled it slowly as if he was trying to figure out how it worked.

"This," he said stiffly, pointing a finger at it. "This can resurrect someone?"

"The murdered," Fiiorha clarified. "We need their remains as well as the blood of whoever killed them, or the killer's offspring."

"Then. . ." Rhala's face tightened with pain and he fell back against the wall, a low, guttural moan escaped his throat. He sank down to the floor, where he pulled his knees up and buried his face in his arms. He was still for a long time, but when a quaking tremor passed through his body, Salidus realized he was crying. He slowly moved forward and knelt beside his king, placing a reassuring hand on his shoulder. He exchanged yet another look with Fiiorha, who stared between them. Salidus took notice of her frill lifting and tail spikes twitching with impatience, and he shifted his body to block Rhala's view of her in hopes that his king wouldn't take offense. Salidus winced in sympathy as Rhala's shoulders shook again, and he quietly said, "I am so sorry."

"What do you want," Rhala mumbled, his voice choked with tears. He didn't sound like he cared much for the answer, but Fiiorha responded anyway.

"We need your help."

"With what?" Rhala snapped. "What is so important that you would resurrect a single Rhithien who's been dead for so long?"

Salidus was shocked by his sharp apathy. Sure, he was grieving, but did he not want to be alive?

"The creatures that killed you—"

"Where?" Rhala hissed, raising his head to look at Fiiorha. Salidus knew the expression on his face wasn't directed at him or anyone else in the room, but it was a look that promised murder, and he shrank away from its volatility. He glanced over his shoulder to make sure Nexus had left with the Lucio girl and was relieved to see that they were indeed gone. He feared Rhala would have tried to kill Layla in his rage.

"The planet that is connected to Primaied by the portals is called Earth. It's infested with the creatures that killed you. *Humans*, they're called. We mean to destroy them and take their planet for ourselves."

"You speak of extinction. Genocide. The very thing I fought against Zaidryn for ninety years to stop."

"I speak of justice. Zaidryn committed atrocities that deserved to be stopped, did he not? These humans butchered you and attempted to destroy your legacy when you had done nothing to earn their wrath. If it wasn't for them, you could have protected your fortress from the insurgents who killed your pack. You could have protected your mate. The humans are the cause of the pain you feel now."

Rhala was silent for so long that Salidus began to doubt he'd heard Fiiorha's words. He looked to her for answers, and she gave him a helpless shrug.

When Rhala spoke again, his voice was so soft that it took them a minute to figure out what he was saying.

"What happened to them?"

"Who?"

"My pack!" he snarled, slamming a fist onto the ground. "Aelys, Yundriel, and the rest? And Haraena. What happened to her? What happened to. . ." He trailed off, then swallowed and finished with a cracking voice, "What happened to the cubs she was carrying?"

"I don't want to lie to you," Salidus said slowly, "so I'll tell you everything I know. After your death, a small collection of Zaidryn's remaining loyalists attacked your fortress. Insurgents, as Fiiorha said. Your pack was killed, but the queen escaped. We don't know how. She went to an Oasis and raised her cubs there. We only discovered this recently, when some scholars in that Oasis found an old journal belonging to one of the past elders."

"How did she. . ." Rhala was unable to finish the sentence.

"She lived the rest of her days in peace and safety. It was age that took her."

"And our cubs. . . They lived?"

"I'm sorry to say that one died a few days after its birth, but the other two survived. If they hadn't, we would not be having this conversation."

"What do you mean?" Rhala asked, lifting his head and frowning at Salidus.

"As Fiiorha explained, the ritual calls for the remains and blood of the fallen. We found your heir. Your bloodline has stayed alive all these years, and we found the most current holder. His name is Aremaeid."

"Where is he?" Rhala asked hoarsely, standing and looking around the room like he was trying to decide which of them was the most likely candidate. "Where is my son?"

Salidus considered reminding him that Aremaeid was not, in fact, his direct offspring, but he thought better of it. Rhala was in pain. It wasn't something he needed to hear at that moment.

"He deserted just as we began the ritual. We managed to get some of his blood, but he returned to Earth with—"

Salidus stopped abruptly. He recalled the hatred that had clouded Rhala's face when they brought up the humans. How was he supposed to tell him that his heir had chosen to run off with one?

"With whom?"

272

"A human," Fiiorha finished, shooting Salidus an irritated look. "From what it looked like, one of them somehow corrupted him and convinced him to switch sides. How it accomplished this, I don't know."

Rhala processed the situation in hollow-eyed silence. Fiiorha, Salidus, and the pack waited anxiously for his reaction. It occurred to Salidus that they had no way of knowing what mental state he was in, or how severely the loss of his pack and mate had hit him. Perhaps they were rushing things. Would he even be willing to fight for them? To lead Primaied in battle once more?

At last, Rhala straightened, and a cold, impersonal mask settled over his face, obscuring all emotion and making Salidus feel strangely distant from his king.

"Very well," Rhala declared. "I will lead you if that is what you ask of me. But if I die and any of you resurrect me again, I will kill you all."

The threat hung in the air, but Salidus was hardly listening. Pride bubbled up in his chest at the thought of fighting alongside a living legend. Yes, the war would be long and bloody, but they would fight to the bitter end.

And they would win.

*****

"Let me go!" Layla screamed as the spike-tailed Rhithien carried her down a flight of stairs and into a long hallway.

"Hush, little cub. Let us not fight today."

"Fuck off! I want to go home!" Layla protested, kicking and thrashing. The Rhithien's strength rendered her efforts in vain, however, and it clicked its tongue in disapproval at her defiance.

"I mean you no harm, special one. My name is Nexus."

"I don't care about your fucking name! I want to go home!"

"So said the others before you. But you will learn to like it here, I promise. We treat our humans well. You will not be harmed as long as you are under my care."

Nexus carried her into a small room cluttered with books and knickknacks. Another spike-tailed Rhithien awaited them, though this one was smaller and had shorter horns. It stood by a table, where a thin leather collar lay open. It looked human-sized and had a small metal tag with some sort of inscription carved into its smooth surface. Layla shrieked and resumed her struggle. Nexus gently placed Layla on the table and held her down while the second Rhithien snapped the collar around her neck. It flipped the tag playfully, and Layla was reminded of the way she enjoyed looking at the tags on dogs' collars whenever she got to pet them.

Nexus said something to the other Rhithien in that strange language of theirs, then left the room. The Rhithien grabbed a bundle of scratchy cloth, wrapped it tightly around Layla, and scooped her up. It carried her into another hall and opened one of the many doors lining the sides, revealing a small cell with a cot, a bucket, and a few puzzle games that were battered and stained with a dark substance. It looked suspiciously like old blood. One was a Monopoly set that still had a peeling Walmart price tag on the side. An unlit lamp was mounted high up on the wall where Layla couldn't reach it. On the cot was a flat pillow and a heavy-looking blanket, and the Rhithien gently placed Layla down on the pile.

"Nexus always treats her humans well. You have nothing to worry about. Those puzzles are there if you feel like playing with them," the Rhithien said brightly, smiling and patting Layla tenderly on the head.

She said Nexus is a "her". If Ornathium's pack is all males, then are the ones with spikes females?

It was an intriguing thought, but it flew from Layla's brain as the Rhithien went to the doorway and grabbed the handle.

"Wait, don't leave me here!" she cried. She didn't want to be alone. She didn't want to be with a Rhithien, either, but she lunged clumsily off the edge of the cot and grabbed her captor's ankle, holding her desperately.

"Hush, little cub. You are perfectly safe."

"No, please, I want to go home! Don't leave me alone! Please, I have to. . . I can't. . . please, you can't just. . ." Layla's words dissolved into heavy sobs, and she collapsed against her captor's leg. The Rhithien crouched down, purring gently, and picked her up again. Layla didn't fight this time as the Rhithien cradled her for a moment, then returned her to the cot.

"You will be fine. It is safe for you here. Rest, little cub," the Rhithien said sympathetically. She closed the door, and Layla heard several locks click into place outside. She screamed in anguish as the room was plunged into darkness.

ACKNOWLEDGEMENTS

I've had the Rhithien floating around my head since 2019, but I didn't start writing about them until 2020. It was more or less a coping strategy during the pandemic. Then it bloomed into something bigger than I ever could have imagined. All of the initial writing and story building was mine, but I could not have completed this project on my own. Special thanks to:

My parents, who were my first beta readers. It's part of their job to critique papers, so they gave me legitimate feedback rather than just saying "Oh, that's wonderful, sweetie! I wouldn't change a thing!"

My sister, who always stands by me and is just as avid a writer as I am.

Jessica Young, a good friend of my mother's and the beta reader who provided the most significant developmental edits. Her contribution led to a full-scale reworking of the first few drafts and the version that you, dear reader, have just finished.

My lovely editor, Lisa Rose from The Write Rose Editing, who helped me grow and develop my authorial voice in the final stages of this project.

My Uncle James and Uncle David, who know what the hell they're doing and helped me figure out the business aspect of this mess.

To my teachers, who were willing to promote this book to their other classes. Go knights!

And lastly to you, dear reader, for picking up my book in the first place. These pages would be lost to time without you.

Please be patient. Everything will come together in the end.